Please enjoy -
Feb, '98

To See the Other Side

A "Thru-Hike" of the Appalachian Trail

A Novel by
John M. Wilson

Paint Rock Publishing, Inc.
Kingston, Tennessee
1998

BOOKS BY JOHN M. WILSON

Oh, Yes, I Want To Go Home
(Historical Novel set in the American
War Between The States)

Final Furlough
(Short Stories about the American
War Between The States
and other Subjects of Interest)

I Have Looked Death In The Face
(Civil War Biography of
William Porcher DuBose of South Carolina.
Soldier, Philosopher, Theologian)

To See The Other Side
(A novel of a thru-hike on the Appalachian Trail)

INTRODUCTION

My love affair with the Appalachian Trail started with my first hike in the mid-1950's. Maybe it was the things I experienced, the peace, solitude, beauty, sense of danger, a realization that while I am there I must be self-sustaining. Maybe it was the satisfaction and feeling of accomplishment following a successful hike, even though every part of my body hurt. All these things are an integral part of the trail experience. There is magic in the name and the concept; a continuous trail linking 13 states, Georgia to Maine, along the spine of the eastern United States.

After weekend hikes along the Appalachian Trail or in the Great Smoky Mountains National Park, I resented having to stop and return to things mundane: work and responsibilities. I never saw what was "on the other side of the mountain." So, I had to live a thru-hike vicariously. From people who had the courage and strength of conviction to make a thru-hike, I have read about their experiences in books about thru-hikers I got in my hands. While I continued backpacking treks through the sixties and into the seventies, my four children, Betsy, Jack, Ric, and Kenny, participated in the blood, sweat, tears, and pleasures of backpacking. Through the seventies and early eighties, I made two-a-year treks up to Mt. LeConte Lodge. Satisfying and highly enjoyable, but not quite the same as the backpack. A comfortable bed was waiting for me at the lodge, and there were people to provide food. I wasn't self-reliant. I lost touch with the AT. Then, in 1995, I rediscovered the Trail, strapped a pack on my older, grayer, overweight body and walked again. I was amazed at the proliferation of better, lighter backpacking gear and was pleased that others had continued to hike while I had faded away. But, I guess old hikers are a lot like old soldiers . . .

While I re-discovered hiking, I also found writing for fun and was fortunate to have several books published. I began to take notes of experiences from both my earlier and current backpacking days. These notes accumulated to an extent that I became interested in writing a novel about a thru-hike. To write about a subject, any subject, you must do research; therefore, I studied books essential to a thru-hike. *The Appalachian Trail Data Book* and *The Appalachian Trail Thru-Hikers' Companion*, published by The Appalachian Trail Conference and the Appalachian Long Distance Hikers Association. For my characters I prepared a plan for a thru-hike and was ready to modify the plan when evolution within the story necessitated any change. I prepared a detailed timeline, knowing that if my book was read by a successful thru-hiker, that person would recognize what was out of sequence, or what couldn't have happened. While trying to avoid a "travelogue," I tried to put things where they could have happened. I hope I succeeded.

My characters are fictional, but similar experiences have happened to me and to others. Trail experiences could fill 1000 books. This book is about "Doubting Jon" Parker's and his friends'. If it encourages one person to try a wilderness experience, the time will have been worthwhile.

I would like to acknowledge the assistance of a number of people. First, my wife, Faye, who encouraged me in the hikes I took to get back into the hiking mode. My hiking companions Mike Morris, Steve Perry, John McKinney, Changsheng Lu, Jon Blount, Jack Wilson, Ric Wilson, Andrew Wilson, and Kenny Wilson made this the most enjoyable research I will ever do. Mr. Ric A. Wilson did a remarkable job of book layout and cover design, just as he has done on all my books. Ms. Phyllis Garman did the line-by-line edit. Changsheng Lu's black and white photographs and Steve Baker's sketches grace these pages and give life to the mountains and the characters of the story. A number of people read the rough manuscript and made suggestions that improved the story, including Ed Miller, James Wedekind, Bill Wilson, Sam Jones, and Kenny Wilson. I appreciate the assistance of these people more than I can state.

John M. Wilson
Kingston, Tennessee
1998

Requests for permission to make copies
of any part of the work should be mailed to:
Permissions
Paint Rock Publishing, Inc.
118 Dupont Smith Lane
Kingston, Tennessee 37763
(423) 376-3892

Publisher's Cataloging in Publication

Wilson, John Morris, 1939-
"To See The Other Side" ; A novel of a thru-hike on the Appalachian Trail/ by John M. Wilson
p. cm.
Includes bibliographical references
ISBN 0-9649394-2-8

1. United States — Appalachian Trail—Hiking—Out-of-doors—
Novel. I.
Title.

PS3573I5766 1998 813'.54
QB196-200

Manufactured in the United States of America
First Edition

TABLE OF CONTENTS

1

"THE SEED IS PLANTED"

"I can do it! I'm by God gonna do it!" The voice rings out in the air. Not that there is room for anything else in the air of the pub. The smoke and noise fill the air and your lungs and your ears to overflowing.

The loud pronouncement came from Jon Parker, a young man who just turned twenty-four and is slowly and painfully starting to face the fact that his life isn't going very far very fast. He is enjoying a Friday night out with the boys. So far, he hasn't missed Sissy, his long-time date who is showing signs of more serious intentions than he is ready to face. The corner of the pub where the men are sitting has been getting louder with each passing hour and each passing pitcher of beer.

Andy, Jon's best friend, a long, tall drink of water, says, "Jon, you're full of shit. That's what I say. Just cause you managed to hike eight miles last weekend in the Black Warrior Wilderness Area doesn't mean you're ready for the Appalachian Trail, 'specially a thru-hike! You don't even know enough to call it the AT instead of the Appalachian Trail, that's how damned green you are."

Chuck Boggs chimes in, "Full of shit." He points at each of the five young men seated around the table. "You're fulla it, so're you, and you, and you." He points an unsteady finger at himself–"For that matter, I'm fulla it too. Seems like everybody I know's afflicted with the King Excreta touch. Everything they touch turns to shit."

Jon laughs, "Chuck, you're mostly full of beer. I can tell by the number of trips you've made to the head that your saturation ceiling is way behind you. Why don't you just take your next mug of Mick and dump it straight into the urinal? It'll save you a trip later." Jon returned to the subject of discussion. "Anyway, I'm serious as a heart attack. It's just October. I've got till March to get ready." He stops and tries to count on his fingers. "One, two . . . " Every time he gets to five, he runs out of hand and the beer won't let him figure out what finger to use next.

Andy laughs and stretches out a hand, fingers spread widely. "Here, bud. Use one of mine till you can control your own. How the hell is somebody that can't count to seven gonna hike the AT, much less figure out where he is?"

Jon doesn't answer. He uses Andy's hand and triumphantly counts, "One, two, six! There, by God, I got six months to get into shape and get maps, gear, and . . . "

The others shake their heads in disbelief. Andy says, "Jon, this is just like last summer when you were gonna work as a raft guide for folks who float the Ocoee River, and the summer before that, when you were gonna get a job and work in Alaska or in Montana, and the summer before that, when you were gonna . . . "

"I know, I know. You don't have to recite a litany of all my failures over the years. I understand the science of history, if nothing else. I can count them myself." Jon's shoulders slump and he slides down in the booth seat until he is sitting on his spine, not his butt.

"You're just afraid to get away from home and mom and dad and Sissy, that's all. You gotta grow up some time," Andy says.

Jon mutters, "Damn, Sissy's already decided she's ready to get married and have a kid, that's what she told me last night. There's lots of things I wanna do before I get any more locked in than I already am. Life sucks. Chains everywhere. You can't do this, you can't do that. You have to get married, have kids, get in debt, get a house, get old and gray and fat, and die. It's the American way."

Andy laughs. "Damn, Jon, you're getting more philosophical than Chuck. That's pretty bad. Speaking of Chuck, look at that sorry case." The three turn just in time to see Chuck's head slowly sink below the table top. Chuck was a football player for the University, or as he likes to tell it, he was a tackling dummy for the real football players; there is a man-mountain slowly sinking below the table.

"Hell, he looks like the Titanic going down all over again," says Jon. "I guess we'd best call it a night before we all join him passed out and Tony bans us for a month." He stands and says, "One of you guys better help me get him up off the floor. He weighs a ton, and I got stuck with toting him home the last time he tried to drink Tony's dry."

With substantial pulling, tugging, and cussing, the three friends get an uncooperative Chuck upright and more or less balanced on unsteady legs. As they half-carry, half-drag him out the door, Jon says, "Andy, if you think I'm kidding about hiking the whole AT, think again. This ain't just the beer talking. I mean it."

Andy just smiles. "Yeah, yeah, yeah. Let's see if you even remember tomorrow. Or for that matter, after you tell Sissy, let's see if she'll turn loose of the nose ring she's got hooked on you. That sucker looks awfully tight to me."

Chuck is shepherded down the street by his three human sheep dogs. Andy says, "Thank goodness we live close enough to drag ourselves home. We're in no shape to be driving."

Jon grabs his arm. "Look! What's that down the block?"

Andy laughs. "Looks like a car to me, you damned college-educated grease-monkey. Your eyes getting as bad as your mind?"

Jon responds, "No, not just a car. I think I saw a blue reflection on top. It's a cop!"

Three of the four men sober up right away. Chuck's too far gone to either understand or care. They drag him into a smelly alley, kick aside the trash to clear a space to stand, and press against the damp brick wall. Andy puts his hand over Chuck's mouth to quieten his incoherent mumbling. The others collectively hold their breath as the patrol car drives slowly past the alley entrance. Fortunately, the spotlight the police are using doesn't illuminate the men. The car passes by, and breaths are released.

"All right," exclaims Jon. "They might've kept Chuck forever."

"Keep Chuck, keep Chuck, who wants to keep Chuck?" mumbles the object of the discussion.

"Nobody in their right mind!"

The quartet continues its corporate lurch down the sidewalk and Chuck is deposited on his parents' doorstep. The other four ring the bell and run, leaving him to his fate. Laughter trails their staggering quasi-run down the street as they imagine the scene taking place at Chuck's house. The laughter is mixed with relief that the cops didn't spot them.

One of the men stops and enters his apartment complex and Jon and Andy continue down the road for a few more blocks. The white frame Civil War-vintage house they share is finally in sight. At least they don't have to face parents; the only thing they have to face is the drum-pounding, brain-splitting, sick-gut, beer headache of tomorrow morning. Chuck will have to face his folks tonight plus an abundant dose of a hangover and more parental harassment tomorrow. Ouch! Enough to make you want to quit drinking. Well, almost.

Jon opens the door to his room and is greeted with a thunderous "Woof! Woof," broadcast by a 75- pound black Labrador Retriever dancing around like a month-old puppy. "Pookie!" exclaims Jon, "Damn, I forgot I shut you up in the room. I expect you're ready to go outside."

At the magic word, "outside," Pookie goes down the stairs more like a graceful gazelle than a clumsy Lab and stands, not-so-patiently, by the front door. Jon staggers down the stairs, finds the leash hanging on the doorknob. Once outside, Pookie plays sled dog. He drags an unstable Jon from one side of the yard to the other, with Jon's curses floating behind them. Pookie finally finds just the right spot, completes his business, then drags his unwilling master back to the porch. Jon opens the door and tells Pookie, "Sit, you miserable fleabag. Let me get this damned leash unhooked."

Jon makes his second trip up the stairs under difficult conditions. He falls in his bed, unmade that morning, and Pookie takes his usual place by the door, nominally there to protect Jon from burglars or muggers. Not that he would be much help, because just like most Labs, he loves everybody at first sight and would likely happily offer to hold the flashlight for any would-be burglar.

From Jon's horizontal position, the room spins at dizzying speed, threatening to leave him behind. He mutters, "Stop the Ferris wheel and I'll get off. Wow! This ain't the fun part, that's for damn sure." The room finally quits spinning enough for Jon's mind to start working again. That is problematic. "Hike the AT? All 2000-plus miles ?" He who has three weekend hikes and cheap equipment to his credit is a long way from ready to walk the AT with the big boys. "Let's see, I need to scrounge dollars, get in shape, get off the beer and slim down and, get new equipment . . . " He sleeps, suffering disturbing dreams of sore feet and pursuing bears and imminent failure.

The sun is painfully streaming in the window when Jon awakes. He lies still, hoping against hope that non-activity would forestall the inevitable start to the day. He hopes, just as countless other folks who drank too much beer the night before have also unsuccessfully hoped. He cracks open one eye and the light stabs his nerve ends like a laser.

"Oh, God," he moans, "Never again."

It takes 15 minutes to complete the sitting up process and a few more to stand. He staggers to the kitchen for coffee, detouring to the bathroom for the oft-helpful "plop, plop, fizz, fizz." However, this morning, he has to whisper at the innocent glass, "Shut up, you damned bubbles, you're making too much noise!"

The combination of Alka-Seltzer and a sip of hot, bitter coffee helps. At least enough that he can finally open both eyes fully. Open enough that he jumps when he focuses on Andy, already sitting opposite him at the kitchen table, cuddling his own cup of coffee.

"Mornin', sport," growls Andy. "Damn, your eyes look sorta like road maps. Do they hurt you as bad inside as they pain me looking at em from here?"

"Yeah, I don't feel any too swift. You ought to see your own eyes. Why the hell do we do that, anyway?"

"Don't know. Don't make any sense, does it?"

"Nope. Hey, Andy, you think I'm full of shit 'bout that AT thing?"

"Yeah, I do. Don't surprise me none, though. Makes things exciting to see what you might come up with next. It's been a while since you've had a wild-ass scheme. I'm really surprised that you even remember it from last night."

"I wasn't that drunk. Anyway, this isn't a wild-ass scheme. Well, maybe it is, but I'm dead serious. I was gonna ask you this morning if you'd think about coming with me."

"Go with you? You think I'm crazy as you?"

"Yep, I reckon you are. You live in the same house as me, don't you? Don't hurt none to ask, even if you say no."

"Jon," begins Andy, "have you thought this thing out? You got Sissy to worry about, plus your job. Not that pumping gas down at the local garage is any great shakes, but I seem to remember that it took you four months to find even that job after you graduated."

"Yeah, a degree in history is nothing in the job market. But, the garage is better'n nothin'. Besides, I got that spiffy 50-cent raise last week. I'm not getting rich on 200 bucks a week, but I get by. Those are nice guys there, and Shorty's a good boss. Maybe he'll let me off for five months for a hike? Yeah, sure he will. When hell freezes over." He slumps in his chair, head cradled on his arms.

"Dammit, there you go again," shouts Andy. "Thinking of reasons why you can't do what you want to do. You need a shot of self-confidence in the worst way. Figure out how you can do something instead of why you can't. I don't guess I'm ever gonna get you trained and grown up."

"I thought you were the one that was listing the reasons why I can't possibly do the hike."

"Yeah, yeah, I was, but just so's you can figger out the speed bumps in your path. You got to make a list of possible hiccups, then get after 'em one at a time." Andy gets up and walks out of the room. "Shit, man, get a life!" Andy clips the leash on Pookie's collar, "Come on, boy, I believe you'll make more sense than that damned master of yours. Can't you train him any better?"

Pookie agrees completely with whatever Andy says, or, for that matter, anything that anyone says. He spins in a circle, then gives his usual "Woof! Woof!"

Jon sits by himself, thinking about Andy's advice. At least, he's thinking as hard as his throbbing head will allow. He jumps when Andy and Pookie come back into the house after a 10-minute walk.

An hour later, Jon is still sitting at the table. He's afraid to move too rapidly. The phone rings, and Andy returns to the kitchen and picks up the receiver. "Yeah?" he growls in the mouthpiece. "That bad, huh? We tried to tell you that last night." He listens for a moment, "O.K., see you there." He hangs up and asks Jon, "Chuck needs to escape his folks for a while. You up for a Castle Burger breakfast delight?"

"Yeah, the grease might help. It can't hurt none."

Jon and Andy amble down the street, in no hurry. Chuck is sitting on the curb in front of his house, head in his hands. All 280 pounds of him is in a stagnant condition. As they stand in front of the seated figure, they see right away that this is not the effervescent Chuck they're used to.

Jon starts, "Bedraggled, that's what I'd call him."

Andy replies, "Terminally ill."

"Sad."

"Ruffled."

"Pitiful."

"Hopeless case."

"Call AA."

"Call 911."

"Call the morgue."

"Enough, you damned comedians," growls Chuck, "You ain't funny in the least. Your humor ain't appreciated today, not that it could ever be called humor in its finest hour."

"It's alive, it speaks!" shrieks Andy. Jon falls theatrically to the ground, clutching his chest in the vicinity of his heart.

Chuck painfully rises to his feet and starts walking down the street toward fast-food heaven near the university. "It not only talks, but it walks!" Andy yells, staring in amusement. Chuck keeps walking in wounded dignity and self-righteous indignation. He chooses to ignore his buddies. Not at all discouraged with Chuck's lack of response, Andy and Jon keep the pressure on all the way to Castle Burger.

Safely inside the restaurant at the counter, Chuck orders the breakfast special. In exchange for his three bucks, he receives two patties of sausage, two eggs shimmering with grease, two soggy-looking pieces of toast, and a dollop of "Georgia ice-cream," also known as grits.

Jon feels an attack of terminal nausea as he stares at Chuck's plate. He looks at Andy and sees his feelings mirrored. Jon says, "You next. I need to figure out what my stomach will let me eat."

Andy goes the safe route–he orders two plain cake donuts and a cup of coffee. Maybe digestible, maybe not, but definitely more esthetically pleasing than Chuck's order. Plus, the advantage of fewer stomach lurches.

In an amazing display of talent and much practice, the large woman in the grease-stained Castle Burger uniform never misses a lick on her chewing gum as she clangs, "Whattayawantkid?"

Jon stares, then winces. He fears that if a button pops off the uniform front where it's strained to the breaking point by her huge bazooms, it might hurt. He can visualize the button ricocheting from wall to wall, chipping off the plaster as it flies. He thinks, "What I want is for you to get the Doc to cut that mole off of your chin. Yeah, that one. The one with the trio of inch-long coarse black hairs, each sprouted exactly 120 degrees from the next." Fortunately, diplomacy and sanity take over and he doesn't air his thoughts. Besides, it's obvious that the woman could take him in the best of three falls without breaking a sweat. Instead, he orders four Castle Burger Smalls, complete with grilled onion, mustard, and one small, pitiful, wilted pickle slice perched on top of each soggy bun. An order of fries and a large Coke completes the fare he intends to offer in sacrifice to appease his angry, volcanic, long-suffering stomach.

When he carries his tray to the table, it's his turn to catch grief. "My, God," moans Andy. "Gut bombs, sliders, grease balls. I can't stand it. I can't believe it. For breakfast, for God's sake!"

Jon defends his choice. "Well, they've worked for me before as hangover preventive medicine. Maybe they'll work as a cure."

Andy says, "You're right on the prevention–I don't know if it's the soggy bread, the onions, the grease, or the soybean burger, but something works every time. I think that with all that in you, you're afraid to barf. You can't barf."

Chuck makes the sign of the cross on Jon's forehead and solemnly intones, "In nomine Patris, et Filii et Spiritus Sancti, Amen. Good luck, son. You're gonna need it."

The roundtable harassment ceases as the three settle down to ingest what they hope will bring them back to life. Thirty minutes later, all announce they feel better, at least for the time being. Even Jon's greasy burgers are temporarily settled in his stomach. They all may live.

"Damn," says Jon, "I'm sure glad I don't have to pump gas this afternoon. The smell of gasoline would bring back a case of the queasies. The queasies are hanging around, waiting for me to do something dumb, like move. They'll attack me with a vengeance."

Andy starts, "Jon, let's talk about that AT thing for a minute. How much money you got saved up? Gonna take a bundle for gear and food. How much you got? $500? $300? I figure you're gonna need at least a couple grand, before you're ready."

Jon shuffles his feet under the table before answering. "I got bout 100 bucks, give or take a little. Sissy's been on my ass about saving more so we can get married. Leastwise, that's what she wants. I thought it was what I wanted, but now I'm not so sure."

"Damn, son, where in the world you gonna get the moola you got to have to pull this thing off?"

"Work more hours and save faster, I guess. That means my dates with Sissy are gonna be none too exciting from now on."

Andy laughs. "Friend, I have a feeling that when you tell Sissy what you have on your feeble little mind, spending money on dates with her is gonna be the least of your troubles. I believe you are about to get shot plumb clean out of the saddle. That is, if you've ever been in the saddle." He looked at Jon with a questioning expression.

Jon turns scarlet. "Ain't none of your business whether I've ever done anything with Sissy. Mind your own damned business."

Andy laughs again. "I guess you just gave me your answer, even though you didn't say anything. But, that's not what matters. What matters is that you need to get moving, make that list I talked about. Figure where you plan to come up with mucho bucks. Cause that's what it's gonna take, mucho dinero. A damned big bunch of dinero."

Jon sits pensively for a moment, formulating his response. He thinks, "Damn that Andy, anyway! He always has nasty questions that usually turn out to be the right ones to ask, pinning me down. Maybe I need to be pinned down. I want to do this, but it's a hell of a move." Jon finally speaks. "Andy, I said that I was interested in getting hiking partners, and I still am. You interested?"

Andy shakes his head. "It would be something to talk about if that trip could be made. But I'm not sure I want to do it bad enough. I spect that you need to want to do it more than anything in the world to carry it off. Let me think about it for a bit. I'll let you know."

Chuck pipes in. "You haven't asked me, yet. Ain't I good enough to accompany your majesty on this dream hike?"

Jon says, "Chuck, I'd like it if you want to come along, but I'm afraid you'll have a problem leaving the beer alone for seven months to get in shape, let alone for the four or five months of the hike. A case of beer a day won't fit in a backpack."

Chuck shakes his head sadly. "Damn, son, you're asking a lot of this old country boy. Go beerless for near onto a year? Damn, son." He puts on a hangdog look and collapses into speechlessness, approaching comatose.

The conversation wanes as heads and stomachs announce that hangovers are still in the neighborhood. The friends leave the Castle Burger with little conversation. None of them do anything worthwhile for mankind the rest of the day. They leave Chuck at home to face his parents, who have had enough time in his absence to regain strength for a renewed attack on their son's night-time activities. After walking Pookie around the block so he could mark every bush and tree on the way, Jon cat-naps in front of a football game featuring two losing college teams and Andy retires to his room, likely to sleep as well. Saturday afternoons aren't designed for anything strenuous anyway. Particularly when it follows trying to close down Tony's Pub by seriously depleting his stock of beer.

Pookie finally wakes Jon up at about six o'clock by announcing his intention to tear the neighbor's cat limb from limb. The cheeky cat perches on the outside window sill, where it knows Pookie can see him, but can't get to him. Pookie has absolutely no love for cats. Jon grumbles, but he wakes up with a start, when he remembers he's supposed to have pizza with Sissy at seven that night.

Pookie gets only a short walk before they return to the house, but he feels much better and Jon is a little improved. Jon goes upstairs where a long, hot, steamy shower helps a little more. He forgot to turn on the bathroom vent fan, so he tries to wipe the fogged-up mirror to shave. He nicks himself three times with the Bic. "Damn," he says, "that's what I need, three pieces of T.P. hanging off my face. I can see it now. Sissy, I need to talk with you about something. I'm leaving in March for five or six months to take a hike. She would be pissed if she was listening, but maybe she'll be so busy concentrating on the toilet paper as it twitches when I talk. Hey, that may help! Diversionary tactics! Smart thinking on my part. I'm so clever, sometimes I scare myself."

Fantasies complete, Jon dresses in his favorite pullover and jeans as Pookie watches with interest. If Pookie were capable of thought, he would definitely be thinking in his tiny Lab brain, "Hum, Daddy's getting dressed. Maybe I get to go? If I stay out of his way, maybe, maybe . . . "

Jon has been with Pookie long enough to interpret what he has in mind. "Nope, Pookie, not this time. Don't think the pizza place or Sissy would approve of you. Maybe next time."

Jon completes his preparations and leaves the bedroom just as Andy, yawning and stretching, appears in the hall. "Well, bud, worked up your courage 'to the sticking point,' as old Willie Shakespeare would say? Gonna let Miss Sissy know what's on your agenda? I won't have to listen for the phone to hear her answer."

"I'm gonna clearly and logically tell her about the hike, if that's what you mean. She's a grownup, and she'll take it just fine." The last thing Jon hears as he goes out the front door is Andy, still laughing and choking in the upstairs hall, hanging on to the banister for dear life.

Jon's brain operates in high gear all the way to Sissy's. He parks his pickup truck in front of her folks' two-story Victorian white frame house and approaches the door. She is ready and waiting, and closes the door behind her. Jon at least escapes her Dad's usual not-so-subtle questions as to whether Jon's intentions towards his daughter are honorable. That's okay, he'll probably be waiting when they get back, trying to hide his 250-pound carcass behind the lacy curtains in the living room, so he can jump out like an fat panther and nab him for interrogation. All he needs is a floodlight behind him to look like a scene from *Mission Impossible.* "Where wuz you on de night of April zeventeen? Speak up an we won't hurt you."

Sissy flips her talk mode to chatter, its usual setting. Jon is spared from making conversation. Simply use "Un-huhs" at the right time and intersperse, "That's right, Babe" when responses are called for. He doesn't even have to think until the pickup shudders to a stop by the restaurant.

When they go in, they find that some nervy interloper has had the audacity to park himself in their favorite corner booth, the one Jon had hoped would hide and muffle his conversation with Sissy. They have to sit at a table right in the middle of the room, in public view. "Damn," he thinks. "I knew it had started too well."

They settle in and order a large pepperoni, mushroom, and onion pan pizza, and a Coke for Sissy. He starts to order a pitcher of beer for himself, but changes his mind. He'd has to cut back, if he's serious about this hike. Jon finally focuses in on what Sissy is chattering about. She's busily planning their wedding, complete with how she's going to get even with such-and-such a girl by not asking her to be a bridesmaid, and what size cake they will need, and which apartment over on South Street they could rent. Jon inwardly groans. This isn't going to be easy. They definitely aren't in the same hymnal, much less on the same song sheet. Maybe he'll wait a little longer before he tells her. Nope, this confrontation is the first thing on his mental list, not yet relegated to paper. He clears his throat. The flow of chatter never slows. He takes a swallow of beer and clears his throat again. Sissy finally notices.

"Jon, are you taking a cold? No, I'll bet you just don't feel so good after drinking all the beer Tony had to sell last night. You drink way too much because you still run around with those, those, boys who still haven't grown up and gotten married. After we're married, you'll need to find some mature friends."

Jon's inward groan intensifies. Luckily, he is saved from delivering his semi-prepared speech by the arrival of the pizza. He thinks, "Hum, greasy pizza. I guess this is another one of those things that I'll have to eliminate while I'm getting in shape. I'm getting love handles from all this high living." These lofty thoughts don't stop him from consuming eight of the twelve slices of pizza. His brain rambles on. "The training regime will start tomorrow. A tomorrow diet. That's the diet my mom's been on for years. It hasn't worked for her, but it will have to for me. Wonder if I can really carry this thing off?"

The one-sided conversation goes back to the wedding, which Sissy hasn't really stopped talking about since leaving her house. He "Un-huhs" several more times. He thinks, "Damn, this ain't gonna do. I've gotta break in soon and get this job done. Soon, that's when I'll do it."

But, the chatter is unstoppable and "soon" doesn't come that night. Sissy's Dad is waiting as Jon had expected. Jon gives him no chance to pounce. He accepts Sissy's chaste sisterly kiss on the cheek and dashes to the sanctity of his pickup. Blue smoke trails him. He walks Pookie and escapes Andy's derision for that night by going directly to bed. He sleeps like a log, never stirring until morning.

Jon is still groggy even though he's been up for over an hour. But at least he's not hung over this morning. He walks Pookie, then goes to the kitchen and starts the coffee percolator. About the time it's ready, Andy stumbles into the room, rubbing the sleep from his eyes.

"Ya sleep well, Bud?" Andy asks.

"Nah, I mostly tossed and turned and thought about this wild idea of mine. I don't know, man. I'm not completely convinced I can do it, I guess." Jon sits glumly at the kitchen table.

Andy shakes his head. "Yeah, yeah, yeah. Same old, same old. You ain't changed a lick in all the years I've known you. I can't do this, I can't do that, I ain't never done that. I told you so."

"Don't write me off yet. I just need to make up my mind, that's all. Pour me some coffee and shut the hell up, how 'bout it?"

Andy laughs as he pours. "When do you plan to make up your mind, anyway?"

"I don't know. Just don't bug me, okay?"

"Okay, I'll leave you alone."

They sit in companionable silence and let the coffee do its thing. Nobody's in a rush–it's Sunday.

Pookie loudly announces the arrival of the newspaper as it lands on the front porch with a thump. Jon stumbles out and picks it up. He checks out the football scores on his way back to the kitchen.

For the next hour, status quo reigns. At about 10 o'clock, the telephone rings. Jon's brother Matt asks if Jon wants to meet him, his wife, and two sons for breakfast after church.

Jon agrees, although he rolls and cuts his eyes.

Jon says, "Okay, twelve-thirty it is. See ya then," replacing the telephone receiver carefully in its cradle.

Andy laughs, "What the hell was that all about? You looked like you were accepting an invitation to your own hanging."

"That's pretty accurate. Big Brother Matt wants me to meet his yuppie suburban family at a downtown restaurant. Probably so he can berate me about my life in general, and any recent failures in particular. But, I've got to listen to it every once in a while. Might's well be now."

Once again, coffee and newspaper, and later the Lonesome River Band on the stereo, take away all conversation. After about an hour, Jon stands and stretches and yawns.

"Damn," he says, "I'd just soon hit the sack as go anywhere. Reckon I could get Matt paged in church and cancel lunch?"

Andy laughs, "I can just hear that. The loudspeaker in church blares, 'Will Mr. Matt Parker please come to the service desk at the rear of the sanctuary for a message?'"

Jon also laughs. "Nah, I'd best get ready to go. You mind walking the Pookster? It's been a while."

"No problem. Be glad to. Let's go, Pook." Andy and Pookie exit via the back door and Jon heads for the shower.

On the way to breakfast, Jon thinks about his relationship with his brother. Ever since they were small, Matt had always been the good boy, the one pointed to by their parents. You know, "why can't you do __________ (fill in the blank) like Matt?" Jon tried, Lord knows he tried, until he just flat-out has quit trying. Whatever he did, wherever he went, whichever class he was in, Matt had been there and his shadow lingered over Jon. So, he had relegated himself to just being Jon. Problem is, he isn't sure what Jon is supposed to be. Maybe that's what this crazy hike will do. That is, if he even finds the guts to take the hike.

The closer he gets to the restaurant, the more depressed Jon becomes. He thinks, "Oh well, I'm not gonna sweat it. It's the way it is and I can't do anything about Matt. Make the best of the situation."

Jon goes into the waiting area and is met by his two nephews with hugs and loud high-five greetings that earn them a "Hush boys" from their dad. Matt and Sarah say their hellos, Matt with a handshake, Sarah with a hug.

The hostess calls, "Parker, party of five," and they dutifully follow her to a table back near the hot food bar.

They sit, order, and get their salads with few words exchanged. Jon is beginning to believe that a meal might pass with no unwanted fatherly advice from big brother, when Matt says, "Jon, I'm glad you're getting married. I think Sissy is a mature young lady who might help you grow up, find new friends and a better job, maybe finally become a productive member of society. Maybe you can . . . "

"Maybe you can just get off my back," explodes Jon. "I'm tired of listening to you preach. For your information, my productivity to society is about to take a downward dip. I'm calling off the wedding with Sissy and I'm thinking about dropping out of society for four or five months. I'm gonna make a thru-hike on the Appalachian Trail, all 2000 miles. Least that's what I'm thinking."

Matt throws his head back and laughs out loud. "Hike 2000 miles? You? I remember how you couldn't spend the whole night out in the tent in the backyard because of the night noises. You also lasted one whole night at scout camp before you called Mom to come get you. I can just see you out on the trail for five months. You've never finished anything in your life; I can't see you finishing this, either."

"Yeah? You'd best be picturing it, 'cause it's gonna happen. Listening to you makes me want to take that hike even more than I did before. Thanks. Even though you were just being your usually bossy self, you helped me decide. Here, this should cover my share," and Jon tossed a five-dollar bill on the table as he pushed back his chair.

"But . . . but . . . but . . . " says Sarah. "What about your meal?"

"Don't feel like it, now. But I'm not mad at you or the kids," and Jon hugs Sarah from behind and ruffles the boys' hair as he stalks past them and out the door. He climbs in his pickup truck and drives home. He feels pretty good about telling Matt off, one of the few times in the 20-plus years he has known his brother. He feels good about having made the decision on the hike. For better or worse, he has decided. Lots of quicksand and mine fields out in front before he starts the hike, much less completes it. But, he is going. He is going!

Monday morning comes and with it, Shorty's Garage. At least time has helped Jon feel more human and he is fully recovered from Friday night at Tony's. Shorty is civil, Mac his usual sardonic self, and James isn't quite as bouncy as usual. When Jon was first introduced to James several months earlier, he innocently asked if people called him Jimmy. James glowered at him, flexed his arms, and picked Jon up off the ground as if he were a child. That was when Jon realized how incredibly strong James was. James growled, "Boy, my name is James. Not Jimmy, not nuttin else. Recognize that my name's the only dignity I got. Don't you forgit that, now, you hear me a'talking at you?"

Jon wasn't sure what was going to happen next, but James returned him to his feet, laughed, and said, "Boy, it's Friday afternoon. Let's go next door to the grocery store and get some chocolate milk and cottage cheese. I plan to get wasted tonight, and I've got to get my stomach coated." Thus was Jon's introduction to a character larger than life.

Jon enjoys his job most of the time–there's never any telling what might happen next, particularly with James around. This particular morning, the garage has a surprise visitor. The auto parts places around town found out a year ago that Shorty has an employee with considerable strength. Since that time, when an order is placed for brake shoes, carburetors or such, they send their biggest man to deliver parts and to test James' arm-wrestling skills.

Shorty calls the parts place that morning to get several brake drums resurfaced. When the battered pickup truck pulls in 30 minutes later, it leans several degrees to the driver's side. The man sitting in that seat is huge. His arm, resting on the window sill, is massive. It practically fills the entire window opening. The arm is so big that his sleeve is slit all the way to the armpit to make it possible to get the shirt on. He extracts himself from the seat with considerable effort and strides toward the garage with a purposeful gait. The truck's springs and shocks sigh in temporary relief.

The man-mountain takes the stack of brake drums from Shorty and places them on the floor. He grumbles with a voice that sounds like it's coming from the bottom of a well. "Ain't interested in them damned drums right now. I hear you got a man here that you think is good at arm wrestling. I got enough time to test him. Don't blame me if he's off work for awhile with a dislocated arm. I been known to do that to folks several times before."

Shorty calls, "James, get your butt over here. Got some one you need to meet." James walks over and immediately goes into an act that Jon has seen many times but never tires of. His eyes grow as big as saucers and Jon sees nothing but white. James walks around the man, conducting a survey. He says in a voice that quavers with apparent fear, "White man, dat's the biggest arm I ever seen." He feels the monster's biceps and his hand barely covers the top portion, partially covering the naked lady thereon. He whines again, "Mr. Shorty, dis man gon break my arm or discombobulate my shoulder. Do I haz to do dis?" If his "pore ole darky" act were any more ham-like, it would include the entire hog.

Shorty winks at Jon. "No, James, I don't guess you have to, if you don't want to. I can't afford to be shorthanded around here. If you're afraid of this moose, I can see why. But, maybe he wants to put some money on the wrestling? It shouldn't take all of your drinking money for tonight. Maybe you'll even go home on time and give Sheila what's left of your paycheck, and she won't be calling me tomorrow wanting to know why I didn't pay you much this week. I won't have to lie to cover your lazy black ass for a change. No, if you're afraid . . . "

James lets out the biggest sigh Jon has ever heard. It's from the depths of his soul. "I don't reckon I treats that little lady like I should. I does git drunk more that I oughta. White man, I reckon we'd best git on with it. With dat arm you gots, it shouldn't take long for you to take me out. Be easy on me, you hear?"

Shorty asks the visiting one-man team, "How much you want to put on this, bud? Bout 20 bucks should pay me for James' lost time if you hurt him."

James pipes in, "I needs 20 of that for the pain Ize gwine suffer. Can you handle that?"

Jon puts in his two cents worth, "How about 20 for me? And, I'll be glad to hold the money."

The man counts out 60 dollars from a wad that could choke any mule that Jon had ever seen. He looks at the three bettors, smiles like a crocodile, then counts out another 60. "I'll see your 60 and double it. All right with you guys? My wife needs a new dress."

Following the appropriate moans and groans about how they really couldn't afford such high dollar stakes, the bets are covered and the arena is prepared. A hydraulic grease rack is raised to the correct level and two old wicker-bottomed chairs are placed one on each side of the rack. Shorty pulls a filthy rag out of his back pocket and ceremoniously dusts off the seats of the chairs. "I guess we're ready."

The combatants sit in the chairs. Jon is amazed to see the visitor's butt sticking out on each side of the chair about as far as the chair is wide. James' whining and fear increases to a fever pitch. "White man, don't you hurt James. You chill now, you hear?"

The man scowls, "I ain't worrying about being easy. I'm just gonna set your arm down on this grease rack so hard you're gonna see rivet imprints on the back of your hand for weeks. We'll soon see who's the champ. Now, you gonna whine or wrestle?"

James groans again, this time even deeper than the last groan. "I guess if we gwine do it, we might as well. Somebody get a rag to git us started."

Shorty puts the same rag he used to dust over the two hands. As large as James' hand is, the monster's paw engulfs it like a child's. Shorty says, "When I jerk this rag off, you two get at it. No jumping the gun, or we'll start over. You both ready?"

James and the visitor are jockeying hand grips and are able only to nod. Shorty waits about five seconds, then snatches the rag. "Go!" He shouts. The combatants simultaneously grunt and the veins in both arms pop out like cords. Biceps and triceps swell and tendons make noise as the testing begins. Jon watches James carefully and sees his eyes grow even larger than when he first began his act.

The straining goes on and clasped hands go one way then the other. No more than an inch is gained by either. Jon looks at James' face again. His dark eyes, opened wide by tension, narrow and a look of confidence creeps over his coal-black, sweaty face. James says in a dangerously soft tone, "I reckon I carried you enough. I'm gonna open up a can of whup-ass. You ready white boy?"

The monster grunts, "Do your damnedest, black boy. I can take anything you can dish out."

James gives a rafter-lifting grunt and puts his arm and shoulder into what Jon sees as high gear. He slams the man's hand down on the non-forgiving steel of the grease rack as if no resistance at all had been encountered. Jon hears a snap, and he and Shorty look at each other and wince. "Damn," Shorty says, "That had to hurt. Damned near hurt me, standing over here."

The man yells, "You broke my damned arm! Shit, the boss is gonna kill me when I get back to work."

James grins. "Glad it wasn't my arm. I guess old James was just a mite stronger today."

"Today's ass. I don't want no more part of you. Not now, not never. Going to the hospital."

Shorty uses the rag for the third time and fashions a sling for the man's arm. "Don't worry about returning the rag, unless you want another shot at the champion. Keep that fine piece of cloth as a souvenir. Sure glad you doubled that bet. Thanks!"

As the man folds himself into the seat, the pickup gives a groan just about as loud as James' victory sound. It backfires twice and creaks out of the parking lot. Shorty takes his 40 dollars from Jon and says, "Thanks James. This will come in handy. What're you gonna do with your money?"

James' white teeth flash and gleam in an ear-splitting grin. "Reckon I'm gonna have a fine time tonight. I'll give my whole paycheck to Sheila before I go out. She won't know nothing about this 40. Wine, women, and song, that's what I mean!"

Shorty turns to Jon. "What about you, kid? You ought to get a good night out with 40 bucks. What you going to do?"

Jon shakes his head. "Nope, this is the start of a pot I've got to get together. I've got to get about two grand by next March."

"Two grand? What you need that kind of money for? You planning to get hitched?" Shorty queried.

"Nope, I'm planning a hike. I'm gonna try to hike the whole Appalachian Trail from Georgia to Maine, starting in March when it starts thinkin' 'bout getting warm in Georgia. 'Bout 2000 miles, I understand."

"You gonna be a thru-hiker? You're crazy!" exclaims Shorty. "But, if you've got such an insane itch, you'd best scratch it while you're still a kid." He turns and walks back to the brake job he was working on before the excitement started. "Two thousand miles? Crazy as a loon. Two thousand miles. Shit. The kid's nuts."

The drive-over bell rings and Jon goes back to work. His mind is active for the rest of the day, and he has to be careful to remember what Shorty insists is full service. He forgets to check tires and oil several times and his customers are shaking their heads as they drive away. He makes a decision–he'll go to the library tonight and see if he can find any books about the AT. Maybe even a how-to book. Yeah, that would be a real help. Give me some idea of what I'm getting into, what kind of gear I'm gonna need. I got an idea of what I need, but a list would really help. I reckon that my pack is gonna weigh 30 or 40 pounds, time I load up all the stuff I'll have to carry. Whew, my shoulders and back hurt just thinking about it. Enough thinking. It's time to get out of this place and get to the house.

Just before five o'clock, Jon is interrupted from his musing by Shorty calling from his office. "Hey, Jon, come on in here for a minute. I want to talk with you about this hiking thing. Sit, sit," waving his hand at the old Chevy back seat that serves as a visitor's chair. Jon rakes several piles of well-thumbed copies of *Auto Mechanic's World* and *Car Repair Digest* to the floor and sits.

"I want you to know that I thought about making a long hike like you're talking about, but that was long ago. The years and beers have taken their toll," he said ruefully, patting his stomach. "But you're young and tough. If anyone can make such a trip, I guess it's you. Tell me what you're planning."

Jon thinks for a minute, then starts. "I can't tell you much cause I just came up with the idea a day or so ago. I guess I thought of this hike a couple of weeks ago when I hiked up in the Wilderness and I talked with a guy who'd done a thru-hike. Even though I've always doubted I could do stuff or finish anything, that short hike went okay and I survived just fine. I seemed to be able to make the right decisions when I had to, up there in the woods. No pressure from people, folks wanting me to do things their way."

"Yeah, but what do you know about hiking the AT, the whole thing? It don't worry you none? What if you get hurt or lost? What about food? What about gear? Tell me what you know."

"I don't know much, yet, except it's about 2000 miles and takes most people who make it about five or six months. That guy also told me that parts of the trail were mighty rough–steep and rocky–and you had to be in great shape to think about it. He also said that a nut who hikes from Georgia to Maine is called a 'thru-hiker,' so that's what I'll be, if I can get my act together. Lots of planning to do and money to save up." Jon hung his head. "Damn, I just think about what all has to be done and I get discouraged."

"Dammit, Jon. Cut that out. You've got to think positive." Shorty leans forward, and Jon sees a spark in his eyes that he had never seen before. "I'm excited for you. I'd love to do it, but I'm way too fat and old and have too many responsibilities to go. If you get this together, you've got to take lots of pictures. In fact, I'll donate 100 bucks to your savings to buy film. That's how excited I am."

"But, but . . .what about my job? Will I still have it when I get back?" Jon returns to worrying and projecting the worst that could happen, always the worst.

"Yeah, yeah, quit sweating stuff you don't have to sweat. Just sweat the stuff you have to. This ain't one of them. Look, Jon, you're a good-looking kid with that curly blond hair and blue eyes. I've heard several giggly girls say to each other that the only reason they get gas here is so's you can wait on them. You're a good foot taller'n me. You're good for business with the womenfolk. I'll hire some kid to replace you, and he'll have to understand that when you get back, you get the job back. That is, unless he turns out to be lots better'n you, then I may have to reconsider."

The twinkle in Shorty's eye lets Jon know that his leg is being pulled. Actually, it's pretty gentle teasing for Shorty. His practical jokes are known far and wide, and Jon avoids as best he can being the butt of the complicated, oft-times rough, locker-room humor. "Thanks, Shorty. I appreciate the hell out of that. Over the next few months, I'll come in and let you know how it's going and maybe get your advice. I sure will be able to use any overtime you can throw my way. With the 40 dollars James won for me today, the 150 I have in the savings and the 100 from you, that makes me, let's see, $1710 shy of what I need. Whew, that's lots of bucks."

"Enough whining," says Shorty. "Get your butt out of here and get to thinking about what you need to get together. If you really want to start whining, I think you're looking at needing more like four grand, not two."

Jon says, "What? Where do you get four grand? Two thousand is bad enough. Where in the world am I going to get that kind of money in six months? Stick up a bank?"

"I reckon you're gonna need money when you are out on the trail. Somebody told me once that it costs you about a buck a mile when you're hiking, not counting the gear. It's for food, motel, restaurants, hiker fees, stuff like that. You got lots of research to do. When you get a list, come and talk with me about it; maybe I can make a few suggestions. But, remember I've been out of the hiking business for a long time. Wait a minute, I just thought of something. Move your butt out of that seat."

Shorty begins digging in the pile of magazines like a dog hunting a rabbit. Jon ducks as magazines fly by his head and slam into the opposite wall. Shorty is just about at the bottom of the pile when he triumphantly holds a magazine over his head. "Here, I knew it was somewhere in this pile of shit. Look, it's a REI catalog. It's 10 years old, but it'll give you an idea of what real gear looks like. You don't need to even think about any cheap stuff–it'll never hold up on the trail. Not for four or five months."

Jon says, "Thanks, Shorty. But, what's a REI?"

"Boy, you are green. That's a hiking and climbing outfit out west somewhere, in Washington or Oregon. They ain't cheap, but they carry nothing but the best stuff. Look through it for ideas, maybe write for a new catalog. Now, get the hell out of here. I've still got to figure the books for the day. I'm going to be late for dinner and the old lady's gonna raise hell, maybe put a knot on my head. When you're as bald as I am, you try to avoid knots on your head 'cause they show up so bad. Now, git!"

Jon leaves the office. He makes his way to his pickup, stumbling over just about everything lying on the floor of the garage, as he tries to look at the bright pictures and walk at the same time. He succeeds and arrives safely at his chariot, named Rosinante. It's old and wornout like Don Quixote's nag, but it gets him where he needs to go. He resists driving and drooling over pictures at the same time. Ten minutes later, the pickup shudders to a stop at home. Pookie is waiting for him. If he was a human, he would have had his legs crossed, but all he's able to do is to bark excitedly, saying in doggie language, "Where the hell have you been? Get my leash, quickly!"

Jon figures out Pookie's problem and snaps the leash on his dog's collar. Pookie drags Jon straight to the nearest tree, which he paints heavily with his mark, not saving any for other more, fortunate bushes and trees. When he finishes, Jon swears there's a smile on Pookie's face. The two go back into the house. Jon fixes Pookie's dinner. He sees a note from Andy that says he and their buddies are going to Tony's for the evening. Jon says aloud, "I guess this is my first temptation. Nope, can't do it. Got to go to the library and find help for this crazy project. No, I guess to be more accurate, the project's not crazy–the person contemplating it is the crazy one."

Jon leaves a disappointed Pookie behind and drives to the university library, where he still manages to keep a card even though it has been several years since he graduated. He searches the card catalog and finds several references to hiking the Trail. He goes to the section indicated on the card and finds most of the books on hiking and backpacking are gone. He finds one called *The Complete Walker*, which he pulls from the shelf. The book is tattered and well-used, and he surmises it has been checked out many times. He stands between the stacks and flips the pages. Even though it's not about the AT per se, it's filled with suggestions about gear, saving weight, and such. The book reads almost like a novel, and Jon decides that this will be his first reference.

He checks out the book and returns home. After feeding and walking Pookie and eating a bowl of cereal, he retires to his room where he spends two hours deeply immersed in the book. The author, Colin Fletcher, is a preservationist, something Jon hadn't thought about in the past. The last section Jon reads is, "Your mind as well as your body has been honed. You have remembered that happiness has something to do with simplicity. And so, by slow degrees, you regain a sense of harmony with everything you move through–rock and soil, plant and tree and cactus, spider and fly and rattlesnake and coyote, drop of rain and racing cloud shadow. You have long ago outgrown the crass assumption that the world was made for man."

Jon puts the book down, turns the light out, and sleeps, Fletcher's poetic words ringing in his mind. Harmony with his world or the earth is something that he doesn't enjoy now–maybe a walk, such as the one he now dreams of, will help him when he comes back to this world. Maybe it will make him self-confident. If he doesn't believe in himself, it's for damned sure no one else will. This hike will either give him a healthy dose of self-reliance or kill him. Which one is not certain, but Jon avows that he will read, plan, train, and do whatever else is needed to gain that self-confidence and become a successful thru-hiker.

2

"GERMINATION"

The Complete Walker still lies by his head on his pillow when Jon wakes at seven A. M. He lies still for a moment, enjoying the absence of a hangover. He rolls over and greets

Pookie who responds with the distinctive quasi-snarl of a Labrador Retriever "smiler." When many people meet Pookie for the first time, they recoil from him because it looks like he is about to attack. Not true; he's just giving his friendliest greeting. Pookie's a typical Lab in another way; he's a very smart, trainable, dog, but has very little common sense. He loves everybody, whether good, bad, or indifferent, at first meeting.

Jon's had Pookie for almost eight years and can't imagine going anywhere without him. Jon comes up with a question. What about Pookie and the hike? What are the rules on the AT? Are there any rules? He'd have to look into that–back to the library. He has to travel to the other side of town and talk to his parents. They'll worry. And fuss. He also still has Sissy to face. Brrr! The ice maiden is sure to turn volcanic, when she hears that Jon's plans are diverging from hers. Pretty drastic diversion by anybody's definition.

Oh, well, enough thinking–it's time to get ready for work. As Jon showers, his brain continues to work. He's still in a state of shock about Shorty's reaction to the proposed hike next spring. Shorty, an ex-hiker. Who would have thought it? Clean and ready to go, Jon walks Pookie. He drives to the garage, ready to get dirty again. Got to get those bucks! No dinero, no hike.

As Jon walks into the garage, James fixes him with a questioning gaze. "Boy, you still thinking about that hike? I thought about it some last night before I went to sleep, and I woke up later with leg cramps. How you gonna work that?"

Jon grimaces. "The physical part of it worries me a bunch. Say, James, you stay in pretty good shape for your age. You exercise, work out, stuff like that?"

"What you mean for my age? I ain't but 34 years old. No way I'm old. Yeah, I still work out, lift weights, but not as much as I used to. Working, husbanding, partying, all that shit has cut into my time at the gym. What's up with that?"

"Can you help me with an exercise program? Something that'll get me in better shape by next spring, so I might pull this off?"

"Yeah, I could. What's in it for me?"

Jon thinks for a minute. "I guess the best thing for you would be that you wouldn't have to listen to me mope and bitch, if I limp back here unsuccessful next spring or summer. Whine prevention–that's what you'll get."

James laughs. "That's cool–I'll think about it." The shrill ring of the drive-over bell shuts off further talking, and Jon services and gasses the car and forgets the conversation.

During the morning, the dream fades a bit as the garage is extremely busy and Jon is kept hopping. During lunch, Shorty calls Jon into the office. "Here, Jon, I found this old catalog last night. It's like the REI catalog–a bit old, but maybe you can call the 800 number and get a new one. This is a less expensive place than REI so you'll have to look for brand names on decent gear and avoid cheapies. Cheap stuff will let you down every time, particularly when it's most inconvenient."

"Thanks, Shorty, I'll look through it."

Jon heads for his lunch and while eating his sandwich, thumbs through the catalog, turning down pages with gear he spots that he might need. After lunch, he uses the office phone and calls the 800 numbers of both REI and the outfit in Missouri and orders new catalogs.

The afternoon is just as busy as the morning, and Jon swears that every single car in town is buying gas at Shorty's that day. No hike planning can find a place in his head, but the day flies by swiftly. As he goes through the familiar rou-

tine of emptying the cash register that is his pocket, he remembers the first time he got home and discovered a wad of bills in his pocket. He panicked, thinking Shorty would believe he was pilfering from the garage. He called Shorty at home and confessed. To his relief, Shorty got a real laugh and told him, "Don't worry about it, Jon. Happens all the time. Just lock the cash register up tonight and bring it back in the morning. I'll count it then. If I didn't trust you, I'd make you bring the cash from each sale in when they pay you."

The evening passes much like the day before. Walk Pookie, clean up, back to the library. He finds that a book by a guy named Jan Curran, a thru-hiker, had been returned during the day. He snatches it up and checks it out. He sits in Rosinante and scans the book before starting the engine. In the introduction he reads, "The Trail . . . can be a beautiful, but demanding master, who extracts from those who would hike it, an ever increasing measure of dedication and sacrifice . . . the Trail becomes the catalyst for self-knowledge or self-fulfillment." Jon shuts the book. "Damn, sounds like this guy has been there, done that and is looking into my head. 'Self-fulfillment,' he says. I guess that's the idea behind this whole crazy dream. At least I'm not the only person to dream a thru-hike. I guess I'll find out as I read this book whether this guy had as many doubts before he started walking as I do now."

Jon drives home, a confused man. At the house, Andy is sitting at the kitchen table and is full of questions. "Well, you started your to-do list yet? Or have you given up already?"

Jon laughs, then turns serious. "Nope, I haven't given up. Actually, I started scratching a list today. Just a few things that I know I have to get done, but it's not worthy of being called a list yet. If anything, I'm more positive than I was. Shorty's real supportive–turns out he used to backpack before he became a businessman and got old and bald and fat. He gave me a couple of his old camping gear catalogs and I've checked out several library books. To answer your question, no, I haven't started my real list yet cause I don't know enough to even begin. I've got to do research before I start that list."

To Jon's surprise, Andy agrees. "Good idea, Bud, best find out what you're getting yourself into before you go off half-cocked. Damn, you may grow up, yet. I'm gonna miss you down at Tony's. Since you're just getting ready for a hike and not going into a monastery, maybe you can lower yourself every once in a while and join us?"

Jon laughs. "Yeah, I can. I just need to avoid those way-too-many-beer nights with you guys. Yeah, I'll do that. A beer or two won't hurt me any. I don't think it will disturb my training regime."

Andy asks, "The tough question. Sissy?"

Jon shakes his head. "Not yet. I guess it's because I know what her response is gonna be. When I tell her, there's gonna be a scene, and I dread that. It'll happen in a day or so."

Andy responds, "My fatherly advice is that bad news is just like dead fish–it don't smell any better with time. Better get it done."

"I know, I know. Now, how about getting something to eat? Lorenzo's all right with you? I can almost see a plateful of spaghetti and meatballs."

"I'm shocked. All that fat. All that grease. All those cholesterols. What about your training?"

"Since I haven't set it up yet, it's hard to break. Let's go."

After supper they return home and Jon curls up on the couch with the catalogs, wishing that the new ones would come. He wants to begin to get an idea of what this grand scheme is going to cost. He'd checked his savings balance and he is just shy of $200, thanks in part to James' arm wrestling victory. A start, but it has to grow faster. Otherwise he'll be starting his hike in the year 2020.

Jon and Pookie take a slightly longer walk that night and Pookie carefully examines and anoints every tree and bush. Jon has to laugh at him. "Dog, I guess the mountains are gonna wear out your sniffer. More trees than you've ever seen in your life. For that matter, that's true for me, too. All those trees, not many people, all those steep rocky grades, sweat, dirt, blisters, and rain all the time. I'm nuts for thinking this. Maybe I won't lose too much face if I back out before I get any deeper . . . "

Negative thoughts ringing in Jon's brain, man and dog return home. Dog to sleep soundly, man to worry until he falls into a dream-disturbed sleep. More dreams of pain and failure, of people laughing at him–particularly Matt. Jon can even hear his big brother in his dreams. Bad enough that he has to share his life–now he has to share his dreams. Ain't fair. Ain't fair at all.

At work the next morning, Jon is greeted by James as soon as he gets out of his truck. "Home-boy, after your question yesterday about training, I been thinking. I've decided you need a training boss. That's cool. You down for it?"

Jon is amazed. "Thanks, James. I really haven't thought much about it, other than I have to get in shape. What're you thinking about?"

James pulls a tattered piece of paper from his pocket. "I'm thinking we're going to take it light. Here's your orders for the next two weeks. I figure you gotta work on your wind, your legs, and your upper body strength. Show me your biceps and triceps. Let's see what you got."

With flashbacks to his childhood, Jon "makes a muscle" and James places his hand on Jon's arm. His massive hand engulfs Jon's biceps. James whistles. "Boy, we got a hell of a lot of work to do. My momma's got more muscle definition and tone than you do and she's 65 years old. For the rest of this week, we're gonna work on wind and legs. Then, we'll start on muscle tone. You down for it?"

"Yeah, you gotta start somewhere." Jon looks at the paper and it's his turn to whistle. "Wow, I'll be ready for the Olympics. This is just for the first week? Walk a mile each day, checking pulse after each quarter mile. Fat-gram consumption down to 25 grams a day. Twenty sit-ups and 10 push-ups every morning. Whew."

James looks at Jon with a serious expression. "Boy, this is just the beginning. We'll see what you got. Here's a present I got last night for you." James goes to his dilapidated car and reaches into the back seat. He hands Jon a small notebook with the words, "Jon's training" written on the cover. "You need to write what you do and what you eat in this every day. Then, show it to me here at work. If you get behind in your training, I'm gonna whup that ass. I'm serious about this; you'd better be! I ain't doing all this work for nothing. I don't know the word failure."

Jon says, "I am serious. Thanks James, though I'm not sure how thankful I'll be as I get into this. Sounds like work."

"It will be work. You've worked for years to get into such bad shape–we only got six months to recover from it all. We'd best get to work before Shorty starts tripping. You get started on all that today."

Jon puts the notebook in his truck and thinks about the notebook off and on the rest of the day. During lunch, he eats a large hamburger and French fries and James shakes his head. "Boy, you got any idea how many fat grams that thing has? You best get a book with fat-gram counts so you can look them things up. You're a greenhorn, for sure. I've gotten myself in a spot." Shaking his head, he walks away. The instant guilt makes Jon's last few bites of his lunch taste like cardboard.

After work, Jon stops at the drugstore to buy a small pocket-sized calorie and fat-gram booklet. He looks up the hamburger and fries and whistles. "Damn, I can't eat for the next three days!" Nonetheless, he dutifully records the food in his notebook. Pookie enjoys the mile walk that night, "That dog's in better shape than I am," thinks Jon as he huffs back into the house. Both sleep well.

The next morning, Jon manages the 20 sit-ups with no problem, but can only strain his way through six push-ups. He has a fruit bar for breakfast, after discovering it has only a few fat grams, and carefully writes everything in its proper place. James is waiting for him at the garage and looks at the morning's results. "Okay, it's in the works. You need to add a push-up every day till you get up to that 10. Maybe we'll hold it there for a week or so till you can handle more. You get that fat-gram book?"

Jon proudly pulls it out of his shirt pocket. "Right next to my heart. I'll take it to the grocery store tonight when I shop. I guess I'm gonna look like a little old lady comparing coupon prices when I look at every label for fat content, but I'll do it, boss man."

"You'd best do it, or you'll make me unhappy. I'd hate to have to trip on you. I'd take you out."

That night, Jon goes to the library and walks straight to the outdoor sports section where he finds no new books. When he talks to the librarian, she gets interested in his search, and the two pour over her copy of R.R. Bowker's *Books in Print.* Jon points out several thru-hiker books and she agrees to get them on inter-library loans. She says, "It usually takes a couple of days to get books in this way; I'll give you a call when they arrive. This sounds like quite a project you've set out for yourself."

When Jon arrives home, he finds a message from Sissy on the answering machine. He has neglected his daily call to her and she sarcastically asks him to return her call, if he can find time in his busy schedule. She has some more thoughts on the wedding. The tone of her voice and the short, clipped words she uses leave no doubt as to her opinions on one Jon Parker at the present time.

To quote Andy butchering Mr. Shakespeare, Jon can't quite "screw his courage to the sticking point," and the call goes unmade again that night. The walk does get made, although he finds a few muscles in his legs that object when he stretches to get loosened up. He notes this in the ever-present notebook and James grins the next morning as he checks on his pupil's progress.

"How bout your stomach. Any soreness there? I see you managed to do seven pushups. No pain, no gain."

Jon ruefully admits that his arms screamed at the extra pushup but he did it anyway. James claps him on the back and says, "I reckon a lot of muscles gonna scream starting next week when we hit the gym. I still got a membership at the black gym across town, though I've not used it in a while. I reckon them big black fighters gonna wonder why a skinny white boy is messing up the average muscle size and tone in the gym. We start next Monday."

Jon manages to worry about his acceptance in that gym for the rest of the day. Somehow, his mind can seize on just about anything to worry about, exaggerating and projecting until he convinces himself that he can't possibly do whatever it is that he wants to do. Positive thinking, that's what he needs. Right now, he's real positive that he has gotten himself into a real mess and there's no turning back without a serious loss of face. What was it he had heard? "The longest journey begins with but a single step?" Jon guesses he's taken maybe a part of a single step–only time would tell if he could or would keep on walking. No, for now it was to see if he could keep on getting ready to walk. The walk itself would come along soon enough.

Jon successfully avoids Sissy the rest of that week. His two library books come in and he studies them with much more interest than he ever did a textbook while at the University of Alabama. Those books were history texts. Now, his thinking is that these new books, written by thru-hikers, could help keep him alive.

Jon learns about weight. Some of the early thru-hikers carried almost no gear at all–power walkers arranged for friends to meet them at road-crossings to bring them food and supplies. Power-walking, for speed rather than just completing the trail, is apparently frowned on by many of the purist thru-walkers and Jon feels that his goal of completing the hike in five or six months is more attainable for him than the 60 days or less in which some of the power folks complete the trail. His early estimate of 30 pounds has bumped up to about 50 pounds. He reads about weight-conscious hikers who carry it to an extreme. One early hiker carried a Bible with him and would tear out each page as he read it to cut weight. There were those who would make sure they exchanged change to get the lightest possible combination; for example, give two nickels for a dime. Some advocated cutting off the handle of their toothbrush and the little cardboard square from tea bags. Maybe a bit anal-retentive, but it could add up. Weight reduction of gear seemed to be a key to physical success, helping with attitude. With these thoughts running through his mind, Jon begins his list of needed gear. He hopes that the improved attitude would follow along behind the gear.

The new gear catalogs arrive, and Jon pours over them as well as the how-to books. The costs amaze him; he finds a direct reverse correlation between cost and weight. The lighter the gear, the more expensive it is. Jon extends both his list and his cost estimates for gear. He thinks about picking out the few pieces of gear his current cache of money would buy, but decides to wait until he can get a better deal on shipping costs by buying more at one time. His list continues to expand.

The physical part of his program also grows. He finally attains that elusive 10th push-up, and on Friday it hurts less. James keeps on his back about the program, and Jon is beginning to believe that he's selected a monster for a fitness coach. But he keeps on going. And, he keeps on dreading the inevitable confrontation with Sissy. Sooner or later, he needs to get that done. Even though he is making progress with his goal on all other fronts, the entanglement with Sissy is mentally holding him back. He decides that Friday night is the night. He'll get it done.

On Friday, Jon calls Sissy from the garage and listens to her complain about his lack of attention. When she has to stop to catch a breath, he jumps in. "Sissy, let's go to dinner tonight. You can finish chewing on me then. Where do you want to go? Tony's?"

"Not there–it's so noisy. Let's go to the family buffet down the street."

Jon inwardly groans. That's the last place he would have chosen. Family dining, quiet conversation, lots of fat grams and calories. Not the best place for either a knock-down, drag-out or a low-fat diet. Oh, well, he thinks. "Okay. Pick you up at seven?"

He interrupted her acceptance with a hurried, "Whoops, the bell rang. Got to service that car. See ya!"

Jon works on getting through the rest of the day. The more he thinks about the evening's pending confrontation, the more he dreads it. He hates being the center of attention.

Jon imagines the scene at the restaurant. He has to interrupt Sissy's babbling about china patterns and dress-fittings. He tells her of his dream. As he finishes describing his plan, Sissy goes ballistic and throws her full plate of food at him. Spaghetti is dripping over his face. "Six months–are you out of your mind? Plus five to get ready? You're nuts if you think I'm gonna wait over a year while you go live in the woods like some crazy mountain man. Jon, grow up!"

In Jon's fantasizing, the last eight or 10 of Sissy's words are delivered in a force-10 gale. Every single person in the restaurant stops what they are doing. Conversations cease in mid word. Forks pause halfway to mouths. People carrying trays come to a complete halt. Every eye and every ear in the place is turned and tuned to find out what happens next. Jon tries to crawl under the table.

The ringing in Jon's ears turns out to be the drive-over bell rather than increased blood pressure or pulse. He shakes his head to rid his brain of the unwanted images, and gratefully goes out to service the car that may have just saved his imaginary life. That scene was frighteningly real. Maybe even prophetic?

The rest of the afternoon drags by. Jon continues to prepare his speech, writing and rewriting mental notes about the safest way, the most intelligent and grown-up way, the absolute best way to de-fuse explosions. As the work day ends, he's no closer to a potentially successful approach than he was when the day started.

Jon, in spite of little attention paid to his driving, arrives home safely. He scratches Pookie's ears, and they complete their walk. He showers and dresses feeling somewhat like he's dressing for a funeral–his own.

No matter how he stalls and delays, the inexorable movement of the clock hands continues, and seven o'clock comes. He takes a deep, quavering breath, and marches out to the pickup, to drive his own chariot to his own execution. Living up to its namesake, Rosinante finds its way to Sissy's house. and Jon automatically goes through the routine. He greets Sissy, talks man-talk with Mr. Swingle, walks to the truck, holds the door for Sissy, gets in on his side, and drives away. Sissy starts immediately about china, crystal, and silverware, and Jon shifts his brain into neutral.

Five china decisions later, they arrive at the restaurant. As they stand in line, Jon worries about what he could eat and not destroy his fat-gram goal for the day. Let's see, he thought, "Concentrate on salads, vegetables, baked fish. No clam chowder or chicken wings. No butter-soaked rolls. No pecan pie with ice cream." Damn, he'd listed as no-nos, every reason he loved all-you-can-eat buffets.

As Jon and Sissy make their way along the tables groaning with food, she observes his changed eating habits. “Jon, are you feeling okay? You usually need sideboards on your plate to keep from spilling everything. Are you slimming down for the wedding?”

Jon inwardly groans. He covers his distress with a cheerful “Nah, just watching fat grams a bit closer. I’m getting a little thick around the middle.”

“Beer, more than likely.” she sniffs. “Are you still closing Tony’s down every night?”

“Nope, I was there just one night this week and I left at eleven after two beers.” They finish filling their plates and find a table. Eating takes Sissy’s mind off of the wedding for the time being. Jon’s food goes down hard and collects in a large, heavy lump in the middle of his belly. He dreads saying what he knows he has to say tonight. It has to be tonight; he can wait no longer.

Sissy goes back to the dessert line and brings back a piece of pecan pie with soft ice cream and Jon’s mouth waters. Sissy sees the expression on his face and smiles. “I guess this doesn’t fit on your low-fat diet. You’re not even getting dessert? Maybe you’ve got more will power than I thought. I’m impressed.” She attacks and defeats the pie a la mode in short order as Jon helplessly watches his favorite dessert disappear.

Dinner completed, Sissy starts, “Momma said something about a neat house over on Fourth Street she saw yesterday. A two-bedroom white frame house with a fenced-in back yard. I thought we’d go see it tomorrow after you get off of work. What time does the garage close?”

Jon takes a deep breath, and prepares to launch himself over the cliff. “Sissy, I’ve got to talk to you about something, and I guess this is as good a time as any.”

Sissy steamrollers right over the top of Jon’s comment and begins again. “I guess that’s settled, then. We’ll go over there tomorrow at about six o’clock. Are you going to pick me up?”

Jon tries again. “Sissy, that’s what I need to talk about. I can’t look at a house to rent right now. I’m saving all my money for a trip I’m going to make next year, from March or April through September.” His head is spinning, but he plunges forward. He has one foot over the cliff and the other foot is sliding fast on a banana peel. "I've decided I'm going to hike the entire Appalachian Trail, from Georgia to Maine. So I guess the wedding will have to be postponed–for a while, anyway."

"But, why? Why then? What about the plans we've made?" Sissy wails, her voice gaining in decibels and going up an octave.

Jon winces. "Sissy, *you've* been making all the plans. I reckon I love you, so I've gone along with you. But, this is something I've got to do while I still can."

Sissy's eyes narrow and her voice becomes more of a whisper, a deadly, cutting whisper. "Damn you, Jon Parker, if you think I'm going to sit around and wait for six or seven months for you to go climb a mountain and have to explain all of this to my family and friends after all the preparations that have been made, you've got another think coming. The whole thing is over. Forget it! You can go straight to hell! I don't want to see you again. Since you obviously have no consideration for me at all, you don't need to worry about taking me home. I'll go call my Daddy to come over here and get me. I'm leaving! Get away from me! I never want to see you again!"

Sissy rises and flounces away from the table leaving Jon as an object of curiosity and extreme interest to the people sitting close by. The last few words of what had been a whispered tirade had become louder. He thinks, "That really wasn't so bad. At least everybody in this part of Tuscaloosa didn't hear it." He decides that he had better stay where he is for a few minutes, rather than walk by Sissy, stationed at the front door, waiting for her father to come and pick her up. He swears he can see real steam coming from her stiff form.

Jon's waitress stops by the table, a wry smile on her face. "Sounds like your girl isn't too happy with you. Can I get you anything? A Tevlar vest? An aspirin? An icepack?"

"You can get me out of here by another door, if you've got one. I don't want to walk out the front door. I don't like bloodshed, particularly when it's mine."

Her grin becomes even bigger. "Yeah, I can help you out. Blood's tough to get out of the carpet. Come on, you can go out the employee's entrance, back off of the kitchen. The manager might fuss at me, but it's not the first time and probably won't be the last."

Jon is led through the kitchen and he scurries to his truck and leads the blue cloud of smoke home. He arrives just as Andy is walking out the door. Jon says, "The evil deed is done, and I'm still standing, though my knees are weak and shaky. I told Sissy."

Andy grins. "I don't guess she's the type to sit around quietly with the home fires burning and the candle in the window waiting for her man to come back from the wars, huh?"

"Let's just say she didn't take it very well. Not very grownup at all. But, I escaped with my body, if not my dignity, intact. Where are you headed now?"

"Hell, man, it's Friday night. I'm going to close down Tony's. It's a shame you're on your strict diet, or I'd ask you to come along. You look like you could use a beer or three or four."

"Ask me," Jon says.

"Come on."

He went.

3 "THE GROWTH PROCESS BEGINS"

Saturday is usually Jon's day off. But, he's asked Shorty for whatever overtime he could get and Shorty offered Saturdays. Jon figures he needs money more than time right now, so he gladly accepts. His head isn't in the best of shape on this particular Saturday, but it is amazing how good he feels. He feels as if a weight has been removed from his shoulders after last night. His convoluted logic tells him if he had needed lots of nights at Tony's in order to keep his mind willing to stay in a relationship with Sissy, now that that relationship has ended, Tony's beer was necessary last night to put a final exclamation point in place. To get closure.

The drive-over bell hurts his head every time it rings, but he feels free. Really free, for the first time in a long while. He guesses he had loved Sissy, but maybe he just loved the relative freedom of being "spoken for." As such, he didn't have to get into the hunt and pursuit game of new dates, what to talk about, what not to talk about, where to go, where not to go. Sometimes a relationship is as comfortable as an old shoe; however, it can be just as boring.

As the day moves on, Jon comes to another decision. He needs to go across town and talk to his folks about his coming adventure. He dreads it. Part of his feelings of inferiority came from that house on the hill overlooking the river. A regular pastime in that house was asking why Jon wasn't more like his older brother, Matt. Why didn't he make straight A's, why wasn't he class president, why didn't he have a good job with somebody like IBM, the company that had snapped Matt up as soon as he left school. Why wasn't he wearing dark blue suits, white shirts, and blue- and red-striped power ties. Why wasn't he married and producing grandchildren to satisfy his folks. Why didn't he ever complete anything he started. Even though it had been a decade and a half ago, why didn't he even finish his soapbox racer in Cub Scouts, or complete his Eagle Scout award. Why, why, why? Jon's head hurts even worse thinking of the why's. But, he needs to let them know what he is up to.

So, he calls and asks his mother if they will be home tonight. Using her mothers' problem-sensing antenna, she immediately asks, "Why? What's wrong? Are you in trouble?"

Jon responds defensively, "No, no trouble. I just figure it's been a while since I've been over there and I thought I'd just come visit you and Pop. I'll bring Pookie and be over there at about seven. See you then." He hangs up the phone, cutting off the additional questions that seemed to flow from his mother like the Warrior River during the spring floods.

Jon loads Pookie into the truck ready to face the next milestone in his quest. The well-behaved Pookie is always welcome in his folks' house, maybe even more so than Jon. Pookie was just a tiny ball of black fur when his Dad had bought him as a present for Jon's 16th birthday. It had been over his mother's objections as she doubted Jon's ability to take care of anything. But, he had fooled her as he fed and watered the puppy daily and cleaned up the inevitable puppy messes. She was even more amazed as he trained the playful young dog, giving up one evening every week to accompany Pookie to obedience school. Jon always wondered whether it was he or the dog that was trained, but Pookie is well-behaved. He will sit, stay, lie down and keep his muddy feet on the ground. People who normally don't like dogs, love Pookie. Jon has even taught him not to beg for food, and can put a bone under Pookie's nose which he will refuse until Jon nods okay.

Jon and friend arrive at his folk's home and go into the living room where Elizabeth and Richard Parker are watching television. Jon's mother hugs him and holds him at arm's length. Her trouble antenna are still in fine operating order. "Jon, are you sure you're not in any trouble? You feeling all right?"

Jon extracting himself from his mother's hug, laughs, "No, Mom, I'm fine. Honest."

Jon's dad, never removing his eyes from the one-eyed TV monster, grunts his hello, in response to Jon's "Hey, Pop, how are you doing?" Jon and his mom sit on the couch, safely out of the line of sight between his father and the TV. Jon and his brother had learned early in their lives that stepping into that line of sight was a sure way to get into trouble with their soft-spoken, yet intense father.

"Mom, I need to tell you what I'm about to do," begins Jon. "I'm planning to do something different."

Jon's mother wails, "I knew it. I just knew it. Okay, let's have it. What kind of trouble are you in?"

Jon hastens to reassure her. "No, Mom, I told you I'm not in any trouble. I'm just working to grow up. Well, first, I guess Sissy's and my wedding is off."

The wail returns. "Oh, Jon, she's such a nice girl. Did you do something dumb? Why is the wedding off?"

Jon has a fleeting thought that he shuts down as tacky. Maybe the reason his mother likes Sissy so much is because she is a young carbon copy of herself. Jon has no problem visualizing himself sitting in a chair just like Pop's, glued to the TV, responding to questions and comments with "Uh-huh," and never daring to doubt or question anything, 'cause keeping the peace is his number one priority.

"Well, Mom, I guess the reason that the wedding is off is 'cause I told her what I'm going to do next spring. In March or April, I'm going to start a hike on the Appalachian Trail from end to end. All 2000 miles of it, from Georgia to Maine. She didn't take kindly to my plan, because it'll take me five or six months. I won't be finished and back home until probably October. That is, if I can make it."

As Jon finishes, the silence hangs heavy, broken only by the TV characters' dialogue. It's quiet for so long that Jon starts to worry. Then his mother starts.

"Jon, Jon. What are we going to do with you? I thought you were ready to settle down, with a wife and someday give us more grandchildren like Matt has done. Now I hear that you're going off on a wild goose chase, the wildest I've ever heard. What if you get hurt up there? Who's going with you? This isn't something Matt would do; this is crazy stuff." She rests for just a second, gathering her strength for another attack.

Jon sits still, with his hand resting on Pookie's head, figuring out his response. To his complete and utter amazement, the response comes from the other side of the room, from his dad's over-stuffed chair. "Hush, Elizabeth. Leave the boy alone. This is Jon, not Matt. At least Jon won't be a stuffed shirt like his brother. I think it's the neatest thing I've heard of in a long time. Jon, tell me about it. What have you done to get ready? What training program are you going to do? What kind of gear are you going to get? What about food, water? How do you get additional supplies while you are on the trail?"

When Jon is able to draw a breath, he steals a glance at his mother. She puts on her "great stone face," the one she wears when Jon's dad speaks his mind, rare as that is. Jon answers his dad's questions and finishes with the admission that he's beginning to read enough about it to be dangerous: his research is just starting. His doubts are legion.

After Jon finishes, his dad shakes his head in amazement at what his youngest son is proposing. "Jon, if you pull this off, it's something nobody will be able to take from you for the rest of your life. I think it's great. Let me know how I can help."

Jon's mom bustles to the kitchen, and the rattling and banging of pots and pans provide a hint as to her opinion of the conversation. Jon's dad chuckles. "I'll work on her and she'll come around after a while. Now, a practical question–what about money? I doubt you've been able to save much out of your garage paycheck. How much do you guess this is going to cost you? A grand? Maybe two?"

Jon ruefully shakes his head. "Yeah, Pop, that's one of the real problems I see ahead. I figure I'll need to buy all new gear, cause my old stuff is way too heavy and mostly broken down. The gear is gonna cost about two grand. That, plus the expenses on the trail, will total about $4000. They figure a couple of bucks per mile, plus gear. It's gonna be tough, but I'll get it somehow."

Jon's dad then makes a statement that completely floors Jon. He isn't able to respond at all when his father matter of factly says, "I guess you can put me down to help with the gear. I've got a small savings account for a rainy day. Your momma doesn't know anything about it 'cause I never told her. I'm saving for emergencies. Meet me over at the bank at lunchtime day after tomorrow and I'll transfer $2000 over to your checking account."

Jon is speechless. He has been dreading this visit almost as much as he had dreaded talking with Sissy. Now, he not only has his dad's moral support, but financial backing as well. He stands up and gives his dad a hug from behind his chair.

His father says, "Enough mushy stuff. Now, hush–I'm losing out on what these idiots are saying. God knows, the world might come to an end if I don't hear the ending of this mind-numbing story."

"Thanks, Pop, I appreciate it more than you'll ever know. I'll even pay you back if you want."

"I said, hush. I also said that I was giving it to you. What part of the word giving didn't you understand?" The twinkle in his eye softens the words and Jon hushes.

He goes into the kitchen and hugs his Mom. "Mom, I don't expect you to understand what I'm doing, but I think I have to do it. I've never finished anything in my life as everybody is fond of telling me, but I will finish this! I think it's important that I do it."

Elizabeth wipes a tear from her eye, "No, I don't understand why you're doing this crazy thing. Maybe I will, in time. Now, why don't you take that fat mooch over there back home before he eats me out of house and home." She points at Pookie, lying on the floor by the refrigerator. He is sleepily guarding a ham bone that is lying by his head. The bone is clean and polished and it gleams like ivory.

Jon laughs, "Pookie, get your lazy butt up and go thank Mom." Pookie creaks upright, stretches each leg very carefully and smiles, then he walks to Elizabeth. He sits and offers his right paw, still smiling. She has no choice but to laugh. She takes the proffered thanks and he gives her a doggy kiss on the cheek.

"Best kid I ever had, that's for sure. Take him away. By the way, what are you going to do with him while you're up in the mountains playing Grizzly Adams?"

Jon stops in the center of the kitchen. "That's something I haven't completely figured out. I've got several ideas but I haven't made up my mind as of yet."

"We'll be glad to keep him, if you want us to. He's no trouble at all. The truth be told, I've missed him ever since you moved cross town into your own place."

"Mom, I need to think some more about this. I may take him part of the way with me, then get somebody to pick him up and keep him for me till I get back. The books I've been reading are kinda down on taking dogs with you, but I can't imagine not taking him with me. He's my best friend and has been for years now."

During this discourse, the subject being discussed sits and looks back and forth between Jon and his mother. He stands and with a bark, informs Jon that it's time for him to go outside. He is so anxious to depart that he even leaves the ham bone behind.

Jon drives home in a daze, a state in which lately he seems to be in constantly.

Sleep does not come easily and he gets out of bed three times to re-read the catalogs. He realizes that spending the $2000 gift from his father is not going to be a problem. Finally, exhaustion takes over and Jon sleeps, dreaming about the romantic nature that the trail holds for him in just a few short months. Money has calmed the savage beasts of the doubt monster.

The next morning, Jon joins Andy at the coffee pot and blurts out his good news about the gear money. "Damn, bud," says Andy. "That's great! That should get you well along the way. Indicating Pookie, he says, "What are you going to do with this guy?"

`"Mom asked the same thing last night. I told her I would have to think about it. He would be pretty good company and he might scare away someone wanting to hassle me, as long as they didn't know what a wuss he is. I have read that dogs can be a problem, particularly in shelters on rainy days. As soon as your dog shakes once on people's stuff, they're just liable to toss you and the dog out into the rain. I'm also worried about wild critters, skunks and porcupines and bobcats and such. Pookie would have to bark if something didn't seem right. I can't stop him from that. I would also have to carry extra food and water. Taking him will be tough. But, leaving him behind would be even tougher." Jon falls silent, pondering his damned if you do, damned if you don't dilemma.

Andy says, "Well, Pookie is in pretty good shape. That's a plus. He's also pretty well trained and behaves most of the time, anyway. He shouldn't be too much of a nuisance to other hikers. Maybe you could take him for part of the way. I'd be glad to come pick him up along the trail where you plan to stop, anyway."

Jon stares in amazement. "Damn, Andy, you been reading my mail? That's exactly what I was thinking. Maybe take him as far as the northern boundary of the Smokies. From what I read, parts of the northern section of the AT pass through pretty civilized territory, so other dogs and people would be a problem. I guess that the trail would eventually be rough on his feet and I don't want to injure him. If you wouldn't mind meeting us and picking him up there, my folks want to board him the rest of the time."

Andy laughs. "I wouldn't mind keeping him for that time, either. I was actually going to miss the big mutt. But, if he's at your folks' place, I can go see him every once in a while. There, one more challenge met and whipped. See, if you just keep a positive attitude, nothing but good things will come along."

Jon laughs, "Andy, you're the most incurable optimist I know. With my total pessimism, we make a hell of a team."

Later in the day, Jon takes the order blanks from his catalogs to the grocery store and makes several copies of each form. He figures that he'll probably fill them out three or four times each, and this way when he makes his final decisions, he could send in a clean copy. He spends the rest of the day reading the gear sections of the thru-hiker books he has checked out of the library. He makes one decision that he is proud of. He finds that when it comes to hiking boots, there are as many opinions as there are people to give them. The majority of the writers suggest medium-weight boots. These would give support and protection from rocky trails but don't add too much weight to the already substantial weight which will be on his person. His earlier estimate of 25 or 30 pounds has risen to closer to 45 to 50 pounds. He decides to order two pair of boots as soon as possible, so he can break both pairs in while his feet had time to heal from the inevitable blisters. He will wear one pair, and ship the other pair ahead to himself with one of the care packages to be sent every 10 days or so.

Damn, that's another detail to work out. He has to decide on an approximate schedule, without falling into the trap of scheduling himself so tightly that he couldn't enjoy himself, or take a side trail if he feels like it or stay an extra day in a motel in civilization if he needs additional physical or mental healing. This is likely the only time that he will be able to take a long distance trek like this before he is governed by life, so he means to make the most of this possibility.

Jon and Pookie walk two miles instead of the one on his training regime. After they return home, Jon amazes himself by doing two extra push-ups and 10 extra sit-ups. James will be proud of him, tomorrow. James. Damn, he'd forgotten. Tomorrow is the day they will go to the gym. Another confrontation to worry about. He isn't anxious to face that gym full of black fighters. He figures he'll be as welcome as a skunk in a perfume factory, but he had told James he would do it, so he will. He sighs. Damn, one problem after another.

The next morning, Jon leaves home for the garage, feeling good about going to work. Pretty amazing, considering that he usually feels like he is going to the salt mines. His co-workers look strange when he greets them with a cheerful hello and a big smile. Considering the weekend he'd had, successfully cutting Sissy's apron strings plus the surprise of his father's gift of all the gear he would need, it's no wonder he's in such an up-mood.

James responds to his greeting with a sour expression. "You won't be so hyped when my boys take you out."

Jon says, "James, even they don't worry me any. I have to get into shape, and they may be able to help. Nope, I'm looking forward to lunchtime." He sprinted out to service the first car that drove up. James watched him go and muttered, "Damn crazy white boy. I'd shoot him and put him out of his misery, but it'd be a waste of a good bullet."

Jon spends the entire morning being cheerful. To his surprise, three customers tipped him, two a dollar each and one two dollars, when he went out of his way to do favors for them. Even though Dad had come through with flying colors, Jon still had some 1700 bucks to go and every little bit helps.

The long-awaited lunch break comes, and Jon gets into James' old car, clutching his gym bag. As they pull into the parking lot by the building housing the gym, Jon feels a momentary twinge in his belly. A twinge that gets stronger as they walk up the dimly lit staircase. James opens the door to the gym and Jon looks into the smoke-filled room as he takes a step inside. He comes to a complete stop and as he notices every single eye in the place is looking at him. As he glances around, he sees a variety of men, in terms of height. They have two things in common–all are black and all are extremely well-built. Whether tall or short, muscles bulge, some making James look small by comparison.

Several young blacks swagger over to James and greet him with various and sundry handslaps. One asks, “James, what’s up with that? Bringing that skinny white boy over here? You know what the rep of this place is. You know how it is down here.”

James laughs, “Yeah, you’re right. This here’s Jon. He works with me over at Shorty’s Garage. He’s planning on taking a 2000 mile hike next spring and I promised I’d get him in better shape. Not that it’s gonna be too difficult getting him into better shape than he’s in now, cause that’s not saying much. Chill, he’s my homie.”

James leads Jon to the locker room where they change into shorts and tennis shoes. For the next hour, Jon is led through a routine of tortures that he’s positive are medieval in origin. Punching small bags, big bags, having heavy bags thrown at his belly. Rope-skipping, weight-lifting, along with several pieces of exercise equipment that definitely looked like the rack used on the Count of Monte Cristo. But, he survives. Well enough that James even compliments Jon as they drove back to work. “Boy, you did okay. You’re on. We’ll plan to go over there once a week. But, this don’t replace the daily routine. I need to increase your reps on those exercises. We may add a weight belt when you walk every day. Might as well get used to toting something.”

Jon groans, “Right now, I believe I’m enjoying all I can stand, maybe even more than I can stand. If the saying ‘no pain-no gain’ is right, I gained a bunch today.”

James laughs. “It’ll get easier. A little less worse, anyway. Don’t want you to be able to blame me if you don’t make that whole hike. Nope, your body’s gonna be ready. It’s up to you to keep your head together.”

The garage is just about as busy during the afternoon as it had been that morning. Jon continues to be as cheerful to the customers as he could. It does become more difficult because he is sore. Real sore. Parts of his body that he hadn’t really been aware of before, hurt. When he bends over a hood to check oil and water levels, his back hurts. When he stoops to check tire pressures, his legs hurt. When he has to lift a tire from a trunk to repair later, his chest and arms hurt.

James walks by Jon late in the afternoon. He laughs, "Yo, what's up with that sad look? You hurtin'?"

"James, I hurt all over. Every single part of me has aches and pains."

"Well, that just means that we were on. You used muscles today you haven't used in years. If they're hurtin', they exercised. If it makes you feel any better, they'll hurt tomorrow morning even more. But, don't rest tonight–keep your routine going, your walk and reps. This gym thing just comes down once a week–the reps are where it's at."

Jon's cheerfulness, even though forced during the afternoon, pays off again and he garners six more dollars in tips. When the day finally ends, he goes straight home. He finds an old mayonnaise jar in the pantry and places it on his dresser as a tip jar. Jon and Pookie take their evening walk–in truth Pookie walks, runs, and scampers while he sniffs every tree and marks most of them, while Jon hobbles and groans. But they make one and one-half miles and Jon feels a little looser when they return home.

Jon spends his evening re-visiting the gear catalogs, and writes up his first order form–he orders two pair of medium-weight hiking boots and eight pair of socks, four pair of heavy hiking socks and four pair of light-weight silk inner socks. He completes his exercises, albeit with enough moaning and groaning that Pookie sits nearby, cocking his head with worry about his master.

Jon's bed has never felt so comfortable.

In the morning, Jon creaks a bit as he goes through his morning routine, but he has to admit that the exercises the evening before helped alleviate some of the muscle twangs. On the way to the garage, he drives by the post office and mails his order. It feels good, the first of many.

Jon moves through the morning still feeling really good about the progress made thus far. He meets his dad at the bank at lunch and deposits his check in the checking account. He shakes hands with his dad. "Thanks again, Pop. This makes this whole thing seem more possible. I'm working hard on coming up with the rest."

"I said it was no problem. I'm glad to help. Everybody needs a dream of some kind, and this is the first I can remember that you have ever expressed. It's time for you to get out from under Matt's shadow. Now we'd both best get back to work. Come see us!" He walks toward his car and Jon toward Rosinante'. Maybe it's not an impossible dream, after all.

The next few weeks speed by as Jon becomes more and more familiar with the routine. He loses only about five pounds, but his body is definitely getting firmer. The percentage of body fat is going down regularly. James compliments him several times, but Jon learns to take the compliments with a grain of salt, because an increased exercise routine usually follows. The boots are delivered to the house by the delivery service and Jon spends one evening working water-proofing into the leather. He begins wearing the boots on his evening walks. He finds the breaking-in process somewhat painful but tolerable because he is able to wear his grungy tennis shoes to work each morning. The few blisters he gets soon toughen and both pairs of the boots become more and more comfortable.

Jon begins work on his schedule after receiving two books from the Appalachian Trail Conference; *The Appalachian Trail Data Book*, which gives mileage between points along the trail and services available, and *The Appalachian Trail Thru-Hikers' Companion*, which details where the post offices and the services are in towns along the way, and some of the sights he will see. He decides that this is enough information to complete his planning without overdoing it. He plans to take these two books with him on the trail as guides. If he finds he needs more detailed information, he can go to the state-by-state guides which the Appalachian Trail Conference also publishes.

Andy takes more of an interest in the project, and he and Jon sit at the kitchen table several evenings and make and re-make schedules. Andy agrees to handle sending the packages every week or 10 days or so to provide the re-supplying that Jon will need. They schedule the shipping and make a list of the post office addresses and the dates that Jon hopes to arrive at each place.

Jon keeps working on Andy to get him to come along, but Andy doesn't have the same dream. He tells Jon one evening, "Bud, this is your project. In my humble opinion, it's the best thing that's ever happened to you. You're planning ahead, not just worrying. You started in plenty of time, so breaking in your body on the trail won't be quite so painful or take so long. I'll keep helping when I can, but no, I'm not going."

One evening, Jon comes across something in a book that seems to sum up a successful attitude for the hike. In Larry Luxemberg's book, *Walking The Appalachian Trail*, he reads, "Proper attitude, desire, and commitment are essential for a successful thru-hike. Adjust to the trail instead of expecting the trail to adjust to you. Be positive, anticipate the good times ahead instead of concentrating on current misery. Know what you hope to accomplish and what you don't." Jon is so impressed with this that he types it up and goes to the grocery store where he runs it through a laminating machine, because he plans to have it handy to read daily.

Jon orders his pack, a Kelty inside-frame model that is for long-distance hikes and a sleeping bag that is designed for low to moderate temperatures. He also

buys a light-weight bag, to be shipped by Andy after the threat of cold weather is over. This will save weight from that point on as he can ship the first bag home in the same box.

As December rolls around, the evening walks are up to three miles a day and he begins carrying the pack, trying to adjust to the extra weight. He starts with only the sleeping bag in the pack, but begins adding additional weight, ultimately getting up to 25 or 30 pounds.

In mid-December, Jon adds the football stadium to his walking routine several times a week. He climbs the concrete stairs to the top three or four times each visit, a lonely figure, wearing a backpack and trailing visible breath steam in the midst of the concrete structure which usually holds 70- or 80,000 die-hard Alabama football fans. But, the steps get easier, as do the trips to James' gym. He has been adopted by the fighters who train there as their "special skinny white boy project." Several of the guys suggest additional exercises to James, who has blossomed into an excellent training coach and who has been offered a part-time weight coaching job at the gym.

Christmas comes and Jon receives practical gifts from his family and friends. After checking with Andy, Jon's parents give him a Whisper-light stove, touted as the best on the market and Jon spends Christmas Day practicing with it in the back yard. Andy gives him maybe the best gift of all. He had a set of nylon saddle bags made up to fit Pookie so he can carry his food and water. Pookie looks at Jon strangely the first time he straps them on, but the patient Lab quickly gets used to them on the evening walks.

The guys at the gym, the same men Jon was petrified of meeting at first, went together and had a walking stick carved by a local artist. The old man's head which is carved near the top has a smile on his face, rather than the usual evil spirit on such carvings. Jon has read that a stick is an optional piece of equip-

ment. But, as it is useful as a balance point when crossing streams and descending steep grades, and is great as a dog-intimidator particularly in the northern parts of the trail where dogs can be a problem, Jon has already decided to carry one with him. The fact that the fighters gave him this one makes it truly special.

Chuck gets into the spirit of things and presents Jon with a Swiss-Army knife with lots of attachments. He also formally gives his regrets at not being able to accompany Jon on the hike. The regrets are certainly no surprise to Jon.

James, Shorty, and Mac down at the garage go together on a special cooking pot and cup, made out of a titanium alloy, light and strong. They include a utensil set that nests together.

Christmas night, Jon and Pookie sit in the middle of the living room floor, surrounded by the gear accumulated to date. Jon feels great about the support group that is building around him. If he is able to complete his dream, it will be in large part due to the help of his friends and his family.

The day after Christmas, Jon makes a tough decision. Even though he has heard through the grapevine that Sissy has a new beau, he wants to smooth over the way they had separated. He buys a nice scarf and glove set, wraps them, and makes the tough drive over to Sissy's house. When he knocks on the front door, Mr. Swingle opens the door. Jon receives a chilly greeting when he asks to see

Sissy for a minute. Mr. Swingle says, "I'm not sure she will see you. For that matter, I'm not sure I want to see you, myself. You hurt my little girl. But, I'll ask her." He shuts the door, not so politely in Jon's face.

Five minutes later, Sissy opens the door. "I'm not sure why I'm doing this," she says. "I said that I never wanted to see you again. What do you want?"

"I feel badly about the way we parted and I wanted to ask if we could at least be friends. Here," he thrusts the present at her.

She accepts the gift but does not respond. She looks at Jon for a while then finally says, "Maybe us splitting was for the best. I was so wrapped up in plans that I never really asked you what you wanted. We obviously didn't see eye to eye. I'm glad you stopped by, and, yes, we can be friends. I'm not sure Daddy will ever forgive you, though. Are you still planning that crazy hike?"

"Yes, I'm leaving in March and should be finished in August or September, if I'm lucky and stay focused. I've done most of my planning, accumulated most of my gear, and I'm following a training program religiously."

"Jon, maybe you have changed. I believe you will finish if you want to badly enough. This is the first thing I've seen you stay with. Good luck, and I hope you make it. Let's stay in touch." She shuts the door, substantially softer than Mr. Swingle had done earlier. Jon walks away feeling much better. Somehow when you do things that you don't have to but ought to, it makes you feel really good about yourself. The chapter in his life titled "Sissy" is closed.

With the holidays over, Jon returns to work with a vengeance. He increases the portions of his conditioning program that seem to have the most relevance. He climbs stairs at the stadium three days a week and does twice as many steps. He goes to James' gym an extra time each week. Several more of the fighters take him under their wings, suggest additional exercises, and spot him when he lifts weights. The day Jon attains the combination of weights and reps that James had loudly set as a goal several months before, he is startled when he hears the final three lifts counted out by numerous voices. When the spotter helps him return the weight bar to its cradle, Jon looks around and the entire population of the gym has ceased its activities and is standing around his bench. A cheer rings out and Jon is surrounded by dozens of husky black fighters giving their white boy his props. Jon feels a rush of accomplishment like he'd never felt before and he exchanges high fives with everyone within reach.

Jon and Pookie continue their walks and weight is steadily added to their packs and saddlebags. By late February, the loads are almost what they will carry on the trail. Jon writes the various places along the trail where he feels he will need reservations and tells them his estimated date of arrival. He receives confirmations back that suggest he call from down the trail and verify dates about a week before his arrival.

As slowly as the first months of preparation and gear selection and research had gone, the two weeks before departure are going even more slowly. His finances are in good shape. He has spent $1500 of his father's gift on gear, leaving 500 to add to his savings which total about $1,000.

At the garage one morning two weeks from departure date, two men Jon doesn't recognize come into the garage and go straight into Shorty's office. A few minutes later, Shorty comes to the door and beckons to Jon. Puzzled, Jon nonetheless walks to the door where he is introduced to Mr. Wilkins, a reporter for the Tuscaloosa Times daily newspaper. Mr. Wilkins is accompanied by a man he introduces as his photographer, which explains the two cameras hanging around his neck. Mr. Wilkins has heard of Jon's upcoming trip and is interested in doing a human interest story on the whens, whys, and whats involved. The photographer wanders around the office, occasionally snapping pictures of Jon with Mr. Wilkins. Jon sits with the reporter for an hour, although he guiltily jumps each time the drive-over bell rings. He looks out the door of the office once, and sees Shorty out front checking the oil in a car. He shakes his head in amazement, an act he repeats later when Shorty brings Jon three five dollar bills which had been left as tips for "that hiker that works here."

Mr. Wilkins, hearing the exchange, looks at Jon and asks, "You haven't said anything about finances. What is a trek like this likely to cost?"

Jon says, "I figure a total of about $4000, all told. About 2000 for gear and 2000 for expenses along the trail. Supplies, food, motels on occasion, stuff like that."

The reporter asks, "How are you doing on money? Been able to save enough?"

Jon laughs, "Well, it seems to have become a community project. My father made a generous gift and I've received presents of gear from others. But to answer your question, no, I haven't quite gotten there. But it doesn't matter. If I'm short, I'll avoid a few motels and two-night rest stops. It'll work out. All that matters is that I intend to make it all the way to Katahdin, the mountain in Maine where the trail ends, before snow falls. I'll make it."

Mr. Wilkins thanks Jon for his time, shakes hands, and departs. Jon finishes the day and goes home to his usual routine. Pookie even runs over to his saddlebags and waits patiently for Jon to hook him up. Jon laughs, "Pookie, I believe you're good to go, just like I am. We've only got a couple of weeks to wait."

When Jon enters the garage the next morning, Shorty, Mac, and James are standing at the break table looking at something. When Shorty sees Jon, he yells, "Hey, celebrity! Get your butt over here!"

Jon looks at the morning newspaper and is amazed to see a picture of him and a full page article giving details of his coming hike. James proudly points to a line which proclaims, "James Regan, a co-worker of Jon's, is the conditioning coach."

Shorty points out the last line of the article in which Mr. Wilkins says that Jon is still short about $500 of his goal but that he has hopes of getting that before he leaves in two weeks. Shorty says, "Maybe that'll do some good and somebody might feel compelled to send you some bucks. Wherever the money comes from, it'll still spend the same."

Jon answers, "I doubt anybody'll send money to help some crazy guy walk 2000 miles. We'll see."

All of Jon's regular customers come by the garage that day and comment on the article. Most leave five dollars and one man tucks a 20 in Jon's uniform pocket. "Here," he says, "Have one great meal on me." Jon thanks him.

By the end of the day, Jon is amazed to find he is $80 closer to his goal than he was that morning. He shakes his head and says to Shorty, "Damn if I'm not feeling a lot of pressure, now. All these people have been so nice and I've got to make the whole hike or never show my face in Tuscaloosa again. I hope to hell I can do this."

"Nah," says Shorty, "Don't sweat it. Just give it your best shot, that's all. That's all people expect."

Jon shakes his head again, "I'll keep telling myself that, but I still feel a little bit of pressure. Thanks, Shorty, I'll remember."

Jon goes home to an excited Pookie who seems to sense that whatever it is that they have been doing is coming to a climax of some sort. "Bud," says Jon, "I'm gonna feel terrible on that day I send you home with Andy. I believe you're into this as much as I am. I'm really getting excited. I wonder, though if we'll be as excited the first time we get rained on for three or four days in a row, walking and slopping and sleeping in mud. Sounds great, huh? You're lucky–you can't understand a word I'm saying. You can't project or think of all the bad stuff that could happen. Oh, well, let's walk, partner." Pookie has no problem understanding that.

At about ten o'clock the next day, Mr. Wilkins of the newspaper comes by the garage. He seeks out Jon and waits until he finishes servicing a car. "Jon," starts Mr. Wilkins, "We've had an amazing response to that story about your hike. Here's a check from the newspaper for $300, the total sent in by readers. It came in one's and five's and 20's. Checks written to 'that hiking man,' 'Jon,' the newspaper, and lots of other ways. Your story and your dream touched a nerve in our readers. More may still come in."

Jon accepts the check, mouth agape. "Mr. Wilkins, I appreciate this more than I can say. Thanks for writing that story. This gets me real close to my goal."

Mr. Wilkins says, "You're more than welcome. I'm interested in your plan myself. Now, I've some business to work out with you. I talked with my features editor, and she's very excited in the story. She wants you to be a sort of roving reporter for us the whole way through your hike. Keep a journal. Jot down your thoughts, your feelings, the good, the bad, the beautiful and the ugly. Send a pile of notes to me each time you come off the trail to a post office, and I'll clean the notes up, and we'll keep our readers up-to-date on the whereabouts of one Jon Parker, Thru-Hiker. What do you think?"

"I think that would be really neat. I'd enjoy that. I don't think it would be like a travelogue, though. I think that since my whole effort is to learn to stay focused, to stick to something, even to grow up and gain self-reliance, the notes might be a little more along those lines. Will that work? Feelings rather than places?"

"That would be great! I think we'll get a map of the entire 2000 miles of the trail and show a dotted line over the parts you've walked. That way it will really be a way for folks to keep up with you. Sounds good. Do you plan to take a camera?"

Jon answers, "I thought about taking just a light, simple camera. I could get some shots and get the film developed at one-hour photo shops and send them to you."

Mr. Wilkins gets more excited. "Great! That's even better! Here's a stack of 18 addressed and stamped envelopes ready for you to stuff and mail to me. I think you said you'd be coming into towns about every 10 days? I think 18 will be enough. I'm excited about this project 'cause I have a lot of readers who are excited. When exactly do you intend to leave? I'd like to have a photographer at your house to get some shots of your departure."

Jon pauses for a moment. "Well, I'm still trying to figure that out, myself. Early March is asking too much on the weather. I'd likely run into snow. So, I'm thinking about giving it one more week, to March 15. That's a Saturday, so Andy, my roommate doesn't have to take off work to get me up the road to the trail leading to Springer Mountain, Georgia. That's the official beginning of the trail. So, at six o'clock in the morning of March 15, I guess that's the date."

Mr. Wilkins shakes Jon's hand and says, "Jon, this is a fun project. I wish I was younger and in better shape and I'd go with you. But, I'm not either of those things, so I'll stay here in the comfort of civilization and wait for your dispatches. I'll call or come by if any more money comes in. I'll bet there'll be more. See you!"

Jon wasn't to see Mr. Wilkins again until March 15th, but three days before that date, he sends a cub reporter over to the garage with another check, this one for $450. That amount carries Jon to his goal. Even though he feels he would have made it without as many off-trail stops, every book he has read mention how important the "vacations" are for the thru-hikers. Laundry, re-supplying, phone calls home, gear repair, and bug-less and mouse-less sleeping; these things help one recover and get mentally prepared to hit the trail.

On March 14th, Jon makes the final rounds of his supporters. He sees his parents, and his mother, finally accepting that her younger son is really going to do this insanity, hugs him and wishes him luck. His dad shakes hands formally and reiterates that they would take good care of Pookie when Andy delivers him in three and one-half weeks. He says, "Son, we're proud of you. Do your best, and even if you don't make the whole hike, come back with your head held high. You at least have the guts to try it."

Jon swings by the gym where he is greeted by a round of high-fives and hand slaps and a lot of boisterous wishes for good luck. They will be keeping up with Jon's progress in the newspaper and they'll see him when he gets back home in five or six months.

At the garage, Shorty, James, and Mac wish him luck and Shorty draws him to one side. "Jon," he says, "Like I told you earlier, don't give another thought to your job here. It'll be waiting for you when you get back. I've found a college kid who'll fill in part-time for you in your absence. So, anyway, good luck and remember we're all walking with you."

James is standing by himself when Jon walked over to him. "James, I owe you the biggest thanks of all. If you hadn't taken charge of my conditioning program, I expect I wouldn't have made it on the trail for more than a day or two before my body would have seized up tighter than an engine without oil. So, thanks again." He hugs James, who lifts him off the floor as if he is a kid.

On "D-Day," the photographer appears at six a.m. and takes a bunch of shots of Jon and Pookie, both wearing packs and feeling and looking somewhat like human pack mules. Both travelers crawl into Andy's pickup and the great adventure is beginning–it's finally here.

Andy, Jon, and Pookie make good time from Tuscaloosa to Atlanta, then turn north toward the corner of Georgia where Springer Mountain has stood proud for millions of years. Jon believes it has been waiting for him.

Carefully following Jon's notes, the trio find their way to Nimblewill Church and drive 14 miles over a rough, gravel, mountain road to Nimblewill Gap. There is plenty of room for Andy to turn around. When the vehicle comes to a stop, Jon spots the first blaze on a tree that he has seen, a blue blaze on the north side of the clearing indicating a side-trail to the AT. It is the first of thousands of blazes that will provide his road maps for the next five or six months.

Jon lets Pookie out of the car and the dog immediately heads for the nearest tree. After saluting it, he notices the forest around him with an infinite number of trees that call out for marking. He runs out of ammunition and returns to the car where Jon has finished extracting the packs, leaning them against the car. Pookie is put into harness and Jon grunts as he follows suit.

The doubts flood Jon. "Damn, I should have brought that extra cook pot and maybe I should have bought those state-to-state maps from the AT Conference and maybe . . . "

Andy laughs, "Bud, if you were any better prepared you couldn't even walk for the notes and maps. This isn't the time for doubts. Lots of folks have faith in you; listen to them, not yourself." He pulls out his own schedule. "Now, according to this here master plan, I'm to ship your first package in time to get to Franklin, North Carolina in 10 days and I'm to be at Davenport Gap to bring another package and pick up Pookie on day 22. That sound right?"

Jon looks at his copy of the plan. "Yep, that's what it says. That is, unless I call before then and change days. That could happen. In fact, it probably will happen. But I'll try not to let it change too drastically. Who knows–this is the wilderness, as you can see."

Andy looks around, eyes shielded from the sun by his hand. "Yep, this may not be the end of the world, but I definitely think I can see it over there . . . " He points to the north, Jon's route.

Jon laughs again. Then turning serious, he says, "Andy, I really appreciate all the help you've been so far. This is my dream, but lots of folks have helped me to have a chance to realize it. I reckon we'd best be on our way and let you get back to Tuscaloosa."

They shake hands and Jon puts Pookie on the leash. They walk toward the first blue blaze and before entering the forest, turn and wave at Andy who is still standing, leaning against the truck. He waves back.

The adventurers start up the trail. After a few minutes, Jon hears the sound of Andy's truck going down the gravel road. He stops and listens to the sound of civilization going away from him. "Pookie," he says, "Reckon we're truly on our own. It's you and me, bud." Pookie smiles and happily follows Jon up the trail.

About an hour and a half later, they reach the top of Springer Mountain, a hardwood-covered round-topped mountain. Four other hikers are lounging on the ground. They are busy arguing about something, so Jon waves at them and walks to the other side of the clearing. Packs are shucked and Jon rubs his shoulders to relieve soreness. "Damn," he thinks, "I guess they're right when they say the only way to prepare to hike in the mountains with a full pack is to walk in the mountains with a full pack. Sounded silly when I read it, but I understand, now." Jon spots a rock ledge with a bronze plaque fastened to it. The plaque has a picture of a hiker and a statement:

"APPALACHIAN TRAIL
Georgia to Maine
A footpath for those who seek fellowship
with the Wilderness
The Georgia Appalachian Trail Club."

Nearby is a metal mail box which Jon investigates. It contains a sign-in book for hikers. Jon pulls the book and pencil out of the box and sits on the ground. He reads some of the entries, many of which were written by thru-hikers, like himself. He is amazed at the number of thru-hikers who have already come through here this year–hundreds and hundreds. He reads of their goals, their dreams, along with a healthy sprinkling of their doubts and fears. He sketches the symbol of the thru-hiker–a T connected to a capital A. On the side, GA, standing for Georgia, and an arrow pointing to ME, his destination, Maine. He thus becomes official. He writes his name and the time he arrived, and assigns himself an official trail name, "Doubting Jon," a name by which he will be known in the trail hikers' community for the next five or six months. Jon has read that many of the thru-hikers wouldn't know your real name but they would remember your trail name for years to come.

Jon has a sip of water from his water bottle, a task Pookie already accomplished when he found a nearby puddle. Jon stands and looks around the clearing. The other hikers are still discussing their mutual problem, whatever it is. Jon spots his first white blaze; he's officially now on the Appalachian Trail, rather than the side trail from Nimblewill Gap. The two re-enter their packs where Jon notices the pack straps find the most sensitive spots on his shoulders. He shifts in the straps and tightens the waist strap. Enough weight is transferred to his hips that his shoulders feel a bit better. He addresses his canine companion, "Bud, we've still got better than four miles to make. I'm glad I planned a short hike today, 'cause we've got a couple of 11- or 12-mile days coming up. Let's move out!"

Dog and master walk up the trail, each step counting down toward Jon's goal of Katahdin.

4

"THE SPROUT APPEARS"

Jon takes his first official step on the Appalachian Trail. He announces to Pookie, "Well, I've taken one step anyway. At least now, I don't have five-million steps to complete my thru-hike. Now I can say I have four million plus some-odd steps to go." Ritual completed, Jon begins walking in earnest, Pookie trotting by his side. Jon decides that the smart thing to do is keep his dog on leash to start, then when he gets used to the idea, maybe let him run free, as long as he is within easy voice command.

The hikers traverse the four miles to the Gooch Gap camping area with no problems. As Jon approaches the camping area, there are three tents set up, but no hikers in sight. He thinks, "Good, Pookie may have a little more time to get

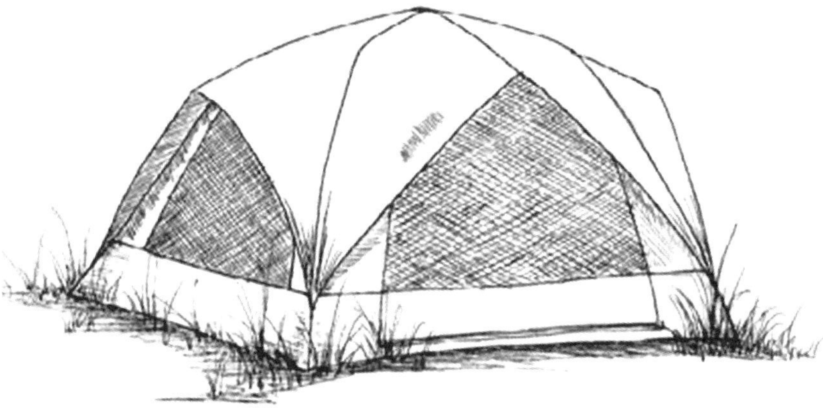

used to this wilderness idea. If he barks now, we can work on cutting that back, before he barks tonight and bothers somebody other than me."

Jon sets his tent up, and he and Pookie walk down the trail and find a nearby spring. He fills a collapsible water bag and returns to his camp. He sets up his Whisperlite stove and opens a baggie. He drops a macaroni and cheese dinner, along with the contents of a can of tuna, into a pot of heating water.

This first dinner is truly a learning experience. Jon had practiced with his Whisperlite before leaving home, but that wasn't the same as on the trail. There's no nice, smooth asphalt or concrete surface on which to set it, so the threat of tipping over is a constant concern. Particularly when dinner is cheerfully bubbling, sending delicious smells into the air. Pookie sits by his side, nose twitching at the aroma. Jon successfully completes preparing the dinner and manages to eat, while ignoring Pookie's pleading eyes. The dog realizes that Jon's dinner smells a lot better than the dried dog food he has to eat. His hopes are dashed when Jon crumbles a doggie-type dinner and puts it into Pookie's bowl. He sniffs it, then returns to his post by Jon, hoping his master will change his mind. Jon laughs, "Okay, bud, I'll flavor your dinner with a little of mine. But you'd best get used to that dried meat. It's your fare for the next three weeks." Pookie flashes his smile and patiently waits.

Refreshed, the two explore the area. They meet three men and a woman, apparently the hikers whose tents are set up in the clearing. They exchange greetings and Jon and Pookie walk on. Jon finds a small pool of water away from the spring and scrubs out his pot and Pookie's bowl. "There," he says, "All ready for tomorrow." The two return to camp and Jon brews a cup of tea and sits under the starry sky while he sips the sweet tea. Dusk is approaching. Jon sits by his tent and begins the notes he will be forwarding to the Tuscaloosa newspaper. He scratches his head, then plunges in. He writes of the near-panic feeling when Andy's car pulled away. He writes of his overwhelming thoughts as he takes the first of five million steps. And, he writes of his appreciation for the conditioning program that his friend, James, had overseen. He has some sore spots and twanging muscles, but if he had not prepared, he fully believes he would now be in complete agony and would be unable to get out of his sleeping bag tomorrow morning. He closes with a description of the clearing in the pine forest in which he is camping, and the silence. The other hikers have already extinguished their candles and they are in their tents. The silence is deafening. A bird sends out three sleepy chirps, but there are no other sounds. Pookie barks once by his side. Jon jumps. He returns to his notes. "My Lab had to try out his barker to make sure it still works. It does."

Notes complete, Jon turns off his flashlight and crawls into the tent, a five-by-seven foot tent with a small vestibule. He had sacrificed the slight extra weight over a smaller tent, so Pookie would be able to join him. Besides, the temperature has dropped to the teens and the extra body heat should help. He spreads a small tarp he carries for Pookie to sleep on, avoiding damage to the floor of the tent from the dog's claws. Pookie happily joins him in their mobile home and curls up, wrapping his tail around his nose so nothing is visible of his face except his eyes. Jon's eyelids become heavy. By this time, Pookie is accustomed to the sounds of the forest and is content to sleep on the floor of the tent, lying next to Jon's sleeping bag and pad. He does have to raise his head every once in a while, listening carefully to the night sounds and sniffing deeply, tests each new smell to determine if it is of friend or foe.

Jon sleeps well. He wakes at about 6 o'clock and lies in his tent for a few minutes for the sleep-fog to lift. It's not light yet though he can sense the imminent appearance of dawn by the faint, ever so faint, glow through the leaf-less, closely-spaced trees.

He lies still for a few more minutes, listening to the silence, and enjoys the warmth of his encasing mummy bag. Before retiring last night, he had placed his coffee making supplies right outside the tent. Maybe he can stay mostly in the tent and start the stove and coffee without leaving the warm sleeping bag. Worth a try, anyway.

Jon unzips the tent and starts the Whisperlite and sets the aluminum coffee pot on top to begin the perk process. He scoots back fully into the sleeping bag and lies still, savoring the warmth. There was a hard frost and the ground is white. It takes twenty minutes for the coffee to perk, and Jon happily waits, inside the bag. He dozes for a moment, until the coffee pot announces perking is happening with the cheerful little blurp, blurp, bluuuuurp the coffee makes as it bubbles up into the glass knob on top of the pot.

He impatiently waits for the coffee to turn dark then pours his first cup. He has heard to be really careful with the metal cup because otherwise, he would qualify for the hot lips award. So, he takes his time and avoids earning that award.

When the light from the rising sun completely invades the thin walls of the tent, both man and dog stir and head immediately to the nearest trees to relieve full bladders. Feeling better, Jon fixes a bowl of cold cereal, dampened with dried milk and water. He shares a few bites with Pookie, cleans his bowl, and pours the remainder of the water from the collapsible bag into his and Pookie's water containers.

Jon slips his feet into the boots. A few sore spots, but nothing requiring moleskin. He's proud that he thoroughly broke them in while carrying weight down on the flatlands. Jon does a few stretching exercises and loosens his leg muscles He puts his loyal pack dog into harness and does the same for himself. Shoulders scream in silent agony, but begrudgingly accept the load. Legs twitch at the weight so unceremoniously returned to them. The two strike out. It's about seven-thirty a.m.; they did well getting out so early after their first night in the wilderness, although not as successful as the other hikers in the clearing. Those people were gone before Jon and Pookie had even stirred.

On this, the second full day on the trail, Jon's mind keeps wandering to one of the books he read in preparation for the hike. All of the books he read were enjoyable and each provided information he used to get ready. One book stood out as the most fascinating. *Blind Courage*, by Bill Irwin. Irwin may be blind, but his blindness cannot be called totally handicapping, because he and his dog, Orient, made a thru-hike in 1990. Irwin estimates he fell about 5,000 times during his hike and tells of navigating errors with devastating results–snowbound for days in the fall in Maine, plus an encounter with a bear. But they made it, in spite of the doubts and fears that threatened to overcome Irwin. Jon has to laugh at his own doubts, so insignificant next to Irwin's.

As he hikes, Jon thinks about the claustrophobia that must have beset Irwin at times. He says to Pookie, "Dog, I know you're not really trained for it, but we're gonna try an experiment. You're my eyes for the next little bit." Jon looks around to make sure nobody is within eyesight of the game. If he falls and busts his butt, he doesn't want to hear the sound of anybody's laughter, but his own.

He shortens the leash until his hand is almost on Pookie's collar, shuts his eyes, and pulls his bandanna headband down over his eyes to prevent cheating. He says to Pookie, "Okay, bud, you're now a seeing eye guide dog. Let's go."

Pookie starts up and Jon stumbles along beside him. Every rock and root suddenly becomes an obstacle that prevents smooth walking. After his fifth stumble and near-fall, he tugs on Pookie's leash and slows down the pace. He says, "That's some better–I'm just tripping once every 20 feet instead of every foot. Damn, how did that guy do this, anyway?"

He takes a few more steps, and his left foot, feeling for terra firma, encounters nothing. Nothing at all. Jon drops his walking staff and releases the leash so he can break his fall with his hands. He has stepped in a small gully that luckily is only a foot or so deep, but he still falls face-first, full-length on the unforgiving ground. He lies there, gasping for breath, and Pookie licks his face in concern.

Jon rubs Pookie's ears. "Dog, not your fault. That was a crazy stunt I tried. The experiment is done. Finished. Kaput!" He unties the bandanna and blinks his eyes at the sudden glare of light.

"Damn. I thought I'd better understand how Irwin made this hike, but now I'm even more amazed. I couldn't even handle a straight, level piece of trail. How did he keep up with where he was or find water or shelters? Damn, I'm flabbergasted."

After putting first-aid cream and a bandage on his skinned knee, they take off again, now using four eyes instead of two. The navigation is much smoother, and all six feet step firmly on terra firma.

When he stops at the shelter for the night, Jon hurts. There's no softer, easier way to put it; he hurts like hell. Starting at the bottom, his feet hurt. He has moleskin on both heels and between several toes. The ends of his toes and his toenails hurt where they've been jammed down into the toes of his boots. One ankle throbs where he turned it on a slippery rock late in the day. His thighs twitch and cramp and his calves ache from ascending and descending mountains. His shoulders and back hurt. The seven or eight hikers already at the campground don't appear to feel any better than Jon and Pookie and nobody is talkative.

Jon turns to Pookie, who is lying next to him, apparently in no better shape. "Hey, Pook, whatchya think? We crazy or what? All that training, all those miles and those stadium steps, and I still hurt. Well, I guess I wouldn't have made it this far, if we hadn't trained. Right, buddy?"

Pookie is plumb tuckered out. He can't even raise his head to respond to Jon. He gives him a weak thump, thump, thump of his tail on the pine-needle strewn ground. Jon checks the pads on Pookie's feet and they look okay. "I guess we'll live,

Bud. Let's see if food will revive us." The night is really cold, with the temperature hovering around zero degrees. It's really tough to get out of the sleeping bag.

For the next few days they hike over and through the 3000- foot peaks of the Chattahoochee National Forest. The 11- and 12-mile days are fairly tough, but Jon had built one easy three- and one-half mile day into his schedule, so they are able to laze around camp at Slaughter Gap until noon, before they start back on the trail. They have seen dozens and dozens of hikers and the campgrounds are usually full. Most folks are still hurting physically, so they keep to themselves.

After a short hike, they arrive at their first sign of civilization since leaving Nimblewill Gap. After a steep descent from Blood Mountain into Neels Gap, they come onto Walasi-Yi hostel, run by Dorothy and Jeff Hansen.

Jon pays for one night and informs Pookie that he's not welcome in the hostel. He ties his dog to a large pine tree and fills a water bowl, trying hard to ignore the sad, expressive eyes characteristic of Black Labs. Jon goes into the store and walks through the aisles of back-packing gear. The flashlight he had been using was not quite right. He can't hold it in his mouth while he accomplishes other tasks with his hands, so he buys a new, smaller light and several extra batteries. He also purchases a candle lantern and several extra candles. He figures he might need to write his notes inside the tent or shelter on late or cold days, and the small lantern is safe inside tents. Jeff Hansen helps him pack his old light and several other pieces of gear that he really hadn't needed so far, and the package is prepared to ship back to Tuscaloosa. Jeff tells him that they annually ship two tons of gear determined to be non-essential by the 800 hikers that visit Walasi-Yi. He compliments Jon on the small amount of returning gear. Stuff Hansen has returned in the past has included such items as a small battery-operated TV set, video cameras, heavy extra clothing, and metal and canvas camp stools and cots.

Jon re-stocks his food supply and returns to the hostel. He has to spend time with Pookie, who still doesn't understand why he's relegated to the outdoors. Jon showers and sleeps well that night, enjoying his return to civilization, even though it's only been four nights on the trail. He knows it will be seven more nights before he plans to hitch-hike to Franklin, North Carolina, where he will retrieve his first "care package" from home, assuming Andy has done his job.

Five of the seven days it will take him to get to Franklin are in the 12- to 14-mile range and include some eight mountains to cross, but when he arrives at Franklin, they will have passed a milestone–100 miles completed on the trail.

After the good night's sleep, Jon's shoulders and feet feel pretty good. He carefully checks Pookie's feet and pads and his back to make sure his pack hasn't rubbed any sore places. Pookie gives him a sloppy kiss, apparently saying, "Let's go, Dad I'm fine! I forgive you for making me sleep outside like a dog." After both of them are harnessed, they start down the trail.

About mid-morning, the skies darken, and they have their first encounter with the nemesis of the mountains–rain. It's certainly not to be their last. Jon stops and tugs his rain gear out of his pack. He has a pack cover for both his and Pookie's packs. He had read that packs are vulnerable to becoming soaked through zippers

and seams, and he's not ready to sleep in a wet sleeping bag, if he can help it. He pulls on his poncho and says to Pookie, "Bud, I guess your hide is water-tight. You can shake dry when we stop. Remember, not on people!" Pookie looks at him as though he understands, and wags his tail in agreement.

They are lucky–this rain ends after an hour or so, and Jon gratefully shucks his poncho. The poncho does a good job of keeping out the rain; it does an equally good job at keeping in your body heat. He's almost as soaked with sweat as he would have been with no poncho in the rain. He removes Pookie's saddlebags and lets him run around, shake, and do doggie tasks for a short while, before he puts the bags back on him.

Their first experience in a shelter on the AT is that night at Whitley Gap. When they arrive, there are three other hikers already there, cooking their meals outside the fenced enclosure. They cast sour looks at Jon's companion, but after Jon instructs Pookie to sit, and he sits and stays, their looks are not quite so sour. Jon introduces himself to the other thru-hikers, and they swap stories about their adventures to this point. Rather than start at Nimblewill Gap, these men had started their hike at Amicalola Falls State Park. It's only six miles farther than going via Nimblewill, but it is an extremely steep trail that catches the uninitiated off-guard, and many end their dream of 2000 miles after getting only to the top of that first grade to Springer Mountain. These three are weary, but undaunted.

Jon takes Pookie and introduces him to the hikers, and after handshakes all around, they brighten up. One says, "He may come in handy tonight, being a Lab. I've already seen hundreds of mice in this blamed shelter. I hope he's a good hunter."

Jon laughs, "Maybe he is. Let's find out." He takes Pookie inside the shelter and ties him up. Pookie looks around the shelter and sniffs in all corners, then lies down and falls immediately to sleep. The four men laugh and Jon adds, "Maybe if the mice run into his mouth, he'll catch them. Otherwise, I'm afraid he won't help much."

The cold night passes quietly, after a fashion. Jon hears the mice for what seems most of the night. The critters obviously feel that they own the shelter, and the humans and dog are interlopers. Jon had read about hikers that carry mouse traps and one who carried a cat and its food, but he doubts that the extra weight is worth it. The three had hung their packs from the rafters and Jon punched a hole in the center of his empty can of chicken from dinner and strung the pack-hanging rope through it. The shelter mice are known to be creative in finding ways to get into your pack and cause substantial damage.

Jon has to laugh out loud when he pictures in his mind the source of a strange sound he hears a few moments after all lights were extinguished. He hears a mouse chattering above him, up in the rafters. It then becomes quiet, then a tiny, metallic sound is followed by a small thud and lots of mouse-cussing. He could see in his mind, the mouse sliding down the rope, then being propelled into space by the swinging, unstable chicken can, landing on the ground with a tiny thud. Jon's pack survives the night intact. It did take a while to get used to additional sounds in the shelter. People moaning in their sleep, turning over, and snoring. Two of the three snored–one in deep, almost continuous roars, and one in falsetto squeaks. Jon sleeps relatively well, considering.

The hikers awaken to a beautiful sight–three or four inches of snow had fallen during the night. It is enough to look spectacular, but not enough to seriously impact hiking. The four men and Pookie leave together, and Jon discovers he is able to keep up with the pace. It turns out that they are heading for the same shelter, up on Blue Mountain, so they walk together for much of the day. At mid-afternoon, two of the three men strike out at a faster pace. Sam, who stays with Jon, laughs and says, "It's been like that since the start of the trail. Mike and David are the athletes. Both played high school football in Memphis, and they run five or ten miles every day and work out at the gym. I'm an Olympic-quality couch potato, and I've still got this damned beer belly, as you can see. Those guys walk faster than I do, so they charge ahead, and we meet at the shelter. It's worked well. It may or may not work for the entire trail. We'll see."

After spending the night at Blue Mountain, Jon and Pookie hike on with the three men. They swap names and addresses, so they could keep up with one another. Crazy Mike, Recovering Sam, and Gotta-be-hiking David are Tennesseans from the flatlands over near Memphis, so the hills and mountains are doubly tough on them. Jon can see improvement in their physical condition, as they hike for the next five days over six rugged mountains.

The hikers cross Bly Gap, where the AT crosses the Georgia-North Carolina line. The trail takes a turn into Nantahala National Forest. Jon reads from his Guide that they will cross and pass a number of mountains with mile-high peaks. In their discussions as they hike, Jon learns that his new friends don't plan to get off the trail at Franklin, so they'll part company at the road crossing. Maybe Jon can catch up with them in a week somewhere in the Smokies.

The four men and the dog shake hands at the road leading to Franklin, and Jon removes his pack and sticks out his thumb. Franklin is about ten miles away; he's not ready to hike that far. After about 30 cars pass, a farmer and his wife stop their pick-up and Jon, Pookie, and their packs are toted down into Franklin, where they find a motel that accepts dogs.

The first task is to take a shower. He enjoys it more than he can ever remember a shower in his life. Actually, he takes three showers, because he has to soap down and scrub three times before his skin looks pink again. He puts Pookie on his leash, and the two walk down the street and drop off Jon's film at a one-hour photo place. They go into a Laundromat where Jon washes his short and shirts that now could stand in a corner by themselves. Before he started the hike, Jon had sworn that he wasn't going the way of most thru-hikers and give off a natural aroma when he reaches civilization. In other words, thru-hikers usually smell. Badly. Au Natural. Jon remembers his American history class where he heard that you could have smelled a Civil War army before you heard or saw them. A Thru-hiker is a bit like that. Jon carries deodorant and washes every day, but he still gets fragrant. Maybe clean clothes and that memorable shower will help until next off-trail time.

Chores finished, Jon takes Pookie back to the motel room and puts out his food and water. He goes back outside and finds a Mexican restaurant, Mi Casa, next door waiting for him. He goes in, now disguised as a normal person, rather than a thru-hiker. He fools the waiter and after devouring the menu with his eyes, places his order–two complete dinners. The waiter innocently asks, "Sir, is someone else joining you? I'll need to get more silverware."

Jon laughs, "Nope, you're doing just fine. Just bring me a pitcher of beer and a mug, then keep the food coming."

The disguise stripped away, the waiter recognizes him as one of them. Those guys and gals who come into town, eat just about everything in sight, drink most of the available beer, then go back to the woods. The waiter leaves and returns quickly with a pitcher of brew. Jon pours a frosty mug full, then downs half of it in one swallow. He leans back in the chair, content as a human can be.

The food is demolished in short order and Jon lets out a soul-satisfying, if somewhat rude and crude belch of which any self-respecting Arab would have been proud. Plates on the next table rattle, but luckily, no one is sitting there. He waddles out of the restaurant and stops by the photo shop to pick up his first developed pictures. As he checks them out, he says, "Not bad for an amateur, not bad at all."

Jon spends the rest of the evening catching up on his notes and selecting photos on which to write identifying notes. He seals the envelope to Mr. Wilkins and will drop it in the mail at the post office in the morning, when he picks up the package Andy addressed to him that should be waiting there.

Jon crawls in the bed, but it takes him a while to become accustomed to the softness of the bed and the presence of a pillow. But slumber finally comes, and he sleeps the sleep of the dead and doesn't wake until eight o'clock the next morning.

Jon walks Pookie, then enjoys a leisurely breakfast, while waiting for the post office to open. He mails the letter to Mr. Wilkins and picks up the package Andy had mailed. "All right, food for the next two weeks. The Pookster and I can eat. Speaking of him, I think I'll get him a can of real dog food and a bone at the grocery store. He deserves a treat just as much as I do."

Jon kills most of the rest of the day piddling around with his gear. He applies another coat of waterproofing to his boots and tightens a strap that has been squeaking and adding an aggravating sound to each step. He de-Madison

Avenues the food in his care package and repacks all the food in plastic bags and tosses the carefully and expensively printed boxes and foil in the trash can. He has struck another blow in his war against his worst enemy, weight.

Jon and Pookie take a long walk and wind up near the shopping center. As he is walking along the sidewalk towards the strip of stores, a car with no muffler, pulls alongside him. As he glances at the car, Jon sees three men, definitely red-necks. Each of them holds a can of beer in his hand. The man in the passenger seat hollers out the window, "Hey, Hippy, you one of them hikers? We don't like your kind here. Get the hell out of town!"

Jon continues walking, but the car keeps pace. The men increase their cussing campaign, and the more Jon tries to ignore them, the more acid their invectives become. Finally, the car lurches ahead; the man in the passenger seat opens his door. The huge specimen of a man has massive arms, long, tangled, red, greasy hair, and a collection of tattoos of which the circus lady would be envious. The beast steps to the sidewalk. His jeans are worn at half-mast, and the top of his butt crack is displayed, as if anyone would want to see it. He takes a last swallow of the beer, crushes the can effortlessly in one hand, and tosses the crumpled metal to the ground at Jon's feet.

The redneck growls, "I reckon you didn't hear what we was sayin to yuh. We said, get the hell out of town, or we're fixin to remove yuh."

Jon notices that a small crowd is looking out store windows and from nearby on the sidewalk. He finally speaks. "We're here for just tonight, then we'll be gone. I'm not looking for any trouble."

The man laughs. "Reckon we're lookin fer trouble. I plan to give it to yuh." He takes several steps toward Jon, body-language definitely indicating his willingness to give that trouble.

Pookie growls deep in his throat. Jon has almost forgotten he is sitting patiently by his side. The man takes two more wobbly steps toward Jon, and Pookie suddenly jerks the leash out of Jon's hand and charges the man. Screaming curses over his shoulder, the man, as best he can, part-staggers and part-runs back toward the car. He puts all his remaining energy into a head-long dive into the window, but not before Pookie nails the seat of his pants and rips away a souvenir. Hanging out the car window as it speeds away, is an incredibly hairy butt that looks for all the world like a picture in a book that Jon had seen of a battle flag belonging to a defeated Civil War regiment retreating at double-quick.

Jon laughs so hard that he has to sit on the sidewalk. Pookie walks back to his side and politely sits, leaning against Jon's shoulder. Jon grabs Pookie in a bear-hug and buries his face against his neck. "Thanks, bud. I really owe you that bone now. I'll never call you a wuss again. You really saved my hide."

When Jon looks up, he finds that the incident had attracted five or six spectators. Included in their number are three very attractive young ladies, all three blondes. An older lady says, "Son, don't judge us all by those ruffians. We like our hikers, and we hope you keep stopping here in our town." Her husband mumbles similar sentiments, and the couple moves away.

One of the girls says, "That's a brave dog. Those clowns hurt a hiker pretty badly a month ago, but the cops couldn't prove it was them, so they weren't arrested. What's the dog's name?"

"Pookie, and mine's Jon. He's always friendly to folks that are friendly in return. For that matter, so am I."

She says in a soft voice, "Is it okay if I pet Pookie?"

"Sure, he'll like that."

She steps toward the hero of the hour. He happily flashes his best Lab smile; she being among the uninitiated, thinks he is snarling at her. She stops dead in her tracks. She wails, "You said he was friendly! Is he going to bite me?"

Jon laughs, "Nope, he's what they call a 'smiler' Lab. That's his greeting to you."

She hesitantly reaches her hand toward Pookie. He immediately inundates it with a slobbery kiss. She laughs as he holds up his paw for a hand-paw shake. The other girls crowd around Pookie, and he delights in the attention. Now Jon is feeling left out.

Then, comes unwanted attention. A car pulls alongside of the group and a very large, red-faced deputy county sheriff gets out. "Son, I've had a complaint about you. Some folks say you've got a vicious dog over here. I came to check you out. Got any ID?"

Jon pulls his Alabama driver's license out and hands it to the deputy. "Here, sir. We weren't causing any trouble; Pookie and I were just walking along the sidewalk . . . "

"Son, when I want any information, I'll ask for it. Now, you one of them hikers?"

"Yes sir, we're down here for a couple of days to re-supply."

The deputy looks at Pookie, still happily sitting surrounded by the girls, one of whom has placed a protective hand on his head. "He don't look too vicious to me. Are his shots up-to-date?"

"Yes, sir," answers Jon. He shows the deputy Pookie's rabies shot tag, hanging from his collar.

"Looks good to me. Now, about this animal attacking one of our fine citizens. You, there, young lady," he says, addressing one of the girls, "Did you see this incident?"

"Yes, Deputy Grisman, I saw the whole thing. Those jerks were hassling Jon, and that ape, Red, was fixing to whip him, like they did that other hiker a while back. Pookie was defending Jon."

She starts giggling, joined by the other girls.

"What's so funny?" asks the deputy.

"You should have seen Red's butt hanging out the window after Pookie grabbed this." She held up Pookie's souvenir, the tattered piece of jeans. "If Red's bare butt isn't indecent exposure, I don't know what is. It was the worst looking thing I've seen in my life!"

The girls giggle. Jon chuckles, and the deputy shows a crack in his official stone face as he breaks into a broad grin. "I kinda figured that was what happened. Son, will you give me a statement so's I can fill out an official report and keep those guys where I've got them now, in my jail?"

Jon demurs. "Sheriff, I'd rather not cause any more trouble. We just want to get back to the trail tomorrow morning and keep on hiking. We're trying to get to Maine before snow flies."

The deputy frowns. "Well, I guess I can keep them for a couple of days on public drunkenness. If a question ever comes up, I've got three witnesses here that I can call on." He takes down Jon's name and address and those of all of the girls. One of the girls adds, "Deputy, Mr. and Mrs. Wilson, Jimmy and Sarah, also saw what happened, and she fussed about those 'ruffians,' too."

"Well, son, I don't reckon I can blame you 'bout not filing a statement. Reckon I'll mosey back down to the jail and sweat them boys some. I may tell them you're wanting to sue them, and mebbe I can get one of them to confess they beat up that boy last month. Then, I can have them a-busting big rocks into little 'uns on the county roads for a year or two. You know, in them designer white coveralls with the numbers across the back. When they get into that place, they find out real quick they ain't as tough as they think. After that experience, they may even turn into model citizens, but I somehow doubt that. Now, son, where you staying while you're here in town?"

"Over at the Franklin Motel, but we're not ready to go back there yet . . . "

"Son, there you go again, offering information I ain't asking for yet. You got a bad habit of doin' that. Now, my question is, what time are you a-leaving tomorrow to go back to the trail?"

"Probably at about six o'clock in the morning."

"Ouch. That's awful early on my day off, but I reckon I'll be there by six to give you a ride to the trailhead. A ride'll be nigh-on to impossible to catch at that time of day. See you, then." He walked back to his car, mumbling about six o'clock and how his old lady was gonna scalp him, a-getting up so early on a Saturday.

Jon and the girls laugh. One of the girls, short with a pug nose and a spectacular figure, says, "Jon, now you may be in even bigger trouble. Sue and Kathy here are spending the night at my house and my daddy's cooking steaks. We've fixing to kidnap you and Pookie for the evening and show you some real Franklin hospitality."

Jon tries to object, mumbling about not wanting to be a bother, although the idea of spending an evening with this group of pretty girls is very tempting.

"Just quit fussing. Sue, go over to that phone and call my house and tell Daddy I said for him to throw on another steak. We're gonna have company." She turns to Jon and links her arm with his. "By the way, my name's Luann and if you haven't figured it, I never quit chattering. I've got lots of questions to ask about your hike."

Sue returns from the phone and reports, "Luann, your daddy says that'll be fine. Nothing you do could ever surprises him, he said."

Luann laughs. "I guess I've just 'bout got him trained. I keep on trying, anyhow. Well, let's go. My car's right over there." She points to a shiny, black Lincoln Towncar.

Jon objects again, "But Pookie can't ride in a car like that. He'll get hair on the seat."

Luann says, "Bullshit. He won't hurt a thing. I'll get it washed tomorrow. I said, let's go."

When Jon is faced with insurmountable odds, in this case being tugged on by three pretty girls, he knows when to surrender. He gives up gracefully and is escorted to the car. Luann, in her organizing mode again, says, "Since Pookie is the hero, he'll sit up front with me. Jon, you get in the middle, between Sue and Kathy. Now, girls, remember that poor boy's been in the mountains for a while, so you two be nice and behave. I'll be watching in the rear-view mirror."

All four do as told, including Pookie. He recognizes an irresistible force when he sees one, so he hops into the front seat, where he puts on his kingly pose, sitting proudly upright, looking over the passing countryside. The two hikers are happily surrounded by the eye- and nose-pleasing sights and odors of leather upholstery and pretty girls.

What follows, Jon has to describe as one of the most enjoyable evenings he has ever spent. Luann's parents are gracious even if they seem to be somewhat overwhelmed by their precocious daughter. Jon tells his story about the trip thus far and his plans and dreams for the next 5 months. His audience is attentive and listens with obvious interest.

Jon asks permission to use their telephone to make an important call to satisfy something that has been bugging him all evening. Luann's father waves away Jon's offer to pay for the call, so Jon dials his own number in Tuscaloosa. Andy's voice answers the phone with, "Home of the wandering Jon, may I help you?"

Jon has to laugh, "I might have known you'd have come up with something crazy. How's it going?"

"Just wonderful. Quiet, though. 'Cept for all the phone calls. How about with you guys, that's the question?"

"Been fine, so far. Pookie and I have rounded into great shape, and we just completed 100 miles. 12- and 15-mile days are possible, if your mind is set, your body is stout and your heart is pure. Say, Andy, I have a favor to ask of you. You know our plans are that you will meet us at Davenport Gap to take Pookie home?"

Andy chortles. "If I don't know those damned plans of yours by heart, it isn't because you haven't told me enough times. What you got on your feeble little mind?"

"Thinking about making a small revision. Would it be possible for you to skip that trip and come up to Damascus, Virginia, instead? We'd meet you at The Place Hostel, right in town on First Street. Will that fit within your busy schedule, you social lion, you?"

Andy rustles papers, looking at the master schedule. He's quiet for a moment, then groans. "You wouldn't believe the tender young thing I have lined up that night. Maybe I can put her off one more weekend, but she'll hate delaying the opportunity to be with me. Sheesh, what I don't give up for my friends. Okay, Damascus it is. What changed your mind about keeping him another two weeks?"

Jon says with obvious feeling, "I owe him one, big time. I'll tell you all about it in Damascus. We've got 18 miles to cover that day, so it'll be close to dark, time we're there. If you get there early, go ahead and get all three of us sleeping space. Thanks, buddy, now I owe you one." Jon hangs up the phone and returns to the gathering.

Jon finally manages to answer all Luann's questions before her parents excuse themselves and go to bed. Pookie is leashed and placed on the back porch and is presented with six steak bones on which he immediately begins work. He exhibits all the skill needed by a surgeon. The bones don't have a chance.

Still playing the self-appointed organizer, Luann turns the stereo on and instructs Jon, Sue, and Kathy that it is time to rock and roll. "Nobody gets to monopolize Jon, ladies. We'll keep a stop watch on dancin' time."

The three proceed to basically wear Jon out. After an hour of non-stop gyrating to the stereo, Luann puts on a slow song. She grabs Jon and begins dancing. He soon suffers the indignity that all men know under such circumstances, and he tries to keep both contact and indication of his condition to a minimum.

Jon gains control by the time he completes his dance card, and bows graciously at his three dates for the evening. "Ladies, this has been a wonderful evening, but the Pookster and I have to make twelve miles tomorrow. We've got to get some sleep. By the way, I hope Pookie is still on the back porch." The quartet looks out the window and sees Pookie, sound asleep on the porch, surrounded by the collection of polished, defeated, Porterhouse bones.

Pookie is awakened, and the Town car is fired up again. They arrive safely at the Franklin Motel. Jon receives a hug and a kiss on the cheek from each girl. Pookie gets his share of good-byes, as well. After addresses are shared so the Franklinites can keep up with his progress, an exhausted Jon and a full Pookie go in for the night. Jon dreams, probably yipping in his sleep like Pookie does when he's chasing rabbits. Neither ever catches his desired prey.

At exactly six o'clock, Deputy Grisman appears, yawning mightily behind the wheel. In jeans and a tattered red checkered shirt, he is slightly less foreboding. "Your chariot awaits, Sir. Sorry it's just a pickumup truck. Hop in and we'll whisk you away from civilization and back into the wilderness."

Jon laughs, "That sounds mighty fine to me. I believe I've seen enough of civilization for a while." He puts his pack in the back, and Pookie jumps in there as well.

The deputy asks, "Will he be okay, back there? Is he used to riding in the back of a truck?"

Jon says, "We don't call him the 'All-terrain-dog' for nothing. He'll ride in anything that moves. By my count, he's ridden in trucks, boats, bulldozers, a wagon behind a tractor, and even in a back-hoe and a Bobcat. He'll be okay. Sit, Pookie. Stay."

Pookie immediately obeys, and Jon crawls in the cab. Fifteen minutes later, Jon and Pookie say good-bye to the deputy and disappear into the woods. They are planning to camp that night at Licklog Gap, some 12 or 13 miles away.

Getting back into the stride that has served them well to this point is tough. Just two days in soft surroundings has temporarily spoiled both of them. They toughen back up and complete that day in good shape. When they awake the next morning, Mother Nature is replenishing her water supply. A cold, steady, drizzle is pinging on the metal roof of the shelter and shows no sign of letting up. That sign proves to be completely accurate, as it rains steadily for the next three days. They slip and slop through those days as Jon sees first-hand proof that the Smokies get the third highest rainfall in the United States, behind Gulf Coast and the Washington state areas. Everything gets wet. When he pulls his boots off, Jon's feet look like dead fish. His sleeping bag gets damp around the edges. Jon sees Pookie giving him strange looks during the evening. He's maybe thinking in his tiny doggie brain, "Boss, you've lost all your marbles, but I'll keep going with you. Crazy, that's what you are, crazy!"

The next day, Jon and Pookie are slowly walking up the trail ascending Rocky Bald. It's been a clear day to mid-morning, but the sky is beginning to appear ominous. They hear the rumble of thunder across several ranges of mountains. Pookie presses against Jon's leg, reminding him that he, Pookie, is the biggest storm wuss in the Western Hemisphere. If he hears thunder, a firecracker, or a gunshot back home, he's quickly hard to find. They begin walking a bit faster but it's not easy to do, going up the slope.

The thunder rumbles closer, until it's almost a continuous noise. Washington Irwin's one alley of ten pins in his story *Rip Van Winkle* is definitely being one-upped. The noise here sounds like a hundred-lane bowling alley. One rumble ends but four more have started; the surface of the ground vibrates and shakes.

Then, the wind starts. Leaves and small things blow across the trail in front of them, and they walk even faster, looking for a place to safely hide. The wind turns nasty and produces almost a micro-burst and tall pines bend at impossible angles. Trees, being strained beyond their capability to recover, snap and pop up the hill. The noise of one falling reaches their ears.

A feeling of panic comes over Jon, and they almost dash up the trail. Near the top, the wind eases off a bit, but Jon can hear the rain over the next valley. It's coming this way. Jon quickly strings his poncho between two trees, and he and Pookie crawl under. They and their packs just fit under the cover.

Jon sits, leaning against his pack, and Pookie leans against Jon. The continual rumble of the thunder has Pookie trembling. Jon scratches his ears and says, "Pup, I guess this is as good a place as we can be. It's all a gamble–which tree's coming down, where lightning's gonna hit–all we can do is be here and hope our number's not up." Lightning hits a nearby tree and sparks and smoke fly. "Damn," says Jon. "Yelp," says Pookie. Another thunderbolt hits farther up the mountain. The thunder continues its sonorous rumble.

The rain reaches their position, and Jon and his dog huddle even closer together. The only consolation is that the thunder seems to be moving on out, as it is becomes fainter and fainter.

Not true for the rain–that portion of the storm seems determined to wash them down the mountain, trying to succeed where the thunder, lightning, and wind had failed.

The old fashioned "frog-strangling" rain storm lasts an hour, but Jon and Pookie stay dry. Jon moves the supporting sticks several times when water builds up in large puddles above their heads. As the rain dwindles down to a mere trickle, the two trekers crawl out from their shelter and pack up, ready to hike again.

They approach Fontana Dam, as they near the half-way point of day 18. Six miles before Birch Spring Shelter, a one-hour break in the heavy, low-hanging clouds gives a view of the dam, a concrete monument to man's engineering achievements. The dam, which backs up the Little Tennessee River, is an overwhelming sight. The mountains provide a focus on the dam, and the Little T gleams like a jewel as it flows around a bend. Jon is glad that writer Colin Fletcher is not there with him, because his views on man-made intrusions into the wilderness such as dams, are clearly and vigorously given in his books. He doesn't care for them, and doesn't mind telling his readers.

Heavy, soaking rains return after giving Jon his spectacular view, and they slog to the Birch Spring Shelter, where they collapse after Jon hangs wet clothes from the rafters of the shelter. The rains finally stop about the time they go to sleep, too late to do them any good, that day anyway. But, it doesn't matter; both sleep hard and neither of them stirs a muscle until daylight makes its appearance. The sky is a beautiful blue with just scattered, fluffy clouds.

5 A RITE OF PASSAGE

Jon and Pookie enter the confines of the Smoky Mountains National Park. The total length of the AT in the Park is only about 70 miles as the crow flies. Jon expects the foot traffic to pick up even now as they travel through the park, with lots of families and groups, but the crowding isn't too bad at first. Jon sees a few day hikers, but for the last three days he has been hiking by himself, trudging in the cold rain. The rain! The damnable rain. It starts in the morning and steadily drizzles, occasionally yielding to a more serious downpour. Several times Jon has to seek shelter under a large tree or rock overhang to duck the worst of a deluge. Pookie is just as miserable as Jon, but is a good trooper and keeps pace with his master. It's possible that the reason there ain't many day–hikers is the fact that anybody with any sense is inside, not hiking through slop.

Walking in the rain wrapped in a poncho cuts off all peripheral vision and limits you literally to tunnel vision. This leads to lots of thinking and reminiscing. Jon's brain whirls and has a difficult time settling in on any one subject. He starts thinking about what it will be like if he completes the hike and returns to Tuscaloosa. He thinks about going to his folks' house, the garage, and the gym. Then, he visualizes an evening at Tony's, where this trek idea started.

Tony's Pub is typical of the wanna-be British pubs that have sprouted all over the United States. The pub is small and intimate. The booths are leather or at least good imitation leather, and the walls are dark paneling. The obligatory dart board is on the wall and after a match or two, the winners go to the sporting goods store to buy a set of official tournament darts. The darts don't help their game that much, but the thrower feels more, well, more official! Every square inch of Tony's is occupied with college students from the University of Alabama, along with some folks like Jon and his buddies who really don't want to admit that they are older than college age.

Near noon, the rain slows to a drizzle, then finally stops. Jon's attitude is lower than a snake's belly; he's been beaten into submission by the constant rain. He's seriously doubting his ability to continue any farther and complete the present hour or day, much less complete the entire trail. Everything he has on his body and his back is wet. His boots are so soaked he squishes with every step and his feet are tender and look horrible. The past two nights he and his dog have been fortunate to sleep in shelters along w/double hand-fulls of thru hikers. Jon has faithfully hung his clothes on un-occupied bunks, but nothing dries. When the humidity is 100 percent, things cannot dry.

Jon hopes to cover 15 miles today and he forces his wet, weary body forward, doubting his sanity and his commitment. The sun finally burns its way through the perpetual cloud cover, peeks through the canopy, and he can actually see steam rising from the clothes he's wearing. His belly loudly growls and informs him that it's time to eat, particularly since he skipped breakfast that morning in an effort to gain distance under adverse conditions.

Jon, walking by himself, looks to his right and sees bright light filtering through the dense forest canopy. He leaves the trail and follows an overgrown path. He emerges from the forest and finds himself on a large, flat, rock ledge by a drop-off of several hundred feet. He shucks his dripping pack and rubs his shoulders to ease the pain. Pookie shakes the last drops of water from his fur and finds a warm spot on the rock. He circles, then lies down, looking at Jon as if daring him to take another step.

"Dog, you got more sense than I do. Good idea!" Jon looks around and can see no people or even another trail. Their perch is completely hidden from the AT, so Jon strips down and lays out everything in his pack, tent and sleeping bag included. Taking off his boots is one of the most pleasurable events he can remember. Spotting a good-sized puddle of water near the trees, he takes advantage of the opportunity and, using his wash cloth and soap, bathes and puts on a new layer of deodorant. He weighs down corners of his gear with rocks to avoid wind-borne escape and stretches himself out on a semi-dry towel. Sighing contentedly, his entire body is enveloped by the warming rays of the sun, and within minutes, he is sound asleep.

Jon and Pookie sleep for an hour until Jon's internal alarm clock prompts him awake. Checking the clothes and gear, he finds all just about dry. After turning them over to complete the process, he enjoys a can of Vienna Sausage for lunch, although sharing them with Pookie forces him to open a second can.

After stowing the trash, Jon dresses, repacks his gear, and slips into the harness. "Hey, dog, this infernal house on my back must be 10 pounds lighter. Let's

try to stay dry from now on, huh? Whata ya think?" Pookie licks Jon's hand in response, agreeing with everything he says, and Jon has to laugh.

"Dog, you're gonna get me out of my blue funk, if you're not careful. I was sorta enjoying wallowing in my misery; now you've messed it up by making me laugh." Pookie agrees again, and they retrace their steps through the thick underbrush and branches lining the quasi-trail and returned to the AT.

When he reaches the trail and bursts through the tangled underbrush, he steps between two large trees guarding the entrance. He runs directly into another hiker, sending them both tumbling to the ground, packs, hiking sticks and all.

"Sorry," he gasps.

"Me, too," agrees a muffled voice, much more musical in tone then the male thru-hikers he has talked with in the past few weeks. "Now, are you as good at helping people up to their feet as you are at knocking them down?"

Jon locates the woman's hand protruding from the midst of a toppled pack. Her face is covered by a sweater that she must have had hanging over the top rail of her pack to keep it out of the way. Jon helps the woman and manages to extract her from the tangled grip of her pack. He lifts her to her feet. The top of her head barely comes to his chin, but as he will discover soon enough, a lack of physical height is the only challenge she doesn't attack head-on.

"That's better," she says and removes the sweater from her face. Jon stares at the pert freckled face framed by reddish-brown curls now in a serious state of disarray.

"Cat got your tongue?" she teases.

"It—it—it's just that you're the prettiest thing I've seen for weeks. I'm used to dirty, hard-ankle men," Jon stammers out.

"Phooey, you've obviously been up here too long. Any female would look good to you. Besides, my nose is too long, I've got too many freckles, and no one has called me pretty in a while. By the way, my name is Gretel," she says, as she extends her hand.

Jon's hand is gripped by surprising strength. He responds, "I'm Jon, and I'm real pleased to be talking to another human. If anyone could hear me talk to my dog, they'd be convinced I'm nuts. This good looking fellow is Pookie," he said, gesturing at the Lab, patiently sitting by the trail.

As Gretel approaches, Pookie smiles. She stops dead in her tracks. Then, Pookie extends his paw to Gretel, and she laughs with delight, kneeling to make his acquaintance. Pookie responds to the attention and leans against her, moaning in happiness as she scratches his ears. "You were smiling at me! I'm glad to meet you, too, Sir."

"He'll sit there for three or four days, as long as you do that," laughs Jon. "I guess we'd better hit the trail. Where're you heading?"

"I've just got four days, but I'm gonna try and make it most of the way through the Park. A friend of mine has a convention of some kind down in Gatlinburg, so I rode with her, and she let me off at Fontana Dam. I climbed to the Appalachian Trail up that steep grade there by Shuckstack. She's going to pick me up at the parking lot at Newfound Gap. What about you? Where're you heading?"

Jon answers with a touch of justifiable pride, "I'm a thru-hiker. I started in Georgia at Springer Mountain in March, and I'm going to Katahdin in Maine. I hope to be there in August, maybe September."

Gretel's jaw drops. "Wow," she manages to croak. "How long a trip is that, anyway?"

Jon replies, "2,158 miles, give or take a foot or so. I'm afraid I've still got a little way to go."

She shakes her head in amazement. "You must have a will of solid iron; what in the world possessed you to undertake something like this?"

"Well, it's hard to explain. I spend a lot of time trying to explain it to myself. I guess it's 'cause I never finish anything, accomplish anything. I start lots of stuff, but never finish them. I hope that this hike will give me a real shot of self-confidence. You know, actually finish what I start. Leastwise, that's what I hope."

"I hope you complete it, too. You seem tough enough to me. You got good gear?"

"The best I could afford–mostly good namebrands. It's holding up pretty good, so far. What about you?"

"Well, I'm afraid most of my gear is blue-light special stuff. Since I'll just be three days on this hike, I didn't want to spend very much. Besides, I just graduated from college a year ago, and I don't have bucks to spare. One of these days I'll splurge and get a set of really good gear, but it'll have to wait for a while."

Jon says, "I expect that gear will hold up pretty well. I made several weekend hikes using the same. Now, I guess we'd best go. You want to hike with us? Pookie'd like the company."

"Oh, you wouldn't?" she teases. "Mr. fancy namebrand gear is embarrassed to walk with Miss blue-light special?"

"No, no. Believe me, I'd like the company as much as Pookie. Hiking by yourself may build character according to books I've read, but it gets old. I'm a people person. I'd love company!"

"Well, if you are completely sure that Pookie will approve, I guess I'll tag along. You lead."

Jon starts up the trail with Pookie beside him. This part of the AT is narrow, so conversation is impossible for a while. He hears her footsteps behind him, and she's keeping up the pace, apparently effortlessly. He thought, "This is quite a gal. A good-looking, smart, athletic woman is the last thing I figured to find up here. Wow, she even seems to like me, in the middle of all her teasing."

He shuts his brain down and concentrates on hiking for the next hour. The walking style he's developed is usually to hike steadily for an hour, then rest for five minutes, then hike. He has to make up time from the slow pace necessitated by the three nasty rain days.

The trio trudges on. Jon glances at his watch and then spots a fallen log by the side of the trail. He stops without a word, unslings his pack, and sits. Pookie stands to get his pack removed, then flops by Jon's side.

Gretel stands in front of him, hands on hips, barely breathing hard. "What's the matter, Tarzan, tired? We've just been walking an hour."

"No, I'm not really tired, but I've found that a quick rest stop, a drink, and a handful of gorp keeps me going longer."

"What the hell is a gorp?" she asks.

"Here, try some. It's a trail snack of raisins, M & M's, sunflower seeds, and peanuts. Gives you energy, plus it tastes great."

She digs in, and they sit in silence disturbed only by munching. She stands first, stretches, and slips her pack on. He follows suit. Gretel says, "Okay, my turn to lead. Let's see if you can keep up with me." She sets out at a brisk pace and Jon has to hustle to keep up. Pookie follows.

It takes 20 minutes for Jon to realize what's different. Something is. He's usually able to shut down his mind and concentrate on the rough trail. Now, he's tripping and stumbling on almost every root and rock in the trail, and there's plenty of both. What's different?

Then he figures it out. Instead of concentrating on the trail and his footing, he blushes as he realizes that his full powers of concentration are zeroed in on the rounded, decidedly feminine rear end, encased in tight, faded Jean shorts that is moving from side to side in front of him. Gretel is framed by the lowest rail on her pack and on either side by the vertical bars. He stares, fascinated, as each hip sways just enough to lightly touch the vertical bars. Jon continues to stare, until he finds walking not only more difficult, but uncomfortable. It's tough to hike a steep, rock-strewn trail toting a 45 pound pack under any circumstances, but doing so with a growing erection is nigh-impossible.

He shakes his head and forces himself to look at the trail, not at the lovely distraction. He even begins whistling a soft, tuneless song. What's he thinking about, fantasizing about, anyway? Gretel's just being nice to him cause she wants company on the hike.

Jon's troubles diminish, and the walking becomes somewhat easier. Whew! That's somewhat better–easier walking, anyway. His mind starts to wander. Here he is, 24 years old and still hasn't made it with a woman. There was that time in his pickup, when kisses became passionate, breathing heavy, and windows fogged over. He groped with his right hand and found Sissy's breast, but barely had time to recognize what he had before the offending hand was quickly and forcibly removed. He received a stern lecture about old-fashioned girls, moral standards and waiting until marriage, along with all other such clichés known to mankind. He never tried that again. Andy and his buddies talk all the time about their successes with the ladies. According to them, their scores were legion, a fact that Jon takes with a large grain of salt, about the size of a cattle-lick block of salt.

It's funny that he's spending time reminiscencing about Sissy, in light of that chilly dismissal she gave him at Ryan's, when he announced this trip. "Never speak to me again, don't ever bother calling, you're inconsiderate, you've never finished anything in your life, why do you think you're going to be able to accomplish this," etc., etc., etc. But his mind keeps on wandering and remembering.

Not only is he classified as a virgin, people don't seem to believe him capable of such an act–make love to a woman? Not good ole Jon–he's to be trusted–he's safe–you don't have to lock up the women and children when Jon's around.

Jon thinks back to last fall, when he and Sissy got a wild hair and drove to Knoxville to watch their beloved Crimson Tide play the hated, despicable Big Orange. It was an afternoon football game, so they didn't plan to stay all night.

As they left the 95,000 disappointed orange-clad fans following an Alabama victory, the skies looked foreboding. The weatherman had predicted rain mixed with snow, but you know you can't trust what they say. You know, how can you tell when a weatherman is guessing? When his lips are moving.

They had decided to take I-40 over to Nashville, then head south on I-65. There was still plenty of daylight left; maybe they'd do some sight-seeing. But, Mother Nature intervened. The snow mixed with rain turned to 100 percent snow mixed with sleet, and the road turned hazardous. Halfway up Rockwood Mountain they turned a curve in time to see an unbelievable sight. Trucks were jackknifed, and 15 or 20 of them were completely blocking the road, shoulders, and ditches. There were 50 cars between Jon and the trucks.

Jon spotted a cross-over–one of those that says, "Official vehicles only." They skidded and slid and accomplished a U-turn. They went back down the mountain, where they found that the road going back towards Knoxville was equally blocked and impassable. They got two rooms in Harriman at an inexpensive motel. They called home to let their folks know where they were and that they were safe, then they had dinner. Jon admitted to having a few lecherous thoughts, but Sissy squelched any possible progress along those lines. When Jon unlocked her door for her, she took the key from his hand, placed a kiss on his cheek, told him good night, and firmly closed the door in his face. "Damn, another chance wasted," he said. He was destined to keep his love (or lust) burning within himself.

The worst thing about the whole incident was when they returned home the next day after the salt trucks and scrapers did their thing. Nobody questioned them, nobody teased them, and Sissy's dad clapped Jon on his shoulder and said, "That was a real grownup decision you made, Jon. Thanks for taking care of my little girl." Jon thought to himself, "You don't need to worry, Mr. Swingle, your little girl is more than capable of taking care of herself."

Gretel brought him back to the present as she stopped by a large rock outcrop. "Well, Tarzan, I admit it–I'm tired. Let's get a drink and try another shot of that gorp."

Jon does a double take–after all the reminiscing he has done about Sissy, he has transposed Sissy's face on Gretel. That doesn't last long. Gretel's cute face reappears as does the present time.

"Shoot, yeah. I've been wondering if you were ever going to poop out. If you're going to call me Tarzan, I'll have to call you Jane. She was always the tough one in that relationship, anyway."

After shucking their packs, they sit and enjoy rest, water, gorp, and a pleasant silence, broken only by the singing of the birds. Jon loves it. They can enjoy each other's company without needing the incessant chatter that always seemed to emanate from Sissy.

Jon says, "It's right about four o'clock. We should be at Russell Field Shelter in about an hour or so. Okay with you if we stop there for the night? That should put you on schedule to be out of the park in three days."

"Whatever you think, Tarzan. With your experience and expertise, I think I'll let you call the shots, for now. Don't get the big head, though. There's not a compliant bone in my body. I'm what you call a thoroughly assertive lady."

Jon laughs, "We'll get along just fine. We can sleep in the shelter, I guess. You don't carry a tent, do you?"

Nope, sure don't. Unfortunately, my sleeping bag is a cheapie and I hope I don't lie awake all night shivering."

"It'll probably keep you warm enough. The real cold weather is behind us. Should be in the 20s tonight."

They proceed along the widening trail and are now able to walk side-by-side with Pookie trailing. He still has to check out all the new smells on that part of the trail and stops dead in his tracks at times. If you follow too closely on his heels, you, dog, and pack would all come together. If Pookie minds his place being usurped by Gretel, he shows no signs of it.

As they walk, Jon finds himself unloading his inferiority complex on Gretel. She is a great listener and confidence-builder and by the time they arrive at the shelter at dusk, Jon is feeling very self-assured. Amazingly, the shelter is unoccupied, and they set their packs on two bunks and prepare to eat dinner. Jon has a dried beef stew concoction he's pretty proud of and Gretel offers candy bars as dessert. Working as a team makes cooking and dish washing an easy task, and they sit back to enjoy a cup of coffee in less than an hour.

The banter continues, and Jon enjoys the third grade word war as much as he had ever enjoyed a conversation in his life. Then, it happens. They hear voices and an approaching commotion. They strain their eyes in the dusk and see, to their horror, a Scout troop approaching. Twelve boys and two adult leaders. A whole lot of khaki cloth and army-surplus gear propelled by 28 legs.

"Oh, shit," exclaims Jon. "Some hikers I walked with back down the trail told me that this happened to them once. If the boys are good guys and well-trained, it can be okay. But if they're complainers, it'll be no fun at all. We'll just have to see. It's too late to move on to the next shelter."

"We'll make it, oh great fearless leader. We'll make it."

They exchange greetings with the Scouts and watch the fire drill that ensues. The boys aren't very organized, and the men are too busy complaining about their feet and their backs to be any help. One of the men goes into the shelter and counts bunks, then counts heads.

"Oh man," he says. "Somebody's going to have to sleep on that hard dirt floor cause of that broken bunk. It sure as hell isn't going to be me!"

Jon looks at Gretel and whispers, "Are you ready for me to make an executive decision? It's for sure we're not going to get any peace and quiet or sleep here."

She whispers back, "That's for damned sure. Those guys have about as much discipline as my little brother, and that's not saying much. Whatcha gonna do, claim squatter's rights?"

"Nope, I'm going to recommend that we retreat in grand style and live to sleep another day."

She groans. She also looks puzzled. "I think you just totally mangled that saying, but whatever. I'll follow your lead."

Jon stands and walks over to the leader, a large man who fits into his official Scout leader shorts and T-shirt like an overstuffed German sausage fits into its skin. His stocky legs are lily-white. Jon says, "Sir, we can't have anybody sleeping on the floor. The AT shelter mice are as unforgiving as the skunks. I've got a tent, so Gretel and I will find a place down the trail a bit to set it up and leave you guys the shelter. That way, even discounting the broken one, everybody will have their own bunk."

The Scout leader's mouth falls open as he tries to digest Jon's message. "Mice? Skunks? What kind of wilderness is this? I'm going to call my congressman when I get back home."

"You'll be O.K. Just get the guys to hang their packs from the shelter roof beams with ropes threaded through paper cups or something, about half-way down the rope. The mice are experts in climbing down ropes and they'll play havoc with your pack. If a skunk wanders in, leave him alone and let him wander. They're pretty tame and won't bother you, if you don't bother them."

The Scoutmaster mumbles his thanks, still thinking about this wilderness experience and wondering why in the hell he's even here. Jon and Gretel re-pack their stuff and move out. They hike about a half-mile until the light of the flashlight reveals a level place under the trees about a 150 feet off the trail.

As they walk to the spot, nicely carpeted with pine needles, Jon says, "Jane, if you'll hold the light, I can get this tent set up in five minutes. It's a pretty nice one; even has a vestibule so the dew won't get on our packs."

He turns the light on Gretel. She's standing still with an incredulous look on her face.

"I don't believe this. Damn, Tarzan, I thought you had no self-confidence. But here I've followed you into the woods in the night to share your cave. I'm glad you didn't revert to a caveman and drag me off by the hair. We might have had a bru-ha-ha, if you'd tried that! The follow-me approach works much better with me."

Gretel holds both flashlights and watches as Jon quickly and efficiently places the groundcloth, spreads the tent, snaps the shock-corded poles into place and stretches the rainfly. He accomplishes the task in the promised five minutes.

"Tarzan, you're good. Really good. I'm impressed. What now?"

"Well, it's just eight o'clock. Since it's such a clear night, want to see if we can find an overlook and do some star-gazing? I don't know much about constellations, but I get totally relaxed just looking."

She agrees, and they carry their ponchos and flashlights, off into the night. Within a quarter of a mile, they find an overlook and lie back on their ponchos. Both are mesmerized by the hypnotic sparkle of the stars. Pookie chooses to lie down on Gretel's poncho beside her, instead of Jon's, and he has to laugh.

"I guess you've been adopted. He definitely has good taste. I'm curious as to what he'll think when I tie him up outside the tent. He won't like it much, but he'll get used to it."

"Why don't we make him a shelter out of my poncho?" asks Gretel. "After all, I'm the one displacing him."

"Yeah, good idea. It will protect him from the dew. He'll like that."

They lie there enjoying the silence and the nearness of the stars and the bright quarter moon. After an hour or so, the temperature has dropped enough that the chilly air is making it hard to enjoy the stars. They roll up their ponchos and walk back to the camp site under the bright stars, barely needing the flashlights, until they enter the heavy canopy of the trees.

Jon and Gretel sit on the ground near the tent. Jon's brain is busy thinking thoughts like, "I sure like this woman. Maybe there's some way I can get her into my life." He decides to explore the idea.

"Gretel, where do you live, anyway? We never swapped addresses."

"I live near Boston College, my alma mater. I work in an office not too far from the school. What about you?"

"I did the same thing after I graduated from the University of Alabama a couple of years ago. I still live and work near the campus. Here," he tore a piece of paper from the small notebook he carried in his shirt pocket after he wrote his address and phone number.

Gretel accepts the paper and says, "I'll give you my telephone number so you can call me after you complete your thru-hike. I'll be pulling for you to make it." She gives him the number, then says, "Now, I'm about to freeze. I'm more than ready to crawl into my sleeping bag."

It takes just a few minutes to fashion a lean-to for Pookie and Jon fastens his leash to a nearby tree. He pours him a night's supply of water and spreads his own poncho under the lean-to, for a bed.

"There, bud, a place fit for a king. Keep the critters away from us." Pookie goes into the shelter, sniffs, then circles a few times, and settles in. He curls up until only eyes show above his tail. Jon turns to Gretel and says, "I'll light my hiker's candle in the tent, so you can see to get ready for bed. I agree with you; I'm getting chilly, too." He crawls into the tent and lights the candle, placing it in the folding lantern. He returns outside, and Gretel goes into the tent.

Jon rubs Pookies' ears for a minute and is rewarded with his usual moan of enjoyment. Gretel calls, "Okay Tarzan, I'm in my sleeping bag. Come on in before you freeze. Brrr, this bag is cold!"

Jon enters the tent and by the dim glow of the lantern, sees a shivering lump in Gretel's sleeping bag, but no visible head. He laughs. "That bag'll warm up in a minute. They say shivering is good for you cause it warms you up. You believe that, don't you?"

"Hell no!" issues through chattering teeth, and Jon has to laugh again. She responds, "Keep on laughing, Tarzan. You still have to warm up your bag. Then it'll be my turn to laugh."

Jon says, "Stay under there for a minute, while I get ready and in the old mummy bag and blow out the light. Then it'll be safe for you to poke your head out."

"I might poke my head out, and I might not ever come out again," chatters Gretel.

Jon strips down to his underwear and quickly crawls into his sleeping bag. He blows out the candle and says to the darkness, "Okay, you can come out now and quit playing hide and seek."

"I'm just fine here, thank you. I hope your sleeping bag is incredibly cold. You really deserve it."

"This kind of bag warms up really fast because the body heat can't sneak by your shoulders. Try folding the corners around your shoulders. It'll help some."

"I'm getting a little warmer. Now, if you'll shut up long enough, maybe we can get some sleep," grumbles Gretel. "Good night."

Silence falls and Jon's eyes close. Just before he drops off into the sleep abyss, Gretel says softly, "Jon, thanks for today. I really enjoyed it, and I learned lots of stuff by just watching you. You're good in this environment. Now, good night, again."

Jon drifts off to sleep, and all conversation ceases. At least for a while. Some time later, about an hour or so, Jon is partially awakened by a small noise. It's the kind of noise that hangs around and you try to ignore, but it's persistent.

Jon drifts in and out of sleep. The noise persists. His foggy brain can't put enough information together to try and put a name on it. The noise intensifies and finally gets Jon's attention to the point that he drifts slightly closer to the waking stage. The noise is coming from his right. He turns over that way. His eyes have adjusted to the dark and with the help of the moon light, he locates the noise as coming from Gretel's sleeping bag. She's not visible at all, still completely burrowed inside the bag.

Jon clears his throat and mumbles, "Gretel, are you okay? You sick or something?"

"No - - o - - o, I'm not sick. I'm freezing! I've not been able to warm up this bag. I haven't slept a wink. Can you get hypothermia at night, in a sleeping bag, for God's sake?"

"I don't think so, but I don't know. We need to do something, or you'll be too tired to walk at all tomorrow."

"Wha - - a - - at," she chatters, "can we do?"

He responds, "We could maybe pile extra clothes on top of your bag. That should help some."

"No, I don't think that would help enough. Why don't you crawl in my bag with me and put your mummy bag on top? Mine is big enough for both of us–in fact, that's the damned problem with it. There's not enough of me to warm it up."

Jon's mind races, and he is suddenly the one who is stammering. "Ok—k—kay. Maybe the combined heat will take care of the problem. Hypothermia can kill you," he added in a granny's tone of voice. More grown up than he feels at the present time. He thinks, "Damned lucky I got that puddle bath today. Otherwise, I'd stink so badly she couldn't stand me, warmth or not."

He unzips his mummy bag as far as it will go. Manufacturers of sleeping bags have determined that zippers are a pathway to let heat escape, no matter how well you insulate them and the tabs that cover them. His bag zips only half-way down.

"Here I come," he stammers. He crawls out of the bag, trying to carefully place his hands to avoid crushing her. He reaches for the top of her bag to lower it and crawl in. His hand meets resistance, but not the material of the sleeping bag he expects. What he encounters is soft and warm and exactly fits his hand. In the split second it takes his mind to recognize he has his hand on her breast, he panics. "Sorry, I thought I was grabbing the sleeping bag." He snatches his hand back as if it were on a hot stove. "Sorry," he says again.

"No big deal," she laughs. "At least a part of me was warm for a second. Now get in here. What little heat there is in the bag is escaping."

He now moves with great care. He cautiously slips into the bag and manages to touch no additional body parts. He zips the bag part of the way up and pulls his mummy bag over the lower part of her blue-light special. He completes zipping the enclosure and lies completely still, hardly twitching a single muscle.

In a barely audible voice, Gretel says, "I'm still cold. Do you mind if I slide over next to you, spoon style? Turn away from me."

He obeys orders very well. She slides next to him, knees bent to fit with his. His stomach feels a slight hiccup as he becomes very much aware of her bare legs against his. Her body conforms rather nicely to his and she slips her arm around his chest. Her breasts, encased in a T-shirt, press softly against his back. No muscles were moving before, but one muscle now quickly responds to it's fullest extent. Luckily, blushes aren't visible at night. His face feels as hot as if he'd just spent four days in the sun at a bluegrass festival. His underwear is strained.

When such night-time problems occur and he is by himself, he can rearrange his Fruit of the Looms for comfort. But now, in these circumstances, he's helpless. Her arm is over his arm; besides, to reach down to rearrange himself would draw attention to his problem. He decides to lie still.

"Tarzan," whispers Gretel, "You're good at more than just hiking and setting up tents. You're warm! Thanks for helping me out."

"G—g—glad to help." Will that damned stutter ever go away? he curses silently.

She wiggles, trying to get even closer, hoping to absorb more body heat. His blushing increases, as does his problem. He wouldn't have thought it possible for either to grow, but both do.

Gretel's hand brushes his face, and she says in surprise, "Jon, your face is hot! You're not getting sick, are you? It feels like you have a fever."

He laughs in embarrassment. "No, I'm not getting sick. I'm used to having Pookie in my tent, not good looking ladies. I reckon I'm blushing."

It's her turn to laugh. "Tarzan, I'm shocked. I would have thought that a good looking jungle man, like you, would just swoop down on a vine and carry off the maiden of your choice. I love it! I've scared Tarzan!"

When she receives no response, she quits laughing and is silent for a moment. She concretely whispers, "Jon, I'm sorry if I embarrassed you. I apologize. Do you want to go back to your sleeping bag? I'm all right now. I'm finally warm."

"No," he says forcefully. "Do you want the truth, or should I give you macho bullshit?"

"The truth, always the truth."

"Oh, shit, I've never told this to anyone in my life. Ah, here goes. I've dated lots of girls, and I even had a steady for three or four years. But I've never even left the batter's box, much less gotten to first base. There, that's the truth. I believe I'm blushing even more."

He lies in silence, crushed and humiliated. Gretel is also silent, although she does tighten her arm around him. "Jon," she whispers, "that took guts. Thanks for telling me the truth."

They lie there as if cased in one skin. Empathy and embarrassment are strange bedfellows, but here they are. Jon's blush slowly dissipates. At least one of his problems is lessened.

Gretel's hand starts moving, inscribing small circles on Jon's chest. He holds his breath, and the slow easy caress continues. No words are spoken. None are needed.

Her hand moves lower to his stomach, still moving in circles. Jon finally has to take a breath, more like a gasp. Her caress continues and moves lower and lower. She traces the elastic on the top of his shorts then slips in her hand. She takes him in her hand and strokes him. Jon groans; his emotions are somewhere halfway between ecstasy and panic. But, he doesn't move.

After a moment of the most intimate contact Jon has ever experienced, she withdraws her hand. "Damn," thinks Jon, "what now?" What's now is she turns away from him and faces the other direction.

Jon lies there in shock. What happened? Why did she leave? Did he do something wrong? He jumps when she whispers, "Okay, Tarzan? It's your turn to warm me."

He turns over and fits himself to her body. The softly rounded rear that he had admired from afar on the trail is now pressed against his manhood, still straining against his jockey shorts. He hesitantly, cautiously puts his arm around her. His hand finds her breast again, this time on purpose. He caresses her and feels the nipple grow in his hand. He caresses the other breast, and it's her turn to moan softly. His other hand feels left out, so he begins rubbing that magnificent rear. The cotton of the T-shirt makes her skin feel like satin, and it slides sensuously over her skin. He kisses the hollow formed where her neck meets her shoulder.

He gets brave and lets his top hand slide down. Down over the tight stomach and between her legs. He rubs, enjoying the feel of the cotton sliding on her body. She rolls over onto her back and slides the T-shirt up. Jon caresses her until she moans again, this time less silently. Her hand stops him.

"Wait," she whispers. "Reach into the top left pocket of my pack and get the protection."

He slips out of the bag, finds the small foil-wrapped pouch and returns to the warmth of the bag and the warmth that is Gretel. Cold and desire motivate him to rapid movement. She helps him remove his shorts and gets him prepared. She pulls him over her and helps him enter. They moan as one.

It's amazing how well such activities can be carried out in a sleeping bag designed for one. But, it works. It works well. They reach release almost simultaneously, and Jon rolls sideways, keeping the connection. They lie there for several minutes, clasping each other in a tight embrace, her face buried in his neck and her soft hair filling his nostrils with fragrant woman-smell.

"Jon, that was wonderful. If that won't keep me warm the rest of the night, there's something wrong. That was your first time? You're as good at lovemaking as you are at wilderness hiking."

Jon laughs. "Yep, that was a first. Being so unexpected, it may also wind up being a best."

"I doubt that. There are lots of things you need to try. Now that you're out of the batter's box, I suspect there'll be lots of ladies who will be happy to be your next hit."

In unspoken agreement, they pull apart and Jon lies beside Gretel in a warming and protective position, with his arm around her. She snuggles to him and practically purrs. They sleep.

At about four in the morning, Gretel wakes him. "Jon, why don't you slide over into your mummy bag, so we can sleep more comfortably. I'm fine now. I'm nice and warm."

Jon sleepily grumbles, then kisses her on the forehead and complies. The interior of his sleeping bag warms quickly, and he sleeps even harder.

It's been daylight for over an hour, when Jon wakes. He sleepily opens his eyes partially, then realization jerks them fully open. Gretel's sleeping bag is gone. He sits up and turns to the vestibule of the tent. Her pack is also missing. "Damn," he says, "Gretel, where are you?" Silence answers. He calls again. Pookie's soft whimper is the only response he receives.

Jon frantically pulls his clothes on, fearing the worst. He crawls out of the tent and sees no sign of her. He crawls back into his portable house. Up by the small pillow he uses lies a small piece of paper. He snatches it up with all the intensity with which a drowning man grabs a life preserver.

As he reads, he can almost hear Gretel's soft low voice: "Dear Tarzan, last night was wonderful! I'm happy I had the privilege of helping you reach first base. It was special. I left early for one reason and one reason only. At this time, I can't handle a relationship. I'm just over one, and I have to concentrate on my job. If I could make a commitment now, I'd choose you. Believe me when I say that! Now get out there and complete your hike. You can do it! Maybe we'll meet again some day. I hope so! For now, good-bye and love, Gretel."

Jon sits for long minutes, face in hands. Then reality sinks in and he stands. Pookie is sitting erect, ears perked up, and he's looking at Jon. If concern is an emotion that can be expressed by a dog, it's plastered all over his furry face. Jon walks over to him and buries his face in Pookie's mane. "Dog, I reckon it's you and me once again. I believe you like her as much as I do."

He unsnaps Pookie's leash, and the dog runs around, having doggie activities to accomplish. Jon watches him for a bit, then starts his stove and soon enjoys a cup of coffee with a fruit bar. He sadly and mechanically rolls, packs, stuffs, hooks, and ties his gear and straps his house on his back. He whistles and a dew-damp Pookie bounds out of the thick woods, a silly Labrador smile on his face.

"Dog, I wish I could recover as fast as you. Look at you–happy-go-lucky." He carefully unfolds Gretel's note from the shirt pocket in which he had placed it. He reads and re-reads the note, until he can quote his favorite parts. "I'd choose you . . . Maybe we'll meet again some day. I hope so . . . Love, Gretel."

Jon and Pookie follow the path and turn north on the trail. Jon walks steadily, quickly, almost as if in a daze. He needs no mind detachment games this morning–there's no question about where his mind is dwelling. Sad, happy, contentment, longing, pride, pain. These and many other emotions run through his mind and chase each other around, until he feels as if he is looking through the business end of a kaleidoscope. Ultimately, happiness, contentment, and pride win the battle, and Jon walks the trail, a huge grin on his face.

6 "THAR'S A BAR OVER THAR!"

After the interlude with Gretel at Russell Field, Jon walks steadily, if absentmindedly and covers 14 1/2 miles. During the day, he and Pookie see many hikers, most of whom are day-hikers or folks with kids in tow. For a change, Jon doesn't see any other thru-hikers. He has to tell his story about why he's doing what he's doing several times to day-hikers, and for the first time in his life, he enjoys being the center of attention. Maybe last night's encounter has been a real confidence-builder. He has to admit to himself that in terms of enjoyment, on a scale of one to 10 the event rated at least a 12 or 13.

They arrive at Silers Bald Shelter at about four in the afternoon, and to his surprise, the first person Jon sees is Recovering Sam. "Sam," begins Jon, "I didn't expect to catch up with you guys quite this soon."

Sam laughs, "Well, I don't know that you have caught up with we guys. The other two are long gone. I see their notes in the trail notebooks, and they're two or three days ahead of me. I doubt I'll catch up with them. So, I've been walking by myself since Fontana Dam. Sometimes I walked with another thru-hiker for an hour or two. I've been at this shelter for most of today, just resting. It felt like the thing to do, so I did it and I'm glad. I feel rested."

"Had any problems traveling by yourself?"

"Nah, in fact I've been enjoying the solitude. Plus, there's been no pressure on me to walk faster than I want, in order to keep up with the two speedsters. How bout you? Been playing the hermit?"

Jon laughs, "Nope, the Pookster's been keeping me pretty good company. I've walked with a few other people since I've been in the park. By the way, did you see a really good looking gal pass you earlier today?"

"Yeah, at about one o'clock this afternoon she came through–said she was trying to get all the way to Icewater Spring by this evening. She was moving super fast. She's definitely the best-looking thing I've seen up in these mountains. Why do you ask, she a friend?"

Jon's jaw drops. "Damn, that's a 30-mile day she's working on. She really is a walker. I'm impressed. Yeah, she's a friend. I was hoping I'd catch up with her again. My feet are sore, so I can't go any farther. I won't be catching up tonight. Damn, 30 miles. I'm afraid she's long gone as far as I'm concerned."

Jon and Sam prepare their dinners in companionable silence, cooking on their stoves just outside the shelter. Jon is still caught halfway between happy and sad. Other hikers trickle in during the late afternoon and early evening, until the shelter is almost a full house. Several campers announce that they had seen a bear

or two that day. Jon puts the leash on a reticent Pookie, figuring he's better off inside the shelter in the event of additional wildlife visits. Particularly the large, furry, black type, complete with large teeth and claws.

At about six o'clock, the weekend hikers are lounging around, still discussing the bears they had seen earlier. They are still hyper about their sightings. Jon is sitting on his bunk in the shelter with his hand resting on Pookie's shoulder, when he feels his dog's muscles tighten up. Pookie shivers, then barks once. Jon commands, "Quiet, Pookie, no barking allowed up here." The dog doesn't like it very much, but he complies and lies down on the floor near the row of bunks. His body is still trembling.

One of the hikers points to the other side of the clearing. "Look, there's one, now!" A rather large bear slowly saunters out of the forest and ambles across the clearing. She knows exactly where she's going, apparently a frequent visitor to that particular shelter. The ensuing movement of campers inside the shelter Jon will later compare to what he imagines Grand Central Station at rush hour is like. Ten men and women and one dog line up against the cyclone fence that protects the front of the rock-walled shelter and become the animals inside the zoo enclosure. The bear, with a red tag in one ear and a white tag in the other, paces outside, eyeing the humans in the cage.

Lagging behind the sow are two cubs. They are apparently last year's litter, because they are about the size of a large German Shepherd. Momma bear lets one of them know that she's no longer worrying about their welfare. The cub, sniffing the ground beside the shelter, finds a few scraps of food, spilled when one of the hikers had prepared their meal. Momma bear sees the cub, and almost faster than the eye can see, she reaches out and cuffs the cub with a resounding thwack! The cub rolls about fifty feet like a furry ball with an occasional paw sticking out. The ball emits squeals until the cub comes to a stop against a sapling. The hikers laugh. Jon feels Pookie quiver again, shaking from head to paws, his instincts telling him that he must either bark or explode. Jon strokes his fur. He whispers, "Quiet, boy, no barking. Just watch." The quivers slow down, ever so slightly. Pookie's muscles are as tight as banjo strings.

Camera shutter clicks fill the air, sounding like a busload of tourists at the Grand Canyon, as Momma bear turns Hollywood, stopping to pose at intervals. The cubs wisely stay their distance, as Momma grubs around in the spots where she finds food scraps. After 15 minutes of exploration, she ambles back across the clearing, joined by the cubs after they see if Momma has left any scraps. When the last furry butt goes out of sight into the forest, the hikers release a collective sigh and Pookie shudders again. Jon says in his ear, "Bud, I guess you are leash-bound in here for the rest of the night. Even the cubs are bigger than you, and I'm not taking any chances."

The hikers exit the shelter; however, none ventures more than eight or ten feet from their safe haven. One hiker says, "I think she's gone. I saw a dead tree back behind the shelter, so I'll get some firewood. She's liable to come back, and maybe she won't like the fire." The hiker's companion follows on his heels, and they start back along the side of the stone wall.

What occurs next happens so fast that it's hard to sort out. Jon hears a loud, "Oh, shit!" and the two men virtually fly back toward the front of the shelter. "Inside, quick," one yells. The ten men and women land in a rugby scrum inside the fence. Luckily, one has the presence of mind to reach up and secure the gate, after slamming it in the face of a charging Momma bear.

"Damn," one of the erstwhile wood gatherers says, "That was way too close for comfort. "I guess she went over the side of the ridge, then doubled back and came up the mountain on the other side. She was waiting at the rear wall, and when we came around the corner, she played grizzly bear and stood on her hind legs. She was trying to scare us, and, believe me, she succeeded. I may have to change my drawers."

Another hiker laughs. "I'll bet she's pulled that stunt off lots of times. She came damned close to getting our packs. If she had gotten inside here, I wouldn't have fought her, that's for sure."

The captives watch as the disgruntled bear prowls the grounds again. She finds nothing else that is of interest, so human pulses cease racing, and adrenaline goes back to normal. She saunters across the clearing. This time, the humans wait for 15 minutes. When they do emerge, the back of the shelter is carefully scrutinized and watchers are posted until the firewood is successfully collected.

Peace and quiet reign for an hour or so, and dusk is creeping over the clearing in the forest. One hiker stops in his tracks. "I hear voices," and he points to the place where the bear had first appeared.

Jon laughs, "You don't reckon she has ventriloquism in her bag of tricks, do you?"

Laughter releases the remainder of the adrenaline as four hikers emerge from the forest. The party consists of two men and two women. As they approach the shelter, one inhabitant tells the saga of Momma bear. "She's liable to come back any time. We'll squeeze together in here, if you want. There's four more bunks."

One of the hikers responds in a self-confident voice, "Nope, we came up here to tent-camp, and that's what we're going to do. I've camped out west and survived grizzly bears; I don't think that an eastern black bear's going to cause me any trouble." The voice is authoritative from one accustomed to being listened to.

The four walk to the edge of the clearing, although Jon sees one of the women cast envying glances at the relative safety of the stone shelter and the fence. The four set up camp and start stoves in preparation for dinner. The dark of the night makes visibility poor, but the shelter dwellers can dimly see the activities, as the self-proclaimed bear expert, a professor at the nearby University of Tennessee, directs his troops. He gives them the benefit of his wisdom in continuous lectures. As he hangs their food sack from a line stretched between two trees, he says, "It's a well-known fact that eastern black bear can't climb trees once they reach maturity. The food'll be safe."

"Uh oh," whispers one of the shelter-bound hikers. "Look over there," pointing to the trail. All eyes see their old friend, Momma bear as she emerges from the forest. "There she comes," he yells at the four tent campers.

The professor has an answer for that; no one doubted for a second that he wouldn't. He picks up a pan and a large spoon and begins banging. "Noises like this will even scare off a grizzly. That black bear won't come any closer." But Momma bear doesn't even slow down as she saunters toward the camp. One of the shelter-dwellers whispers, "That racket might scare off a grizzly, but I think that this Momma believes it's mess call." The others laugh nervously, waiting for the drama to unfold.

Unfold it does. Even with weak eyes, Momma bear spots the bright red nylon food sack hanging from the rope. She sets a course directly for the bag. Unfortunately, one tent is on the straight-line course she has set and she plows right over and through the orange rip-stop nylon, shredding tent and sleeping bags laid out inside. She continues to one of the trees holding the rope that suspends the bag. She is followed by a loud protestation, "But adult eastern black bear can't climb trees." Not knowing any better, she efficiently goes up the tree. She slashes at the rope with one paw until it gives way. The food bag comes down and so does she. Clutching the bag in one paw, she exits the clearing on three legs, ready for a feast.

The campers sit on the ground, and the knowledgeable professor holds his head in his hands, no more lectures to give. His audience of three gather up the remnants of their gear and, without a word, march to the shelter and prepare to sleep there. After a few minutes, the professor picks up his tattered sleeping bag, joins them in the shelter, and has nothing else to say for the remainder of the night.

And, what a night it is. When all of the hikers turn off their flashlights and the activity of the shelter mice begins, most of the humans fall asleep. Pookie is sleeping under Jon's bunk and pays the scampering rodents no mind. But, Momma bear is still determined to cause them more misery; apparently the professor's food hadn't completely satiated her voracious appetite, because she visits them several times that night, shaking the secured gate in the fence, as she tries to get in. Every time the gate rattles, 14 flashlights turn on simultaneously and fix the perpetrator in the spotlight. She grunts and saunters away.

The long night finally passes, and Jon and Sam decide over breakfast to hike together that day. Following a Granola and dried milk and coffee breakfast, they fill their water bottles in the spring and gratefully leave the battlefield. They've got 15 miles to cover today to Icewater Spring Shelter, where Jon hopes to sleep tonight. Their hiking paces are close to the same although several times Jon walks ahead and waits for Sam at rest sites. It works well, because Sam is a slow but steady hiker, and his rest stops are brief.

Jon and Sam pass by Clingman's Dome, the highest elevation the AT attains in the Smokies. The mountain is a spectacular one, with balsam firs and mountain cranberries in several small patches along the trail. The mountain also takes its toll on legs and backs, but Jon and Sam succeed.

Halfway between Double Springs and Icewater Spring, the three walk into a clearing and see Mt. Collins Shelter. A young man is sitting on a log by the shelter, face resting on his arms. He is tall and slim and has a shock of black hair that is tied up in a long ponytail. "Got troubles?" inquires Jon.

"Yeah, I guess I do. Bear got every bit of my damned food last night. I was on the second night of a two-week hike, and I'm not sure what I'm gonna do now."

"What happened," asks Sam. "How did the bear get your food?"

The man points to his tattered pack, resting on the ground by his feet. "I was cooking my dinner last night at the edge of the clearing, when I heard a grunt. I swung my flashlight around just in time to see a big, black, hairy arm grab my pack and take off through the woods. I yelled, but nobody would come out of the shelter."

After taking a deep breath, the man gestures wildly and continues. "An hour later, I talked five guys into coming with me, and we walked down the trail for a couple of hundred yards. We found my pack, and the bear had ripped the food section off as neatly as if he'd been a surgeon. He ate two weeks worth of freeze-dried food."

Jon and Sam look at each other. Jon asks, "Did the bear have any tags in its ears? The rangers tag the bears who bother people."

"Yeah, one in each ear. A red one and a white one."

Jon and Sam choke off laughs. The young man says, "I don't think it's so damned funny. What's funny?"

Sam says, "Sorry about that, we weren't laughing at you. We were visited by that same bottomless pit last night over at Silers Bald; she had her snack before she came over here. She must visit these shelters on a regular basis. You know, though, you might have gotten revenge and didn't even know it. That freeze-dried food expands four or five times in volume when it contacts water. If that old sow didn't belch a bunch of times, that food might've swelled and split her wide open. It might've killed her. Even though she's a pest, I hope it didn't."

"Don't make me feel any better. I still don't know what I'm gonna do. Damn, no food. I'm pissed."

"You're only four or five miles from Newfound Gap, where the road to Gatlinburg crosses the trail. Maybe you can hitch a ride into town and get more food and get your pack sewn up."

Jon and Sam shake their heads in admiration at what has been the scavenging of a resourceful bear. She has successfully pulled off every trick in the book.

"The town part sounds pretty good. I guess my hiking's over for this trip, anyway. I think I'll go back to campus and tell a bunch of lies about what a great hike I had." The man points at Pookie, "You know, I think I heard somewhere that dogs aren't allowed in the Park. How'd you get around that?"

Jon's face falls. "But, but, he's on a leash."

"I don't think that matters. Here," he thrusts a colored brochure on the Great Smoky Mountains Park at Jon. "I picked this up at Sugarlands, the Ranger station where I registered. Read for yourself."

Jon reads the flyer and his face falls. "Damn, it does say that! I wasn't as well planned as I thought I was. I never heard that. What am I gonna do? My buddy's not scheduled to pick up Pookie for another 17 or 18 days. I can't lose my hiking partner." He slumps to the ground, worrying. His posture shows his unhappiness.

Sam says, "Look at you two! I've never seen such long faces. We can get around this, somehow. Tell you what. How many rangers have you seen on the trail?" addressing both men.

Jon says, "None, so far."

The foodless man says, "I've just seen one and that was back a day or so ago. He had a rifle and a flashlight and said he was hunting wild boar–the Park Service is trying to reduce their population. But, that's the only one I've seen."

"Okay, I've not seen any at all. Where are we most likely to see one? Newfound Gap is coming up shortly. Since that's a place where lots of tourists stop to see the view, there'll probably be plenty of police protection there. Jon, you stay in the woods, while I go into the Gap and check for rangers. When the coast is clear, I'll come get you and we'll go across the road in a hurry and we'll likely not see any more rangers until we get out of the Park."

The young man gets interested, in spite of his desire to wallow in his self-pity. "Yeah, that'll work. I'll stay on the trail halfway between you two and be a runner, so you guys can get across quicker."

Plan in place, the three men and the illegal dog proceed. The few times they hear voices, Jon and Pookie leave the trail and hide in the forest. Their caution isn't needed; no rangers are spotted.

A half-mile from Newfound Gap, man and dog hide once again, and the interim runner takes his place a little farther along the trail and tries to look innocent, as he munches on a handful of Gorp that Jon has given him. Sam walks down to the stone monument that decorates the parking lot at Newfound Gap. He spots two rangers talking to a covey of tourists, marked as such by Bermuda shorts with dark socks. Sam takes a long drink of cold water from the fountain and casually sits on a bench by the monument. He's prepared to wait out the authorities.

It takes an hour, but at long last, both rangers drive off. Sam trots back up the trail and alerts their co-conspirator, who relays the message to Jon. The tourists at the Gap stare in amazement fifteen minutes later, when three stubble-bearded men wearing packs and accompanied by one dog sprint out of the woods and across the road. One of the men stops in the parking lot and yells at the retreating backs of Sam and Jon, "See you guys! Good luck!" He laughs out loud, forgetting his misery, at least temporarily.

As they re-enter the concealing shelter of the forest, the trio continues at a fast pace, until they are forced to stop and rest. "Damn, that was close," pants Jon. "Thanks, Sam, I appreciate your help. I guess I'll stay paranoid for the next several days."

"No problem, Pookie's good company. For a while, I felt like we were involved in 007 activity. It was fun. We'll maybe have to do the same thing at other road crossings, but we shouldn't see any rangers on the trail. I hope not, anyway. I enjoy the Pookster's company."

The trio starts up the trail again, and Sam and Jon laugh about their mad dash across the Newfound Gap parking lot. Jon is worried about what kind of trouble he would get in if a ranger caught him with Pookie on the trail. Sending Pookie home prematurely and paying a large fine aren't in his itinerary. He knows he has two weeks left to enjoy Pookie's company; however, only two days are in the borders of the park. If they are careful, they should make it undetected. With Sam helping as lookout, Jon and Pookie take to the woods three times during the afternoon; all three times are false alarms.

They arrive at Icewater Springs Shelter at about six o'clock and to their surprise, find only a few thru-hikers as residents for the night. That shelter is closed to all but thru-hikers due to overuse in the past, and the three enjoy the almost vacant shelter. While dinner is cooking, Jon subjects Pookie to a careful inspection. Pookie rolls over on his back for a tummy rub, displaying his complete lack of dignity. Jon finds a small place on the dog's shoulder, where the saddlebags have chafed him, and he applies salve. He checks the harness and finds a rough place, that he trims smooth with his Swiss Army knife. Pookie's foot pads still look good, and there are no cracks or bruises. Jon is afraid that one of the quasi-tame bears of the Smokies might be around, so the leash is brought into use, once again.

Pookie lies down in the shelter and manages to look abused. Jon and Sam give him a lot of attention and dinner helps raise his spirits. The two men sit around and enjoy talking about everything. Sam is an architect and has been in business for six years. He was at the burn-out stage and walked out of the office one Friday, telling his boss he was quitting. The boss told Sam to call him when he gets back to Memphis, and if he has an opening, he will re-hire Sam. Sam's not sure if he wants to go back into the architectural field again, but he has no idea as to what he might do. His goal on the AT thru-hike is to examine his priorities, and decide what direction he wants his life to go. Sam asks Jon, "What about you? Why are you up here? You running from something or somebody like many of us are?"

Jon pauses for a moment to think about the question. "Well, if I'm running from something, it's probably avoiding getting stuck in any commitments I might regret later. I also have something big to prove to myself–that I can complete something that I start. That's been a real problem for me all my life."

Jon and Sam are getting along well, both in temperament and walking speed. They discuss what their schedules are for the next several weeks to determine whether they might continue to travel together. Jon is looking ahead to when Pookie is back in Tuscaloosa, and he is on the trail by himself. He plans to exit the trail at Davenport Gap, Tennessee, at the boundary of the Great Smoky Mountains Park, because he should have a re-supply package waiting there. Sam's schedule is slightly different, as he has a package at Hot Springs, North

Carolina, about four days further up the trail. They settle on a plan to walk together until Jon exits at Davenport, while Sam continues until he goes to Hot Springs. Then, they will meet at Jerry Cabin Shelter, up the trail from Hot Springs.

Plans and schemes are thus set as well as can be when you depend on the vagaries of the trail. Silence settles in, and Jon, Sam, and Pookie try to sleep and prepare to allow the mice to do their thing. When they are almost asleep, Pookie stiffens and a low growl sounds menacingly in his throat. "Quiet, boy," warns Jon. "What is it?"

Sam and Jon sit completely still, ears straining to hear the faint noises. "I can't figure it out," says Sam. "Doesn't sound too close to us, though. Maybe not threatening."

Silence falls, but Pookie's vigilance of the background noise continues. He's not happy with the noise, whatever it is, but he settles down. It's a restless night and Pookie and Jon wake a few times.

In the morning, Sam admits he was awakened several times as well. The source of last night's disturbance has still not been identified.

They begin hiking along the slight upward grade of the trail. After several hundred feet they notice something really strange along and on both sides of the trail. The underbrush is cleared out, small trees have been uprooted, and the thin topsoil has been scoured and disturbed. The land has been literally plowed for hundreds of yards up the hills on both sides.

Sam and Jon stand still in wonder. "What the hell did this," asks Sam.

"Don't know-looks like small bulldozers worked all night."

After poking around in the soil for several minutes, Sam points with his walking stick to a footprint. "Lookie here-it was either hogs or the devil came to see us, one. Look at the cloven hoofprints." Sam points around him on the ground at other tell-tale prints. "Damn, musta been a whole herd of them to have plowed up this much territory. No wonder we were awakened so many times. They were rooting all night."

"I should have turned Pookie loose. He might have brought us some bacon for breakfast," says Jon.

"Bullshit!" answers Sam. "Those boars go 450 to 500 pounds and have huge, curved tusks. I read somewhere that they are a crossbreed between domestic hogs and Russian boars that some bankrupt wild game ranchers turned loose a few years ago. Pookie wouldn't have had a chance against those tusked guys!"

"Damn, I'm glad he was in the shelter. You reckon we were in any danger, ourselves?"

"Nah, they're pretty shy. The rangers are hunting them, trying to reduce the population, so the hogs eat all night and sleep all day."

In the morning, Jon checks his inventory of food and finds he mis-calculated on Pookie's rations; he is short of food by a day or so. Happily, he has enough of his own to share. "Pookie," he says, "I know you're gonna hate this, but you get human food for the next few days."

Sam answers for the dog, "I guess you can call pasta and canned meat human food. I'm not tired of them yet, but I'm beginning to understand why thru-hikers talk about never wanting to see some foods again after they go back to civilization. Variety is tough to get. At least, a variety of light, easy to fix foods."

It seems that the more carefully you plan, the more likely it is that things will go awry. In the middle of the morning, Sam places his foot on a slippery rock near Charlie's Bunion and twists his ankle. He sits in the middle of the trail, groaning while Jon carefully removes Sam's boot and thick hiking sock. "Sam, you're lucky. Nothing seems to be broken but I can already see that sucker swelling. I'll wrap it, and we'll try to get to Pecks Corner Shelter, where you're gonna need to lay up for a day or so."

Sam objects, "But that's gonna mess up your schedule. I can make it okay by myself."

"Bullshit. It won't hurt a damned thing. We'll just stay one night at Davenport, and we'll be right back on track. Besides, those damned schedules are supposed to work for us, not the other way around. But if we don't wrap that ankle and get your boot back on now, you're gonna be hiking in your sock."

It turns out that Sam is made of strong stuff. Jon cuts him a walking staff. To this point, Sam has not carried one, but he now needs the extra support. They struggle into Peck's Corner around nine o'clock that night. Jon has to transfer 10 pounds of Sam's gear to his own pack, but they make it. Sam wearily collapses into a bunk and eats a portion of the dinner that Jon prepares.

While sitting quietly in the dark by himself, Jon has time to think. He thought he was over the mourning of Gretel's disappearance. He finds he isn't, when he has time to think. What a night. He doubts he'll ever forget it. Or her. He goes to bed, a smile on his face.

After spending one full day and a night at the shelter, Sam announces the next morning that he is ready to try to proceed. His ankle is rainbow-hued, but not nearly as swollen. They struggle, but manage to make it to Tri-Corner Knob shelter. That night Jon consults his ever-present *Appalachian Trail Data Book* and announces to Sam, "I believe I've got a Plan B. If your ankle is up to it, we'll make it to Davenport Gap tomorrow, and you'll exit with us. I planned a two-nighter there, anyway. Two days ought to bring your ankle around. Then, you can pick up your package at Hot Springs, and we'll keep on going. Right back on schedule without a hiccup. Whata you think?"

Sam moans. "You're as tough a taskmaster as the boss I'm escaping. Yeah, that'll work. Tomorrow will be a bitch. What is it, 12 or 15 miles to Davenport?"

"Yeah, that's about right. We'll leave at the crack of dawn. You know, it sounds strange, but we're lucky we're just about out of food. The packs are a good bit lighter, anyway."

After eating, the men settle into their sleeping bags early. They leave the shelter just as the sun is barely visible through the huge conifer trees. The fifteen miles is a struggle, but they meet the challenge. They catch a ride the couple of miles to Mountain Mommas. Pookie is boarded, and Jon and Sam terrorize the cook at the short-order grill with multiple orders of food. Luckily, the cook is used to thru-hikers and keeps the food coming until the men are completely full. Jon spends much of one day catching up on his notes and gets several rolls of film developed. He mails a package back to Tuscaloosa to Mr. Wilkins at the newspaper and vows to himself to become more regular in his promise to mail packages weekly. Tuscaloosa seems much farther away than the 240 miles covered on the trail. Farther away both physically and mentally.

The two days in civilization pass swiftly and, after re-supplying, they set out for the short hop of three days to Hot Springs. They had discussed passing up staying at Hot Springs to catch up the day they are behind, but the town has a serious draw on the thru-hikers, so they decide to stay. At lunch the next day, they demolish several hamburgers and fries at the Hot Springs Cafe, a place a thru-hiker bragged on. Jon knows that he will have Pookie's company for only 11 or 12 more days, and his mood turns grumpy when he contemplates that fact. Jon makes himself feel better when he buys one more order of hamburger and fries, to the amazement of the cook, "I thought you was about to bust! Another order for you?"

Jon answers, "Not for me. My buddy out there under the tree needs a pick-me-up." He points to Pookie, looking abandoned in the grass under a large shade tree.

The cook laughs. "Okay, I'll go heavy on the burger and light on the pickle and onion. You reckon he likes mustard or mayo?"

Jon laughs, "If you go heavy on the meat, I don't think it matters what's on it. He'll be happy."

Pookie's mood improves, and Jon and Sam laugh as they watch the Pookster attack the burger and fries. The dog goes over to the pile of gear left for him to guard while the men were inside; he tugs at a corner of his saddlebag. He drags it over to Jon, who has to laugh. "You ready to go, big guy? I never could have guessed." The quick return to civilization is enjoyable.

The next four nights and 80 miles pass relatively quickly, and they go into Erwin, Tennessee. Two hikers have warned Jon and Sam that some residents of the town are not particularly friendly to thru-hikers, so they stick out their thumbs on the highway leading to Erwin with some trepidation. A car with several local rednecks passes and obscenities and empty beer cans are tossed in their general direction, but two men with a rather large dog seem to provide enough of a challenge to the harassers, that the old car speeds on by, trailing blue smoke and clattering valves. A farmer on his way to town gives them a lift. They enjoy an all-you-can-eat buffet at a restaurant; each makes his way through a half gallon of ice cream. Before he started this hike, Jon considered himself an ice cream monster, but he never in his wildest dreams would have believed himself capable of eating a half gallon at one sitting. No problem, now.

Since they still have about eight miles to cover before they reach Indian Grave Gap campground, they cut their time in town short. After unsuccessfully trying to catch a ride, they call one of the local shuttle services and cheerfully pay the five dollars rather than walk the four miles back to the trail.

As they approach the trail head, Jon feels a strange sensation come over him. He tries to express it to Sam: "You know, it's funny, but I feel that I'm safer and more at home back here on the AT. Here, I just have to worry about myself and, for another week anyway, Pookie. But I don't have to worry about making my plans mesh with somebody else's, or worry about whether they like me, or anything else. Even though I'm walking on a rough trail looking like a scruffy turtle with my house on my back, I'm freer here than home."

Sam nods in agreement, and musing is the order of the rest of the day.

Two days after leaving Indian Grave Gap, the hikers cross several grassy balds, some of the most spectacular views of the Smokies. Three-hundred degree panoramas of mountains literally take their breaths away. They continue along the state line, and for quite a ways, they alternate stepping in the two states–one foot in Tennessee and the other in North Carolina. At Roan Mountain, they leave North Carolina behind and enter completely into Tennessee. They follow the trail down to the magnificent waterfall in Laurel Fork Gorge and then, cross Watauga Lake Dam. They traverse a long, narrow ridge, called the Tennessee Turnpike by some folks, and head into Virginia.

Even though 12- to 15-mile days are still ahead of them before they reach Damascus, Virginia, the eight days pass without incident. The views and hiking in this stretch of the AT are some of the prettiest in the entire 2000 plus miles, and Jon and Sam have enjoyed the beautiful, yet wearying, days.

Jon finds a pay phone near the trail near Hampton, Tennessee, and calls Andy. "Hey, bud, how the hell are you?"

Andy responds, "Doing okay. Life goes on. How about you guys? Hey, you sent a package to Mr. Wilkins lately? He's bugging me 'bout daily. Says he's getting calls from readers wanting to know where their wandering boy is now and what he's doing. I wish you'd send some notes and get him off my back."

Jon laughs, "Yep, took care of that a few days ago. Sent him a bunch of notes and photos. I'm gonna try to be more regular."

"Good. Shorty's also called a few times, and . . . guess who else called? Sissy! She said she was interested in how you were doing. Did you guys make up before you left?"

"Not exactly. I did go by to see her and talk for a few minutes. Said I hoped we could be friends."

"It musta worked. By the way, the paper's been full of announcements of her up-coming wedding. She's gonna finally get her wish. Somebody's hooked."

"Good, I'm glad. I don't need that complication. You all set to meet us at Damascus? We should be there in about a week, the good Lord willin' and the creek don't rise. Why don't you reserve rooms at The Place Hostel for us. By the way, I'm walking with a guy, Sam, so make him a reservation, too."

"No problem. You looking forward to sending Pookie home?"

"No, I'll miss him when he goes home. He's not really been a bother. I guess I'll like losing a few ounces in my pack, but he's done just fine. Like I said earlier, I owe him one. See you in a few."

The next seven days hurry by and they reach Damascus, called by many thru-hikers the friendliest city on the trail. The AT follows the main street of town, and the men and the dog find The Place with no trouble. Andy has arrived a while ago and is just walking out the front door of the hostel. Pookie greets Andy with a Lab hug and a sloppy kiss across his entire face–ear to ear. Andy laughs, "I guess you're glad to see me. We'll see how glad you are when you have to get into the truck."

Jon says, "Let's not even talk about that until we have to. You get our rooms?"

"Yep. But, I first checked at the Appalachian Inn; they want 75 bucks a day. I figured you'd rather stay at the hostel for two dollars, since you're such a miser. By the way, here's another 200 bucks that's trickled into the newspaper office. And, look at this, you celebrity, you."

Andy pulls a newspaper out of the truck, and Jon is shocked to see his photo on the front page. "Hum, must not have been anything going on in the world that day. Wow, look at that! Even the Pookster."

On hearing his name, Pookie runs in circles and lets his infamous bark tell of his happiness. All three men laugh at the clown. Jon says, "Since he knows it's a no-no to bark up on the trail or in the shelters, I guess he's trying to make sure that his barker still works. It does! Pook, hush! Enough, already!"

Pookie calms down and hardly fusses when, once again, he is boarded, while the humans get their rooms ready for the night. After several pointed comments from Andy about the harm the two hikers are causing to the ambient air of the hostel, Jon and Sam head directly for the shower, where the now-familiar ritual of two or three showers are required to find skin under the multiple layers of trail grime. No matter how hard you try, trail grime accumulates, but they are finally ready for polite society again.

The three decide after minimal discussion that the local pizza place is to be the choice of cuisine for the evening. Located close to the hostel and the AT, the folks at the restaurant are accustomed to thru-hikers, most of whom consume a large pizza by themselves, washed down with copious quantities of beer. Not-so-polite belches announce their pleasure with the meal and the fact that they are all stuffed. Totally stuffed.

The thru-hikers say they are in favor of early bedtimes tonight, and maybe they'll try to find some activities tomorrow night. Andy doesn't argue after his 300 mile drive. After Pookie is fed and walked, all settle in for the night. Their sleep is disturbed for a short time by the arrival of a wild bunch of men and women, who are participating in a long-distance bicycle race. Luckily, the bikers are just as tired as the hikers and hit the sack quickly themselves.

In the morning, Jon and Sam both have repairs to make on their gear, and they slap another coat of water-proofing on their boots. Jon walks up the street to Mt. Rogers Outfitter's to buy a small sack of strap clips to replace several on his pack that are in danger of breaking; it's easier to replace them here than on the trail. He also buys some freeze-dried food for a few dinners to break the monotony of the pasta and meat meals that he eats most nights.

Following lunch, the three pile into Andy's pickup and drive twelve miles to Abingdon, Virginia, where they find an all-you-can eat restaurant. When they depart, the kitchen help that keeps the food bar filled look at each other in amazement at the quantities of food the men have consumed. Looking around the streets of Abingdon, they spot a movie theater and go in to watch Steven Segal's newest thriller. Halfway through the movie, the soft seat and the air conditioning take their effect on Jon, and he is soon happily snoring. Andy looks over at him and says to Sam, "Damned if I can see how anybody can sleep through one of these movies. By my rough calculation, somewhere in the neighborhood of 35 bad guys have gone down for the final count so far. It's tough to sleep through Segal's brand of justice. But Jon goes to sleep. He didn't even get any popcorn."

When the movie is over and Jon's been rousted, a banana split at the local Dairy Queen finishes off the evening, and they head back to the hostel. A cross Pookie is waiting inside the pen fence and ignores Jon until he finds the right tree and gets relief. Then, and only then, he is willing to lean against Jon's leg and give him a sloppy kiss on the cheek.

Jon stays outside with his dog for quite a while, dreading tomorrow and Pookie's departure for Tuscaloosa. He's been good company, and Jon feels he still deserves a hero badge for his help back in Franklin, when he protected Jon from the rednecks. "Oh, well, Andy and Mom and Dad will take good care of Pookie," he thinks. Jon says to the dog, "Pookie, I wish I could take you all the way with me, but those rocky trails up in Pennsylvania and all those city dogs up in New York and New Jersey just won't cut it. Nope, it's home you go. I'm gonna miss you."

Pookie looks at him questioningly and gives him another kiss as Jon leads him back into the pen. He goes to a corner and curls up with only his eyes showing above his tail, wrapped around his face. "Night, buddy," says Jon as he enters the dark hostel, where the rest of the population is already sound asleep.

Hikers and bikers wake at the same time, and the resulting activity is akin to madness. Toilet facilities and showers are strained to their maximum capacity. Somehow the men and women manage to get ready for their particular form of physical torture for the day. Bike saddlebags get packed; backpacks get loaded. All the packs but one, that is. When Jon puts Pookie's small, empty pack in Andy's truck, the dog sees him from his spot in the pen. He barks, questioningly.

When the two hikers are ready to proceed, they sling their packs in the back of the pickup and Pookie willingly jumps in. As the truck drives away, Jon says,

"Andy, I need to make this quick or else I'll change my mind. When we get there we'll move the packs and I'll put Pookie in here. You leave then."

Andy feels his friend's misery and responds, "No problem. The Pookster and I will do just fine. I'm glad you and Sam are hiking together. Maybe it'll make it not so hard."

"I don't know, maybe it will. I just know I'm gonna miss him. We trained and hiked together, and he saved my ass. Now I'm sending him home." Jon slumps down in the seat. His mind works the pros and cons. Concern for his dog's safety wins out, once again.

At the trail head, the plan works. Pookie isn't entirely happy about jumping in the truck, but he obeys. Jon buries his face in the black, shiny mane. Pookie gives him his usual sloppy kiss in the ear, and Jon turns from the truck as Andy starts the engine and drives away. As the truck leaves the parking lot, Jon steals a glance and sees Pookie's face against the glass of the truck window, looking for all the world like a kid locked out of the candy shop.

"Damn," chokes Jon, "That was one of the hardest things I ever had to do. I know it was what I had to do, but that don't make it any easier."

"Well, just keep telling yourself that it is the right thing. From what I've read about parts of the northern trail, we're gonna have enough trouble ourselves. You did right," says Sam.

The two start their trek. They know that their pending hike up the backbone of the Commonwealth of Virginia stretches out some 535 miles in front of them. Before they arrive at the Appalachian Trail Conference Center in Harpers Ferry, West Virginia, they will have hiked roughly the same distance they have already covered to this point in their hike. But when, and if, they make it, they will be almost halfway in the thru-hike.

As Jon walks, he keeps on telling himself that it is the right thing, it was a grownup decision, he's showing responsibility; he tells himself all the right words, but few sink in. He walks, a miserable young man, with one more milestone reached in his life. A milestone that he is not appreciative of at this time.

Sam gives Jon all the space he needs and doesn't offer any conversation or consoling words. He also doesn't speed up his pace when Jon accelerates, trying to leave behind all his doubts. "See you at Lost Mountain Shelter tonight," he shouts at Jon's disappearing back. Jon acknowledges with a wave of his arm and strides ahead, the tears in his eyes blurring his vision. He's trying unsuccessfully to walk away from them as well.

Jon walks solo all day. He passes a few dozen thru- hikers, some going north, some going south. The only conversation he offers is a curt "hi," and a nod of his head. Nobody pushes him. He arrives at the shelter and sighs with relief when, amazingly enough, he finds it unoccupied. He putters around and fixes himself a cup of tea which he doctors with two spoonfuls of sugar. He finds a small overlook and sits with his tea, legs swinging over the edge.

After an hour of self-analysis, he comes to a realization. The deed is done, and he can't undo it. He might as well make the best of the situation. If he continues to roll around in self pity, he's going to turn Sam off, and he'll have no hiking partner at all. Sam is turning out to be a really good friend, and right now Jon needs friends.

Maybe it's the self analysis, maybe it's the sugar rush, but whatever it is, Jon walks back to the shelter in a much better frame of mind. He arrives just as Sam pants into the clearing and slides to the ground, worn out. Jon helps him shuck his pack, "Gee, coach, you look like you could use some Gatorade. Here, I'll brew you a cup of tea; you'll feel better. It sure helped me."

Jon starts his stove, and before Sam can regain his strength, Jon places a steaming cup in his hand. Jon continues to move around with renewed energy and has dinner bubbling in the pot. "You know, Sam, this is the only part of coming back on the trail after civilization that I hate. A Domino's pizza would be mighty tasty now, but I guess macaroni and cheese and chicken'll have to do. Yum, yum."

Sam has to laugh. "Pysched yourself out, have you? I think the Domino's sounds better, but I'll settle for the macchicken. Damn, I made a pun. Even a Golden Arches burger sounds good."

They start eating, and Jon provides dinnertime entertainment by reading from his guide. "This thing says that we're in for some beautiful mountains in Virginia. It also says that we have seen our last 3000-foot climbs, until we get all the way up into Maine, that is. That sounds all right, eh?"

Sam laughs. "You, my man, are truly an incurable optimist. I'm sure some of the mountains we'll cross between Virginia and Maine will get our attention, even if they're not 3000 feet high."

As Jon and Sam are enjoying their dinner, several more hikers appear at the shelter. George and Charlie are a young couple, who hail from St. Louis. When Jon and Sam introduce themselves, Charlie says, "We're trying to do thru-hikes, but we couldn't get enough time off to do the whole thing at once. We did Springer Mountain to the Tennessee-North Carolina state line last summer. This year we started from there and hope to get to Katahdin. We've just been on the trail for a day. My shoulders are killing me. Here, rub them."

She sits and presents her back to Jon who hesitates, looking over at George, who is cooking her dinner. George sees Jon's look and laughs, "Go ahead, Jon. You'll learn that she usually gets what she wants. If you can help her shoulders, maybe she'll whine less."

Charlie comes back with, "Me whine? Who was it that whimpered all day about how his legs felt like somebody was beating them with a 2 by 4? I'm thinking about giving him a new trail name. I'll call him Whining George. Go ahead, Jon. Go to work."

Jon starts rubbing the back of the small, pert, black-headed, young woman. She is obviously into shoulder and back rubs and continuously gives Jon directions. "There, that's good, lower, no, not so low, ouch! There! Harder! Man, that's good, George. I think I'll keep this guy–he knows how to do this. He's the original All-State guy, you know, you're in good hands."

George and Sam laugh at Jon's discomfort, marked by an extremely red face. "Jon, I told you she always gets what she wants. She's *the* woman of the 90's. Here, Honey, here's your dinner," bringing her a steaming plateful of stew."

George is a large, clumsy man who is just shy of homely. His feelings for the vivacious Charlie are obviously deep. He is always hovering around her, and she just as obviously feels the same way about him and enjoys his bumbling efforts to make things easier for her. Their repartee livens up the evening, and the four sit outside the shelter after dish-washing time and talk until the bright stars light up the clearing almost as bright as day.

Charlie, who is lying on her poncho with her head on George's leg, sighs. "Look at those stars. I think that's one of the things I like best about being up here. You can almost reach out and touch them." She extends her arm, as if trying to do just that.

Jon says, "You know Sam, I've almost forgotten about sending the Pookster home. I expect they're back in Tuscaloosa by now. Wonder how he's doing? Maybe I can call the next time we leave the trail. I don't remember when we see civilization next."

Charlie says, "What the hell is a Pookster? Man, or beast?"

Jon gives the saga of Pookie and receives the appropriate commiseration. Charlie adds, "You asked about civilization? We checked over our *Appalachian Trail Data Book* last evening, and we cross either the Blue Ridge Parkway or the Skyline Drive a total of 63 times as we hike through Virginia. I don't think that finding civilization is gonna be any problem, at all."

Jon sits upright, startled. "63 times? Damn, what happens to the wilderness walk we're taking? Up to now, we've only crossed a few roads. 63? Damn," and he lies back.

"Yeah, but I hear it's not really too bad. Those roads may be full of tourists in station wagons and mini-vans, but the roads are pretty, natural drives. You know, lots of green grass and trees. slow speed limits, and plenty of pull-offs, so the tourists can stop and take pictures and go home and bore their friends with slide shows about their mountain wilderness experience," offers George.

"Hush, George, you're letting your sarcasm show," responds Charlie. "Someday you'll be a driving tail-gate camper yourself, when you're not able to hike anymore."

"I hope that's a long way off. I really enjoy this way of seeing the world. Kinda like a turtle, but we see more about what's out here when we hike." George sighs. "I guess it's time to go do war with the shelter mice. Jon, have the mice retired since last year? I was kinda hoping that."

Jon laughs, "Nope, alive and well and fat from robbing the hikers blind. There's no deficit of mice."

They walk slowly toward the shelter, Charlie in the lead. She stops at the shelter gate with a shriek. "Look, over there in the corner. What the hell is that?"

Four flashlights combine to form a bright spotlight on a visitor–a large skunk is slowly checking out the shelter floor and at the present, is scratching his back against the corner of Jon's pack. Sam says, "Shh, don't spook him. None of us will be able to use our stuff for a week. Turn your lights off–we can see him by starlight."

They back up to give the skunk his space. He's obviously in no hurry. He saunters around the shelter floor. Jon and Charlie's packs are on the dirt floor, the other two are up on bunks. Luckily, the two reachable packs were fastened before their owners had gone outside to enjoy the celestial show, and the visitor can't get in them.

After 30 minutes of the skunk watch, Charlie shivers. "Damn, it's getting chilly out here. I wish Brer Skunk would give up and leave. I'm ready for my sleeping bag."

George laughs, "You're on his time-clock, Babe. He'll leave when he's ready to leave. When he's good and ready."

Another 30 minutes pass, while Mr. Skunk checks and re-checks the two packs. When he can't find a way to get in, he waddles out the gate. The hikers back up, willing him to depart. When he moves out and they can skirt him, they move into the shelter and fasten the gate. "There," says George. "Maybe that'll keep the little stinking bugger out. You guys see any places where he can wriggle in? I'd hate to have that little guy sneak back in here later." He shivers. "Can you imagine getting sprayed while you're trapped in your sleeping bag?"

Sam laughs, "Nope, I for one ain't at all interested in that experience." All four hikers become busily involved in crawling around the floor of the shelter, plugging even small holes to assure that the skunk can't get back in and pay them a surprise visit. Charlie and Jon hang their packs, a night-time mice-prevention chore that nobody forgets more than once.

"There, that ought to keep him out," says Charlie. "It's bedtime, boys and girl." She makes a dash for her sleeping bag, and the men follow suit. Soon, sleeping bags are warmed up and all sleep. They are fortunate–Mr. Skunk doesn't come back, but the mice scamper and chatter most of the night, disturbing George and Charlie's sleep. Jon and Sam are basically immune to their frolics by now, and neither of them stirs until dawn.

The four hikers travel together for two days, enjoying each other's company. The third day, Jon and Sam have planned a 23-mile day, from Fox Creek to Sugar Grove, and Charlie, as usual, expresses her opinion. "Not me, buckos. It's 10 miles for me. We're stopping at Raccoon Branch shelter. Ten is enough for me. I love you guys, but I'm just a poor, weak, defenseless woman. You, know, the weaker sex and all that?"

The three men laugh heartily. "If you belong to a weaker sex, Charlie, then I'm Snow White," says George.

"I'm Cinderella," adds Jon.

"And I'm Tinker Bell," from Sam.

"Okay, you three cartoon characters. I'm serious, guys. Not for me. I'm still trying to get in shape."

So, the four reluctantly part company at Raccoon Branch. Jon and Sam reshoulder their packs and trudge on, questioning their sanity. They sleep in a motel that night and the comfort convinces them that they may be sane after all. After breakfast they head north again, knowing they face several 18- to 23-mile days stretching ahead of them before each night's rest, complete with nine mountains to cross. The two-man team is still working well, so they continue.

Three long days get them to Pearisburg, Virginia, where both men have care packages waiting for them. The mountain ascents and descents seem endless, but they persevere. They get there after the post office has closed on Friday evening, so they fake unhappiness at having to stay in the Holy Family Church Hostel for two nights. As there's a buffet near the hostel, they attack the buffet and eat entirely too much. Jon spends the evening catching up on his notes and gets a package ready to send Mr. Wilkins when they visit the post office tomorrow.

7 "TWENTY-TWENTY HINDSIGHT"

Saturday and Sunday are filled with nothing. The men sleep late, eat lots of food, and hang around the store where thru-hikers re-supply. They spend hours swapping tales, tall and otherwise, with their compatriots. Relaxation time and soft beds are welcome gifts, and both men are feeling better after Sunday night's sleep. After a leisurely breakfast, Jon and Sam strap on their packs and stroll to the post office. Jon goes in first, while Sam sits and watches the packs. Jon picks up his package, sent by Andy, and mails his report to Mr. Wilkins. He exits and swaps places with Sam, who enters the post office.

After he sits down on the curb, Jon spots a telephone booth near the front door and enters it. He calls Tuscaloosa and Andy answers the phone after only one ring.

"Hey, bud, how's it going?" queries Jon.

"Well . . . okay, how about with you?"

"We've made it to Pearisburg, Virginia, in pretty good shape. Obviously you got back to Tuscaloosa in one piece and . . . "

"Jon, I'm afraid I've got some bad news for you. Real bad news."

Jon's heart feels like it goes to his throat. "What is it?"

"It's Pookie. He's gone."

"What do you mean, gone? Has he run away?"

"No, much worse than that. I mean gone–dead."

Jon stands stock-still. Waves of emotion roll over him. He feels lightheaded, and he can hear his pulse hammering in his ears. It's hard to form words. "Wha . . . wha . . . what happened? How did it happen?"

Andy swallows. "Damn, bud, this is tough. Really tough, but here goes. When we got back to town, I called your folks and got their answering machine. We drove to their house, and a neighbor told us they'd gone out of town for a long weekend. We left there and went over to Anita's. She's my new girl friend. I went in and told her I was dog-sitting with Pookie, and she told mc to bring him on in cause her black Lab, Mollie, got along with anybody and there's a fenced-in backyard. So, we went in. I wish to God we hadn't, but we did." Andy pauses to catch a breath, and Jon is incapable of speech.

Andy starts again, "We went in the house, and Pookie and Mollie got along great. We put them in the backyard and watched them play like a couple of big puppies. Chased each other around and mock-fought while we stood there. They wore themselves out, came to the porch to get a drink, then lay down side by side under a big oak tree. Anita and I went back inside to watch a movie on the television.

"We didn't forget about the dogs; I checked on them several times, and everything was okay. They would play for a while, then rest for a while. I know about an hour and a half passed, cause the movie we were watching ended. I stood up and stretched and we walked to the back porch. Pook and Mollie were playing again. Then it happened. The neighbor's cat walked by, just outside the fence. Pookie ran over there, barking and raising hell. The cat started running, and Pookie ran alongside of the fence. Then he jumped and crawled up on the fence and climbed over. I was yelling and so was Anita, but he didn't pay any attention to us at all. The cat dashed into the road with Pookie right on its tail.

"They ran right into the path of a delivery truck that hit them both. The driver didn't even have time to step on his brakes. Pookie and the cat never knew what hit them–they didn't suffer 'cause it was so quick. Man, I hate like hell to tell you. I thought about waiting till you got home, but you know how I feel about bad news–it don't get any better with time. So, there it is. I'm sorry; that's all I can say."

Silence lies heavily over the telephone line.

Andy breaks the quiet. "Jon, you okay? Damn, I hate this. I never would have gone over there if I'd known . . . "

"It's okay, Andy. I don't blame you. That mutt could never resist chasing a cat. He'd broken a chain to get after one. Damn, I wish I'd kept him with me. Damn, damn, damn."

Heavy silence reigns once more. The only sound is the electric hum of the wires, weighing heavy on the ears.

Jon breaks the silence this time. "Andy, like I said, I don't blame you. I'm grieving. I can't deny that. I'm hurting, but I can't quit. I may sound grown-up right now, but believe me, I'm a kid inside right now. But I'll make it. I've got to make it."

"Bud, I'm sorry. I feel for you, and I miss the Pookster like hell. Anything I can do?"

"I don't think so. It's going to take a while for this to sink in–I dread it when it does. There'll likely be a few tear stains on my journal tonight. Well, I'd best go. I'll talk with you in a week or so. Thanks for the package–it was sitting here right on time. Bye."

"Bye, Jon. I'm sorry again."

Jon hangs up the phone and mechanically pulls his pack on and Sam follows suit. He has noticed that Jon's body language showed whatever news he had just received wasn't good. Not good at all. He simply follows Jon and asks no questions.

The men had scheduled a long hike that day, to the Pine Swamp Branch Shelter, almost 20 miles away. As it turned out, that unknowingly was a good decision, because it takes all 20 miles for Jon to work the devils of doubt, out of his mind. The debate over whether he should have kept Pookie with him, rather than send him home rages over and over again. For every reason he thinks of for why he should have kept him, two reasons for why he made the correct decision surface. The decision–doubt devils are joined by more devils: "Why am I doing this, anyway?"

During lunch, Jon tells Sam the essence of the phone call and talks about the internal battle he is having. Sam says, "I understand, man. I'll give you the space you need, or talk when you want to talk. I'm here. Damn, I hate this." Jon nods his head, but says nothing.

By the time they reach the shelter, Jon is fresh out of arguments, pro and con. He feels like he had made the best decision he could make at the time, but re-evaluating his decision was tearing him up. During the now-routine housekeeping chores of fetching and treating water, cooking dinner, and hanging packs, Jon slowly returns to his normal self. When the men finish washing dishes and go outside to sit with steaming cups of hot chocolate, he is finally at peace with himself. They swap stories about Pookie, the smart and clever things he had done, along with the really dumb, Lab-type actions. Jon closes the conversation with the thought that he doubts he'll bother with another dog. He loves them almost as much as he loves any people he can think of, but it hurts too bad when they're gone. The two enjoy the peace and quiet of an otherwise unoccupied shelter and sleep well, and for a change, the mice also sleep.

For the next five days and 75 miles, Jon slowly heals. By the fifth day, he thinks of his dog only a few times. Sam is a perfect hiking companion during this time, giving Jon the solitude when he needs it and company when he needs that. There is very little laughter shared, a rare situation for the friends.

To their great surprise at Fullhardt Knob Shelter, they catch up with Charlie and George. They are both lounging on the needle-covered ground in front of the shelter, people of leisure.

Jon asks, "How did you guys get here?"

"We bypassed Pearisburg and kept on trucking, slow but sure. We musta passed you guys while you were in town," answers Charlie. "Good to see you two. We thought you'd maybe slipped by us in the dead of night or something. I hate to admit it, but we've missed your company."

"Nope, we didn't do any slipping around. We just did the city lights of Pearisburg. Such as they were; they roll up the sidewalks there at eight," says Sam.

As they are preparing supper, Jon notices Sam as he slips over to Charlie and says something to her in a quiet tone of voice.

A little later, Charlie walks over to Jon and gives him a hug. Surprised, Jon asks, "Not that I mind, but what was that for?"

"We're sorry about your dog. I remember how much you hated sending him home, back when we first met you. I know it's tough. You making it okay?"

"Yeah, I'm fine. It's one of those damned things where there's nothing I can do 'cept go on. So I'm just going on. Thanks for your concern, Charlie."

The four hikers sit outside the shelter and swap trail stories after dinner is finished and the dishes are washed. George asks, "Hey, you guys remember back at Raccoon Branch when I talked about seeing fat, sun-burned tourists in mini-vans 63 times? Well, tomorrow it starts, according to our trusty *Trail Guide*. Tomorrow it begins. I think we cross the Blue Ridge Parkway four times. I'm not sure I can still walk on pavement, but we'll give it a shot."

George lies back with his head on Charlie's lap. Silence reigns as the imminent darkness slowly closes around them like a shroud. The hot day has cooled down so that a jacket or wool shirt feels really nice. Clouds cover the stars and moon; the darkness becomes complete.

Charlie's voice comes out of the dark, startling the three men. "How far are you guys going tomorrow? We were looking at Bobblets' Gap, 'bout 13 miles. I'm slowly getting in shape. Maybe we've got a shot at Katahdin before snow falls. Good Lord willing and the creek don't rise."

Jon answers, "That's where we're heading also. After that, I think we've got two or three 17-mile days in a row. Think you can make those, Charlie?"

Charlie groans, "I guess I'm gonna have to sooner or later. I was hoping it was gonna be later rather than sooner, but we enjoy being with you guys. If you don't mind, we'd like to hike along with you for a while, if you don't mind George's whining."

George laughs, "Talk about the pot calling the kettle black. I'll second what Charlie said, if it's okay."

Sam and Jon answer in unison, "Sure, sounds good."

Jon laughs, "Damn, Sam, we've been together too long. We're even thinking alike. The next thing will be that we finish each other's sentences. Yeah, guys, come on along. If one of us gets antsy and moves on off, we'll wait at the agreed-on shelter. Company sounds good."

Conversations wane as bedtime approaches, heralded by Charlie's huge yawn. The four crawl into their sleeping bags, and all lights but one are extinguished. Writin' Jon has not scribbled notes in his journal for several days, and he needs to catch up. The light doesn't bother the others; they are soon asleep.

After 30 minutes of writing, Jon notices a noise–tiny, but audible–in the quiet of the shelter. To be accurate, he hears a bunch of noises. He casts the glow of his flashlight around, but doesn't spot anything. He sees movement out of the corner of his eye; this time his light stops a small gray field mouse dead in its tracks. He laughs and says softly, "What say, Mickey? Where's your buddy Minnie?"

Another shape speeds across the floor, followed by another, then another until Jon sees six or eight bold rodents. Scurrying around the shelter, they basically ignore Jon. Amazed at their brazen attitudes, Jon watches in fascination as they cover every single inch of the floor. His eyelids grow heavy, and he turns off the light and sleeps.

They all sleep for a while, maybe an hour. Charlie's blood-curdling scream results in the three men bolting upright, flashlights on, grabbing walking sticks, looking for an intruder.

"What the hell was it, Charlie?" asks George.

"A mouse," she replies.

"All that noise for an itsy-bitsy mouse?"

"You let a damned itsy-bitsy mouse run over your damned face and see if you damned well don't scream."

Jon tells them about the mice's fearless behavior under his flashlight spotlight. George says in amazement, "Those mice. Damnedest thing I've ever seen." All return to sleep, this time with sleeping bags all the way over their faces. Caution pays off, sometimes.

It is truly the night of the mice. The shelter is their home, and they plan to have the run of the place whether there are hikers or not. One manages to crawl into Jon's sleeping bag; man and rodent exit the bag simultaneously, man yelling and rodent squeaking. Everyone else wakes up, and it's Charlie's turn to laugh. "Man, I thought somebody'd been killed. I don't want to hear anything else about how I screamed when I was attacked by that man-eating mouse earlier."

Jon has to laugh. "Yeah, I wasn't sure what had crawled in with me. I thought I'd been had. You know, I heard about a guy with a long beard who wasn't the cleanest person in the world, if you can imagine that for a thru-hiker. Anyway, he ate his pasta and chicken and didn't bother to wash his face before he went to bed. Apparently he had spilled a bit of his dinner in his beard, maybe saving it for a midnight snack. When a mouse smelled it, he tried to finish the pasta. It was doing okay until he tried to crawl in the guy's open mouth. I understand that every hiker for miles woke up when that man yelled."

All four of the hikers laughed; Charlie shudders. "Damn, that little guy crawling across my face was bad enough. In your mouth? Ugh, too much for me."

The friends swap mouse stories long enough for the adrenaline to go away and sleep to overcome them once again. Apparently the mouse who wanted to get familiar with Jon went back to his buddies and told them that the hikers weren't very friendly, because attacks on humans died out. The critters stay active, squeaking from all corners, and a few tried sliding down ropes that had been used to suspend packs from the rafters, but all attempts to gain entrance into the food compartments of packs were unsuccessful.

Jon is the first one up in the morning, and he stumbles out of the shelter door and finds himself in a cloud. Visibility is about four feet, and the air feels wet and heavy. He starts his stove and soon has his first cup of coffee. As he sits enjoying the hot, life-giving brew, he is joined by Charlie. "Mornin', handsome," she growls.

"Mornin' yourself, good-lookin'," he responds. "You ready for 13 fun-filled miles after that wonderful night of sleep we had?"

"Yeah. I want you to know that George and I are dead serious about making Katahdin before they shut the park down for the winter. I 'spect that we'll hike along with you guys as long as you can stand us. When it's just two of us, I get a little lazy, so I need inspiration."

"Well, you're more than welcome. It's funny that somebody is looking to me for inspiration. That's a new concept. I ain't got much inspiration to give, I'm afraid. Not that I've ever had much confidence, but I'm still grieving 'bout Pookie. I'll get quiet at times, 'cause that's the way I handle bad stuff. I've always done that."

Charlie says, "Don't sweat it. Go ahead and get quiet, and we'll leave you be. But, don't keep beating yourself up about sending him back, though. You made the best decision you could make, even with 20-20 hindsight, isn't it still the best decision? We're all good at second guessing. Shoot, I'm world-class. But, enough philosophy. Hey, you gonna hog all that coffee, or you gonna share? I've been holding my empty cup for fifteen minutes waiting for you to offer me some. I guess I'll abandon my basically shy nature and just ask."

Jon laughs as he pours her a cup. "Charlie, I don't think you have a shy bone in your body. I think you are the best thing that could happen to me to help me get over my hurt. It's gonna be tough to withdraw and feel sorry for myself with you guys around."

Charlie gives him a hug, and they quietly enjoy their coffee. They equally enjoy waking up the still-sleeping George and Sam with a feather that a bird had kindly left by the shelter door. Drawing a feather across somebody's nose resembles a mouse. The wanted effect is achieved and, after the fussing and cussing dies down, all the hikers prepare for another day.

The day and the four crossings of the Blue Ridge Parkway pass without incident, and they arrive at Bobblets Gap Shelter in mid-afternoon. There's a little bit of dead wood lying around. They gather it to have a small campfire that night. Sam laughs, "It's gonna be real funny, having a fire tonight. I always figured that a campfire was an integral part of camping, but the herd of locusts that call themselves hikers clear off the dead wood completely along the AT. Somehow, they missed a bit here. This'll be neat tonight."

Sitting around the glow of the tiny campfire that night, they wax philosophical once again. Charlie starts it with, "I got a question for you guys. You having fun? There are days, times when this seems more like work or a job than fun to me."

Silence reins for a moment, broken by Sam. "The job I had in Memphis was no fun at all. Even though hiking does get to be like work, the good times make up for the sweating, climbing over rocks, stinking, and the rain. Good times like this, I mean."

Silence falls again. Jon says, "Yeah, I guess I second Sam. A job in a garage is no great shakes, but I think I'm gonna improve that when I get back to Tuscaloosa. Here, it's really simple. Walk, survive, no tough decisions to make. No, this has been a great opportunity for me; I intend to make the most of it. I don't see how I'll ever get another chance at something like this hike again. You know, once I get awful things like responsibility, a real job, a wife, house payments, stuff like that. Yuck, sounds terrible."

George laughs, "Better be careful, bud. In case you haven't noticed, there's one of those w . . . i . . . f . . . e types sitting close enough to you to reach you. And she's got a dandy right hook, let me tell you."

"Yeah, but Charlie's different. She may be a wife, but she's also one of the guys."

Charlie defends herself, "I'm not sure whether I'm complimented or insulted. I'll accept the former in order to avoid a fight. I'd hate to break the serenity of the forest by mopping up the pine needles with you, Jon."

The four laugh; peace and quiet descend on the small outpost of civilization. George stands, yawns and stretches. "I'm ready for bed. Jon, what does your magic plan show in store for us tomorrow?"

"Oh, nothing much, just 17 miles, three mountains, and two Parkway crossings before we reach Cornelius Creek Shelter. No big deal I 'spect."

Charlie groans, "Damn, sounds like a big deal to me. I'm tired just thinking about it. Fact is, it tires me enough that I think I'll hit the sleeping bag. Night, guys."

A chorus of "Night, Charlie," follows her into the shelter.

8 SAME OLD, SAME OLD (WELL, ALMOST)

At daybreak, Sam wakes his sleeping companions, as he loudly announces, "Up and at 'em you happy campers. Another day, another cup of crappy instant oatmeal plus yucky Tang. Yum, Yum. When this hike is over and done with, I hope I read in the paper that some terrorist group claims credit for simultaneous attacks on every oatmeal factory in the world on the night before. Nobody makes oatmeal at night, so nobody'll get hurt, 'cept the oatmeal. But there'll be no more oatmeal! Yay!"

"Sam, you've been out here too long. You're crazy as a loon," growls Charlie, echoed by Jon and George. Nonetheless, stoves are soon bubbling, producing hot water for coffee and, what else, but instant oatmeal. Dishes cleaned and water bottles filled, the friends leave the shelter relatively early that morning.

The day starts with all in cheerful moods and spewing lots of chatter. Conversations wane, then cease altogether as Cove Mountain looms ahead, and the upward trek begins. Steep slopes, plus loose rock talus, result in treacherous hiking and everyone concentrates on every step.

At the top, after catching her breath and taking in the view, Charlie asks, "You said there are three mountains today, Jon. How much elevation gain is there on the other two?"

Jon checks his trail guide, "Not nearly as bad as Cove Mountain. None of these mountains in Virginia are as rough as the ones in Georgia, North Carolina, and Tennessee. You've already conquered the best they have to offer. No sweat, Charlie."

For once, Charlie has no snappy return comment, and George looks at her with a strange expression on his face. "Babe, you okay?" he asks.

"Yeah, yeah, we women of the 90's are tough. Tougher than you guys. I'll make it."

"There, that's better. More like the smart-ass Charlie we know and love. It worries me when you get quiet."

They pull their packs back on and head north once again. Seven miles up the trail they whip Fork Mountain. Then six miles farther, Floyd Mountain becomes molehill number three, last for the day. When they limp into Cornelius Creek Shelter near dark, all four drop their packs on the ground and themselves right by them. Nary a muscle stirs for 15 or 20 minutes, until Charlie announces, "Well folks, I don't know if I'm ready for 17 miles at a clip or not. I think not, but I won't know for sure till in the morning. I'm about as close to being whipped as I've been since we started on this trail."

Jon says, "What will you do if you're not ready for those longer days, split with us? We'd hate that."

Charlie laughs, "I'm on to you guys. I know exactly why you want me around. I'm no dummy."

Sam innocently asks, "Why, Charlie? Your cheerful disposition? Nah, can't be that. Impossible."

Jon asks, "We give up, why?"

Charlie says, "I heard a discussion about how fast a bear can run. The consensus was that a three-legged black bear could outrun a hiker with no problem. The rest of the consensus was that you don't need to be faster than a bear to get away. You just have to be faster than at least one of the people in your hiking party. That's why you guys like me, 'cause you all figure you can outrun me. That's why."

The three men loudly profess innocence, along with how much they love and respect Charlie and that they would never, ever, in a million years, abandon her to a hungry bear.

Charlie responds with a resounding, "Bullshit. You guys think I don't know what goes on in your feeble little brains behind those vacant, glassy eyes?"

George replies, "Besides, Babe, we're all conservationists here. No way would we ever do that to a poor, innocent bear. No way!"

For the next half hour, George has to concentrate on staying out of harm's way–in other words, out of Charlie's reach.

For some reason, the mice are quiet that night. For that matter, all the wildlife are quiet. No bears, skunks, humans; no visitors at all, and the four sleep well. As usually happens, Jon and Charlie awaken first, and stoves produce cups of coffee to open sleep-closed eyes and to sharpen sleep-drugged minds. As they sit on a nearby log, Jon asks, "Well, Charlie, did you think more about the longer days that Sam and I are trying? Do you think you can make it?"

"Yeah, I even woke up once worrying about that question. Let's see your schedule–maybe I can come up with something."

Jon gets the schedule from the upper flap on his pack and returned to sit by Charlie. They poured over the map and Charlie groans at Jon's proposed daily mileage. She points them out–18, 14, 18, 17, 18, 18. "Wow, looks tough to me. I'm not sure my knees are ready for that. But, look there–you plan to spend two nights at Waynesboro. Maybe, if George and I make a few less miles daily between here and Waynesboro, we can plan to spend just one night there and be ready to go again. We can leave when you guys leave."

Jon asks, "You sure one night in civilization will give you enough rest to get going again?"

"Yeah, we've been staying just one night so far at most off-trail sites, anyway. Saving our bucks. So, we'll go for that. We'll miss you guys' company, but we'll see you in Waynesboro. Leave us encouraging notes in the trail registers, so we'll know how far ahead you are. Now, let's get these slug-a-beds moving. What do you think? Pour water on their heads? The old ear-tickle routine? How mean do you feel?"

"Ah, not too ornery. I don't guess either of us wants to listen to non-stop bitching. Just a bird feather in the nose. That'll work."

It works, and Sam and George are roused and informed of the plan. Following breakfast and repacking, they leave. Four miles up the trail, they approach Apple Orchard Mountain. They stop for water and gorp, and Charlie says, "Well, here's what separates you power walkers from wusses like me. I think it's the up parts of the mountains that hurt me. You two guys go on and play charge that slope–I'll poke along and play slow but steady tortoise. Poor George is stuck with me. Make sure to leave a message at Matt's Creek Shelter so we'll see it. We'll be through there tomorrow morning." Jon and Sam start up the slope while Charlie and George lag behind.

After an hour of trudging, Jon moves ahead of Sam. Sam waves his hand and says, "Go ahead. I'm moving a bit slower today. I'll catch up with you at the shelter." Jon is feeling particularly good, so he steps out, up the shale-covered trail.

When he reaches the top of the mountain, Jon sits on a warm, flat rock. He looks around and says aloud, "If I were a drop of water and fell right here, I'd have to split in four parts and go in all directions. Damn if I'm not smack-dab on top! Neat!"

He lies back on the rock and quickly becomes lost in the azure sky, framed by the canopy of large conifer trees. He closes his eyes and lets his mind wander. He thinks back to the beginning of this trek. Back to the help he received from his family and friends. Back to the blowup with Sissy. The success in his physical training with the help of James and the guys at the gym. The response from the readers of the newspaper and their generosity. Jon feels as though all those people were up on the mountaintop with him. "Thanks," he whispers at the blue sky. "Thanks to all of you for making this possible." When he finishes his litany of thoughts, his mind continues to wander. It stops on Gretel. A big sigh escapes. The physical activities aren't what stand out in his mind, pleasurable as they had been. It was the compatibility–the ease of conversation–the person.

A nap attack stops reflection time and creative thought and Jon dozes. When he awakes, the mountaintop seems still and quiet. But as he lies there, the noises around him become clearer and clearer. The background noise of the cicadas down the mountainside. The sound of a pileated woodpecker's raucous call, then the drumming noise as he attacks a tree in the next valley. A hawk screams as it circles in giant, lazy arcs, looking for prey below. The wind gently ruffles the leaves and adds a low, rustling, continuous sound to that of the cicadas, and the orchestral movement is complete.

When Jon decides it's time to move on to the shelter, he takes a last look around him. Gratitude for the opportunity to take the hike swells up in him again, because enjoyment of something in nature, like the symphony he has just experienced, has never happened to him before. Maybe because he has never sat still long enough.

That night while enjoying cups of tea, Jon and Sam enter what they call Philosophy Hour. They solve many of the world's problems, but both admit they miss Charlie's sharp wit and George's moderate approach to just about everything. "Oh, well," says Sam, "we'll see them in two or three days. When they are with us, they definitely make walking more fun."

"Yep, they do. Makes you wonder about whether 20-mile days really make any sense. I'll take a look at my magic plan and see what I can switch around to get rid of some of the really long days. We're doing well, and I think we will make Katahdin before winter, Good Lord willin' and the creek don't rise, and the knees hold out."

"Good idea. Maybe we can still keep walking in a herd. It's clear that changing Charlie's mind ain't so easy."

Jon laughs, "Nope, that's a given. Now, I'd best get working on my pearls of wisdom for Mr. Wilkins. As usual, I'm way behind." He heads straight for his sleeping bag in the shelter, lights his candle lantern, and begins writing.

Sam putters around for a while longer, then joins Jon in the shelter. Quiet takes over. That is, until the men see lights bobbing up the trail from the south. "Damn," says Sam, "Nobody but crazy people would be out at this time of the night. It's almost ten o'clock."

Two men appear at the shelter gate. They look exhausted, but get right to work. One starts a stove and cooks dinner, while the other man lays out their sleeping bags in an obviously well-practiced drill. The man inside is not real talkative, but Sam manages to extract enough grunts from him to learn that the two men are "power walker" thru-hikers and their usual day is at least 17 to 18 hours of fast hiking. They plan to be up at five the next morning and will hike two or three hours before they stop for breakfast.

"Damn," says Jon, "no way could I get started without my caffeine wake up call. Please get up in the morning quiet. I hope to be waking up about the time you guys have breakfast down the trail."

"No sweat. We're up and gone before anyone hears us."

Quiet descends again, and Jon and Sam sleep. The domestic chores the two power walkers perform don't bother them at all.

When Jon awakes at seven o'clock, the two power hikers are long gone. and Jon and Sam agree that they would rather move a little slower and stop to smell the flowers and enjoy the sights. They again discuss modifying their schedule so Charlie and George can walk with them once they re-connect in Waynesboro. That way maybe they can indeed stop and smell the flowers.

But, smelling the flowers that day proves to be difficult, if not impossible. Thirty minutes after they start hiking, the heavens open up and the rain starts and continues all day. They arrive at the un-occupied Matt's Creek Shelter at about five o'clock and gratefully remove wet packs, boots, and clothes. Wet gear fills the rafters, and the two men play nudist colony.

About the time they finish their tuna mac, they hear voices. Sam looks at Jon and says, "You reckon we'd better get our butts up and get decent? Nah, I'm too tired."

"No rush. I'm sure they'll be as wet as we are. They'll likely be dressed like us soon as they get here."

"Yeah, you're probably right. But, hey, let's look at your schedule again. What've we got to Waynesboro, two, three nights?"

Jon says, "Yep, something like that."

The men bend over the schedule and map and forget how they're dressed as they discuss possible Plans B and C. They forget, that is, until the shelter gate squeaks open and three women slosh in.

"Oh shit!" says Sam, echoed by Jon.

Jon pleads, "Wait a second, ladies, please. Turn your backs and we'll get decent."

The three women laugh, and one says, "Nah, I think we'll just stand here and see if you guys can turn any redder than you already are. Okay, start shuffling around."

To Jon and Sam's total amazement, the three women stand their ground. They refuse to turn around.

Jon tries negotiating. "Now ladies, you're gonna have to change into dry clothes, too. What if we're as unreasonable then as you're being now?"

The women laugh again, then condescend to turn their backs on the two extremely embarrassed men. Jon and Sam move quickly to their packs to dig out dry shorts.

Ten minutes later they return the favor and turn their backs as the women don dry clothes. Conversations are lively that evening. As the women are southbound hikers, trail conditions and gossip are swapped until bedtime.

The unofficial spokeswoman for the female contingent stands, stretches, and yawns as she announces, "I guess we might as well hit the sack. I'd suggest we play strip poker, but even if we win, there'd be no surprises for us ladies. We've already seen everything you guys have to offer. It'd be a waste of our time."

Red male faces are again the order of the moment, and Jon and Sam pile into their sleeping bags to the music of female laughter.

That night, Jon dreams. He has what would have to be called a true thru-hiker's dream. No sex, no wild animals, no zombies, monsters, or vampires. He dreams of food. In his dream, he's tied to a chair, hand and foot. The chair is in front of a table on which sits a huge bowl of macaroni and cheese and tuna fish. Gallons of it. If he leans forward, he can reach the hiker food with his mouth. But, he doesn't want that, because just beyond the small table is a long, long table. It stretches as far as the eye can see. The table is covered with food. Fried chicken and fish. Roast beef and leg-of-lamb and pork chops. Every imaginable vegetable–corn-on-the-cob, green beans, broccoli with hollandaise sauce, potatoes and gravy. Hot biscuits, rolls, and cornbread. Desserts–pecan and apple pie, ice cream with caramel sauce topped with a cherry, Boston cream pie and bread pudding with raisins and hard sauce. Jon strains, trying to break his bonds. The ropes bind into his arms, cutting off circulation. His mouth is watering and he wants badly to get to the food; his eyes tear up and he pleads, "I won't eat it all–just let me have a bite. Please!"

Jon wakes to find his pillow soaked from drooling. Luckily, his pleas to the unseen torturer were unheard by other shelter dwellers; he's the only one awake. At least he's spared further embarrassment and ego deflation. He drifts into a blessedly dreamless sleep.

9 "THE PEOPLE YOU MEET . . . "

The men are awakened by the sound of female voices. Loud voices, as the three co-inhabitants of the shelter fiercely argue about their route for the day. The unofficial spokeswoman for the group, Beth, announces, "Okay, you guys. Here we are, at Punchbowl, and that gives us Matts Creek, Cornelius Creek, Bobblet's Gap, and Fullhardt Knob to go before Troutville and the city lights." She punctuates her travelogue with jabs of her finger at the map. "We can do this in three days, if we hump it."

The other two women object to the strenuous schedule. "No way, Beth," yells one. "No way!"

Jon looks at Sam and whispers, "Damn–we took four days to cover that stretch. That's about 65 miles. She's crazy . . . "

The women finish their morning chores and struggle into their packs, and as for Brer Jon and Brer Sam–they just lay low. Beth and her disciples start up the trail and as they walk out of sight, the continuing argument trails in the air behind them.

Sam and Jon, still encased in their sleeping bags, can only laugh. Sam says, "Jon, I think I'll keep you as my fearless leader. You're mean enough and, although I may have thought at one time about switching teams, I believe I'll just stay put. I believe that Beth is too tough for me."

The men prepare to start their 18-mile day and remember to leave a note for their trailing hiking companions. A few months ago, a day this long would have been unconscionable, but now they seem to face them with some regularity. Laying out hikes on paper, when you're doing the planning, is easy, but they become real on the ground. The obstacles become real.

Shortly after lunch, they hear the sound of running water. A half-mile farther, they exit the woods and see a stream. Jon and Sam stop at the edge of the rapidly moving stream. It doesn't appear to be more than a foot or so deep; just deep enough to cause all sorts of boot problems. It is close to 50 feet wide.

Jon says, "What do you think, Sam? No rocks to hop here."

Sam looks upstream. "I don't see anything there either. Let's look below us."

He shucks his pack and walks downstream for several hundred yards, until he finds a string of large rocks crossing the stream. Returning to the trail ford, he says, "Jon, there's a way to get across down there but it may be tricky. Those rocks look slippery–lots of moss, but I think we can make it okay. Of course, we could always slip off our boots and wade in sandals, if we weren't so lazy."

Jon groans, "Man, I hate that pulling off your boots, wading across, pulling them back on. I guess I am lazy."

They wearily crunch downstream until they reach the rocks Sam had spotted. They again debate rock-hopping versus wading, and rock-hopping wins unanimously.

"Tell you what, Jon, I'll try it first, if you'll hold out your hiking staff for me to use for balance."

"Okay, we'll try it. Be careful. Some of those rocks look damned slick." Jon holds his staff for Sam to gain balance as he slowly inches onto the first rock, then on to the second and third. When he reaches the end of Jon's staff, Sam moves even slower.

Sam safely reaches the other side and stands there with his walking staff. "Bud, I can't help until you get halfway over. You're on your own. Good luck and move slowly."

Jon inches out onto the green-encased rocks. Even using his walking staff doesn't help much and, when he lurches forward or back for balance, the heavy backpack adds to the "opposite and equal reaction." He nearly loses his balance several times, but manages to catch himself.

Jon gets within two feet of being able to reach Sam's hiking staff. As he looks down, his right foot is about to come down on a particularly treacherous looking green rock. He makes a mid-air correction and reaches out farther with his right foot, aiming for a drier rock. As his foot touches the dry rock, the pack's momentum slams him forward, and he falls face first into the water.

"Damn," he yells, scrambling to this feet. "Did my pack go under?"

"Couldn't tell from here," says Sam. "Wade on over here and we'll assess the damage. You went under, that's for certain."

Jon hurries, sloshing through the knee-deep, icy cold water to the other side of the stream. As Sam helps him up onto the bank, the chill of the air cuts through him like a knife. "Dam…n… It's co…o…old!"

Sam moves fast setting up the tent. He lays out Jon's sleeping pad and bag. The stuff sack had protected them from the water.

"Jon, get in there and get stripped off and in the sleeping bag. Hand me the wet clothes and I'll try to dry them over a fire. Move quick 'fore hypothermia gets you!"

Jon does as he is told and, after a few minutes in his mummy bag, the chattering teeth quiet; he begins feeling warm. Sam has a fire blazing outside and has Jon's soaking wet clothes and boots around the fire. He wrings about a quart of water out of the shorts and shirt.

"Hey, Sam, how much of my stuff got wet?" asks Jon.

"Not too bad. The pack was in the water and back out so fast it didn't have time to soak up much. I've got the stuff laid out, but it's mainly the clothes you had on. They won't be dry for hours. Don't sweat it. It ain't like we got dates or something."

"Yeah, you're right. I'm in no hurry to get out of this bag–it feels pretty good."

Sam brings a cup of sweetened tea, which Jon consumes with great gusto. He then slowly fades into a nap. Sam continues with domestic chores until he, too, nods off while sitting by the fire.

When Jon wakes, he can handle the not-yet dry clothes. Amidst the curses and moans called for by donning cold, damp clothes, he dresses. They pack the tent and start up the trail. They hope to get to Hog Camp Shelter, and not impact the schedule.

That night at the shelter, Jon and Sam meet a real character. "I'm going-my-way Andrew" is a bearded man in his forties who seems to be enjoying his wilderness trek. Jon and Sam swap stories with Andrew, as they cook their dinners. Over coffee after dinner, they get around to home towns and families, Jon is amazed to learn that Andrew is married and has left his wife and five children at home.

"Five kids? How in the world did you . . . could you . . . what about your wife-how did she take this hike?" Jon asks.

"No sweat, really. When we met 10 years ago and decided to get hitched, we agreed to basically live our separate lives, the way we did before we met. The only rule was monogamy. But, we discovered that we make good-looking, smart, neat kids, so we get together ever so often and breed. Our last youngun's just now two years old."

"But, what about your wife?" How can she stand you being gone for four or five months like this?"

"Well, I call home every time I get off the trail, and she knows my schedule, so she could reach me in an emergency. I'd saved up enough money for her to live on while I'm on the hike, so it all worked out. When I get back, she's going to spend a month in New Orleans with an artist's colony she's read about. We each get to do our own thing. Best deal I've ever heard about, that's for sure."

"I guess it's the best deal I ever heard of, too," agrees Jon. Darkness obscures Sam and Jon's incredulous expressions and their shaking heads. Unreal. Damned unreal!

The next two days and 28 miles pass without incident or encounters with strange folks. There are still plenty of thru-hikers, both north and south bound, but everybody seems to have their own agenda and their own schedule. So, Jon and Sam put all their energy into covering the miles to Waynesboro, where they will enjoy their last civilization before 10 days on the trail. At that time, they will be at the Appalachian Trail Conference Center, headquartered in Harper's Ferry, West Virginia. Half of this self-inflicted, strange combination of pain and agony and good times will be over. The philosopher's question of half-empty versus half-full will come into play.

10 THE CITY LIFE

Following a hard, 18-mile day, Jon and Sam trudge into the intersection of the AT with U.S. Highway 250, which leads into Waynesboro. As dusk is approaching, they attempt to hitch a ride. Both men are soaked with sweat and admit that they smell. Jon laughs at their appearance and their odor. "Sam, you reckon if someone even stops for us, they would let us into their car?"

Sam makes a face. "God, I hope so. I'm just about dead. A warm shower and piles of food are all I can think of. How far is Waynesboro, in case we have to walk, heaven forbid?"

Jon checks in his handy-dandy trail guide and groans. "Four and a half miles, I'm afraid. What do you . . ."

An old and battered pickup truck pulls to a stop, surrounding the weary travelers with a cloud of dust. "You guys need a ride to town?" the man in the truck asks.

"You bet we do," responds Jon. We'd better crawl in the back of your truck. Believe me, you don't want us up there with you."

"No problem. Where're you heading?"

"Going to the Cabin Court Motel in town."

"That's a pretty nice place, and not too expensive. You got it," and the old truck clanks and grinds and belches forth blue smoke, as it slowly picks up speed.

The old man drops them off at the motel after about a ten-minute ride. "Here you be. Enjoy all the night life we got to offer. Course, that ain't much. The convenience store and the Laundromat are open 24 hours. That's about the extent of the night life. See ya!" and the truck lurches away.

Five minutes later, after winning two out of three at rock, paper, and scissors, Jon is standing in the shower under a stream of hot water. Ten minutes later, Sam is banging on the bathroom door. "Hey, bro, if you use all of that hot water, I may have to kill you. Nothing personal, you know."

Jon says, "Yeah, yeah. I'm just about done. Give me about five more minutes, then I'll let you have it."

After Sam finishes his shower, the men pack their dirty clothes in motel laundry bags and set off down the main street of Waynesboro. A block away, they find the Laundromat and settle in to wash clothes that are capable of walking to the machine, by themselves. They are wearing their last pairs of clean shorts. Sam reads year-old magazines, while Jon passes the time talking with a pretty young woman who collapses in a chair after chasing her two-year old boy around the room. Jon pursues the boy, and they spend the next 15 minutes playing on the floor with toy trucks. The young mother enjoys the respite. When Jon's dryer buzzes, he starts to get up from the floor, but she gestures for him to stay where he is.

"You keep him occupied and out of my hair, and I'll fold your clothes," she says.

Jon sits back down, "Sounds like a deal to me, as long as you can stand clothes that have been on the trail for months."

"No problem, my husband works down at Tatum's garage, and I have to try to get his grease-covered clothes clean every day. Your hiking clothes couldn't be much worse than that."

Jon and his young friend play trucks until Jon's clothes are all neatly folded and stacked back in the laundry sack. "Here you go, almost clean as ever," she says.

"Thanks, they look a whole lot neater than I ever folded them. They're almost too neat to wear."

She laughs, "I guess you'd better put them on, anyway. I reckon you'd get arrested walking without clothes on. Besides, I owe you the thanks. That's the longest time I've had without chasing Mikey, that I can remember. I love him, but he gets to be a real handful sometimes. Thanks."

Jon and Sam walk on down the road until they come to Weasie's Kitchen, a restaurant several thru-hikers had told them about. They are famous for their all-you-can-eat pancake breakfasts. As they were seated, Jon asks the waitress, a tiny lady who looks as if she's eighty years old, "Ma'am, can you get the pancake breakfast just in the morning?"

"That's right, Sonny. Does this look like morning to you?" and she points outside at the dark skies.

Jon and Sam look as if someone has stolen their last friend, and the waitress' banter can't cheer them up. "Wait a second boys. I need to check something with the cook. Hold your horses," and she walks back to the kitchen. When she reappears a few minutes later, she is beaming from ear to ear. "Well, guys, I don't know why you're having such good luck, but the regular cook's not here tonight."

Jon and Sam look at each other blankly. "Why is that our good luck," asks Jon.

"Because, Dummy, that means the breakfast cook's standing in for the night-time cook. Geez, can't you hikers understand anything?" She walks away from the men, shaking her head.

Jon and Sam look at each other once again. "Okay," says Sam, "What have I missed in all this? We gonna get to order anything, or not? I'm 'bout starved."

Jon laughs, "Doesn't look like it to me. Maybe we can get Granny back over here and order burgers, or something." But this proves to be a vain hope, because the old lady avoids them for the next few minutes and waits on others in the restaurant. The bell rings in the kitchen, and she scurries through the swinging door, reappearing with two platters of pancakes and link sausages. She places them in front of Jon and Sam, and returns with steaming cups of coffee. "Now, boys, when you want more, give me a warning cause Pete in the kitchen gets grumpy when I rush him. Now, enjoy."

Not another word comes from that table for 15 minutes, except for placing a re-order for more pancakes and butter and syrup. After finishing, the hikers lean back in their chairs, scarcely able to move, much less talk. Jon waves at the waitress, and she walks back over to their table. "Don't tell me you guys want more. You've already 'bout cleaned out the kitchen."

"No, Ma'am, I honestly don't think I could eat another bite. But I do have a question I'd like you to ask Pete," says Jon.

The old lady looks puzzled. "Ask Pete? What the heck you want me to ask Pete?"

"Ask him if he'd consider walking the Appalachian Trail with Sam and me. All he'd have to carry is his cast-iron skillet, pancake mix and a cooler full of sausage. We'll carry everything he needs."

The old lady laughs. "Tell you what, I'll go get Pete, and you ask him yourself," and off she scurries into the kitchen. Jon and Sam are still laughing a minute later when she reappears, a man trailing behind her. "Here, you ask him."

Jon and Sam look at a man that makes the old waitress look like a school girl. He must be pushing the century mark, and when he smiles, it's obvious that he doesn't have a tooth in his head. Jon and Sam manage to choke back laughter, and Sam tells Pete how much they had enjoyed his pancakes. Pete flashes his gums and toddles back into his kingdom. Then, the laughter starts. The two men, joined by the waitress, laugh until they can hardly draw a breath.

"Oh, man, I don't ever think I've laughed so hard. My side hurts," stammers Jon. "Thanks, Granny, but I think we'll pass on taking Pete with us. We might have to carry him as well as all the pancake stuff. I guess we'll just have to come back here before we hit the trail again."

The waitress says, "You'd be surprised at how well that old fossil moves. Probably walk away and leave you whippersnappers. He's always chasing me around the tables here, and I can barely keep ahead of that dirty old man. Here's your bill. Pay up front."

She hurries away to take care of several new customers. Jon and Sam pay and walk back to the motel, where they turn on the TV. Both men go to sleep, waking to the strains of the Star-Spangled Banner, as the station signs off for the night.

When the hikers awake early the next morning, they realize that they are lying comfortably in soft beds rather than on the ground or on wire bunks, and promptly go back to sleep. They wake again at 10 o'clock and go find breakfast. They spend the rest of the morning re-stocking for the next leg of the trip, and both pick up packages at the post office.

When they arrive back at the motel, it takes an hour to de-Madison Avenue the food and repack the packs. They lounge around the motel for several hours, alternating naps with television, a luxury they haven't had for some time. At five-thirty, Charlie and George arrive at the motel, riding in style in the back of a pickup truck that is almost as dilapidated as their chariot had been. The friends exchange group hugs, and the new arrivals disappear into their room and hit the shower as quickly as had Jon and Sam. At seven o'clock or so, they return to the restaurant where the old waitress had taken such good care of them the night before, but neither she nor Pete are working that night. They couldn't get pancakes, but they console themselves with piles of equally delicious food.

After they are satiated, Jon asks Charlie, "Are you sure that you are gonna be ready to head back out tomorrow? One night's rest may not give you back all your strength."

Charlie responds, "No, we said we'd be ready to go back out after one night, if you guys waited for us. You waited, so we'll be ready in the morning."

Later, Sam took George aside and asks, "George, I know Charlie's tough, but this is asking a lot. We don't mind staying another night. Jon and I talked about it, and it's cool with us."

George says, "Well, as you know, she's about as stubborn as she is tough. I'll check with her and see what she says. I have to admit that two nights in a soft bed sounds pretty good to me."

Apparently, George convinced Charlie that Jon and Sam really didn't mind, because when a tap sounds on their room door and Jon opens it, Charlie greets him with a big hug. She runs to the bed where Sam is lounging and gives him the same. "You guys are jerks 'cause you don't believe I can go tomorrow. But, you're nice jerks. Two nights would help. You sure it doesn't mess up the schedule?"

"Nah," says Jon. "I was just looking at the *Trail Guide* and, although we've got 161 miles to Harper's Ferry, there are only two mountains listed. Most of our hiking is on top of the Skyline Drive, but we cross that damned road 48 times. Forty-eight! Damn, we'll have shin-splints and pavement blisters. Since our first day out is a 20 miler, I figured that since you're one of them weaker sex people . . ."

George comes out of his room in time to see Charlie right on Jon's heels, swinging at him with a commode plunger as they run across the motel parking lot and up the road until they are out of sight. George's mouth stayed open, and Sam walks out of his room holding his side with laughter.

"What the hell was that all about?" George asks.

"Jon called her a member of the weaker sex; she took serious offense. He didn't get a chance to finish what he was gonna say. If he comes back alive, maybe he'll tell us. I guess we'll find out which of them is in better shape."

Thirty minutes later, Jon and Charlie walk arm-in-arm back into the room where George and Sam await. The combatants are laughing, so Sam says, "I guess that murder is no longer eminent. Does this mean we're all friends again?"

Charlie laughs, "Yeah, I've forgiven this low-life, but he owes me a banana split. That's the bribe. Come on you guys. We've got to find a place that's still open."

As they walk across the parking lot, George quietly asks, "Uh, Dear. Don't you guess that we'll get better service if you lay down your weapon and come along peaceable-like?"

Charlie looks at the plunger in her hand and laughs, "Yeah, I reckon. Here, slave, take this back to the room." She thrusts the necessary tool at Jon, and he meekly takes it, returns it to the room and quickly rejoins the three. They find a Dairy Queen, and all animosity is immediately buried in banana splits.

Jon and Sam have to admit that the third night in the relative lap of luxury is welcome. Most of the accumulated sores on feet, legs, and arms heal nicely.

On the evening before their departure, the hikers call a local man who agrees to serve as their taxi driver in the morning. He arrives at six o'clock, and the hikers are off again. As they settle into their packs, the straps immediately find sore spots that had not completely gone away during the sojourn. Knees crack and pop and thighs twang, but the walking soon smoothes out as they move off together.

That first day on the way to Blackrock Hut Shelter, they cross the Skyline Drive a total of ten times. For all their complaining about the closeness of civilization, they have to admit that they enjoy the looks they get when they stride purposefully past tourists in station wagons and vans, and they make a game out of cataloging the looks they get. Some are envious, these usually coming from men who have two or three small children hanging onto their pants legs. Some looks say without words, "You guys are crazy. Why in the world would anybody leave the creature comforts of civilization to do this?" Some looks from older folks, instantly categorize them as, them damned hippies. "Go and get a real job." Some folks are downright curious and interested, and the hikers enjoy pulling off their packs for a minute and talking with these people. Their questions are, "What is it like, to walk day after day? Aren't you scared in the forest? What about bears? How heavy is that pack? What if something breaks?" After a while, there are very few new questions posed.

The first day, a 20-miler, is a long one, but the foursome arrives at the shelter together. They find the shelter almost full, and Jon and Sam opt for tents. The next day, Charlie and George sing the usual litany of thru-hikers about the crowded conditions, the snores, them damned mice and the stupid amateur hikers who forget to hang their packs or, who don't take advice of those who have been there. The mice make a real racket all night as they feast on those hikers' food, a noise that is only surpassed by the noise the hikers make the next morning, when they wake up and see the mess.

The hiking is along beautiful stretches of trail with vistas on all sides. They see flowers such as sunflowers, daisies, black-eyed Susan's, growing in profusion by the roadside and from the tiny dirt-filled crevices in the rock walls that were cut when the road was built. The Blue Ridge in Virginia, along which they are making their way, consists of a chain of individual mountains that stretch like a chain of green pop-beads in the Shenandoah National Park. The hikers pronounce that both God and the National Park Service did well when the mountains and the park were formed. The hike is truly enjoyable.

The following two days go well, although Charlie is beginning to lag behind more and more. At Hightop Hut Shelter, Charlie announces, "Okay, guys, you power walkers have once again done it. I ain't ready for no damned 20 miles tomorrow. George and I are gonna slow down a bit like we did before Waynesboro and catch you guys at Harper's Ferry. This time, though, we're gonna stay one night and be ready to go. I've impacted the schedule too much, already." She ignores the other's protestations.

Halfway through the morning, Charlie and George fall behind Jon and Sam, and the foursome is once again two pairs. During that day, Jon and Sam hit an interesting new terrain problem. They encounter a portion of the trail that meanders along and follows the creek bed. The rocks in the bottom of the creek are definitely not homogeneous in nature, as they vary from sand particles to automobile-sized blocks. Most of those rocks underfoot seem to be just the right size and shape–about the size of your clenched fist and round and smooth, to make walking difficult

After several hundred yards of the noisy clatter, Jon says, "Damn, we sound like a troop of cavalry horses. We couldn't sneak up on anyone, unless they were as deaf as a post."

Sam grunts, "I'd laugh, but these damned rocks hurt too much. If it was first thing in the morning, it wouldn't be so bad. But my legs are tired and this hurts my ankles."

Jon says, "Yeah, seems like they're close to turning every step. But at least we're not having to wade across the stream. I hate that decision you make with every

creek crossing. Should I rock-hop and take the chance of another swan dive? If not, is it shallow enough that my water-resistant boots won't leak, or do I have to sit and take my boots off and wade across in my sandals. Sit back down and put the boots on again. Walk another hundred yards and go through the process all over again. I hate it! Decisions, decisions, decisions."

Sam does have to laugh now, and they clatter along the gravel for a half-mile or so, until to their delight, the trail turns up a hill and away from the creek bed.

"All right," says Sam, "Never thought I'd be happy to face an uphill. But, this looks good to me!" The trail is a pretty stretch, winding slowly up through thick forest cover. The sides of the trail are covered with fern thickets growing upward through moss-covered rocks. Noise seems to be non-existent, as the ground cover muffles even the sounds of their boots as they walk along. The spot they camp in that night is more of the same, and the men sleep soundly and even wake up a bit late, at about eight o'clock.

The next three days are relatively uneventful, and all three nights are spent in shelters. Jon and Sam find themselves leap-frogging with dozens of other hikers, some whose company they enjoy, and some they don't. The length of days people are willing to walk varies, particularly now that mid-June has passed and the days are getting warmer and warmer.

The men find themselves soaking wet with sweat by the middle of the morning. Finding clothes each day that aren't so smelly that they can be tolerated, is a challenge. No complaints are voiced as they try to enjoy the relatively smooth trail, knowing that soon after Harper's Ferry they have to face the infamous rocky trails of Pennsylvania. From all thru-hiker accounts, those trails can be deadly–both to the legs, to the feet. and to morale.

Jon pulls out his small, laminated spirit-booster quote just about every day, and Sam has to laugh at him, as he shakes his head from side to side. Jon mumbles, "All right, all right, dammit. I'll keep looking for the fun stuff. The pretty stuff. Never mind that my feet hurt, never mind that we're getting closer to those damned rocks. Gosh, those are pretty flowers. I'm really enjoying myself. Oh, great! We're coming closer to that road with those pasty-white tourists and their damned stupid questions. Boy, I'm having fun, now!"

At lunchtime one day, Sam and Jon find themselves at one of the multitude of Parkway crossings. There is a picnic ground with lots of picnic tables and grills and all the amenities required by car-traveling tourists. The weary hikers find an empty table, and they remove their packs, slumping down on the benches of the table. Sam looks at Jon. "Bud, I don't know about you, but I'm too damned tired to eat. Dried shit and cardboard crackers have lost their appeal."

Jon agrees. "Yeah, I know exactly what you mean. I'm going to fill my water bottles over there at the water fountain and get a drink of ice cold water. That sounds as good as food to me. Well, maybe not quite as good, but that's what I'm trying to convince myself. Do I look convinced?"

As he walks to the fountain, he stops several times to answer the inevitable questions from the flatland tourists about what they're doing and why. Jon does his best to answer each question politely, even for the umpteenth time. He returns to the table, where Sam is silently laughing at him.

A few minutes later, as Jon and Sam still sit, resting their heads on the picnic table. A lady, trailed by two kids, approaches them. She carries a sack in her hand. "Fellas," she begins hesitantly, "my husband and I noticed that you were worn out. We've finished our picnic, and we have some fried chicken left over. If you want it, you're welcome to it. And, here is some potato salad to go with it."

Jon and Sam thank the lady and as she walks away, they look at each other and decide they're not too tired to eat, then they tear into the food. As they are finishing up, another lady walks over, bringing them iced tea in plastic cups and several sandwiches, followed by a man with two bowls of banana pudding and plastic spoons.

Full and refreshed now, Jon looks at Sam. "You know, I believe that we've been successful at what somebody told me about back down the trail. We've been 'yogi-ing'. That guy told me that the rules of the game are that you can't ask for food. You just look pitiful enough that people feel sorry for you and give you all kinds of goodies. I think Yogi Bear would be proud of us. We did good."

Sam's grin is Jon's answer.

11 "HALF FINISHED, HALF TO GO"

On the evening before they are to arrive at the Blackburn AT Hostel, one day from Harper's Ferry, Jon and Sam struggle into Rod Hollow Shelter just before dark and shuck their packs. A man, seated in the dark corner of the shelter, calls their names. They start, then peer into the shadows.

"David! Mike!" Where the hell did you guys come from?" exclaims Sam. "I guessed that you power hikers were halfway through Pennsylvania and those damned rocks by now." Neither of the two men look anything like the athletes they looked like at the start of the trail.

David responds, "Naw, the last little bit we haven't been pushing it too much, and Mike sprained his ankle pretty badly a couple of days ago. We've been resting here ever since. When he can move again, we're gonna try to make it to the AT Hostel and get a ride to Harper's Ferry. We'll call it a day. We quit."

"Man, you can't mean that!" says Sam. "You guys are the reason I'm even out here. What happened to that drive and ambition?"

"Don't really know. I guess we lost it down the trail somewhere. Every day seemed to get harder and harder. It's been a struggle to even get out of our sleeping bags and get going in the morning. We're going back to Memphis and get on with our lives." David sits quietly, his slumped shoulders showing his dejection.

Sam and Jon sit just as still. "Man," says Sam, "is there any way we can change your minds? It'd be a bummer to get this far and not go all the way to Katahdin. I'd hate like hell to even think about quitting at this stage of the game."

"Naw, no way. We've been considering dropping off the trail for several weeks. I guess we've lost the spark. When you can't find anything fun from day to day, you can't keep on going. Nope, we're gone; we're outta here. Maybe think about trying the other half next year. Maybe. I'm afraid the AT can claim the two of us as victims. How about you guys? Having any doubts creep into your minds?"

Sam thinks a minute, then responds, "Not any serious thoughts about dropping off. I question my sanity, or lack of it, daily. But it's making me get my head together about what I want to do when I get home. Nope, not ready to quit. Not yet, anyway."

Jon nods his head in agreement. "Me either," he says. "Practical thought, though. How long before you figure you'll be able to hike this last 17-mile stretch?"

"I guess a couple of more days. My ankle's still a combination of greens, oranges, and purples." Mike pulls off his sock, and both Jon and Sam's guts wrench.

"Man," says Sam, "that sucker looks awful. You don't think it may be broken?"

"I don't think so. I can still move it a little, and I've stopped screaming in agony. Plus, it hasn't swelled any more after the first day. I don't think anything is broken; I think it's just a bad sprain."

"Well, we need to get you to town and have a doctor take an x-ray to make sure," says Jon. "Tell you what. Let's come up with a plan. I've got a good, heavy duty, bandage. We can fix you up tomorrow; maybe put on two socks and the ankle wrap. I'll go find a small tree that'll work as a crutch. David, Sam and I can split up all of your stuff and share the load. We'll move slowly, take our time and we should get to the Hostel tomorrow. If we don't make it, no big deal. We'll set up our tents and stay a night on the way."

David and Mike swap glances. "What do you think, Mike?" asks David. "Can you do it?"

"Maybe so. Having these two share the load might just do it. Yeah. I feel better already. But, it's gonna hurt like a big dog." He sits, dreading the forthcoming pain, but still looking forward to returning to civilization a little earlier that he had thought he could.

Sam and Jon start on their evening chores–getting water and rolling out sleeping bags. "Tell you what, man," says David. "Let's lighten the load a bit. Here, I'll lay out the food that Mike and I have, and let's fix a feast. We might as well celebrate the halfway point for you guys and the end for us. We'll eat like camper kings tonight."

The three pick through the packages, and four stoves are soon roaring and food is bubbling. The men eat until they can eat no more, then lean back with cups of coffee. "Even though that was all freeze-dried hiker food, it was damned good," says David. "I think we lightened the load by six or eight pounds. At least, we redistributed it." "Belch," responds Mike, Sam, and Jon. "Belch."

The next day is a nightmare. Even though the men are in the best physical shape of their lives, the extra 15 or 20 pounds the three now carry, really bends their backs. Mike is having the toughest time of all. The crutch is padded heavily, but by mid-morning, his armpit is as sore as a boil. But he gamely keeps going. Frequent rest stops are taken, and water and Gorp have never tasted so good.

As the afternoon wears on, it becomes increasingly obvious that they are not going to make it to the AT Hostel that day. At the 10 mile mark of the day, they come to the side trail to Bears Den Hostel and, as dusk is coming on, decide to call it a day. When they arrive at the hostel, they find themselves the only inhabitants. No rides to civilization to be found.

While Mike sits, propped up against a tree, the other three men set up housekeeping. The meal they prepare is quite a bit more Spartan than the night before when they thought they would be resupplying tonight. And they also thought they would be dining on all-you-can-eat pizza and beer. One of life's little disappointments.

Mike is dosed with extra-strength aspirin, and they get a good night's sleep, though dreading the morning. The morning adds additional torture, as the sky opens up and gives them a dose of liquid sunshine. But, they persevere and make it to the Blackburn AT Center. To their delight, they find a work crew that agrees to take Mike and David to Harper's Ferry to a doctor. The men say good-byes, and the Memphis contingency agree to call Sam's family and friends and let them know their wandering boy is doing well. Much slimmer now and tanned. They also agree to withhold the not-so-pleasant parts, like he is covered with bug bites, and he stinks like a Civil War soldier after a week-long battle. Non thru-hikers wouldn't understand that part of the mystique.

Jon and Sam feel like their packs have gone to zero weight, as they move toward Harper's Ferry the next day. They laugh at the speed they are able to attain. However they stop short of agreeing to carry super-heavy packs once in a while just so they would feel lighter when they shed the extra weight. Not a particularly attractive scenario.

They arrive in Harper's Ferry early in the afternoon and go directly to the Appalachian Trail Conference Headquarters for the near-obligatory photograph with Jean Cashin, the Trail Mother to all who attempt thru-hikes. Jean holds her nose, hands them a bar of soap and points to the outside faucet, before she agrees to go outside with them and stand close enough for a picture to be taken.

Back inside, after Jon and Sam are more socially acceptable, she shares trail gossip that she has heard from hikers coming from both north and south. They learn which parts of the trail are in particularly bad shape that year, which dogs are more bothersome than usual, and which trail romances have either bloomed or faded. The several hours they spend there are a delight, and Jon and Sam almost hate to leave to find the AT Hostel. Jean promises to let George and Charlie know of their progress when they arrive.

Jon and Sam spend the rest of the day playing tourist–walking around the hills and marveling at the embankments and installations left from the Civil War. Both armies occupied and fought over this key city, and many buildings from those times have been preserved. They also find the Hilltop House, famous among hikers for their all-you-can-eat buffets and the men indeed eat all they can eat and more. The beds feel particularly soft that night, and Jon makes himself a pallet on the floor, because his body can't adjust to the softness. Sam wakes up and sees what Jon is doing, shakes his head, mumbles something about Jon's lack of sanity, then falls back to sleep.

The men laze around for most of the morning, then go into the now-familiar routine of visiting the post office and the nearby resupply store, then make the food ready for backpacking. They go to the movies in the early afternoon, and this time Jon manages to stay awake during the entire show. It does take large tubs of buttered popcorn and a giant coke for him to make it, but he toughs it through.

Charlie and George wander in before dusk, and the reunion takes place at the buffet. At this center of the hiking universe, the workers at the buffet aren't even surprised, much less amazed at the quantities of food the friends consume, washed down with gallons of iced tea and followed with two or three desserts each.

As the next day's hike is only 11 miles, Charlie and George sleep in, and the late start is not a problem. They complete the miles and enjoy the company of other hikers they encounter at Crampton's Gap Shelter that night. There are several women hikers, and Charlie has an extremely good time swapping stories about how dumb men can be, particularly men of the thru-hiker type.

Three nights after Crampton's, they arrive at Antietam Shelter. George and Charlie lag behind, swearing they will catch up. Jon and Sam's interest in history of the Civil War had been piqued at Harper's Ferry, so they stay there an extra day in order to tour the battlefield. They are amazed at the stories the rangers tell about this battle, the scene of the single bloodiest day in the history of the United States. As they leave, Jon shakes his head and says, "I don't think I'll bitch anymore about carrying this pack. At least we've got boots, and we don't have guns and ammo and we don't have anybody shooting at us or lobbing cannon balls or canister at our heads."

As they celebrate 80 days on the trail, they move through Quarry Gap and Pine Grove Furnace and make an unscheduled stop at Boiling Springs, Pennsylvania. They really can't explain an extra night in civilization; maybe it is the dread of the rocky trails to come now that they are in Pennsylvania. Or maybe, as Sam expresses it, "I think it's because we've been spoiled with 12- and 13-mile days. This planned 20-mile day hike to the Thelma Parks Memorial is too much for me to face. I'll have to build back up to that. I ain't ready, yet."

It has been a long day. A really long day. The rain had started about ten in the morning and drizzled all day. It finally quits when the men reach the shelter.

Thelma Parks Shelter proves to be one of the many grubby, over-crowded shelters that are found along the trail, but like all of them, it serves as a welcome port in the storm. Jon and Sam gladly join the half-dozen, bedraggled hikers already sitting around on the wooden bunks.

"What say, guys," greets Jon. He speaks to one grizzled veteran of the trail. "Hey, Pete, we haven't seen you for quite a while. You making it okay?"

"Yeah, getting on getting on, I guess. I hate this damned rain, though. Seems to make the days go on forever. Slopping and sliding, sliding and slopping." He points at the wet, muddy clothes hanging on every available corner of the shelter and on the nails that hikers have pounded into the walls over the years of the shelter's existence. "You can see it looks like washing day down home in the country. I hope some of this stuff'll dry. That's my last pair of useable socks hanging right over there. Walking tomorrow will be a bitch."

The whole group sits for a while. Off-hand comments made up here on the trail, when you're tired, somehow take on an aura of great philosophical importance, and you have to contemplate at length. Kinda like comments made on a CB radio. If someone made CB statements to you in the normal course of day-to-day life, you'd shake your head and walk away, thinking that this person is an idiot. They can't speak English. But, if it's on the airwaves, it must be important. Jon thinks, "I guess this is one more piece of proof that your mind gets somewhat warped on the AT. In some ways it becomes clearer than it has ever been before, but in a warped sort of way."

Pete breaks the silence, "You know, I saw a pair of red-tailed hawks circling early this morning, way before the clouds moved in and the rain started. Maybe that old wive's tale about birds sensing rain coming is right. They were circling faster and faster, the more I watched them. I guess they were looking for their breakfast before the rain drove the little critters under cover." Silence reigns once more.

"Yeah, I saw a couple of oak trees yesterday with their leaves turned bottom side up," pipes in a hiker, a short slim man with thick glasses. "Looked as if they were getting ready to get a drink. I didn't always believe that tale–my Granddaddy always used to tell us that when we were little tykes. But, old granddad was right, once again." More silence while the hikers contemplate that new pearl of wisdom.

Then, from another corner, "My two-cents worth is that I saw the mist rise all the way up to the shelter last night. I had to get up last night to get rid of those two cups of tea I drank. I guess it was two in the morning, and the fog was real heavy. I looked for bears behind every tree. It was so spooky that I was glad to get back into my bag."

"I didn't see any mist or fog this morning, you dummy," interrupts another hiker.

"That's because you broke in before I finished what I was saying, you rude, crude goof. They say that if you don't see the mist in the morning, it means you're 'bout to get wet."

More contemplation. More discussion. They conclude that maybe there's something to the old wives' tales. At least they're right enough of the time that it's worth being prepared. Put your maps and notebooks and T.P. in baggies. Stuff everything into the pack. Have the pack rain cover and the poncho where you can get to them easily. Use a plastic bag to cover your sleeping bag before you put it into the stuff sack. All these things may take a couple of minutes, but they could save considerable aggravation later that night.

One man points at his sleeping bag, hanging draped over a roof truss. "Every corner and edge and seam of that damned thing is soaked. I'm not gonna sleep worth a damn tonight. Wish we'd had this discussion last night instead of tonight. I guess I'm now a member of the old wives' club. This initiation is a bit rough. I reckon I've been initiated enough times. Maybe I'll pay a little more attention to what's going on around me."

Jon adds, "Yeah, me too. I forget sometimes that the critters and trees live here all the time, and we're just trespassers. We can learn from them, that's for sure. What did I read somewhere before I came up here? Oh, yeah, you've got to become one with the wilderness in order to survive. Sounds hokey, but now we're saying it's for real. I'm gonna start paying more attention from now on. I hate a soggy night. Nothing ever gets dry up here anyway, so I mean to try to keep it from getting wet in the first place."

More philosophical conversation is stopped in favor of collecting firewood that is dry enough to burn. Soon, everyone is huddled around a fire that although barely flaming, is putting off enough smoke to signal Tonto from 100 miles away. Coughs are the only conversation that occur until the fire gains a good purchase on the wood. Snaps and pops of quickly drying wood add a staccato background noise to the coughs. At least socks draped on sticks, and boots and pant-leg bottoms get dry, and feet and hands get warm before still damp sleeping bags call the weary hikers to bed.

The next day, the hikers begin to find that locating good water sources on this stretch of the trail is difficult. The clear, cold springs of the Appalachians aren't present here, and they find themselves more and more asking nearby houses if they can fill their water bottles. The locals are agreeable, and the requests are nothing new to them. One has even stretched a garden hose through his backyard to the side of the trail. He lettered a sign which says, "help yourself, but turn it off when you finish." The hikers comply with his request.

Jon encounters a minor crisis; the filter in his small water purifier clogs. Rather than use one of the other hikers' filters, he drinks from a roadside spring. The resulting three days of stomach ache and diarrhea and cramps prove conclusively to Jon that the cardinal rule on the trail–to never, never, never drink untreated water–is a rule to be followed religiously. But, he is fortunate in that he's not been infected with Giardia, a particularly vicious parasite picked up in water that can end a hike, even with proper treatment. Hiking under the pressure of diarrhea does not make for pleasant conditions. Sam gets used to the sight of Jon saying, "Oh, man," shucking his pack and leaving it in the middle of the trail, and dashing into the woods.

The section of trail north of Boiling Springs and Thelma Park Shelter is a particularly hot and steamy stretch. As the trail winds along hedgerows and through the beautiful Pennsylvania farmland, water becomes extremely hard to find But, they enjoy the hike through that stretch, even with the water problems, probably because they know that as they hike north of Duncannon, they will hit the geologic hazard they have been dreading–the infamous rocky trails. They will become intimately familiar with the worrisome, nasty rocks that attack your feet and your well-being with every step. Although many times anticipation is worse than reality, this hazard is commonly griped about, unfortunately, they suspect that this reality will be just as bad.

12 THOSE DAMNED ROCKS

Sam says, "Jon, I don't know whether to be happy or sad. Seems like all we've heard about for months, is Pennsylvania and those damned rocks. Here we are. Well, at least, we're in the state." They have both a fear of the infamous Pennsylvania rock-strewn trail and a wish to get it over and behind them.

Jon agrees, "Yeah, right above Duncannon I think is where the trouble begins. Somebody told me that the other day. Anyway, this part of the trail isn't too bad. Looks just like Virginia and Maryland to me." "Yeah, shame it isn't quite as pretty as down in Georgia and the Smokies. I kinda miss those lush green mountains and less civilization. Although, God knows we saw enough people on the trail and we certainly experienced enough rain to satisfy me for a long time. I read somewhere that we'll be hiking on the eastern ridge of the Allegheny Mountains. Right pretty, I understand."

Jon sits on a rock studying his trail guide. He says, "Well, Sam, according to my handy-dandy, always-present guide, we get the pleasurable experience of 11 miles of rocks and trail before we rest our bones at Peters Mountain. At least it's a shelter, so we won't have to mess with tents." He studies further and announces, "Actually, we've got shelters for the next four nights, 'till we hit Ashfield. I've got a care package waiting for me there. What about you, Sam?"

A nod. While his hiking companion continues with lunchtime chores and food, Jon digs his tattered notebook out of his pack and scribbles notes for the last two or three days. It sometimes feels like the notes for the newspaper are more trouble than they are worth, but a promise is a promise. Besides, he probably wouldn't even be here if it weren't for the newspaper and the readers. So, he scribbles. He will post the latest scribbles and newest photos in a now-familiar routine, while he is in Ashfield. Maybe Mr. Wilkins will send the latest article, so he can see how his immortal words look in print.

The morning's hike has not been too bad. They have made pretty good progress and arrive at Duncannon well before lunch, but don't bother to go the six-tenths of a mile into town; they eat on the trail so they don't lose time. After another mile and a half, they cross the Susquehanna River and are rewarded with nice views from the bridge. While they are enjoying the beauty of the scene, to their surprise and delight, George and Charlie catch up with them. The pride, back together again, proceeds up the trail.

The hikers lapse into a companionable silence in which each withdraws into his own thoughts. Minds are shifted into neutral, walking smoothly and flowingly is the most important thing of the moment. When you quit thinking and concentrate on just the rhythm of hiking, the miles seem to move ever so slightly more quickly.

The trail has slowly become more difficult to negotiate. Rock rubble has replaced smooth packed soil as the main material on which they walk. They stop for a Gorp break.

"Well, guys," says Sam. "What do you think of the rock trail so far?"

Jon answers, "Not too bad, but I'd say we haven't seen the worst by any stretch of the imagination. I'll reserve judgment till later." He returns to his Gorp and water break, which the others have never ceased. They leave the break, and the slipping and sliding on the rocks continues to increase in severity.

Six miles later they arrive at Table Rock and stop for a breather. All four are breathing heavily and are soaked with sweat. Sam sprawls on the ground next to Jon. "Hey, buddy, how about looking at that damned Trail Guide of yours and see if we can negotiate another schedule. I'm thinking that 16- or 18-mile days may be a bit too much on this trail. Charlie hasn't bitched, but look at her–she's pooped. Hell, look at me–I'm pooped!"

Jon nods his head in agreement. He digs out his guide and starts adding numbers. After a few minutes, he says, "Yeah, but we'll have to be illegal for a night. If we stay at Clarks Ferry Shelter at about a mile from here, we can go 13 tomorrow and camp at the spring. We'll have to be off of the trail, so we won't be seen. Then, 12 the next day to Rausch Gap. That'll add one more day, but I think we're okay on our schedule. Let's try this on Charlie and George."

Their two companions have no objections at all to the new schedule, particularly since it means they have only a mile more to go today. Weary nods indicate agreement, and they move on to at Clarks Ferry Shelter. Around the campfire that night, they discuss the trials and tribulations of Pennsylvania's rocky trails.

Charlie says, "Hey, guys, you know those folks that do the maintenance along the trail? The volunteer groups that I think are called trail angels? I've heard that there are some trail devils that sneak around in this area."

"Trail devils?" asks Jon. "Okay, Charlie, I'll bite. What the hell are trail devils?"

"Well, since you ask, I'll be glad to tell you and get a little information into that pea brain of yours. For that matter, all of you guys. The trail devils are the folks that bring big steel files instead of the clippers, chain saws, and grass trimmers."

"Okay, I give up. What the hell are you talking about?"

"How else do you think these damned rocks get so sharp? Look at my knees–cut and scraped. I can just see those little red devils sitting on the ground, hour after hour, sharpening each and every rock with their files to get the hikers. Scrape, scrape, scrape. . . "

The three men laugh as they visualize Charlie's fantasy. Sam, serious look on his face, says, "I believe you've got it, Charlie. That must be why the rocks are so sharp. I'm sure that the geology of the rock has nothing to do with it. It's a man-made conspiracy. That's what it is. Those trail devils are out to get us, to make us quit."

Tea is sipped and silence reigns until the weary hikers give up and hit the sleeping bags. Tomorrow's another day. Another day of two steps forward and one step back–frequently on their knees or back-sides.

The dread and the imaginative pictures prove to be accurate, and the trail for the next three days is as bad as they feared. From Clark's Ferry Shelter, to the spring near Clark's Valley, to Rausch Gap Shelter, then a long day to William Penn Shelter. They drag themselves into Pine Grove, Pennsylvania, where they all have packages waiting. The motel beds have never felt so soft and comfortable, the pizza parlor so inviting. After a rest of a full day, they feel almost human again.

At dinner that night, they discuss the 10 days, or so, it will take them to get to the New Jersey state line, their next major milestone. "A mere 100 miles," says Sam. "What's a 100 miles for folks that have already come 1160 some odd miles? That's no step for us steppers."

His companions agree with him. That is, partially agree. Charlie adds, "100 miles is 100 miles. But, on these damned rocky trails, it's more like 200 miles, time you add slipping and sliding to your forward progress. Maybe the trails aren't so bad as you go north. Maybe. Lord, I hope they're better."

Glum nods add the hopes of the three men to those of Charlie's. Anyway, their choices are simple: tolerate the rocky trails and continue toward the goal, or give up and call for a ride home, defeated. Nobody's ready to give up yet, so the next morning, bright and early, the four set out once again. The indomitable Charlie leads the way, singing, "We're off to see the Wizard, the wonderful Wizard of Oz . . . " With or without the yellow brick road. After all, only 60 miles to go to the next town, Palmerton.

Just like Dorothy and Toto, the Scarecrow, the Cowardly Lion, and the Tin Woodsman, the spirits of the hikers start high, but drop off, as they walk deeper into the woods. There are no wicked witches that they know of, at least none that they see, but the rocky trail is still their constant companion. Maybe the trail represents the Wicked Witch? Today, 14 miles of it to face. By mid-morning Gorp break, complaining is the order of the day. The four are sitting on fallen logs, fussing about and at the rocks as they rub sore ankles.

"Damn, Jon," says Charlie, "How many miles do we have to make according to that schedule of yours?"

Jon shows his frustration with the trail conditions, as he is somewhat short with his answer. He says, "Fourteen miles, but it isn't my schedule. I thought it was our schedule. I just carry it. "

Quiet settles on the four, broken by Charlie. "Sorry, Jon, I didn't mean to give you any shit. At least, no more than you deserve. You didn't put these damned rocks out here. Did you?"

Jon has to laugh. "Nope, sure didn't. If I had, I'd be using an ATV instead of my own two feet. This bitching isn't making it go any faster. We gotta face the trail, no matter what it throws us, or give up. I'm not ready for that; are you, Charlie?"

"Nope, got too much invested to quit. But, one thing I gotta make clear. I still get to bitch. That's part of my God-given right. It's on my job description–designated bitcher. But, I'll try to bitch at the trail, not at you guys. Now, why don't you two power-walkers get going up the trail, and George and I'll catch up with you later. If we don't get to Eagle's Nest Shelter today, we'll catch up with you two in Palmerton. Okay? Forgive me for whining at you?"

"Yeah, yeah, yeah. Nothing to forgive," growls Jon. To his amazement, Charlie rises from her spot on the log, runs over to Jon, and hits him with a perfect body block. As she knocks him off the log, Charlie sits on top of him, astride his stomach. She grabs him by the neck and hisses, "I said, forgive me? You'd better do it now, if you ever want to use this scrawny neck again!"

Jon is laughing so hard he can't say anything. As Charlie isn't moving and the rocks under him aren't getting any softer, he chokes out, "Yes, your majesty, I forgive you. You are in my good graces, never from which to tumble again. Now, get the hell off of me!"

Charlie rolls off him onto her back, laughing. George and Sam are also laughing so hard it's difficult to catch a breath. George says, "Jon, when this trail is over, you fortunate stiffs get to go back south to Alabama and Tennessee. On the other hand, I'm lucky enough to take this wildcat home with me."

Jon and Sam proceed up the trail, and George and Charlie rest a bit longer before they proceed at a slower pace. They don't get as far that day as the first pair, choosing to camp near water off the side of the trail.

Jon and Sam do pretty well on the schedule, as they make Eagle's Nest Shelter that night and Windsor Furnace Shelter the next night, but they fall behind as they don't complete the 18 miles projected the following day. Instead, they get only as far as the Eckville Shelter, 10 miles up the trail.

"Hey, Jon," pants Sam in mid-afternoon as they are sprawled alongside the still-rocky trail. I don't think I've got another 8 or 10 miles left in me today. How's about we stop one shelter short of the Allentown Hiking Club Shelter? I seem to remember that there's one a bit closer. These rocks are killing me."

Jon verifies in the guide that there is, indeed, a closer shelter, and he puts up very little fuss to stopping short for the day. Besides, George and Charlie are probably getting farther and farther behind with each passing hour on the trail. Their company is so enjoyable that Jon and Sam want to keep on hiking with them. So, they agree on Eckville shelter and opt to stop there for the night.

After an early dinner and a wash with water carried from the stream, the friends are lying on the lush pine needle carpet by their small campfire. Jon says, "I hope that George and Charlie catch up with us by the time we get to Palmerton. I believe that George could probably keep up with us by himself, but he's so thoughtful and protective of Charlie that he lags back."

After a moment, Sam responds, "Damn, bud. You sound a bit sexist. Good thing Charlie's not here."

A voice responds, "Why's it a good thing Charlie's not here?"

Jon and Sam shine their flashlights down the trail, and to their amazement, Charlie is leading an obviously pooped George up the final hundred feet of t he trail.

"You macho men thought that this poor little weak female couldn't keep up with you? Well, here we are. Got any more of that tea?" She deposits her pack on the ground and pours a cup, sitting by the fire. She turns and looks at Jon and Sam, "Jon, best close your mouth. There are bugs everywhere and you might swallow one. Damn, lucky for you guys that your Den Mother is as tough as she is. There's no way you could take care of yourself."

George fixes his and Charlie's macaroni and cheese. The four hit the bed early, determined to make an early start on the self-inflicted torture of the rocks.

The foursome makes pretty good time for the next two days and arrives in Palmerton late in the afternoon. There are no motels in town, but the city lets hikers sleep in the basement of the town hall. Happily, the bunk room comes complete with showers. After several showers each, they find a Laundromat and wash their clothes. They then visit Bert's Steakhouse and shock those patrons who haven't seen thru-hikers do their food thing. After dinner, they walk to a line of pay phones and make calls home. Sam hears from Andy that everything is fine in Alabama. Andy teases him about the irregularity of the articles in the newspaper. The teasing reminds Jon that he has to catch up with his notes that evening in order to keep his star status.

Jon hangs up and looks toward his friends. Sam is also finished with his call home, so they wait for Charlie and George, huddled together sharing one phone. They must be getting information of some kind, because Charlie is writing notes on the back of a scrap of paper. George hangs up and walks toward Jon and Sam, with an extremely long face. "Well, guys, got bad news. My father had a serious heart attack, and they are planning quintuple bypass surgery day after tomorrow. I guess that fate has thrown us another curve ball, and we won't complete the Trail this year either. Charlie's checking on bus schedules and, if we can set on one, we'll leave tonight."

Sam and Jon look like they feel–shell shocked, and they murmur sorrow and regret. George says, "Well, they say that Pop's chances are real good. He's a tough old bird: he's always said that he's not going anywhere until Charlie and I give him his first grandchild. Now that finishing this trail is off for another year, that grandbaby is also off for another year. That means Pop will have to hang around for that year. 'Cause we're gonna finish this trail. There's no way we won't."

Hugs and "good lucks" are exchanged all around. They walk to the Greyhound Bus Station at the general store, and Charlie gets them tickets for a bus leaving in a few hours–at midnight. They exchange addresses and telephone numbers, and the departing hikers give Jon and Sam odds and ends of dried food. The time passes quickly. Charlie, George and their packs are soon on the bus, leaving their saddened companions behind.

"Damn," says Jon, "that happened so fast. One minute we're enjoying those monstrous steaks and laughing as hard as usual; the next minute they're on a bus and gone. Gonna miss the hell out of those two. Not gonna be the same."

Mouths drooping like their spirits, Jon and Sam walk back to the town hall, where they toss and turn more than sleep. The next morning they decide that it's time to move on. Their spirits are still low and, since Palmerton is an unscheduled stop, neither man has a package waiting there. The Post office has no hold on them. Those next care packages should be waiting for them in Wind Gap, Pennsylvania, some 21 miles further north. So, they take off. They leave as the sun rises–walking slowly, buried in their own thoughts, remembering the good times shared with Charlie and George.

After a couple of hours of silent walking, Jon tests the sound of his own voice. "Sam, I think we ought to call them in a week or so to see how George's father did with the surgery. We can find out how they're adapting to civilian lowland life. I hear that the transition from the trail is plenty rough. I can't say that I'm looking forward to facing that myself, when, and if, this hike is ever over. I envy them in some ways. You have all the creature comforts of civilization within the reach of your arm, but I'll miss the solitude, the physical shape, the necessity of being self-reliant. I'll miss all that, big time."

Sam doesn't respond. Jon's soliloquy needs no answer. In fact, it is several hours before either of them says anything else. It just isn't necessary to talk sometimes.

That night, at the Leroy A. Smith Shelter, the withdrawn silence continues. Even though there are a dozen thru-hikers, the absence of quiet stables George and the effervescent Charlie, who obviously never met a stranger, puts a real damper on moods, but the two men begin to work through it. The 16-mile day, that the two had clattered and slipped through on the rocky trails, had worked much of the sadness out of them. The weary hikers hit their sleeping bags early and sleep soundly. Even the arrival of three more hikers long after dark wakes them for only a few minutes and, after passing greetings, they slip back into a hard, healing sleep.

The next morning their moods have improved, and they prepare for another hard, rocky day. One of the hikers, who had arrived late the night before says, "I envy you guys, heading north. We've just come from that way; you've got the worst of the rocky trails behind you. We've still got them to face."

Jon and Sam looked at each other. Jon breaks into a smile as he says, "That's the best news I've heard in many moons. We thought those damned rocky trails kept on forever. It's better to the north?"

The hiker says, "Yeah, though it's still not what I would call a nice, smooth forest path. The rocks are a little bit more scattered, and you'll even take a few steps on dirt. I've been down that trail south of here once before, and I've been dreading doing it again ever since. Fact is, I'm crazy for doing it again. Did you know that the rumor is that the trail workers carry files so they can . . . "

Sam laughs, "We heard that story down the trail. It may be true, but somehow I doubt it. Mother Nature has done a fine job sharpening those rocks all by herself–with no help. Thanks for the good news, though. We appreciate it a bunch. We weren't sure how far the bad stretch of trails went."

Jon and Sam sling on their packs and stride away. Somehow, after the discussion with the other hiker about the trail ahead, the loads don't seem so heavy, and the trail definitely feels better. The departure of George and Charlie's gets further away.

Wind Gap is a short four and a half mile hike over the slightly improved trails, and the men arrive well before noon. Both care packages are waiting at the post office, as is that for George and Charlie. Their departed companions' package is returned to the sender. The men again de-Madison Avenue the new packages of dried and processed food while sitting on a curb in the warm sun. Jon finishes before Sam, and his eyelids grow heavy as he sits. During a meal at

Tony's Pizza Parlor, Jon and Sam take a look at the map and the Trail Guide. Jon says, "You know, Sam, Kirkridge Shelter is only eight and a half miles up the trail. You got any energy left?"

Sam thinks a minute and says, "Yeah, I never thought I'd agree to leaving creature comforts to hit the trail, but let's do it. That should help our progress. Yeah, let's do it."

Jon says, "It does put us back on my guesses as to the best places to stay, you know, 12 miles to here, 14 miles to here, and such. I still don't intend for this damned schedule to rule us, but it has helped so far."

Sam laughs, "What's the matter? The teasing from Charlie about the schedule being the boss hit a nerve? Don't pay it any attention. That schedule has really helped. Now, if we're gonna do eight and a half miles before the wilderness god of darkness covers us up, we'd best git." They got.

They huff and puff into Kirkridge Shelter just ahead of darkness. Darkness in the mountains can be a little on the scary side, particularly when it's the first time you've ever been there. Jon and Sam have been caught before trying to make a few more miles, and they try to avoid hiking in the dark, whenever they can. This time, they succeed.

Several hikers are already set up at the shelter. Greetings, gossip, and news–about what has happened to hikers they know in common, are the order of business. Trail names are an integral part of the AT culture, though sometimes strange sounding. The thru-hikers recognize the names they hear. Dinner passes and sack time approaches. This night, shelter mice are numerous and extremely active. Jon is awakened by their racket, as they chatter at one another and hustle around on micely errands. One of the hikers has a melodious snore. It's repetitive in nature, and Jon gets used to it. That is, he would if the snore didn't have a break near the end, making Jon jump every time it occurs. Finally, weariness wins the battle, and neither mice nor snores keep Jon from getting enough sleep.

At breakfast Jon and Sam pore over the guide and realize that on this day, they will pass another milestone. What the psychologists would call an interim reward.

Fancy words that are real in a day-to-day way for the thru-hiker. The interim rewards keep a hiker going. Only a few miles to such-and-such. Never mind that it's 1000 to the end. Focus on the distance of a few miles. That's attainable. A thousand miles is incomprehensible, unattainable. In this case, in six and a half miles Jon and Sam will cross the Pennsylvania-New Jersey state line. One more state conquered and left in the dust! Although in the case of Pennsylvania's infamous rocks, maybe a draw? Hopefully, the trails will continue to improve. Jon asks Sam, "Hey, Bud, You reckon that rocks can read maps? Surely they know that we're about to be in another state, and they ain't welcome?"

Sam laughs, "I bet they can't read. We can, though. Let's hit the trail. Somebody told me that the Delaware River Bridge is right pretty. According to your guide, we still have three miles to the campsite past the bridge. Let's roll!"

Jon says, "Don't you mean Roll, Tide? You know where I went to school."

Sam grimaces. "Nah, whatever I meant, it wasn't that. Remember I went to the University of Memphis. More like, Go, Big Blue!"

The men sling on their packs and start up the trail. They earn strange looks as they proceed, because Jon and Sam are simultaneously singing school songs at the top of their voices. Both men obviously go with the theory that quantity can replace quality.

Summer heat is beginning to be a problem, and heat rashes become aggravating to both men. Lotion becomes an important part of their gear, and they now stow it in an easy to reach pocket of the pack. To add to their misery, water is also not as easy to find as it was to the south, and their small water purification systems get a real workout. They keep on going and arrive at Campsite Number 1 in mid-afternoon. They realize that they need plenty of rest tonight, because the next shelter up the line requires a walk of 21 miles tomorrow.

When Jon points that out, Sam makes a face, even though he already knows that tomorrow will be a rough day. Sam says, "Tomorrow, tomorrow. I get tired of that word sometimes."

Jon strikes a dramatic pose. "Tomorrow and tomorrow and tomorrow, creeps in this petty pace from day to day . . . Sorry, Mr. Shakespeare. But you know, you're right. Did you ever realize that tomorrow is a non-entity? Tomorrow never gets here. Tomorrow becomes today and is no longer tomorrow. Then, the next day, it becomes yesterday. Damn, it's enough to make your head hurt–too deep and philosophical for me."

Jon rolls off the log on which he is sitting and lies flat on his back, looking at the darkening sky through the gently waving branches. "Plumb pretty up here. Makes you a bit closer to God. Physically as well as mentally."

With his silence Sam agrees, and the friends rest. A sort of pre-bedtime nap. One from which you have to wake to go to bed.

13 "THE 'NEW STATES WILDERNESS IN THE MEGALOPOLIS"

"Well," says Sam, after he goes through his stretching, yawning, toe-touching routine. "Here we are, in the middle of nowhere, surrounded by all the Northerners in the world. I feel a little like Lee musta felt at Appomattox Courthouse. How civilized is the trail as we go through New Jersey, anyway?"

"Well, according to the handy-dandy guide, the AT is really pretty remote through Jersey. More remote than in New York and Connecticut, anyway. We've got 70 miles of the first of the "New" states with a few tough climbs. No tough climbs today."

"How many miles did you say we got in front of us today?"

Jon mumbles, "I didn't say. But, it's tw-w-w-w . . ."

"I can't hear you–speak up."

"I didn't want to say it too loud. Twenty-one. Lucky number if you're playing Blackjack. Tough number if you're hiking."

"Damn, damn, damn. We got any other choice?"

"Not really. At least none I can see. No shelters, no campsites. 'Cept for one that's only a mile and a half up the trail."

"Mile and a half–sounds good to me. Just the right distance to hike in a day. Let's get started. What's it called?"

"Campsite Number 2. Creative name, eh what?"

"Ayah, reckon so. There, I'm practicing my Maine-ese. Getting ready so's we can communicate with those folks when we get there."

Jon just shakes his head. Sam has turned into a different person over the miles. They groan into their packs and hit the trail.

Later that morning, during slip-into-your-own-mind-time, Jon meditates on the thought he had earlier that morning–the one about Sam changing. If changes in Sam's attitude and personality are that obvious, what about his own? What about Jon Parker? He knows inside himself, that he's changed. Much more confident. He'd set a goal and was still pursuing it. No quitting. Plenty of doubts, pain, sweat, even a few tears. If this hike had been several years ago, something as traumatic as Pookie's death would have turned his brain into cornmeal mush. A good excuse to quit, withdraw, go back to more familiar people, places, and things, where his failures were already accepted. Yet, here he is, pounding a hard trail, soaked with sweat, but still hiking. Damn, maybe I'm finally growing up. Downright scary!

It's been a long morning. At lunch, Jon and Sam and Humpin' Joe, another hiker who has hooked up with them, shed their packs and collapse gratefully in the leaves next to a small spring trickling out of the base of a rock bluff. Below the bluff lie large boulders, separated from the in-place rocks by thousands of years of Mother Nature's patient weathering process. The men are enjoying doing absolutely nothing.

Joe asks, "What's this spring called?"

Jon says, "The guide says it's Rattlesnake Spring. Hopefully, there aren't any of those critters around."

Joe looks up with a spark of interest shining in his eyes. "I wonder if there are any rattlers here. I used to go snake hunting with my brothers and cousins back in Texas. I think I'll go see what I can scare up."

Sam gets up from the ground and follows Joe towards the bluff. Sam says, "These rocks look like a giant's been tossing building blocks around. Some of these things are the size of a trailer."

Joe climbs onto one large boulder and jumps to the next, followed closely by Sam. The men rock hop until they get near the rock bluff.

"See anything? asks Jon.

"Nah, I think the name's a fraud," answers Joe.

Joe looks around for a good place to put his hand to climb onto the bluff. He reaches out, then freezes at a sudden sound as loud as a troop of Spanish castanet dancers. Jon later says that he would have given anything to have had a video camera to record for posterity what happens next. Joe takes a tentative step back into Sam. The two men slowly inch back, feet moving as if choreographed; then they turn and run over the loose boulders with Olympic-class speed. They tumble in a pile at Jon's feet.

"Welcome back, fellas. What happened to the great white hunters?"

"Snakes," stammers Sam. "Not snake, but snakes! Dozens of them. Slithering everywhere. Damn! My skin's still crawling."

"I never saw such a nest," adds Joe.

Jon adds a needle. "I thought you were an old hand at rattler catching, back in Texas."

"I am! I was!" stammers Joe. "But, I caught 'em one at a time. Not bunches of 'em."

"Excuses, excuses," teases Jon. "Boy, if we're ever starving, no rattler meat for us. I'll have to find better, braver hunters somewhere else."

"Huh." says Sam.

"I agree," adds Joe.

Breaktime is mutually agreed to be concluded, and the pace north on the trail is somewhat brisker for the next mile. At the first water break, Jon checks his ever-present *Trail Guide*. "If it makes you guys feel any better, 'bout eight miles from here, you'll have another chance. We climb Rattlesnake Mountain there."

"Seen enough snakes for a while," mumbles Joe.

"Seen enough snakes for a lifetime," adds Sam.

Jon's only response is laughter. Lots of it.

They safely navigate the mountain with no signs of reptilian companions and arrive at Brink Road Shelter. After they remove their packs, Jon announces, "Well, guys, I'm gonna order a rattler to be placed every mile or two up the trail the rest of the way to Maine."

"Are you nuts?" queries Sam.

"Nope, just smart. Do you realize we've covered 21 and a half miles today without a single whine? The adrenaline rush those little fellas gave us drove us along with a single thought–get the hell out of there."

"Little fellas, my ass," says Joe. "Them were keepers. More than I care for."

Sam says, "Okay, Jon, you gonna rag us for the next 1000 miles about those snakes?"

"Nope," says Jon, and Sam's face brightens. "Nope, just until you guys quit turning red every time I mention them. When it's no fun anymore, then I'll quit."

"Shit," says Sam, and Joe just shakes his head.

"I'll make a deal with you snake hunters, though. I've got a fair proposition for you guys."

"We've listening," comes a chorus.

"You guys get water, cook dinner, wash the dishes, and build a fire and make my tea," and I won't mention the snakes the rest of this evening."

"Damned blackmailer," says Sam. "I won't do it just to shut you up. Fix your own damn dinner."

With Hollywood-quality scheduling, voices sound from the woods outside the clearing. Jon smiles, much like a crocodile eyeing his next meal. "Okay, just for tonight. Shut the hell up," growls Sam.

"Okay," says Jon in an extremely cheerful tone of voice. "Best hop to it, to buy my silence."

It is a very good evening for Jon. The four hikers, who had arrived with impeccable timing, watched in amazement as Sam and Joe wait on Jon, hand

and foot, for the entire evening. Early the next morning, Joe, the mighty snake hunter, sneaks away and heads up the trail before anyone else wakes up. He isn't seen again.

At Rutherford Shelter, Jon, Sam and Pete, agree to stop for the night. Staying in this shelter is against their better judgment, because it's a short distance from Highway 23, and easily accessible to the local folks. Compounding their feelings of uneasiness is the fact that it's Saturday night, and in some areas, the local red-necks count harassing hikers as a close third to their two favorite occupations, drinking beer and chasing women. After copious quantities of the first and unsuccessful attempts at the second, priority three moves up.

Uneasy or not, the weary hikers prepare to spend the night. It has been a rough day. The trail in the area is covered with loose shale rock, and ankles and legs are tired from straining to remain vertical. Even with the extra attempts at balance, the hikers have each fallen at least once during the day, and bruises and battered elbows are painful. Jon says, "I don't think we'd better have a campfire tonight. No sense in advertising our presence."

Sam gestures at the floor of the shelter and the ground outside, strewn with beer cans, chip bags, and other items indicative of frequent partying. "Don't look to me as if we need to advertise. The rednecks definitely know this shelter's here. You reckon we ought to reconsider and set up our tents up the trail a bit?" "Nah" gives him the answer, and majority rules for the shelter. Dinner and bedtime preparations take their minds off of any possible problems.

At eleven o'clock, several hours after the hikers have fallen asleep, a noise awakens them. It's the sound of a car with either twin fiberglass mufflers or no muffler at all. The three hikers lie awake in their sleeping bags and will the noise to go away, to no avail. The car comes to a stop down the road from the shelter, rumbles as it is shut down, and the sound of voices reaches their ears. "Damn, guys," says Pete. "Shoulda taken your advice, Sam. I guess we'd best get up."

The three men crawl out of their sleeping bags, determined to be ready for the worst. The voices get louder, and they see flashlights sweeping the woods on either side, as the car's inhabitants loudly discuss a variety of subjects ranging from the relative merits of different types of beer to why Suzy Jane won't put out. The conversations become clearer as the men draw near.

"You wanna know why she won't put out for you? I'll tell you why. It's cause you grab for her tits as soon as she gets in the car, that's why."

"Yeah Zack, you dumbass. Women gotta feel good about you. You gotta spend some money on them first. You know, buy her a beer or something. Then you got a shot. Don't you know nothing?"

Zack retorts, "Damned if I'm gonna spend any bucks on her. I barely got enough money to buy my own beer."

His two harassers chime in, "Then you ain't gonna get any, dummy. That's what we're trying to tell you."

This enlightened conversation gets the men into the clearing surrounding the shelter, and the hikers can see the drunks. "Damn," whispers Jon, "there are five, no six of them! I hope they don't think hikers are fair game. This reminds me of Deliverance."

To the surprise of the hikers, nobody comes near the shelter as the six drunks stagger around through the woods collecting wood to start a fire. They continue to add wood, until the blaze illuminates the trees and bushes with an eerie light. As the branches gently move in the breeze and as the men outside move around the fire, the scene takes on a surrealistic look. Happily for the hikers, no one has yet visited the shelter, and their presence is undetected. Sam, Jon, and Pete continue to lurk in the protective shadows of the shelter walls.

That situation is bound to change. It does, as one of the drunks stands up and wanders toward the shelter. He announces that he's gonna see if any of them damned hikers have left anything worthwhile in the shelter. His light bounces and sweeps the ground and the tree tops in succession as he approaches.

His light passes by Jon, standing in the dark corner, then returns to illuminate his face. "Lookee here, guys, I got a hiker." His light finds Sam and Pete. "Shit, I got three of them hikers. Com'ere!"

The other drunks stumble over, and the hikers find themselves uncomfortably in the glare of six bright flashlights. "Whatta ya reckon we ought to do with them, now that we caught them?" asks Zack, obviously the leader of the group.

"Don't know, but we gotta teach them a lesson–so's they won't come back and bother us no more," says one of the men.

"Yeah, like we did with that camper couple of months ago. Don't reckon he'll be back, will he?"

The six drunks laugh at the memory of the lone hiker they had pounded. One man says, "Just in case you three get any ideas, I got my equalizer here," and to the horror of the hikers, he unsteadily waves a large revolver around his head. "You three come on out here to the fire, where we can get a good look at you while we decide what to do. Now, dammit!" he yells.

Jon, Sam, and Pete do as instructed. They are then roughly pushed to the ground by the bonfire. Several of the drunks dump the packs on the ground and begin pawing through the contents, looking for anything of value. The first thing they find that they deem of value is the small flask that Pete carries, filled with brandy. A swallow apiece, and the flask is emptied in a minute. The search continues.

Jon tries reasoning with the armed man. "Hey, man, we're not going to bother you guys. Go on with your partying and let us go. We'll go on up the trail and be out of here and won't be back."

The man laughs derisively and waves the revolver around for emphasis. "I reckon you'll leave when, and if, we decide you will. Not before. Now, shut the hell up before I shut your mouth for you."

Jon shuts up. After the booty hunters decide that there is very little worth stealing, except for a few small items like flashlights and knives, they come back to the fire and divide the spoils. Their conversation continues. Suggestions, as to the fate of the hikers fly around the campfire, ranging from killing them and hiding their bodies to beating them.

Zack yells at one of his buddies, whose head has dropped to his chest, victim of too much beer. "Hey Billy! Wake your ass up. It ain't bedtime yet. Not till I say so."

Billy's head snaps upright, but he loses the struggle, and his chin slowly sinks back to his chest. Zack tries again with no success. "Damn, we're either gonna have to carry him or leave his ass here in the woods. Shit, Joey, you 'bout gone too?" He yells at the man with the gun, whose head is nodding deeper and deeper. "Shit, you guys ain't worth nothing. Okay, you shits, got any money?"

Sam digs in his pockets, "Yeah, I got ten bucks. Here, take it." Jon and Pete follow suit and hand over 15 more dollars, which Zack stuffs into his dirty Jean pockets.

"This'll buy us more beer. But, y'all better get the hell out of here. We don't like no damn hikers. This here is our party place, and we don't want no stinkin' hikers here. Come on you guys, let's go get some more brew."

Zack kicks the two men passed out by the fire. He succeeds in rousing Joey who responds by firing three shots into the air. Everybody jumps: the sound is loud as a cannon. Billy proves too far gone and the other five drag him along behind them as they unsteadily lurch out of the clearing. The three trembling hikers hear the sound of the car grumbling to life, and gravel is slung behind as it roars away. Zack yells out the window, "Hey, hikers, we'll be back!"

Collective breaths are released. The men look at each other. "Damn! I thought we were gonners," says Jon. I 'bout peed in my pants when that asshole fired that gun."

"I don't know about you guys, but my butt is outta here. Lucky I keep my small flashlight under my pillow, when I sleep. At least we can see." responds Pete. Packs are hurriedly loaded, they extinguish the fire, and the three make their way by the one flashlight for a mile and a half until they feel they are safe from pursuit. They leave the trail and set up their tents several hundred yards from the trail well out of sight. The ground is uneven and rocky and not a place they would ordinarily choose for camping, but the tents look like the finest motels to the three. They crawl in and restlessly sleep with no further interruptions for the rest of the night.

Sunrise the next morning finds the three men drinking coffee while sitting on logs near their tents, somberly considering the "coulda-beens" of their adventure. They decide that they will listen to the sage words of other thru-hikers about not using shelters frequented by the locals. Definitely a hazard to your health. Jon shakes his head, "Fellas, it scared the hell out of me. If I even think about occupying a shelter within a mile of a road again, go ahead and have me committed. Never again."

Sam agrees. "Yeah, we were sure lucky that nobody was hurt. I wonder if those crazies came back again."

Jon has to laugh, "Well, I don't doubt that Zack was capable of downing more beer. But if he came back, he had to have found a new supporting cast. The one he had was 'bout wasted."

All three men laugh, releasing the remnants of the tension that had kept them from sleeping very well. It's difficult for your body to relax and sleep well when you've got one ear listening hard for any sounds that don't belong in the forest. They wash their breakfast dishes and make a quick inventory of what is missing from their packs. They decide to replace the odds and ends that the drunks had ripped off at the next supply store. All three have more money, secreted in places in their packs that the drunks did not or could not find. Packing complete, they hoist their packs and continue up the trail, resolved to report the incident to the authorities, when they arrive at their next off-trail stop.

They cover the 16 miles to Rutherford Shelter and share the bunk space with three south-bound hikers. Jon writes about the redneck encounter in the trail register in the shelter. The discussion after dinner is about the wild night they had spent, and the south-bounders vow to move through that area quickly and stay in the forest. They warn Jon, Sam, and Pete that the next shelter, Pochunk Mountain, is a pretty one, but has a distinct disadvantage. It has no water supply, so they have to carry enough water for two days.

Jon scratches his head. "Damn, all I've got are the two one-liter bottles I carry every day. That won't work for two days. I guess I'll have to fill my collapsible container with a gallon or so. That'll have to work, although it'll be a pain, carrying it in my hands all day."

One of the southbounders laughs. "Naw, man, it's not that bad. Look at your handy-dandy *Trail Guide*."

Jon slaps his forehead, Three Stooges style. "Damn, I guess I thought I knew the trail by heart. What a dummy." He pulls the guide from his pack and turns the well-worn pages. "Lookie there. We cross a stream four tenths of a mile before the shelter. That's a lot better."

Sam and Pete agree, and the sounds of silence descend on the shelter. They sleep much better than they did the night before. Compared to a thundering herd of drunken rednecks, mice and strange snores are no problem at all.

The next morning the three pack up and start on their next to last day in New Jersey. After one more night, they'll begin the 100 miles of AT in New York State. One more state traversed. Seven states down, six to go. The miles of trail they still have to face don't sound quite so bad that way.

The 15-mile hike that day to Pochuck Mountain Shelter is not bad. The relief from the rocks of Pennsylvania make about any trail more tolerable. They stop and fill their water bottles and jugs at the stream and arrive at the shelter with no problems. As they deposit their packs, Jon flexes his hands. "You know, guys, that water container could get to be pretty painful, if you had to carry it for miles. I guess I'd better keep a better eye on the guide, so we'll know when that sort of torture is called for. Remind me every once in a while, okay?"

Sam and Pete agree and they start setting up their beds and cooking gear. The shelter gets louder as four college students arrive, and the quiet of the mountain is definitely disturbed. The seven get along well, and Jon and Sam enjoy hearing about the modern-day college life. The only problem is, it makes them feel like the old men in the crowd. Particularly when one cute coed calls Jon "Sir." His ego is crushed. Their days in college seem like they were eons ago. For that matter, the day they started on their thru-hike seems like it was eons ago, not just a few months.

The following morning the college students move on south. Pete hikes on ahead and Jon and Sam complete their chores. Jon sits back on a log and says, "Sam, I'm suddenly feeling very much tired and very old. I don't know what it is, but I don't like it. I haven't had thoughts for quite a while about giving up, but that's the dammit way I feel today. How about you? Want to quit?"

"Well, I won't go that far, but I know where you're coming from. I'm kinda in a blue funk myself. I guess it's partly because Charlie and George are gone. It's really quiet around here. Too quiet."

Jon agrees, "I think you're right. It's also maybe because we've got seven more nights and 90 miles to go before we get a motel break. This was a long stretch–I maybe shoulda scheduled a little better, but I couldn't figure a way just looking at the guidebook."

Sam says, "Don't beat yourself up. You didn't have a crystal ball–just that *Trail Guide*. You did the best you could."

Sam's explanation not withstanding, gloom and doom settle over the two as surely as the black cloud used to settle over the Lil' Abner character. Accompanied by sighs and groans, the men struggle up the trail.

At lunch Jon pulls out the ever-present guide and announces to Sam, "Hey, guy, I just noticed something. Sometime today we'll break a barrier. We'll have less than 1000 miles to go. Plus, tomorrow we'll cross into New York state. Another milestone. Damn, we're good."

Sam chuckles, "What're you trying to do, cheer me up? That does sound pretty good, though. Damned good, in fact."

Spirits somewhat revived, they move on. Progress is good for the next few days. They get a neat interlude two days later, as they tour the Trailside Museum and Zoo the night before getting to Hemlock Springs. It's the first non-shelter campsite they've stayed at in a while, at least since their run-in with the rednecks. Sometimes the tents are enjoyable, particularly if the shelter is crowded. But when you're exhausted after a long day, the shelters are convenient, even when crowded with other stinky thru-hikers.

That night, while sitting around the stoves willing them to boil the tea water, Jon says, "Well, we're almost to civilization. We camp tomorrow night at Dennytown Road, then a shelter at Hortontown Road, then town. I may make it! How about you?"

"Yeah, I think so. I'm getting mighty low on supplies. 'Bout out of everything. The big city can't come fast enough for me."

"You betcha. I can't wait. I can taste pizza, fried chicken, eggs and bacon, pancakes . . ."

"Whoa! Enough, already. Here I am burping pasta and cheese, and you're dangling real food out there."

The men get rained on the next day, but by early afternoon it quits, and the hot sunshine sends clouds of vapor ascending above them. The sunshine lifts their spirits again, and they're downright cheerful as they arrive at Dennytown Road Shelter. The good moods continue the next day to Hortontown Road.

They share that shelter with six south-bound thru-hikers. The inevitable trail gossip and conditions, mean dogs, and redneck alert warnings are swapped, and all are a little more up to date on what they'll face farther along their trail.

The 12-mile day to Poughquaq, New York, is a piece of cake for Sam and Jon. At the same time, it seems to take forever, particularly because it's been 15 days since their last care package, back in Ashfield, Pennsylvania. Their food supply has dwindled to almost nothing, and they had to share dinner last night. They somehow managed to make two cups of tea out of one bag. It was more like colored water than tea.

During lunch, what there is of it, Jon works on his feet. He removes his boots and carefully inspects his right big toe, which has become increasingly more painful and has turned an angry red. Sam says, "Damn, bud, if it were nighttime, we could use that toe of yours to light up the trail. Sore, huh?"

"You bet. I used my last scrap of Moleskin yesterday. That place where my boot upper has popped some stitches is driving me nuts. First thing I find in town has to be a shoe repair place. Maybe they can stitch it to last for a while, anyway."

Sam digs in his pack and finds one large bandage. "Here, Jon, not as good as Moleskin, but it oughta help some." Jon puts the bandage on, and gingerly tests his boot.

"Yeah, I should make it now. Let's rock 'n roll."

They arrive at the road to Poughquaq in mid-afternoon and catch a ride for the mile and a half trip to town within a half hour. They are dropped off at the motel and thank the driver. As Jon turns to enter the office, a young couple comes out. Jon's jaw drops open.

"Charlie! George! Where the hell did you guys come from? What're you doing here?"

"One question at a time," laughs Charlie. "Now shut up and give me a hug." Jon complies.

Jon says, "Charlie, you smell good. Like–like–soap."

Charlie pushes him to arm's length. "I hate to be the one to tell you, but you don't smell so good. Pretty bad, in fact. Now hush up and go shower. We can answer questions later, when we can stand being in the same room. Phew!"

Sam receives his hug, and the two hikers head for the showers. After donning clean shorts and T-shirts, they stuff their filthy clothes into laundry bags. They exit their room and find their seemingly resurrected friends sitting in lawn chairs by the swimming pool. Jon says, "Okay, now, what are you doing here? Just visiting?"

George responds, "Nope, we're back to stay. Pop came through his bypass surgery with flying colors. He was up and about two days after the operation and out of the hospital in a week. He says the only thing he vaguely remembers about the operating room was that he had some pretty wild dreams and the doctor told him that that was normal. Doc was pleased with Pop's progress, and Pop insisted that we come back out here. We've still got to pick up that part of the trail that we missed to be full-fledged thru-hikers, but we decided that we'd rather finish the rest of what's ahead with you guys."

Jon asks, "How the hell did you find us?"

Charlie laughs. "Well, we bought our very own *Trail Guide*, figured that you guys would make a bit better time without dragging poor Charlie along, and guessed you'd be here yesterday or today. We got a ride here with my aunt yesterday, and we've been enjoying the night lights of Poughquaq since. Now, you guys gonna shut up and get something to eat, or are you gonna keep on ratchet jawing?"

Jon laughs, "Same old Charlie. I don't know how we survived on the trail without you."

"Me either," she responds. "Come on, guys, tell Momma all about it. What went wrong, what'd you see, what'd you do. Tell me everything."

Charlie links arms with Jon and Sam, leaving George to bring up the rear of the procession, and they do serious damage to the local pizza parlor's profit margin. The chattering is punctuated with bites of pizza, and plans are laid for the next assault on the trail.

After sleeping late, house keeping is next on tap, and Jon finds a local shoe repair place. The cobbler inspects the offending boot and agrees to stitch the split seam. He warns, "This should hold up for a while, but no guarantees. You aren't gonna make it to Maine on these boots. I suggest you get another pair."

Jon groans. He admits that this is his second and last pre-broken in boots, and says, "Boy, I hate to think about breaking in another pair. Hurts to think about it."

The man proves to be a good salesman, and Jon leaves the store wearing stiff new boots. He figures he can stand them for an hour or so and will work with them a little bit at a time. At the Laundromat he rubs leather dressing into the boot and flexes them with his hands, trying to rub the agony out of them. Some of it, anyway.

Jon and Sam link up again with George and Charlie, and they enjoy additional catching up over lunch. All four need re-supply, so they visit the grocery store and the outfitter shop. Back at the motel, they stow the new goodies in their packs and proclaim themselves ready to go in the morning.

The evening is spent enjoying dinner and a movie, and the four rest well that night. Early in the morning, they depart, filled with optimism and grateful to be hiking again as a herd. Adding to their excitement is the fact that in two days they will cross the New York-Connecticut line and be that much closer to their ultimate goal.

Fourteen miles and one night later, the together– again foursome complete that milestone and cross into Connecticut. Eight states down, five to go. Jon says to his companions, "Well, guys, if you're interested in definitions, I heard or read somewhere that we just completed the middle section of the trail. Now, we're on the upper section. If you look at it that way, we've got two down and one to go. Sounds as if we're even closer to the end of the trail, huh?"

Sam, George, and Charlie aren't really interested in Jon's definition. They just keep on walking.

14 "TRUE CONNECTICUT YANKEES (BUT, NO KING ARTHUR IN SIGHT)"

At their first water break in Connecticut, Jon reads from his ever-present information packet. "Okay, guys, it seems that we're about to go back into wilderness, at least compared with New Jersey and New York. Bigger mountains with better views and fewer local yokels. The only trouble I've found with pretty views is that you've got to climb to there. Strange how that works, isn't it?"

Charlie announces, "You know, guys, I've just come to a momentous decision. You interested?"

"Sure, Charlie, we've always interested in hearing what you've got to say," says Sam. "Is it about philosophy, logistics, or what you're gonna do with your life when you finally decide to grow up? Seems like everything any of us have to say up here is about one of those subjects."

"It falls in the category of meta-physical philosophy and borders on geology. It occurs to me that the trail pays no attention at all to what state it happens to be in at the time. You know, this trail isn't a bit different from that in New York. The trail just goes on and on and on. It decides whether it's gonna be flat or steep, smooth or rocky, or whatever. It just goes on and on, forever."

"Forever, huh," says George. "You reckon that this trail really stops at a place called Katahdin? Or does it go on to infinity, and they're just yanking our chains to keep us going?"

Charlie laughs, "Lots of times when I think the end of the trail is just a myth. But, today it's nice, and, for some strange reason, I'm enjoying you guys' company. I'm sure I'll have reason to change that feeling as the day goes on. Now, we'd best get going. Which one of you gentlemen offers to carry my pack for the next few miles?"

The three men ignore Charlie's question, strap on their packs, and walk up the trail. They leave Charlie sitting on a log in the small clearing. She catches up with them in 10 minutes, still sputtering and loudly doubting their chivalry and manners.

They arrive at Rattlesnake Den, their camping site for the night. As they shuck their packs, Sam looks at Jon with a stern expression on his face. "Before you even start on the name of this place, don't."

Jon laughs so hard that he rolls on the ground, holding his side. Charlie and George look at him with puzzled expressions. "Okay," says Charlie, "You gonna let us in on the joke?"

"No," says Jon. "That is, as long as Sam goes along with our deal."

"Shit no," responds Sam. "I'll be damned if I'm gonna go along with blackmail for another 1000 miles. Go ahead; tell it; get it over with." He walks away, looking for firewood. Jon tells George and Charlie the saga of the mighty hunters, and they're still laughing when Sam comes back 15 minutes later, bearing an armload of branches. "Hey, Sam," says Charlie. "Did you check real good to see if there were any snakes in that wood?"

Sam mumbles something and turns beet red. When he doesn't respond to any of their teasing during the evening, eventually they let up. When you get no response, teasing isn't much fun.

The following morning, George asks Jon, "Hey, fearless leader, sneak a peek at that magic guide, and tell me how many nights we have to go before we resupply. I'm just curious."

Jon pulls the guide out and reads as he walks. "Let's see, we've got nine nights to go. Let me count. That's eight shelters and one campsite. Why, you got a hot date in North Adams?"

Charlie laughs a chuckle that contains little mirth. "The only hot date this guy has is with me. That is, unless he aspires to being hurt. Physically hurt, that is."

"No, I was just curious. I was trying to take care of my sweet little wife, that's all. How long are the days?"

Jon returns to the guide. "Well, pretty short to start. The first five days are in the 8- to 10-mile range. Then the last four days are pretty long. Sixteen to 21 miles. We can check tonight to see if we can shorten those."

George says, "Yeah, that's a good idea. Charlie's knees have been doing pretty well, and I don't want to push it."

Charlie, who is leading the pack at the time, stops dead in the center of the trail, causing a chain-reaction pile-up. "Why don't you guys just talk about me as if I'm not even here? What am I, chopped liver? I've told you before and I'll tell you again, I can do whatever you men can do. Now, we gonna talk or hike?"

As she stomps away, the three men look at each other in amazement. "Damn," says Sam, "I never saw anybody who could walk with a definite flounce while carrying a 35-pound pack. Damned if she doesn't pull it off with style and grace."

George holds a number of whispered conversations with Charlie the rest of the way to Stewart Hollow Brook Lean-to, to convince her that he isn't doubting her ability to keep up with the men. She stretches his discomfort out as long as she can before laughing at him. "I'll tell you what, Dummy. I reckon I'm good enough to become a Hollywood actress, seeing that you can't tell when I'm serious or funning you. But, thanks for worrying about my knees. They're fine. If I see trouble ahead with those few long days, you'll be the first to know after me. Now, how about serving my dinner, while I rest in my sleeping bag." She dramatically holds the back of her wrist to her forehead. "You know we Southern women are frail and can't do for ourselves. Hop to it, froggy."

Off the hook, George does as instructed, and Jon and Sam have a good time laughing at his discomfort.

The next morning the group moves out, all carrying their own gear and passing out no new harassment. The weather is gray and overcast, and the wind is blowing slightly. But, no rain. At least, not yet. It's a fairly short day, only 11 miles or so, and the hardened hikers breeze through the day with no problems. They share the shelter with two north-bound hikers and two south-bounders, and the conversations about up-coming attractions are lively.

The shelter mice are quite active, and a skunk tries to visit, but it is persuaded to move on where there's less commotion. They sleep well. In the morning, the weather looks like the day before, but a bit more threatening. In fact, it sprinkles on them off and on during the morning. Today is a 12-mile day. As they take a mid-morning rest break, Jon looks through the *Trail Guide* and discovers that Falls Village is only a half-mile off the trail, and they should be there right at lunch time. He suggests a break, and, not being able to resist temptation, they decide to go to the country restaurant in the village.

After being seated around the table in The Inn, Jon says, "See, a lazy leader can be a good leader. I wasn't ready for a can of Vienna Sausage and crackers. We deserve it, let's enjoy it. Besides, I can resist anything but temptation."

The waitress takes their order and asks, "Are you guys going to weather out the storm here, or go back on the trail?"

Sam asks, "We're not aware of any storm. We haven't seen a newspaper in days."

The waitress brings a copy of the morning paper to the table, then she takes their orders. The four read the headline, which announces that the northern seaboard of the United States is expected to be in the path of a tropical storm, named Sally. Sam says, "Damn, that's my ex-wife's name. That's not a good sign. She was steps above a tropical storm. Did I ever tell you guys about my allergies?"

Charlie laughs, "What in the world do your allergies have to do with a tropical storm or your ex-wife? I don't see the connection."

"Well, no connection with the storm. I just thought it was a funny story. But if you don't want to hear it, that's okay. It won't hurt my feelings." He pouts.

"No, no, go ahead. We wouldn't want to hurt your feelings, Sam."

"Okay, I'll tell you. A few years ago, I became inflicted with hives. Skin hives that really hurt when they swelled up, and they were driving me crazy. I went to a skin doctor who specialized in allergies, and he put me through that medieval torture. The one where they prick you with 200 needles that have different substances. I went back two days later, and the red whelps made it obvious which represented allergies. Turns out I was allergic to dust, mold, seafood, and several trees. For several months, I avoided dust and seafood, and stayed out of the woods. The seafood denial really hurt–I love seafood! All kinds of seafood. But, the hives didn't get any better. They still hurt."

He falls silent; the other three wait patiently for the conclusion of his story. Charlie finally asks, "Okay, Sam, you have us on the hook. What happened next?"

"Well, about that time, my wife and I were really having problems, and she finally moved out. It turned out that what I was mainly allergic to was my wife. When she left, the hives left with her and haven't come back since. Boy, I enjoy seafood. No hives at all." He falls silent again, and Jon, Sam, and Charlie shake their heads in amazement at their friend and his stories. The waitress brings their food, and they shake their heads again. Sam has ordered a huge fried seafood platter, the Admiral's Feast, and he attacks it with great gusto.

While enjoying coffee after lunch, they discuss the coming storm. Jon reads from the newspaper, "It says that the storm may or may not hit this part of the country. You know how weather forecasters are. I think we should go on about our business. The most we may get is heavy rain for a day or so. We can handle that."

Charlie asks, "Will we have shelters for the next three or four days, or will we have to put up tents?"

Jon pulls out his guide. "Let's see, shelter, shelter, camp, then four shelters in a row. Looks like tents on the third night only. That shouldn't be too bad. What do you guys think?"

The decision is to go on, and they catch a ride back to the trail. In no time, they cover the three miles to Limestone Springs Lean-to for the night. They keep a close eye on the weather, and it looks about the same as it has for the past two days. No problem. They don't even have to share the shelter with other hikers that night.

Early in the morning, Jon is the first to wake. He brews his coffee and sits by the shelter. After his head clears, he retrieves his notebook and spends 30 minutes catching up on his notes to Mr. Wilkins. For the first time in weeks, he is completely up to date. As he puts his notes away, his companions begin stirring, one by one.

Charlie goes outside and stretches, trying to remove the kinks that you get from sleeping on a wooden bunk, no matter how good a sleeping pad you have. Wood is singularly unforgiving. Charlie casts an eye at the sky and says, "Well, Jon, doesn't look any worse up there. You guess we're still gonna get that storm?"

Jon moves to stand by her and agrees. "Sky looks about the same. Real overcast. Those high clouds are moving pretty fast, but there's not much wind down here. Maybe that sucker's headed farther north or south. Maybe it's even blown itself out."

Charlie says, "Well, the idea of a tropical storm out here in the wilderness isn't too appealing. I hope it's gone somewhere else."

Breakfast is completed, and they prepare to depart for the day, a short hop of less than 10 miles with no mountains. This area is extremely pretty, and the hikers find themselves stopping and enjoying the view whenever they can. As the day proceeds, the weather becomes more and more threatening, and they get a smattering of rain in the afternoon accompanied by increasing wind. As they hike, ponchos flap in the wind, and they have to tie the corners down. They arrive at Brassie Brook Shelter by three o'clock and enjoy being out of the wind.

They hold a pow-wow over cups of tea. Sam starts, "Well, if this is the worst we get out of that storm, I'll be happy. We're still making progress in spite of it."

Jon looks at his guide. "Yeah, we are. We've got only two miles to go to the Massachusetts state line, and we've got another easy hike tomorrow. I'd call that progress."

Charlie, who's lying on the ground with her head resting in George's lap, yawns. "I'd call this progress right now. This progress is pretty restful. Are there any mountains tomorrow?"

"Yeah, just one. We cross Bear Mountain right before the state line. No, wait a minute. There's another. Race Mountain's about three miles past that. Sorry, Charlie, two's the count."

Water is collected, and all four hikers enjoy an easy afternoon, even though the weather continues to deteriorate. The wind picks up slightly and the dark, heavily laden clouds spit rain every once in a while in brief bursts–a portent of possible things to come. The protection of the shelter is welcome and they cook dinner inside, avoiding the rain. Bedtime comes early.

Jon's sleep is interrupted by a slight sound. He tries to ignore it, and falls back to sleep. He hears faint noises again. He lies quietly, trying to identify the disturbance. He and Sam are in bunks near the shelter door, and Charlie and George are in bunks at the other end of the shelter. That is, when they went to bed, they were in bunks. Jon figures out that now, they are in a bunk. Singular. Charlie giggles, "George, we'll wake the guys. Quiet!"

George whispers, "What if I do this or this or this? Can you be quiet?"

"When you do that, I don't want to be quiet. Oh, George. Don't stop."

Jon lies still, a big grin on his face. He'll have to remember that George and Charlie need their privacy. He and Sam will both have to remember that. His mind shifts. "Damn, I wish Gretel was here. How can I still miss somebody I only knew for one day? I never believed in love at first sight. Now, I wonder." He drifts off to sleep.

When Jon wakes in the morning, the weather is worse. The wind is stronger, and the dark clouds scurry across the sky. No rain, for now. Jon thinks, "Gonna be decision time soon. Let's see, we need to inventory supplies, 'cause we got six days till re-supply ."

His musings are interrupted by a yawning, stretching Charlie, and Jon goes over his thoughts with her, as they brew coffee. They decide to forestall any decision as to go or no-go, until the other two awake. Over breakfast, the hikers are somewhat ambivalent. The discussion, as to whether to wait on the weather or not, swings one way, then the other. Lots of miles and six nights to go before re-supply and the lack of rain convince them that they might as well continue. The short hike is also a factor. They pack up and leave.

The rain holds off, and they conquer Bear Mountain and cross safely into Massachusetts. Standing on top of the mountain, the skies look frightening, and the air has a strange color. Pale yellowish green is the best way to describe it. Huge clouds are visible to the east, and rain seems eminent. They start down the mountain, and the situation gets worse. The wind is getting stronger and stronger and threatens to move them around like pawns on a chess board.

As they struggle against the wind, huge drops of rain begin falling, making things even worse. They can barely hear each other over the wind, even with shouting. Charlie yells at Jon, "Damn–you reckon we're in that storm they predicted? Looks pretty bad. Don't you think we ought to stop somewhere?"

Jon agrees, "Yeah, but tents aren't an option. They couldn't stand up to this wind. Let's keep on going and look for a place up the trail." Charlie nods in agreement; they struggle on.

After a half-mile of increasingly horrible conditions, they come to a deep valley, and the wind is slightly better down in the bottom. The four stand in a tight circle and discuss their options by screaming over the roar of the wind. Sam says, "I vote we set up a lean-to with our ponchos down in this valley. Maybe set it next to the east bank, and some of this wind might pass over us. I believe we're in the middle of that damned tropical storm Sally. We may be in it even worse. It may be a full-fledged hurricane on its way."

Jon gets no relief from the guide. This is the one night out of a bunch of nights where there is no shelter. Murphy strikes again. Whatever can go wrong will go wrong.

With worry threatening to overcome them, they begin fighting the wind to set up what shelter they can. It takes all four to hold the corners of a poncho to get it anchored against the east bank of the ravine, next to a ten-foot rock outcrop that offers some shelter. They tie ponchos together to form a lean-to that's

large enough for all four hikers and their packs. They use the rope all of them carry to tie things down the best they can. All the while, the wind gets stronger and stronger. The wail it makes as it passes through the trees is the scream of a banshee, and the rain is getting worse. The drops are so large that they hurt as they strike unprotected parts of their faces, arms, and legs. Having done the best they could with the materials they have on hand, they crawl into their cozy shelter and prepare to weather out the storm. Whatever it is.

The weather gets progressively worse. The rain is coming down in torrents. The lean-to does a fair job of keeping most of the direct rain off of them, but plenty is still getting through. The four huddle closer for warmth and for moral support. The wind increases and the trees are beyond swaying to the point where wood is straining. Sam yells in Jon's ear, "Them damn trees are making the loudest snap, crackle, and pop I ever heard!"

Jon nods agreement. Conversation is difficult, if not impossible. The sky is completely black, and the hikers can't see the other's faces. The northeast corner of the shelter breaks free of the restraining rope. George lunges for the wildly flapping plastic and snags it. He looks for something to tie it down, but is unsuccessful. He clutches the flap with a death grip and pulls it closer to him, at least keeping the bulk of the rain out. But, the wind increases even when it seems impossible to get stronger. Charlie reaches across George and grabs the plastic to help him. The wind is blowing so hard that it seems alive, and it maliciously yanks on the loose corner of the poncho, practically lifting the hikers off of the ground.

A loud crack is heard above the noise of the wind, and, to their horror, a large tree 15 feet in front of the shelter looses its grip in the shallow soil of the mountain and falls, luckily away from them. "Damn," yells Jon. He yells it to his own ears because the noise of the wind is louder still. It announces that it is not yet through increasing in intensity. The noise approaches the sound of several jet planes on takeoff; several more trees give up the fight and crash to the ground.

Charlie screams, unheard by the men. Something warm and wet is moving next to her leg. She thrashes around, but the thing is insistent and crawls farther up. She gets control of her fear and reaches down. She touches a small furry creature that is trying to find shelter in the storm. She picks up a small rabbit and hugs it to her, providing whatever support she could. The rabbit apparently makes a rabbit-like decision that fear of this human is secondary to its fear of the storm; the animal and human find an uneasy truce.

Another shriek of the wind is followed by more crashing. Then one of the trees serving as an upright for the lean-to falls, pulling the southern-most poncho with it. The remainder of the shelter roof threatens to go with it–the ropes and plastic are taut and vibrating. Jon turns on his flashlight, reaches for his knife, and slashes the rope that is threatening to bring down the entire shelter. The rope parts, and he grabs the corner of the next poncho and pulls, wrapping it around him. The four squeeze closer together.

The storm shows a new side of its ugly nature: massive streaks of lightning are followed by rumbles of thunder that shake the very ground on which they lie. The wind no longer is a continuous roar. Now it gusts and subsides, the gusts even more frightening because of the momentary pauses in its destructive power. Then, suddenly, it all stops. The rain quits, as surely as if someone has turned off the faucet, and the wind ceases the gusts. The sky becomes light, although it is still that frightening yellowish-green color that it was when this whole thing started.

George looks up with wide eyes at the others, "Damn, is it over? I've never gone through anything like that in my life."

Sam responds, "I'm afraid you'd best get ready for it to come again. I suspect that we're in the eye. That damned thing is what's left of a hurricane, not a tropical storm."

Charlie lies still, near-paralyzed with fear. She still clutches the rabbit, and it wriggles even closer to her. She stammers, "How long do we have before it comes back?"

"Don't know," says Sam. "I was in the fringe of one years ago when I was a kid. I think it lasts a few minutes. We'd better tie down what we can, cause it won't be long." The hikers busy themselves taking the rope off of the poncho still tied to the fallen support tree and double up ropes wherever they can. They crawl back inside the shelter.

Sure enough, two or three minutes later, the beast is back. The wind hits like a freight train, and rain follows immediately. The sky goes black and the hikers call on whatever inner reserves they have. This storm is so all-pervasive that closing your eyes to will it away doesn't really help, although all four try. The roar of the wind intensifies, and the crashing of trees adds to near-panic feelings. Another nearby tree falls, missing the shelter by inches. It actually does some good in repose, because it blocks the rain and some of the wind from the north end of the lean-to.

The trailing edge of the hurricane takes almost 30 minutes to pass through; the inner clocks of the hikers tell them it is hours, not minutes. As the wind goes into a pattern of bursts and calm, disaster strikes. One of the bursts is particularly violent, and a tree on the bank above the shelter falls, right on the front of the shelter, bringing it down on them. All of the hikers are exposed to the full fury of the wind and rain. They can't even check on each other–all they can do is hold on for dear life.

Then, as suddenly as it came, it departs. Dead calm. No wind. No rain. Jon yells, "Who's hurt? Charlie, you okay? George?"

"I'm okay," she says. "But I'm trapped by branches. They're holding me down. I don't think anything is broken, but I'm pretty scraped up. George! Are you all right?"

"Yeah, Babe, that tree fell right beside me, but it mostly missed me. Just a few scratches. Sam is here, and I think he's okay, too. Let's get you loose, so we can make sure you're okay."

It takes the three men the better part of an hour to remove the tree, a branch at a time. The whole time, Charlie and the rabbit lie still, not daring to move. The small roll-up saws that most hikers carry work okay on small firewood, but they aren't made to cut larger branches. But, they finally succeed, and Charlie stands upright. She gently places the rabbit on the ground, where it sits still, wriggling its nose. Instinct takes over and it hops away, slowly at first, then he runs–as if a fox is on his tail. Laughter follows him, releasing a tiny part of the stress. Group hugs follow.

The hikers take an inventory of their persons and are delighted when they find nothing broken. Charlie's legs look like she lost a fight with a wildcat, and the three men all have scrapes and scratches on legs, arms, and faces. First-aid cream is applied to abrasions and bandages are taped on the worst scratches. Charlie says, "I guess we owe the man in the sky big time. Look at this place."

The four look around them for the first time since the storm abated and can't believe their eyes. The trees, for as far as the eye can see, are strewn around like a giant game of jackstraws. The trees have the distinctive shape of mountain trees that have been uprooted; a giant biscuit of roots holding the soil that did its best to support the tree against the incredible strength of the hurricane winds, but failed.

"Damn," says Jon, "We're gonna play hell getting out of here. I haven't climbed trees for years, but we'll have to now."

"Guys, look here. You're not gonna be happy," says George who is standing by the jumbled-together packs. "What a mess."

"Oh, man," groans Sam. "My pack is trashed." He holds up a pack that is almost bent back on itself. "Look at yours, Jon."

Jon sits down by his pack. A large branch of the tree, that had almost killed them, had surely killed his pack. It's nearly flattened. He starts pulling gear out of the wreckage and lays it on the ground. Sam does the same with his. Items like candle lanterns and flashlights and stoves are demolished, but things that could give with the force, like clothes and sleeping bags, have survived in fair shape. The men shake their heads in disbelief. "Man," says Sam, "I'm not gonna bitch. It coulda been us, looking like this, instead of this stuff. We can buy more gear at the next resupply."

Jon has to agree. He starts trying to force his pack's internal frame back into it's original shape, but he proves to be weaker than the storm. The four hikers work together and use tree branches as levers and fulcrums and straighten the pack, more or less. Jon laughs, "I hope my back doesn't change shape to fit this battle-scarred veteran of the wars. But, at least I should be able to carry my stuff."

The process is repeated on Sam's pack, and it is more or less straightened. It is an outside-frame pack, and several clevis pins have been snapped, but Sam has extras, and his pack is repaired. George and Charlie's packs were spared direct hits by the tree branches, so all in all, they proclaim themselves lucky. They pack their gear and prepare for a long trip, though the distance is only a few miles.

The anticipation of a tough hike is surpassed by reality. There are trees across the trail every 20 or 30 feet, and they have to either climb over them or walk around them in order to keep going. Jon and Sam's packs hold together. The modified shapes rub sores on hips and backs. As if they don't have enough misery, the rain starts again. They have to fashion the scraps of ponchos that survived the storm into a semblance of rain protection, but they keep going. The temperature has dropped substantially since the storm went through. Just at dusk, they arrive at Race Brook Trail, the place they intend to camp. Though exhausted, they set up tents, and the miserable hikers shuck wet clothes and crawl into sleeping bags to ward off hypothermia. All four fall asleep almost immediately.

At about nine o'clock that night, Jon is awakened by someone shaking his shoulder insistently. He mumbles, "No, Mom, I don't want to go to school today."

Charlie, the shaker, laughs heartily. "No, Jon, I'm not your mom. Here," she says, thrusting a Sierra cup at him. "Drink this soup. I decided to play mom, even though I'm not."

"Thanks, Charlie. That was damned nice of you," and Jon accepts the cup gratefully. Charlie makes the rounds, delivering hot soup to the others.

"What made you get up, Charlie?" asks Jon as he finishes his soup.

"I don't really know. I was sleeping well, then I woke up with my belly growling. I was lying in my sleeping bag trying to feel grateful that we hadn't been hurt, but the longer I lay there, the hungrier I got. I fixed myself soup, then felt guilty, so I cooked a whole pot. That's my domesticity for today. Don't expect more."

"Charlie, You're a jewel, even if you won't accept thanks," says Sam. "Thanks anyway."

"You're welcome. Now, I don't know about you guys, but it's back to the sack for me. I think that brief respite in the rain is coming to an end. I felt a drop on my nose." She crawls back into her tent, next to George. "Goodnight, Jon-boy," she shouts. "Goodnight Bubba-Sam."

"Good night, Charlie Jane," comes the reply. "Good night, George Bob." The Walton game exhausted, silence descends, and sleep begins the healing process.

15 TRAUMA RECOVERY

It's nine o'clock in the morning before the tired and battered travelers wake. Over coffee and oatmeal, they discuss their predicament. Hiking under conditions like yesterday effectively doubles the distance.

Jon says, "What about supplies–food stock okay? We've still got five days before North Adams." The conversation ceases while packs are searched. The consensus is that there is enough food to keep everyone fed.

Sam asks, "What you got inside that head of yours, Jon?"

"I'm thinking we ought to move two miles up the trail and stay at Glen Brook Shelter. The shelter will protect us, if it survived the wrath of Sally. We could stay there a couple of days. I figure we can use the rest. I'm stiff as a board."

Agreement all around. Charlie says, "I never would have been the first to admit it, but, yeah. I feel like I've been in a car wreck."

George pipes in, "You know, staying there might also help in another way. It gives the volunteer groups an extra day to use their chain saws. We're in the center of two trail accesses, but they may be working this way. Least wise, I hope they are."

The decision is a no-brainer and they cover the two miles in a couple of hours. Then, relaxation is the order of the day. Jon and Sam work on their packs, getting support bars straightened and padding taped on spots that rubbed sores.

The hikers do some landscaping–cutting and removing branches that had fallen on and near the shelter, creating a large pile of firewood. Charlie surveys the scene, hands on hips. "There ought to be some happy campers for a while. Collecting firewood is a real pain around these shelters. Momma Nature has provided. The hard way."

They keep an ear tuned for the sound of chain saws, but hear nothing. Nightfall descends, and they sleep soundly.

In the morning, there's no chain-saw noise. They decide to depart anyway and leave by eight o'clock. The trail is just as treacherous as it had been two days before. Trees are down in all directions, but at least it is not raining. They cover seven tough miles by lunchtime. They sit on rocks bewailing their new collection of scratches on top of their earlier ones. Still no trail crew-racket.

They push forward, fighting through and around tree falls. Going through a fallen tree results in the pack being caught by a branch that you can't duck low enough to miss. They grab you. Every time. The hikers are brought to a screeching halt time after time by low branches, and it adds to their weariness.

At four in the afternoon, Jon stops, bringing the train to a halt. "What's that?" he asks, cupping his ear. All listen intently.

Sam says, "I believe it's a sound that I never thought I'd appreciate in the wilderness. That's either a huge flock of beaver or a trail clearing crew, and there ain't no beaver up here."

"Yeah, man!" yells Charlie.

"All right," adds George.

As it turns out, they get to Ice Gulch Shelter before they actually see the work crew. There are two older men and two high school students. The workers are as worn out as the hikers, who welcome the men and their chain saws with open arms.

"Man, are we glad to see you guys," says Charlie. "You're a sight for sore eyes."

"Where were you folks when Sally hit?" asks the crew chief.

Jon responds, "About two miles the other side of Race Brook Trail Lean-to.

We hunkered down in a deep gully and somehow missed the falling trees. We were mighty lucky."

"I'll say you were. You must have been in Sages Ravine. Several hikers were badly hurt a couple miles south of where you were. A big tree fell on them, and the hospital's not sure one of them is gonna make it. It was a bad storm–the worst we've seen in 20 years. It's gonna take weeks or months to get the trail clear again. Volunteer work proves to be a full-time job after storms like this one. I just thought I'd retired."

"Well, we appreciate the hell out of what you guys are doing. These past few miles have been rough," says George. "Thanks again. How far are you guys going tonight?"

"We've gone all we're gonna go. We've got packs down the trail a bit. We're staying here. Hope you don't mind the company."

"The day I mind sharing space with trail angels is the day I'm getting off this trail for good," says Charlie. "You're more than welcome. We'll enjoy your company."

The chief says, "By the way, my name is Adam. I used to be a nuclear engineer till I retired. Now I'm a chain-saw artist." Adam introduces the rest of his crew.

Charlie says, "Like I said before, we're truly glad to see you guys. Where did you say your packs were?"

"Just about a quarter mile back that way," pointing north. Charlie doesn't say a word, but strides purposefully in that direction . Jon, Sam, and George follow her, leaving the work crew standing at the shelter, wondering. Twenty minutes later, the four hikers return with the crew's packs and place them on the ground in front of the speechless men. "Here," says Charlie, "That's the least we can do for you guys, since you're out here doing for us."

"We appreciate that," says Adam. "If we'd gone after them, we might have just stayed there." The cast of eight begins necessary evening chores. Even hiker food smells and tastes great, and appetites are even higher than pre-storm levels.

After dinner and dishes, coffee and conversation prevail. "Well, what are you guys' plans," asks Adam.

Jon replies, "Well, our original goal was to get to North Adams. We've all got care packages waiting at the post office there. My guide shows that is about 66 miles up the trail."

"What kind of shape are you in after weathering the storm?"

"I guess I'd have to say fair at best. We're sorta bruised and battered, but nobody was really hurt. Our gear was hurt more than we were." He pulls his pack from thc shelter.

Adam examines the crippled veteran pack and shakes his head. "Damn, son, that thing has more tape and wire on it than it has metal. That sucker deserves a Purple Heart and maybe a DSC. I don't see how it has survived this far. I tell you what. I don't like getting into other people's business . . . "

"Jump right in," says Charlie. We'll welcome any advice you have."

"Well, what I was going to say was, I believe I'd recommend that you folks leave the trail two miles up the way and go to Great Barrington. It may be four miles or so off the trail, but they have a good outfitter and motel and meals. Fact is, I heard that one of the churches has a dormitory set up free for hikers, and the town folks are fixing meals. I 'spect that you'd better be calling home and let folks know that you're all right after the storm. The police department has received lots of calls from worried parents and friends."

The hikers look crestfallen. "Damn," says Jon, "I'm a real dummy. I never even thought of that. When you're up here, the world doesn't extend past your little cocoon of existence. We knew we were okay, so we figured the rest of the world would know that too."

"Sally's been on national news for a couple of days now, and I believe that would be the thing to do," says Adam. "I'd also say that you've got a real good chance of catching a ride from either workers or locals at the road to Barrington. We've ferried a few folks out of here already, mostly south-bounders."

"Adam," says George, "Thanks for bringing us back from our selfishness. Damn, I have a dad who's recovering from heart surgery. I sure don't need to put any extra stress on him. Yeah, we'll take your advice. I have to admit it, but a few days rest and relaxation in civilization sounds really good to me."

Jon asks, "By the way, how far up the trail has it been cleared? Are there lots of crews out?"

Adam says, "I believe there are. You were in the worst of it, but remember that the civilian folks got hit pretty hard, too. Not much damage in North Barrington, but there's folks doing cleanup there, too. It'll be weeks, months even, before the trail is back to normal, whatever that is. A couple of days in Barrington won't hurt a thing. Maybe a few miles more of trail will be cleared. I know that walking through tree tops is not easy. Even when they are horizontal."

In the morning, Jon struggles back to consciousness after a hard sleep. He looks outside the shelter. To his amazement, George and Sam are fixing coffee. He crawls out of his sleeping bag and looks around. The work crew is still snoozing, as is Charlie.

"Damn, guys, whatever possessed you to be first up? I believe that's a first. It's usually Charlie and me."

"Well, we thought we'd let the lazy ones sleep," says Sam. "Truth is, I think that both of us felt guilty, and we're ready to get to town and make some phone calls. Adam told me last night after you went to bed that he didn't think your poor old pack could possibly last more than a mile or two."

Jon gratefully accepts a cup of coffee and takes a sip. "Thanks man. That tastes great. Now maybe I can think. My first thought is an important one. I trust they've got ATM machines in Barrington. I don't have enough travelers checks to buy a pack and all the rest of the stuff I'm gonna need. What about you, Sam? You got enough wherewithall to go shopping?"

Sam looks a bit glum. "Not with me. I guess I'm gonna do what I hate to do more than anything in the world. One of the calls I gotta make is to my folks to bum some money. I'll hear about lack of responsibility for months. Maybe they will put money in my account and I can get it with my ATM. My credit card is maxed; no space at all on that sucker."

"Well, don't humble yourself just yet, pard. One call I'm gonna make is to Mr. Wilkins of the Tuscaloosa newspaper. Seems that last time I talked to him, a few more bucks were still trickling in because of the stories he's been doing about this hike. If there's enough there, we'll share. He can wire it up here, and we both can re-supply."

Sam looks at Jon. "Damn, man, you're a real friend. I'll pay you back, when I get back home and make some bucks."

"Nope, not really my money, anyway. I don't think that the folks sending in the money will mind at all. Fact is, when I write about the storm, I'll tell them what I'm doing. They know all you guys, anyway. You've been in the story for weeks. What do you reckon it's gonna take to get us set back up? Maybe 300 apiece?"

"I really hadn't thought about it. I guess you're about right. Pack, flashlight, candle lantern, stove, water bottles. Yeah, maybe just a hair more. And, thanks again."

"No sweat. You'd do the same. We'd best get these lazy louts, no, make that one lazy lout up and going. She's the one that always gets a kick out of waking you guys up. What can we do that's particularly diabolical? Feathers? Water?"

George nixes the water, but it's amazing how loud Charlie can yell when three bird feathers work simultaneously on nose and ears. She and the trail crew are definitely awake.

Over coffee, she more or less forgives them. That is, until George says, "Yeah guys, myself, sometimes I wake up grumpy. Then, there are times when I just let her sleep." He deftly ducks the missiles hurled his way by the strong arm of Charlie.

The groups part, one heading north to placate family and friends, one heading south to continue clearing fallen trees. Waves and yells cease as the chain saws begin their less than melodic, but welcome, racket. Birds squawk and fly in all directions and the hikers laugh at the ballet of swooping.

The newly cleared trail is like a super highway for the next mile. Then, Adam's prophecy proves accurate, but for the wrong person, as Sam's pack falls halfway off his back. One of the main upright supports yields to metal fatigue, and the rod parts. The hikers place a splint, and they limp up the trail.

At the trail head, there are several pickup trucks parked and the drivers are sharing coffee out of a thermos. One sees the straggling group and says, "You guys look a bit bedraggled. Need a lift to town?"

"You bet," says Charlie. "We really appreciate it, guys."

The hikers are deposited at the Northside Baptist Church where ladies with the woman's group cluck over them like the proverbial mother hens. They take Charlie and in thirty minutes, she reappears, all scratches dressed, looking somewhat different.

All three men, cleaned up themselves, stare in amazement. Charlie snaps, "Close your mouths, fellas. Haven't you ever seen a lady in a dress before?"

Jon says, "Yes, but not you. Look, guys, she's got legs! Damn, George, you're gonna have to watch her closely or some good-looking town fella's gonna carry her off." He walks over and hugs Charlie. "Love you, Charlie."

"Love you guys, too. Now, you gonna shut up long enough for us to make these calls and get some city food to eat?"

The church ladies cluck again at the obvious feelings the hikers have for each other. "Now you folks don't have to go anywhere for now. There are three phones upstairs in the office, and, when you're finished, the ladies' social circle will have a little lunch over here for you."

In the office, Jon calls his parents, Sam his folks, and Charlie and George make several calls. The pastor won't hear of offers to pay for the calls. Jon calls Mr. Wilkins to let him know that he's okay and asks, "I haven't asked this before, but is there any money left in the pot? Two of us have some seriously busted gear, and we need to go shopping."

Mr. Wilkins rustles papers that are apparently lying on the desk in front of him. "Let's see, Jon. Yes, I count 700 dollars. Why don't you find out what the nearest bank is, and I'll get money wired up right away. Will that be enough?"

"You bet, that'll resupply both of us just fine. Make sure you let the people know how much they've helped."

"Speaking of that, how quickly can you get notes to me? This'll be the hottest story since we started this project. Quite a few folks have called to see if we've had any word from you guys."

Jon turns to the pastor. "Sir, do you have a fax machine? I need to send some information back to Tuscaloosa this afternoon."

"Yes, son, we're in this century. Fact is, you're welcome to use my computer here and you can e-mail your information. Have you got any pictures? We can scan them and e-mail them as well."

Jon relays this to Mr. Wilkins, and his excitement is obvious. "Do you believe you can get all of that to me by five o'clock? I can just hit tomorrow morning's paper that way."

Jon agrees and hangs up. He asks his friends. "Hey, guys, you want to be newspaper reporters? I'll have to get your help on this story." Smiles all around show willingness.

The pastor says, "Folks, I just got word that your small lunch is ready downstairs. I think I'll join you. The ladies don't normally feed me. But, he adds, patting his ample stomach, "I don't miss many meals."

The little lunch turns out to be a spread of home-cooked food that makes first the tables, then the hikers, groan. Several are nodding, naps threatening. Jon says, "Okay, guys, you promised. Naps will have to wait. We've got a story to write." More groans and grumbles, but the three get up from the table and go back to the office.

The pastor has everything laid out for them. Tablets and pencils on tables for each of them, and his secretary poised by the computer. A young man runs into the office, bearing photographs fresh from the one-hour developers. Jon selects five that he thinks show the devastation that the storm has left, and the secretary scans them and gets them ready to transmit to Tuscaloosa. The hikers divide the last week into parts, and soon all four are busily writing their thoughts. Jon pulls them together, and the secretary quickly types a draft, which Jon edits. She transmits the text and photos to Tuscaloosa, and 15 minutes later, Mr. Wilkins calls and raves about their work. "I may have to offer you guys jobs as reporters when this is all over. You made my job easy. I can hit the morning paper deadline with ease. Thanks."

Task complete and thanks passed around, Jon and Sam go to the bank where the banker, already apprised of the situation, has the money waiting. Mr. Wilkins has been busy while they were stuffing themselves. They spend most of the rest of the afternoon at the outfitters, and the money from the newspaper proves adequate. Jon and Sam shop carefully and purchase new packs after substantial discussions with the outfitter about the relative merits of this pack over that pack. Both men feel like they are able to shop more intelligently than they had before they left home months ago. They carry their new packs, stuffed with other replacement items, back to the church, where they carefully lay out all their gear, and more discussions follow. They certainly have more a comfortable feeling than they did when they first saw their mangled packs.

Charlie and George return to the church from their sight-seeing excursion with one of their new mother hens, and they also inspect the new gear. Charlie says, "You know, the best thing is that none of this stuff needs breaking in very much. The packs will feel funny for a while, but not for long. Looks good, fellas. Now, I don't know about you guys, but I'm ready for food."

The four head for the local pizza parlor for food. The beer ain't bad, either. To their amazement, the restaurant manager refuses to take their money, despite their protestations. "You know guys," muses Charlie. "I'm never again gonna brag about Southern hospitality, as good as it is. We couldn't be much deeper in the North, but I've never seen hospitality like this before."

"Yeah," adds Sam, "Corny as it sounds, I guess people are the same everywhere. Doing good comes natural to lots of folks."

Back at the church, the ladies have laid out half-a-dozen pies, and a note that says not to forget the ice cream that awaits in the kitchen freezer. Somehow, even after all the pizza, they manage to demolish several pies and a gallon of ice cream before they toddle off to bed to crash and burn until ten o'clock the next morning.

The hikers spend the next day checking on the status of the trail to the north. The damage that Sally caused was relatively widespread, centered near the ravine where they had weathered her. They find Adam's home and go to visit his wife. She is in contact with Adam by means of a cellular phone he carries, and he has recently talked with crew chiefs working the northern stretches of the trail. Progress is slow. Jon says, "You know guys, we probably move three or four times faster than the cleanup crews, so no matter how long we wait, we're still gonna have to face downed trees."

Sam adds, "Yeah, you're right. The only good thing is that the damage should be less as we move north and get out of the range of the hurricane. What are you thinking, Jon?"

"Well, I'm not sure what I'm thinking. Maybe another day or so here so we can completely heal and they can do more clearing."

George adds, "I feel much better after just a day here. I believe my mind was messed up by that damned storm as much as my body was."

Charlie says, "Well, if we're taking a vote, I vote we stay two more nights before we go back out. I keep having flashbacks about those damned trees and branches everywhere. I feel better, but I'm not quite mentally or physically ready to face the jungle again."

Decision made, they kill the afternoon by going to a movie. Sitting around is difficult for the hikers, whose world has been one of activity, but they manage nicely. The ladies have made dinner for them and the two other hikers who have made it out of the woods that afternoon, and the six survivors swap stories of their struggles with Sally. Sleep on the cots continues the healing process.

In the morning the hikers decide over mountains of pancakes that they need to revise their overall schedule, particularly with respect to care packages from home. Jon calls Andy, and they change the dates Andy is to ship packages by four days. The Post offices will hold packages for a while, but there's no sense in taking a chance. They also call the Post office in North Adams, and the postmaster agrees to hold the three packages waiting there until they arrive. Feeling better, they force themselves to take a nap until lunchtime. It takes very little effort or convincing.

When they awake, Charlie says, "Have you ever noticed how important meal times are in this hiking game? Everything we do is centered around food. Where we go, when we go, when we sleep or wake, when we hike or stop? Everything."

Jon says, "Yeah, you're right. Okay, you've convinced me. Let's go eat. I'm hungry."

"Okay," says Charlie. They go out to lunch. Philosophy is important, but, after all, food is even more so.

The rest of the day is spent in checking new gear, getting the food they have bought ready to carry, filling water bottles, and other domestic chores that always fill their time just prior to hiking. They sleep well and are as ready to go as they can be.

16 "ON THE ROAD AGAIN . . . "

The church folks have rides to the trail head, and the hikers feel that the thanks they have expressed for the hospitality are inadequate. Nonetheless, they are back on the trail. Progress toward Katahdin has been slowed by Sally, but not stopped.

The first eight miles of the trail toward Upper Goose Pond Cabin, their avowed destination, goes smoothly. The trail crews have cleared the fallen trees and the walk is normal. As they stop for lunch, Sam says, "I'm afraid I hear bad news, guys. Listen."

After a moment of silence, they all hear the sounds of chain saws on the wind. "Damn, we've caught up with them. Reckon how far they are away?" asks Charlie.

"Can't be but a mile or two," guesses Jon. "Maybe three, but no more. What do you think we ought to do? We've already passed the last shelter we'll see before Upper Goose. Maybe there is something else. Let me take a look." He pours over the guide, then shakes his head. "Nope, no shelters or campsites. There is a town–Tyringham, but they don't list a motel. I guess we'll have to camp."

George says, "Well, I propose we go ahead and pass the crew and fight the trees. There have been fewer and fewer cut as we've been hiking. Maybe we're getting close to the edge of the storm damage. I hope so, anyway."

"How much farther do you want to go after we pass them?" asks Jon, to the group in general.

"Just far enough so we can't hear them," suggests Charlie. "For that matter, maybe one of the crew will have a suggestion as to a place we can camp a few more miles north."

A plan more or less set in place, they continue hiking. Although nobody said it, it seems that no one is ready yet for 20-mile days. Maybe too much good city living has spoiled them.

It takes an hour and a half to get there, but the hikers walk around a curve in the trail and see four men busily cutting fallen trees from across the trail. One of the men sees the hikers and waves at the other workers. They shut their chain saws down. "Hey, folks, how's it going?" he asks.

"It has been going pretty well, thanks to you guys," says Jon. "But I'm afraid that the clear trail is about to be behind us."

"Yeah, afraid so," says the crew chief. "You've probably got some 15 or 20 miles left of bad tree falls as you go north. But it is getting a little bit better. Fewer trees as we work our way north." How far you planning to get tonight?"

"Well," says Jon. "We had originally planned to stay at Upper Goose Pond Shelter, but I'm afraid that we won't make it. Do you guys know of any place we can camp closer than that? With water?"

"Let's see. When you cross Webster Road, 'bout another five miles or so, there's a good spring there. You could find a clearing a half-mile or so on up the road and camp there. You're not supposed to, but this isn't a normal time, so we'll look the other way."

Jon inspects his guide. "Yeah, that will work. If we can make 14 miles the next day, we can stay at October Mountain Lean-to, then get back on track the next day. Thanks for the suggestion, fellas. We appreciate it. You heard the man, guys.

Five and a half miles of trees to go. If we want to get there before dark, we'd best get humpin'."

His announcement is greeted with groans and boos, but it's on with the packs and up the trail. Instead of "Over the river and through the woods," it's more like "Over the trees and through the boughs," but they keep going. In spite of the obstacles, they get their water from the spring and find a clearing well before dark. They set up camp and actually enjoy hiker food once again.

After dinner they all lie around the fire sipping tea and spouting philosophy. The main subject of discussion is the hospitality of the good folks of Great Barrington. Charlie says, "I don't know about you guys, but I plan to write them a thank-you letter as soon as I can. We owe them big time."

Jon agrees. "Yep, me too. If you guys remember, we did say nice things about them in the article we sent to Mr. Wilkins. I asked him to send a copy of the newspaper to the pastor of the church, and maybe he'll spread our thanks that way."

"Yeah," says Charlie. "I had completely forgotten about that. I don't know about you guys, but this lady's tired. I'm hitting the sleeping bag. Good night."

"Night, Charlie," follows her to her tent. The men last another half hour, and snores are the only sounds that now disturb the quiet of the wilderness.

The 48 miles to North Adams, the next re-supply location, take four long, hard days. There are fewer and fewer fallen trees to detour around, but twelve-mile days are tough enough without those distractions. When they arrive at North Adams, it feels like they had left civilization weeks before, not just five days. They are scratched and bruised and battered, but they are now that much closer to their goal. The storm may have slowed them down and battered them, physically and mentally, but with determination and with the help of some hands held out to them, they had persevered.

The original plan was to pick up their packages in North Adams and not stay there. Instead, they planned to hike two miles up the trail to the next shelter. As the hikers are sitting outside the post office, Jon reminds them of this plan. Sam says, "Boss man, I usually go along with the plan. Even when it hurts. But this time, I don't have the energy. My scratches need doctoring and my back needs a bed. I place a nomination on the floor that we revise the plan and stay here."

George says, "I second the motion."

Charlie adds, "All in favor say aye: there are no no's."

Jon has to laugh. "It's a good thing that this is a volunteer position, 'cause what just passed, might not be constitutional. But I also vote aye. I was just bringing up what the paper says, not what our bodies say. To the motel, troops." Several of the local folks stare in amazement as four scruffy, dirty, scratched-up hikers pass them, marching in close-order drill–all the way to the motel.

The hikers either didn't see or care about the stares. Showers and hot food, non-pasta type, is all that is on their minds. A seafood restaurant is their choice for the evening, and they do their part to prevent the seafood from over-populating and taking over the world. The beds feel marvelous, and spirits are in better shape the next morning. Over breakfast they discuss and revise the plan, cutting down the next few days to more manageable chunks of 13 or 14 miles, rather than the longer days proposed.

Before lunch the hikers cross the Massachusetts-Vermont state line, and celebrate with cheers and Rebel yells, startling into flight a flock of birds that are peacefully sitting in the trees above. Three states to go: never mind that one of those is Maine–a long stretch of trail. Three to go is an interim reward that feels good.

That night, they stay at Cogdon Camp Shelter and celebrate again. Both for the state milestone crossed and the fact that almost no trees are down in this area and hiking is much better. They make 14 miles to Goddard Shelter, then get back in place on the schedule, as they reach Story Spring Shelter the next night. During this stretch, the AT has become a grinding, day-to-day job rather than an enjoyable experience. But, circumstances have a way of changing that. At the shelter, they share space with five other hikers, including "I'm going my way Andrew," the character Jon and Sam met back down the trail in Virginia. Now, George and Charlie are able to judge for themselves whether he is as much of a character as Jon has told them.

Jon greets Andrew, "Hey, man, we didn't expect to ever see you again. What made you slow down? We figured you'd be almost through by now."

"Good to see you," says Andrew. "Who are these fine folks?" Jon introduces George and Charlie, Andrew shakes hands with George, then delights Charlie bowing deeply and kissing her hand.

"Well, Jon, I did lose a week or so along the way. When I talked to my wife over the telephone back down in Pennsylvania, she mentioned that she was getting a bit lonely and a lot horny. She said that she was able to convince her folks that since she wanted to catch a bus to meet me, they should keep the kids for a week. In other words, she proposed a conjugal visit. So, I escaped the confinement of the AT, played hooky from hiking, and we spent a truly decadent week in a resort motel. Charged my batteries, I'll tell you. Sorry, little lady, didn't mean to get suggestive with my story."

Charlie is laughing so hard that she can't answer him. She finally chokes out, "You don't reckon you guys succeeded in breeding, do you? Sam and Jon told us that story."

"Well, guys, I'm shocked that you would spread my little personal secrets like that. I'm shocked," and he turns and walks away. However, Jon notices that his shoulders are shaking with laughter, not anger. So, the hikers get down to business and start their evening chores. Beds are made, dinners started and eaten, and tea is brewed and enjoyed outside under the stars. Andrew keeps all of the hikers in stitches for the rest of the evening, leaving several of them complaining about how badly their sides hurt.

As they head for bed, Jon says to Sam, "I guess that this shelter is the most aptly-named shelter on the whole trail–Story Spring Shelter. There's the spring over there, and Andrew certainly took care of the stories. What an entertaining guy."

Sam agrees.

As he is heating coffee water in the morning, Jon notices that Andrew is gone. He is apparently an early riser and has "folded his tent and slipped away" in the morning mist. As Jon leans back against a tree, he enjoys the complete stillness of the morning. There are no bird songs; no hiker talk; nothing at all. He closes his eyes and reflects on the past few weeks. Sometimes it's hard to think back on more than a few weeks, because much of the earlier times seem to run together. Except for meeting Gretel. That day and night certainly stand out in his memories. Was it really four months ago that he started? Back in the dark ages. The storm? Clear as a bell in the memory banks. He thinks once again about how lucky they were and how lucky that part of the eastern seaboard was, as the hurricane had seemingly threaded its way between the larger cities. It did plenty of damage on the seashore area, but cost very few lives.

Jon's meditations are disturbed by a tiny noise. He opens his eyes and looks for the intruder. The breakfast bar he is holding in his hand, is uneaten. He looks around on the ground and locks eyes with a pair of small, dark eyes. A chipmunk, half hidden by a large leaf, is moving his eyes between Jon's eyes and the breakfast bar. Jon softly laughs. "Is it breakfast time, buddy? Come over here, and I'll share." He breaks off a small piece of the bar and holds it in the palm of his hand, extended toward the chipmunk. The animal takes several steps toward Jon, coming out from under the protective leaf. He stops, testing the air for danger. Any danger he senses is overcome by the delicious smell of the breakfast bar, and he moves again, hesitantly.

Jon speaks again, "Come on, I won't hurt you. Just a few more steps." The tiny critter, nose twitching, takes a few more steps, then stops again. He makes a mad dash, grabs the piece of food, then runs away just as quickly. Jon has to laugh. Two minutes later, the chipmunk is back, although not so far away this time. Jon breaks off another piece of bar and extends his hand. This time, the chipmunk sits in Jon's hand while he delicately holds the food in his tiny paws and eats it. He finishes, then waits expectantly for more. Jon laughs out loud, and the chipmunk trembles at the vibrations. But he doesn't run. Jon places another piece of food on the palm of his hand, near the chipmunk, a process that is repeated until the breakfast bar is gone.

Jon looks up, and Charlie is standing behind him, watching. She softly asks, "You got a new buddy? It looks like you are about out of bribes. Here, try some of mine. It's blueberry–he might like that just as well as he did yours." Jon places a piece of the blueberry bar in his hand, and the chipmunk gobbles that down as well. Then, just as quickly as he had come, he departs, scurrying through the leaves and into a hole at the base of a large tree. Jon releases his breath, which he has been holding, trying not to scare the animal.

"That little guy is a real successful mooch. I bet he pulls that shy act on lots of hikers. It probably works on all of us with soft hearts who like animals. You know, Charlie, I was sitting here thinking about Pookie, and how much I miss that guy. It's gonna be strange when I go home and that big dummy isn't there to greet me."

"I thought you weren't gonna do any more second guessing about sending him home."

"Yeah, yeah. I'm not second guessing, really. I'm just reminiscencing. He was a good friend for a lot of years, that's all."

Charlie reaches over and wipes away the fat tear that is trickling down Jon's cheek. "I like a man that's not ashamed to shed a tear. Or, for that matter, feed a chipmunk in his hand. Jon Parker, you're all right in my book. You and Sam have been good friends. But, you, there is one thing that you could do to be an even better friend to George and me. One tiny thing."

"What's that, Charlie? Name it and it's yours."

"If you would ever learn to share the damned coffee. Here I am, cup in hand, looking every bit as pitiful as that chipmunk, and you haven't noticed yet."

Jon laughs, "Okay, Charlie. Sorry." He pours her a cup, and she sits on the log and sips. The quiet moment passes as the other hikers appear, one by one, and breakfast is punctuated by discussions of the trail expected for the day.

"What's today, Jon," asks George. "Nice, easy day?"

"Actually, yes," answers Jon. " We've got five nights to Killington, our next resupply. I'd read in the guide about the Inn At The Long Trail, and I plan to stay there for several nights. The days are all relatively short. The longest is 13 miles, and there are several less than 10. How does that sound, George?"

"Damned nice. Almost a vacation. What's our destination tonight?"

"Lye Shelter, a mere 101/2 miles up the trail. But you know what? That 10 miles isn't getting any shorter, unless we saddle up and move out. You guys about ready?"

The others signal their readiness by pulling on packs, and they move out, this time to the theme song from the old western TV show, Rawhide. The chorus, "Rolling, rolling, rolling, though the streams are swollen," rings out and the song birds, rudely awakened, spring into flight and depart this crazy place and the crazy interlopers.

The five days to Killington pass without incident. The hiking is pretty good, even the 13-mile day that offers three mountains to cross, and George and Charlie keep up. The foursome arrives at The Inn in mid-afternoon. They collect care packages and hit the showers. This first night, they eat at the restaurant at the Inn and laze around, not going to Killington, two miles away. The inactivity feels good, even after the relatively easy hikes of the last week.

In the morning the hikers call Ray Cartozzi, a trail angel who is known as a friend to hikers, and he picks them up at 10 o'clock and transports them to the Mountain Travelers Outdoor Shop. Here they purchase a few items to replace worn out gear and a few new odds and ends. After completing their shopping, they hitch a ride back to Killington and enjoy a lunch at a deli, where it takes a foot-and-a-half of sandwich to satisfy hunger. As their eyelids are getting heavy, they catch a ride back to the Inn, and satisfy that urge. After napping, the Laundromat awaits, and they accomplish that chore.

All domestic tasks finished, they rest until dinner time comes and eat once again at The Inn. One more night in soft beds cures the last of their aches and pains, and the foursome is ready, almost eager, to depart early in the morning: only 46 more miles of Vermont to traverse. Then, only two more states to cross. Granted, rather long states, but only two. Only two. In some ways, they are eager to finish and accomplish their goal. In other ways, they want the good times to continue forever. Messes your mind up, that's for sure.

Spirits soaring, the foursome arrives at Stony Brook Shelter early in the afternoon and almost get bored with inactivity. Jon warns, "You guys don't get too lazy. We've got almost 20 miles to make tomorrow. We've been spoiled; no 20-milers for quite a while."

"Okay, doom-sayer," laughs Charlie. "Ole Charlie's ready for it. No problem. Just try to walk away and leave me behind."

As it turns out, the best laid schemes of mice and men, and for that matter, Charlie's, goes astray. Ten miles into the day, Charlie steps on a rock and turns her ankle. She twists it badly enough that they are forced to leave the trail and catch a ride over to Woodstock, Vermont, where a doctor x-rays and pronounces it badly sprained, and the foursome are motel-bound for an unscheduled two days while she recuperates. Not that anybody objects to soft beds and city food again, but Jon is beginning to harbor a few doubts in his mind. He's worried about the overall schedule ahead of them. Katahdin's early snows are the constant subject of conversation between hikers, and many times delay the last hike for days or weeks or even until the next season. But, he doesn't say anything to the others.

As it turns out, Charlie's on the pittypot that night at dinner, and she says, "I really feel bad about holding you guys up, once again. Damn, I hate this. Here I am, a tough woman of the nineties, and I can't even keep up with you guys."

Sam says, "Charlie, don't worry about it. We're gonna make it. You know, it reminds me of a story." Eyes roll and groans rise in a chorus. They have heard Sam's stories many times in the past and the response most of those times, is boos. Completely undaunted by their reaction, he plows ahead.

"It seems there was this golfer who came home three hours late from a golf game. He's late to supper, and his wife's plenty pissed and worried. He tells her, "Now, don't be mad. I had a terrible day." She says, "But you love golf. How could it have been a terrible day?" He says, "Well, you know old Charley, my golfing partner for the last 20 years?" She says, "Of course. What about him?" "Well, on the third hole, old Charley has a heart attack. Laid down on the ground and died, on the third green." She says, "That's terrible! Poor old Charley. No wonder you were late. I guess hospitals, ambulances, all of that made you late, huh?" He says, "Well, not exactly. From the third hole on, it was hit the ball, drag Charley. Hit the ball, drag Charley. It was awful. Wore me out, I'll tell you."

Following the groans, Sam moves further away from their Charlie, whose eyes are about as narrow as they can be and still be open. He says, "Here, it's just a little bit different. Here, it's hike a mile, drag Charlie. Hike a mile, drag . . ." That's as far as he gets, and the patrons of the restaurant look agape at a bearded hiker, dashing out of the restaurant, just ahead of an attractive lady hiker, who is limping after him and swinging a cane around her head, threatening death and destruction.

Sam escapes and returns to the table, but no Charlie. George and Jon look around. "Where's the killer lady?" asks Jon.

"I don't know. I was lucky. Since she's crippled up, I lost her a block down the road. I'm sure she'll find me. She has a memory like an elephant, particularly for jokes she perceives as slamming her female machismo. You know . . . " That's as far as he gets, before his words are choked in a flood. A flood that comes from a very large pitcher of water that Charlie has borrowed from a waiter and is dumping over Sam's head. Everybody in the restaurant is laughing as Charlie places the now empty pitcher on top of Sam's head, balanced perfectly, then she sits, lady-like and demurely places her napkin in her lap. "Now, sweety, what was it you were saying?"

"Nothing, darling," says Sam, sitting very still to avoid dumping the pitcher. "I guess I deserved that, huh? But, I had to get you out of that 'poor me' frame of mind."

"Well, it's gone, now. And it was fun getting rid of it. You guys ready to hit the bright lights of this here town? I think I saw a pub down the road." The group leaves, animosity forgotten and try to drink the pub dry, leading to the first hangover any of them has suffered for months. The next morning, Jon groans, "Damn, guys, I've forgotten how much I hate this. My clean living has let me avoid this feeling for nigh on to a year, and it ain't no better. Damn, my head hurts."

Sympathetic groans are his only answer. Nobody minds an extra night in town, because Charlie's ankle still needs healing. So, they rest, healing bodies, ankles, and heads. Over lunch, Charlie asks Jon, "What's up for tomorrow, oh great leader?"

Jon has been practically memorizing the plan, trying to dislodge his feeling of uneasiness about the overall schedule. He says, "Right at eight miles to Cloudland. Then it's six to West Hartford for re-supply. We can see how your ankle is doing when we get there, and stay or not. One night won't hurt our progress. That sound doable, Charlie?"

She sits quietly for a moment. "I think so. I'm barely limping now and hopefully in the morning that will be gone."

Sam says, "We three mules of the trail will take on part of your load until you are back to full strength. Maybe that'll help some."

Charlie's eyes are getting that narrowed look, so Sam hastens to add, "Of course, we've done that before for a friend of mine. A male friend, Charlie."

"Of course, friend Sam. I knew you meant that as a non-sexist comment. However, just to teach you a lesson for aggravating a physically handicapped person last night, I will try to save the heaviest parts of my pack, just for you. Okay, Sweetie?"

Sam leaves well enough alone, and his only response is an affirmative nod. No sense in pushing his luck. Lunch is finished in peace, and headache recovery continues with naps.

Following breakfast, the four divide much of Charlie's load, and distribute small items to their packs, leaving her with about 18 pounds in her pack. She puts the pack on, takes a few experimental steps around outside the motel, and says, "I believe this will work, guys. I'll take back my stuff as soon as I can. Thanks."

They catch a ride back to the trailhead and start up the trail. Charlie gamely keeps up for much of the morning, but falls behind before lunch. Jon and Sam hike on ahead. When they stop for lunch, they worriedly discuss whether or not she will be able to make the full eight miles for the day. Sam says, "I'll bet you dish washing tonight that Charlie will get to Happy Hill tonight."

Jon laughs, "Man, that's a sucker bet if I ever heard one. No way I'll bet against Charlie. That gal's tough. No, she'll be there."

The men arrive at the shelter by three o'clock, and the shelter is empty. They lay out their bedrolls and place some clothing on two other bunks, reserving them for Charlie and George. It proves a good thing that they did this, because by four o'clock, the shelter is rapidly filling with hikers. At four-thirty, Sam spots their friends moving slowly across the clearing to the shelter. He breathes a sigh of relief. "Welcome, guys. How's the ankle, Charlie?"

"Sore, but workable. We just took our time. I'm grateful that there were no real mountains during the day."

Sam helps her with her pack, and she sits on her bunk. "Whew, that feels better already. "George, I think I'll play lady of leisure tonight, if you don't mind. I've got to take this boot off."

Jon kneels in front of her and carefully unties her boot and removes it. Her ankle is somewhat swollen, but the colors are subsiding. He pours cool water from the spring over her foot and ankle. She sighs again. "Thanks, Jon. That feels even better. Now, slaves, take care of your queen. Hop to it."

The three men laugh, as much because of relief as anything else. Charlie's back. They hop to it and serve her dinner in bed. Bunk, that is. She hobbles outside after eating and has a cup of tea. Bedtime comes early, and snores and mice bother no one.

The six miles to Hanover, Vermont, look like a long day, particularly for Charlie. She does keep up, and they catch a ride to town and check into a motel before dark.

Over dinner, she asks Jon, "What's on tap for tomorrow? Long or short?"

Jon has to check the guide this time. "Real short, Charlie. Six miles tomorrow, then 10 the next day, then eight the day following. On the eight-mile day, we cross into New Hampshire. Next to the last state. Sounds good. My guide says that it's one of the prettiest parts of the AT. We go into the White Mountains. Lots of 3000-foot climbs with spectacular views. You can see where you're going as well as you can see where you've been. Sounds neat. What about you guys?"

"Yep, sounds okay, except for that 'lots of 3000-foot climbs. I can probably start taking back some of my stuff tomorrow. I'm walking better now, and, while you guys have suffered in silence, I can still see that that extra six or eight pounds hurts. So, we'll divy some gear back to my pack." The men protest, but not much. Extra weight does make an impact on a person. They all sleep well.

At breakfast the next morning Jon says, "You know guys, I guess I enjoy breakfast off the trail more than any other meal. Mainly because I don't have to do the dishes. I hate doing dishes in the morning. You're ready to hit the trail, to move on. But there you are, squatting by a puddle, washing dishes. I guess that's why most of my breakfasts are coffee and breakfast bar. These pancakes this morning are great. But I'm ready to move on up the trail." Jon's three companions have not slowed up at all in pursuing their share of the pancakes and they let him ramble on in his soliloquy.

They load up and pay a local shuttle driver to take them to the trailhead. They complete the hike by one o'clock, not bothering to stop for lunch on the trail, but eat at Cloudland Shelter. The 10-mile day to Happy Hill Cabin also passes smoothly. At noon the following day, they cross the Connecticut River, crossing one more state line.

17

"TWO BOTTLES OF BEER ON THE WALL . . . "

On day 130, the hikers cross a significant milestone–the Vermont-New Hampshire state line, which means that they have only two states left to cross before they succeed in their quest for Katahdin. Granted, they have 160 miles to hike in New Hampshire, then they face the final 280 miles of the trail through Maine. Even though it is only early September, the evenings are gaining a definite nip, and Jon and Sam are glad that they had a discussion with Charlie and George a few weeks ago. They had agreed to have Jon call Andy, when they were in Killington, to have him send up a four-man tent. It should be waiting for them in North Woodstock. As the four continue to move northward and fall proceeds with them, shared body heat in the larger tent will help ward off cold. Plus, they send back three smaller tents and lose a few ounces of pack weight. Get rid of those ounces whenever possible. When they had started this hike, they needed to get rid of pounds. As they got smarter with increasing miles, they got smarter with decreasing weight. Whatever isn't used almost every day, has to go, and it does go.

A half-mile from the state line, the men enter Hanover, New Hampshire, and find a pizza restaurant near the Dartmouth College campus. They had decided to wait there for Charlie and George, trailing behind only a few miles. They go into the restaurant and order the buffet line. Ah, yes, bless those all-you-can-eat places. Some six or eight trips through the serving line, Jon leans back in his chair. "Well, Sam, did you get enough to eat? We could find another all-you-can-eat restaurant and see what they have to offer."

"Nah, I believe I've had sufficient. Couldn't eat another bite if my life depended on it. But, our buddies aren't here yet. Got anything in mind to kill a little time?"

"Well, that little park across the street has several empty benches. You reckon the policemen will haul our respective asses away, if we avail ourselves of a spot and catch some z's? That sounds like a productive way to kill time."

"There's a cop right over there. I think I'll go ask and see what he says." Sam walks over to the police officer and engages him in conversation. He returns to the glass store front of the restaurant, and beckons at Jon.

They carry their packs over to the park and put them under the benches and soon fill the air with snores. The snores cease when Charlie pinches each of their noses in turn, and they struggle awake from the depths of sleep. Charlie says, "Damn, guys, we leave you in charge of keeping watch and the only thing you watch is the inside of your eyelids. Here, watch our packs while we go have a close encounter with that restaurant." Jon looks at Sam, who is looking at him. They both shake their heads and return to their naps.

Thirty minutes later, either Charlie and George eat their fill, or the restaurant runs out of pizza. They return to the park benches where Jon and Sam sleep, oblivious to any surroundings. Students passing by, hurrying to classes, laugh at the scene. Charlie and George count to three, and two park benches are dumped over, landing on top of their loads. Both men wake rather rudely. Packs back in place, the four hikers stride out of Hanover, back onto the trail.

It is only a mile and a half to Velvet Rocks Shelter, but it seems like more. It had been only a brief stint in civilization, but once again, they had been spoiled. After dinner, Charlie says, "Okay, Jon-boy. How long do we have to go before we get to really sample the soft life again? An hour in town doesn't remove very many cobwebs."

Jon digs the *Trail Guide* out of his pack and scans the schedule. "Well, let's see. Five more nights, all of them at shelters. Sixty-eight miles and five mountains listed. Any more information you desire, Madam?"

"Ugh, that's enough. I think you gave me more information than I really wanted. Sixty-eight miles over six days. Well, that's not too bad. Eleven miles a day. I can handle that. Now, please pour me another cup of tea, Jeeves. Two lumps instead of one, this time. Thank you, Sir."

It may only be six days, but when it is raining hard for four of those days, things get pretty uncomfortable and slushy. Add to that, three substantial mountains, and you have a formula for misery. The hikers barely get dry in the scarce sun when the heavens open up, and the torrents start again. Every night the shelters are filled with clothes and gear hanging in the rafters, and the hikers are hoping in vain for them to dry. Feet are as white as ghosts and muscles hurt, mainly from the constant slipping and sliding on the muddy trail.

At Eliza Brook Shelter, only eight miles from North Woodstock, Sam says, "Well, not far to civilization, now. I can feel that soft bed and taste that real food and cold beer. I'm looking forward to getting my re-supply carton. Jon, isn't this where the new tent is supposed to be waiting for us?"

Jon nods affirmatively. "Yep, if Andy did his job. We can take the three tents we've been toting and send them back home. Even though the new tent is a bit heavier, when we split it four ways, we ought to lose a pound or two between us. Sounds good to me."

Charlie adds, "Jon, I hate to ask this, but are there any mountains tomorrow?"

"Unhuh; I guess they're cousins. At least they're related."

"What the hell do you mean?"

"Well, the first is known as South Kinsman Mountain. And the second is . . . "

"Don't tell me, let me guess. North Kinsman Mountain. Yep, they're definitely kin. Quite a pun, chief. Your humor is completely underwhelming and appreciated very little."

Jon laughs at his attempt at a joke. Sometimes you have to laugh at things to keep from crying. He feels that this upcoming stay in town is maybe one of the most welcome since the hike had begun those many months ago. It has only been nine days since their last stay in a town, but the rain has made it feel like much, much longer.

The exhausted hikers sleep, and the sleeping bags, damp around every corner and seam in spite of all the care, bother no one. In the morning, spirits are high, and laughter and jokes sound around the cooking area and the stoves. The eight and a half mile hike seems like nothing, even with two mountains to cross. Charlie amazes the men, as she not only keeps up, but leads for most of the day. They arrive at the road crossing in the middle of the afternoon, and that proves fortuitous. By the time a truck stops hours later to offer a ride to town, dark is closing in fast. Since it's almost six miles to town and the post office, walking there had been out of the question, so they had waited. The driver drops them off at the motel, and dry rooms and hot, wet, showers claim all of their attention for almost an hour.

After checking the yellow pages, Jon yells at Sam, still camped out in the shower. "Hey, Sam, how does a place called Truants Tavern sound for eats? I guess we're all too old to worry about the truant officer, so it will be safe. You about done? I can't imagine your body accepting any more water after the last week. I was super-saturated, if I remember my chemistry correctly."

"All right, all right. I'm hurrying. Go see if the odd couple is ready to go while I get dressed."

Jon walks next door as Charlie and George are exiting their room, definitely ready for food and beer. They go back to Jon and Sam's room and take turns yelling at Sam through the closed bathroom door, until he finally comes out and they head up the road, wet hair slicked back. On their way to the restaurant, they spot a Laundromat and an ice-cream store. Nobody's interested in laundry tonight, but they check the closing time for the ice cream store and verify that it will still be open when they finish dinner. You've got to get your priorities in order.

An hour and a half later, after huge hamburgers, mountains of fries and copious quantities of beer, the foursome half walks, half staggers back up the street and completes their evening. Each proceeds to eat two desserts, including a "Matterhorn" each. The Matterhorn, a mountain of ice cream and every topping known to mankind, is designed to satiate a normal human being, but these are no longer normal human beings. They are hikers. Thru-hikers. What's a mere Matterhorn after all the mountains they have crossed? Just one more. Back to the motel and the sleep of the exhausted.

In the morning, Jon calls a representative of the hiking club and gets information about what is available in the area. He gets the phone number of the Hikers Shuttle Connection, where a pleasant young lady agrees to pick them up at eleven o'clock and take them to a town where there is an outfitter, Alpine Wilderness Equipment. Each hiker plans to purchase items they need. First, breakfast calls, then package pickup. Included in the packages should be the four-man tent they are utilizing the rest of the trip, when shelters aren't available.

The tent is at the post office, and, after taking it outside, they unroll it. They check for poles, stakes, and ropes, and they realize that there is no ground cloth. They add that piece of important equipment to the list of gear they plan to purchase at the outfitters.

Following their return from the purchase of the gear, the hikers opt for naps, even before lunch. An hour later, stomachs rumble, and they visit the nearest fast food restaurant, where additional hamburgers and fries are required to satisfy the rumbles. The afternoon is whiled away with the TV, and dinnertime comes on them before they know it. The only problem with this dinnertime is that it signifies that their departure time back to the trail is also quite near. Jon calls the shuttle place again and arranges for transportation the next morning back to the trail head at seven o'clock.

Over dinner, they check the guide and Charlie groans, "Guys, guys, guys. Look at this–three mountains. The only good thing is that it's only a 12-mile day. Listen to me! <u>Only</u> 12 miles. My attitude toward mileage has sure changed over the past few months. When we started, 12 miles was eternity. Now it's only 12 miles. I'm tougher or crazier. Don't answer that question if you value your lives."

Her three companions closed their mouths. They had each been prepared to say something smart prior to Charlie's warning. But, discretion pays off and they all live. At seven-thirty a.m., they are on the trail, heading for Garfield Ridge, where they will get a chance to try out the new tent. The three tents, that had served them well to this time, had been boxed and sent home, so it is togetherness from now on. Charlie explains the Gospel according to Charlie. "I am to be in the tent by myself until I change clothes and am in the sleeping bag. Then, and only then, are you men allowed to enter."

"What if it's raining?" the men wail.

"I doubt that any of you guys will melt. It won't hurt you. A lady has to have her privacy, and this lady intends to have hers." Even though only one position is given in the debate, the argument is over. The men never had a chance; there is no sense in even trying.

Seven hours later, the troop staggers into the campsite and learns once again that setting up a new tent for the first time is a real struggle. Even with the help of, no, make that in spite of, the instructions. They succeed, and they take turns laying out sleeping mats and bags. The tent is quite roomy, and the add-on vestibule has enough space to place all four packs out of the night air and the dew. All of the hikers are pleased with their accommodations and get down to work with evening chores.

Following dinner, tea time brings discussions until heavy eyes and tired bodies necessitate a close to the evening. All four quickly fall asleep. The next day is long–17 miles, and it offers two mountains for their hiking pleasure. Eighty miles and six nights and 13 mountains are between them and the New Hampshire-Maine line, their next milestone. Nearly the last, actually.

18 "NEXT TO THE LAST"

In the morning, Jon is sitting by his stove. He is not fixing coffee for a simple reason. His stove, which is almost brand new, won't work. Something is stopped up, and the fuel won't flow to the burner. He glares at it. His coffee is important, and this inanimate object won't cooperate. "Damn," he says, perhaps a little louder than he intends.

"Damn what?" asks Charlie, who has quietly walked up behind him.

Jon jumps. "I didn't hear you come out of the tent. "Damn this stove. It won't make a sound, much less a roar. I can't share any coffee with you this morning, Charlie."

"Well, I believe we fix that," she says. She returns to the tent and pulls a stove out of her pack. They light it, and it makes the satisfying roar that signifies progress on boiling water. "Now, tell me all about it. What's troubling you today, Bucko? The stove-fighting you were doing wouldn't usually aggravate you that much."

"I don't know. When I woke up this morning, I was in a blue funk. Can't even tell you why. Just grumpy, I guess."

"We're not used to you being grumpy, oh Fearless Leader. We can't have that," she says. "Tell me about today's hike. What have we got in front of us? 37 miles and 14 mountains?"

Jon laughs, "Well, so much for my grump. I can't laugh and keep a good pout going on. Charlie, I'm gonna pay you a strange compliment. You remind me of Pookie. He could sense whenever I was out of sorts. He would sit close to me, looking sad. If that didn't work, he'd act the clown. He would do whatever it took to make me laugh and get me back into a better mood."

Charlie has to laugh, "Well, at least my nose isn't cold and wet. I'll take that comparison as a compliment. A real good compliment, being compared to a four-legged dog rather than to a person. Now, drink your coffee and start your day over again. You know, we can start our days over and over again, if we want to, until we get it right. Now, what's in store for us today?"

Jon checks the omnipresent guide. "Well, certainly not as bad as you said, but maybe not too good. Seventeen miles and four mountains. We're gonna stay at Crawford Notch Campsite tonight. Then tomorrow night, I thought we'd try one of the Huts. I read somewhere that they are big places, like motels right on the trail, and there are folks working there. They are just like motels, right up here in the White Mountains. Hold up to 90 people, so there will be plenty of flatlanders. If we fix our dinners, it's $40 with breakfast. You know how I feel about washing breakfast dishes. They say, if you're low on bucks, they will find you work to pay off your stay. We've got three or four nights of the Huts to stay in, so if it gets to be a money problem, we can try that."

"Sounds different. Our definition of wilderness is gonna change a bit, eh what? Something to look forward to, anyway. What say we rouse these lazy ones and move on down the road?"

The morning goes better than it started for Jon. At lunchtime, they have climbed the second of their quartet of mountains for the day and are sitting on top of Mt. Jackson. The foot traffic in this part of the Whites has increased substantially, and they pass almost as many people as they did back down in the Smokies. Two miles farther, they pass one of the huts and are impressed at the size of the place. They take a rest break, and Jon wanders over to talk to one of the staff.

"How's it going?" he asks.

"Well, there could be better places to work than here, but I can't imagine where it would be. I love it up here."

"What do you do in the real world?"

"I'm a student at Dartmouth, but the day after school is out, I head up here. This is my third year of this, and I guess I'll go on and get a Master's, so I can do this during the summer for one more year, before I have to become a real person and go to work. What about you?"

"Well, I'm through with school, but the only job I could find in Tuscaloosa was in a garage. I'm doing this hike sorta to see if I can decide what to do. I'm still not sure, but I've decided that a change is necessary for my sanity. I've got a question. Are these Huts first come, first serve?"

"No way, Jose'. They need reservations and are usually pretty crowded. You're heading for Lakes of the Clouds?"

"Yeah, that's the plan."

"Tell you what. I've got to go over there to bring back a spare part for our stove. I'll be going over there light, so if you will give me a little headstart, I'll be over there way before you turtles. I'll get you four reservations, if I can. A lot of people wander in without reservations, so it should work okay. It's only five miles, so it won't take me long. I do it about every other day. What's your name?"

"Jon Parker, and there's four of us. Thanks, man, I appreciate your help. These crazy people have elected me their pro-forma leader, and what they don't know is, I don't know what the hell I'm doing most of the time."

The man laughs, "No sweat, see you over there." He goes into the hut, grabs an empty pack, and with a wave of his hand, disappears into the forest. Jon returns to his companions and tells them what has transpired. They laze around for another 15 minutes and head up the trail.

Two mountains later they are within a mile and a half of the Hut, and Jon's new friend appears on the trail, walking briskly in spite of the rather large metal piece strapped to the pack on his back. "Hey, Jon, you enjoy those little hills of ours?"

Jon unslings his pack and sits heavily on the ground. "Rough enough, though they are sure pretty. It's hard to see pretty when you're gasping for breath like we were."

The man says, "Well, I got your reservations, but it was close. There was one space left, after I pulled in a favor from Fran over there, and there were five city hikers fighting over that space. You'd best get there and claim your bunks."

"Thanks, we really appreciate your help. I think that the thought of a real bunk has been part of what's kept us going."

"Glad to help. Good luck with whatever you decide to do with your real life. Come on back, and let me know. Bye," waving his hand and walking away.

"Okay, I'll try to. Thanks again."

Jon and his companions rise and walk. They soon arrive at the Hut, where they get glares from some despondent hikers sitting on the porch. "Lucky ducks, wish I had gotten a reservation," one of the hikers says. "We've got to move on down the trail six miles to Israel Ridge Path before we can stay the night."

Jon doesn't mention how lucky he was to get the reservations. He, like Brer Fox, just "lays low."

Jon and the others decide to be lazy tonight and be waited on. Charlie says, "This sounds good for tonight, but we're getting a bit low on wherewithal, so we may have to become indentured servants at the other huts we stop at."

"Hum," says Jon. "I hope I don't run out of money. Having you wait on me hand and foot sounds like it could be really interesting."

"You wouldn't do that, would you? You dirty rat. I believe that you would indeed. George," she wails, "listen to this," and she stomps away. Jon stands there and laughs.

In the morning after enjoying breakfast with no dirty dishes, the herd begins an easy hike-only six miles. When they arrive at the Hut, Jon goes into the office. He is able to get four places and pays for the night. When he goes back out, he says to Charlie, "Well, don't ever say that I've never done anything nice for you. Here is your reservation."

Charlie stands there, mouth agape. "Thanks, Jon, you didn't have to do that. I appreciate it. By the way, how about reservations for the rest of the huts we want to stay in?"

Jon pulls the Three Stooges head slap routine again. "Damn, I'm dumb. I guess maybe we ought to try and do that. Wonder if they can make the reservations here."

Going back into the office, Jon finds that he can, indeed, make the reservations for the next night, at Madison Springs Hut. From there, they will stay in a shelter and then tent camp. The day following the camping, they will cross into Maine. State number last. Fini'. Twelve down, one to go. That night over tea, the four friends discuss this thought. Jon says, "Well guys, I really don't know whether to be happy or sad. I'm tickled to death that I will have finished a goal I set for myself. But I'm not sure I'm thrilled to be going back to the real world." He sits, pondering his own philosophical words.

George responds, "I'm with you. Charlie and I still have to go back and pick up that 180 miles we missed during Pop's surgery before we can call ourselves Thru-hikers. How long did it take you guys to cover that stretch, Jon?"

Jon pulls out his Guide. "Let's see, right at two weeks. What are you thinking, George?"

"Yeah, George, what are you thinking," says Charlie.

"Well, what month is it now? I've lost track of time."

A discussion follows; they agree that it is early September. George asks, "Okay, what have we got left to Katahdin if we stay on track? "

Back to the schedule. Jon adds, and subtracts, and figures. More discussion. Jon rocks back on his heels. "Best I can cipher it, right at 30 days. One short month. I suspect that it will be getting cold up on Katahdin, but we should be able to make it okay."

George sits and ponders the possibilities and permutations. "I reckon that, if we finish with you guys, we're gonna be about out of money. That may present a real problem, but I'm interested in catching a ride to Pennsylvania and finishing that last leg. I hate to not complete something I start. How about you, sweets? Sound doable?"

Charlie's turn to ponder. "Yeah, I guess I'll have two more weeks left in me. But you'd better ask me again as we walk down Katahdin."

Jon is getting excited for George and Charlie. "Tell you what, guys. If it looks like it may happen like that and if there's any money left in the newspaper bankroll, I'll help with that part of the two weeks. There is a catch. You have to call me and let me know when you finish. Weather shouldn't be a problem back down in Pennsylvania. Shouldn't be as cold as it will be in northern Maine."

George and Charlie are overwhelmed by their friend's generosity. Both give him a hug, and quiet reigns.

The next few days go relatively smoothly. Fourteen, then 12, then 11 miles are ticked off, and they arrive at Trident Col Tentsite, only 10 miles from the Maine state line. From that point, they have a mere 281 miles of Maine to traverse to Katahdin.

19 ONE MORE, ONLY ONE MORE

At lunchtime, the hikers sit, almost straddling the New Hampshire-Maine line. "Well, we made it, guys," says Jon. "We, by God, made it. State number last on our hit parade." High five's are exchanged, and they settle down to lunch. Jon checks the schedule. "Well, a bit of bad news. I was so excited about reaching the state line that I forgot to check on re-supply. We've still got nine days till then. How are you guys fixed for food?"

Everyone does an inventory and they agree that they have enough, but barely. No feasts for the next week and a half. Jon checks and re-checks the Guide. "There's really no possible relief in sight, either. The nearest towns are eight and nine miles away from the trail. I guess we're back in the wilderness, huh?"

"Yep," says Charlie. "No rest for the weary. We can make it though. If we can sit calmly through a hurricane, we ought to be able to handle this small hiccup."

Sam adds, "I don't see how you can say that with a straight face. I don't remember sitting there calmly. I seem to remember that I was paralyzed with total and complete fear."

"Well, fear, calm, whatever. We made it, anyway."

The hikers arrive at Carlo Col Shelter relatively early and enjoy the inactivity. Doing nothing is exactly what is called for, so that's what they do. Absolutely nothing.

During dinner, Charlie says, "You know, guys, it may be strange, but I don't feel any different."

Sam, Jon, and George share blank looks. "Okay," says Sam, "I might as well bite. Why, Charlie, should you feel any different?"

"Well, it's because we're in Maine. I somehow thought I'd feel different. But, it is awfully pretty here. These trees have been getting more and more beautiful the past week or so. Look at the size of these guys," gesturing at the surrounding forest with her hand.

Sam says, "Gee, Toto, it sure don't look like Kansas. I think I know what you mean, Charlie. Sometimes as we move along, the area starts to change, but we walk so slowly that it's hard to recognize it. I do know what you can do some day, if you're interested in seeing the changes in flora more quickly."

"Okay, what?"

"Go back to Tennessee and climb Mt. LeConte. If you hike it from Gatlinburg, it's a vertical mile from there to the top. I read somewhere that the change in flora on that mountain is the same as if you hiked from Georgia to Maine. Plus, you get to stay at the lodge up there and get waited on like in the huts in New Hampshire."

"Damn," says Charlie.

"What do you mean, Damn?"

"Hiking up one mountain sounds a lot easier that what we've done for the past five months." She laughs. "Just kidding. But, that does sound interesting. We may do that some day after this is all over." The sounds of approaching hikers ends philosophy hour, and they greet the party of six hikers coming down Carlo Col Trail.

The next few days go smoothly, as the shelters in this part of Maine are spaced in 10-mile increments. They move past Speck Pond Shelter, Frye Notch Lean-to, and Hall Mountain Lean-to, arriving at Bemis Mountain Lean-to. That night, they do an inventory of food and realize that supplies are getting sparse. Jon says, "Old Mother Hubbard went to the cupboard, to get her poor daughter a dress . . . "

Silence. Charlie casts a glance at him. More silence. "Jon!" she yells. "I've never heard that version. Finish it!"

" . . . But when she got there, the cupboard was bare, and so was her daughter, I guess."

The only question is whether the groans are louder than the laughs. It's close. Jon says, "Well guys, sorry 'bout that. That's the best humor I'm capable of. All seriousness aside . . . "

Charlie laughs, "All seriousness is usually aside, with this group. But, go ahead. What's on your mind?"

"Well, I've been looking at this guide, and, if you guys are up to it, we can maybe modify schedule and get to Stratton a day earlier. It'll mean 14-mile days rather than these 10's. What do you think?"

The others crowd around Jon, and he shows them what he means. "Not bad," says Charlie. "I believe we can do it. I'd rather walk a little farther and get to re-supply a day earlier. The way it's going now, we might be looking for wild game the last day, and I think that's illegal. No, wait a minute. I forgot. We have a world-renown big game hunter in our midst. Sam, tell us about that day you caught all those rattlesnakes . . . "

Sam turns red. "Damn, Charlie, I was hoping you guys had forgotten about that. I was sure trying to forget. Nope, count me out. I ain't hunting no rattlers."

The decision made, the hikers hit the sack early. Longer days call for more rest. The next day, they by-pass Sabbath Day Pond Lean-to and camp for the night at Little Swift River Campsite, then make 16 miles the next day to Poplar Ridge Lean-to. Fourteen miles the next day takes them to Crocker Cirque Campsite, and they collapse on the ground in a heap as they arrive. "Okay, guys, you've done it," gasps Charlie.

"Done what?" asks Jon.

"Done wore me out, that's what," she says. "Jon, this accelerated schedule was your idea. Why don't you fix my supper. I'm too tired. And, look at poor old George. His tongue is actually hanging out."

Jon laughs. "Okay, okay. Since we'll be at Stratton tomorrow shortly after lunch, let's combine all of our tasty pasta dishes and make a mulligan stew. Sam, what do you have?"

The mulligan stew proves good. Different, anyway. When you mix canned chicken, tuna, ham, and three kinds of pasta, the taste is unusual. During philosophy hour, Charlie asks a question. "I've been wondering something. Jon, didn't you take a course in geology?"

"Guilty as charged. I hope you're not gonna ask very complicated questions. I've slept since then."

"No, not too complicated. It's a given that they talk kinda funny up here, right?"

A chorus of "Ayh ah" answers her question.

"But, they also name things up here strangely as well. I thought maybe some of it might be geologic in nature. Where we're staying, for example. What the hell is a cirque?"

"Good guess, Charlie. It's geology. I remember that much. Some of the stuff up here is named after glaciers. A cirque is rounded out of a mountain by a glacier where it begins. The ice sorta chews on the rocks and carves out something that looks like an outdoor amphitheater. That's where we are. I recognized another name, where we stayed a few days ago–a col is the low point on a ridge that has a bunch of cirques backing up to each other. The high points are horns. Those are strange names to us, because there weren't any glaciers where we live. There, that's the extent of my glacial knowledge. I hope you don't have any more questions, 'cause I'm out of answers."

"Thanks, Jon. Even I can understand that. You know, maybe you've missed your calling. You just might be a good teacher. What was your major at Alabama?"

"History. That's why I'm working at a garage. There's nothing at all you can do with a Bachelor's Degree in history except maybe work at a garage or flip hamburgers. Teacher, huh. Interesting. I'll have to think on that a bit." Philosophy hour ends, and the hikers prepare for bed. All are looking forward to civilization tomorrow.

They arrive at Stratton at two o'clock in the afternoon and catch a shuttle to Widow's Walk Bed and Breakfast. Following showers, they wander to Kathy's White Wolf Cafe. Their attempts to shock the workers there by the amount of food they consume falls short, because those folks are used to thru-hikers and very little shocks them. Their waitress says, "I'm disappointed. I thought you guys were gonna eat a lot. You ought to see what some folks consume. It takes three or four meals to fill them up."

She gives them directions to a good re-supply place, the Laundromat, and the tavern where the younger folks in the town hang out. Jon says, "I don't know about you guys, but I'm not up to a tavern tonight. Maybe tomorrow night. My soft bed is calling me."

Another tough decision made, they return to the B & B and sleep hard that night. Never do today what you can put off until tomorrow, that's their motto. At least for tonight. Jon dreams of Gretel. He wakes, and vows to call her when he gets back to civilization and tell her that he completed the hike. Filled with resolve, he drifts off to sleep.

The next day is spent in the mundane, off-trail day-to-day tasks of the thru-hiker. Several washings of their clothes, buying and preparing packages of food, and replacing the little odds and ends of gear that have worn out in the stress of the trail. Civilization is wonderful and they enjoy themselves immensely. Eat, drink, and be merry, for tomorrow you hike. Another apropos corny motto.

The Stratton visit is a restful one. The morning following the second night dawns clear. No clouds mar the bright, blue sky. There is a crisp feel in the air, and the hikers stride out at a brisk pace following their shuttle ride to the trailhead.

During the mid-morning break, Charlie reads to them from her copy of the *Thru-Hiker's Companion*.. "Hey, guys, did you know that this area we're walking through was nearly developed into vacation homes and ski-lifts, before they stopped the development?"

"No kidding," says Jon. "When was that?"

"Back in the seventies, this almost became the Aspen of the East. Can't you see this trail surrounded by civilization?"

"Nope," says Sam. "I like it just fine the way it is."

"By the way, Jon, you forgot to give me my mountain warning report this morning, about crossings we have to make," gripes Charlie. "Look at this–Bigelow Mountain, just three miles from here. You're slipping, Bud. You are liable to get fired from your job, if you aren't careful. You're supposed to keep me informed."

"Fire me, fire me," says Jon. "Anybody that wants this job and the bitching that comes with it, is welcome."

The others look at each other and shake their heads. "Nope," says Charlie. "You're still the tour guide by acclamation. Just try to do better, if you're capable." Charlie deftly dodges the pine cones that Jon tosses at her.

The mountain is whipped, and they arrive at Myron Avery Lean-to. There are already half-a-dozen hikers set up in the shelter, and Jon and crew quickly claim bunks.

The scene after dinner reminds Jon of his early days in summer camp. One of the south-bound hikers starts singing in a low voice and is soon joined by the others. John Denver, Gordon Lightfoot, and James Taylor songs get a real workout. The following morning, Jon and Sam discuss the previous evening. Jon says, "Kinda hokey, but lots of fun, huh?"

"Yeah, I enjoyed that. Shame I can't sing worth a flip. But, there's safety in numbers 'cause nobody can hear me in a crowd."

"Oh, shit," says Jon softly.

"What's the matter?"

"I forgot something. I'd better fix it. Oh Charlie, there's a mountain ahead. The other end of Bigelow Mountain. Just to make it up to you for not telling you earlier, I've arranged for a real short hike today. A little more than seven miles. Sound okay?"

"Seven miles? I guess I can stand one mountain. Good job, Jon. Good arranging. You move those rocks and mountains around as well as God and Mother Nature."

"Shucks," says Jon. "I screw up, and she gives me compliments, no less. I'll manage to get fired, yet."

The banter continues all the way to little Bigelow Lean-to. Strange how banter and trail length seem inversely proportional. The shorter the trail, the more ratchet-jawing.

The next two days pass smoothly until they arrive at Pierce Pond Lean-to. The shelter is full. There's no room at the inn. Jon and crew find a likely place and set up their tent, grumbling all the way.

"Hope a ranger doesn't nab us," says George. "We don't need a fine."

"Maybe since we're thru-hikers, he'll have mercy on us," says Jon.

Luckily, at this time, police protection is sparse, and no ranger appears. During tea time, Charlie is taking her new self-proclaimed job as recreation director in a serious way. "Hey fellas, three miles up the trail tomorrow we hit the most dangerous river crossing on the whole AT-the Kennebee River. A guy drowned there about 10 years ago, trying to ford."

"Damn," says Jon. "That doesn't sound so good. No fun."

"Well," says Charlie. "I saved the best for last. All we have to do is hop on the ferry and we'll be okay. No problem."

"A ferry? Damn if you didn't get me that time, Charlie. See what trust I place in you?' I believe every word you say."

Charlie laughs, "Yep, sure did. You ford if you want, Jon. I don't think I will." Charlie is still chuckling, as she crawls into the tent and prepares for bed. She is soon joined by the three men.

Spirits are still high as the group heads out in the morning. They are out and about early, although a light mist obscures visibility.

Charlie, who is in the lead, walks around a curve in the trail, followed by the men. She comes to a sudden stop, which leads to a four-car pile up. "Wait guys," she says. "Something's out there."

They stand still, but can't detect any movement or identify any noises. "What did it sound like, Charlie?" asks Jon.

"Don't know. It was a . . . a soft grunt, right out in front of me. I don't hear it now, though." She starts slowly forward. She stops again. "There it is again. Around that curve in the trail."

The foursome creeps ahead. Charlie stops once more. "Damn, guys, there it is," and she points a trembling finger at an enormous animal standing in the trail. "It's a moose!"

"Are they dangerous?" asks Sam.

"I think just during rutting season. But the way I figure it, anything that big has got to be dangerous."

The object of the discussion stands still, placidly chewing on his cud and gazing over the side of a drop-off on the left side of the trail. His rack of velvet-covered antlers slowly turns, as he continues to chew his cud.

The hikers hold their ground. The moose holds his. Ten minutes pass, and the hikers get restive. "I'm ready to move out," whispers Charlie. "What can we do?"

"He doesn't look so dangerous. Ask him politely to move over so we can get past," whispers Jon.

"You ask him!"

"You're in the lead. Go ahead, start walking slowly toward him. See what happens."

Charlie sends a look at Jon that holds a promise of revenge later. She takes a step toward the moose, then another, and another. The moose watches with no reaction. The hikers keep going, reducing the distance. Charlie stops. "He ain't budging. Shoo, big guy," and she waves her hands. His head sways up in alarm. "Shoo!" says a trembling Charlie. The moose gives a sigh, then turns and saunters down the trail, happily away from the hikers and into the forest. Charlie sits down, right in the middle of the trail. "Whew, Bullwinkle is gone. I don't believe that. What was that, a ton of critter?"

"'Bout that," says George. "Moose are usually quite skittish, but I still can't believe you shooed him away with a wave of your hands. I guess this particular one liked you, Charlie."

"Well. I'm not so crazy about him. I'm glad he's gone. Now I'm outta here. Help me up, somebody."

The crew arrives at the Kennebee River and is ferried across. Three hours later, midafternoon finds the group at Pleasant Pond Lean-to, the first hikers to arrive. They stake claims on bunks with sleeping bags and wander into the thick forest, playing tourist.

It's a peaceful evening, with plenty of repartee' with the other hikers at the shelter. The next day is uneventful as they arrive at Bald Mountain Lean-to at three o'clock in the afternoon. Once again, they are the first hikers there, so they have their pick of bunks.

As they are still two days and one night before re-supply, the hikers conduct an inventory on food and are relieved to find adequate supplies. Tomorrow plans call for a 13-mile hike, so they eat early and hit the sleeping bags by nine.

It proves fortuitous that they get plenty of sleep. After lunch the next day, eight miles from the shelter, they exit the woods to the banks of the Piscataquis River, where they prepare to ford the stream.

They see on the other side of the river, eight people are clearly agitated. There are five backpackers, a ranger, and two day-hikers.

Charlie says, "Well guys, I guess we ought to go on and ford, so we can find out what's going on. Looks like there's trouble of some kind."

They remove their boots and wade the shallow river in their sandals. When they get across, a female day-hiker runs over to them. She is clearly upset. "Have you seen a little girl, 10 years old? She's wearing a red plaid shirt and blue jeans."

"No ma'am, we sure haven't." Jon says. "How long has she been missing?"

"She was with us all morning while we were hiking. When we stopped here for lunch, she ate her lunch, then wandered around the clearing for a little while. Joe and I dozed off in the warm sun for a few minutes. When I woke up and called, I didn't get an answer. I woke Joe, and we both started looking and yelling. But nothing. Nothing." She buries her face in her hands and sobs. Charlie moves to her and puts her arms around her.

The ranger walks over to the women and adds his concern to that of Charlie's. "Ma'am, I've called for the search-and-rescue team and they should be here in an hour. We'll find Julie, don't worry."

Turning to Jon and his companions, he asks, "How 'bout you folks. Can you help us hunt?"

"Absolutely," says Jon. "If somebody will keep an eye on our packs, we'll start right now. Ready, guys?"

"Yeah, let's go," says Sam. "Let's see, if I were a 10-year-old girl, would I wander upstream or downstream?" They look around and decide that downstream looks more inviting. They spread out and start walking, calling Julie's name every few feet. They occasionally stop and look around fallen trees and by bluffs.

After an hour, they've neither seen nor heard anything at all. No footprints. They spread out more and retrace their steps to the ford where they find Julie's mother sitting with a female hiker, anxiously waiting for any news from the searchers. No news from anyone.

Jon asks, "What directions have other searchers gone in?"

The mother looks around. "Some went that way," pointing upstream. "Several crossed the river and split up and went both ways. Oh God, where could she be? It's almost dark! She'll die out there!"

Jon and Sam scurry around and set up their tent to use as a command center. The other hikers help them build a fire. The cheerful blaze doesn't really help the distraught mother.

Jon looks at George and Charlie. "What do you think, guys? Enough energy for another swing through the woods?"

"Shoot yeah," says George. "What direction you thinking?"

"Well, seems to me that nobody's gone the way that Julie and her folks came from. I think that's the way we ought to try."

They agree and pull flashlights from their packs, and the four hikers start back on the trail. It's not quite dark yet, but it's not far off. Once again, they spread out and begin calling Julie's name. The two searchers on the outside of the line have it really rough. The brush is thick in places, and the flashlights cast only a small, if cheerful beam of light as it gets darker. The plaintive ghostly cries of "Julie! Juuuuu . . . lie!" echo through the woods, but there is no response. Nothing but the silence of the deep woods.

Jon, Sam, George, and Charlie walk an hour, and cover a mile. Distance off-trail is tough. The four stop to take a breather. They discuss what to do. Charlie says, "I think we ought to go for another hour. If she went this way, she couldn't have gone farther."

Jon agrees, "Yeah, but I'm worried that we may not be far enough off the trail. If she got off the trail, she could have moved perpendicular to it. Do you guys think maybe we could spread out on one side of the trail and keep going an hour, then turn around and work the other side on the way back?"

Sam says, "We would cover more territory, but we have to be really careful to stay within voice distance of each other. Otherwise they might be searching for one of us, as well."

Though weary, they start through the forest on the north side of the trail, the direction from which Julie and her parents arrived. An hour later, still no sign of the lost child and the hikers are getting quite discouraged. They convene on the trail and spread out on the south side to begin their trek back.

A half hour later, Sam, who is on the outside of the line, calls out. "Hey guys, look here." The other three thrash their way through the brush.

"What have you found," asks Charlie. Sam, who is lying on his side, points to the ground.

"They look like a small footprints, to me," says Charlie. She puts her boot next to the print. "See, it's even smaller than mine." She places her hand on Sam's shoulder. "Damn, Samuel, you've got good eyes."

Sam laughs, "Well, more blind running luck than good eyes. I tripped over a root, and my flashlight and my nose found the footprint at the same time."

"Well, however you found it, great!" says Charlie. "What direction is the footprint pointed? Look, it's away from the trail. We'll have to be careful not to get lost ourselves. Let's go. Spread out!"

The hikers start walking and yelling, "Julie! Julie!"

Charlie yells out. "Guys, I found a couple more footprints. We're on the right trail!" She yells louder, "Julie!" They continue for another 15 minutes, but still no sight of the little girl.

Then, George yells, "Guys! Come over here! Quick!"

Jon, Sam, and Charlie hurry to George's side. George holds out his arm to warn them. "Watch out" he says. "There's a real drop–off here. My flashlight

beam won't go all the way to the bottom. We gotta move carefully. But, I think I heard something"

Silence falls and the four friends listen intently. "There," says George, pointing to his right. "Hear that?"

"Yeah, " says Jon, "It sounds sorta like a kitten."

"Julie," calls Charlie. "Are you down there?"

"Help," came a plaintive cry. "Help! I fell and I can't see where I am."

"Just sit still, honey," calls Charlie. "Don't move – we'll get down there to you. Just sit still."

The four hikers gather for a brief conference. "How much rope we got?" asks Jon.

"Fifty feet of nylon," says George. "It's not very thick, maybe 500 pound test line, but it'll do for support line." The other three have no rope at all.

"Damn," says Jon. "We have no idea how far down she is. I hope it's less than 50 feet."

"How are we gonna work this?" asks Charlie.

"I'm the lightest," responds Jon. "I'll go down. You guys can keep the support line taut."

In less than a minute, the others have Jon rigged up. He's wearing Sam's flashlight strapped to his head with elastic bands and the nylon rope is tied around his waist in the best bowline knot George can tie. Charlie is standing at the top of the embankment, closest to where they thought they had heard Julie's cry.

Charlie cups her hands and shouts down the hill. "Julie! Can you hear me, baby? One of us is coming down to help you. We need you to yell out every once in a while so we can find you. Now yell again – where are you?"

"Here," comes Julie's faint reply. "Here."

"Okay," says Jon. "I'm on my way. Let the line out as I go." He starts backing his way down the slope, and Sam begins paying the rope out, hand over hand. Jon descends down about 35 feet and stops. He yells up at Sam, "Hang on a minute. I've got a vertical bluff to deal with here. It's pretty rough. I can see her, though."

The hikers on top can't hear the whole conversation but they can hear enough to understand that Julie is lying on a rock shelf below where Jon is trying to navigate his way. Sam can feel the pull and release of the rope as Jon carefully moves his way from side to side trying to find the safest way to descend the bluff.

Jon says, "Julie, I need you to help me. Can you do that?"

"Yee.e.eess," comes the answer. "Wha. . .at do you want me to do?"

"Well, I'm going to get my buddies down here, where I am, so they can help me too. They've all got flashlights, so it'll be bright down here. That sound good?"

"Yes–I've been really scared 'cause it's so cold and dark."

"Okay, tell you what I'm gonna do. I'm gonna have to go back up to my buddies to figure out what we'll have to do. Will you be okay, for just a few minutes?"

Terror laces her words as Julie says, "Noooo–don't leave me–I've been so alone and I'm scared–please..."

"Calm down, Julie. Tell you what I'll do. I'll leave my light here on the ground so you can see it. Will that help?"

"How long will you be gone?"

"Just a few minutes. That's all. Then all four of us will be down here to get you out. Okay?"

"Okay, but please hurry."

"I will. Just lie real still. It's a pretty narrow ledge we're on, so we'll have to be careful. Okay?"

"Okay."

Jon starts making his way back up the hill. A few feet away from the light on the ground, the darkness envelops him completely. He stumbles and trips over every root and shrub and runs directly into several trees. If it wasn't for the nylon rope serving as both guide and support, there is no way he could have climbed the slope.

On top, Jon briefs his companions on the situation. Charlie asks. "Do you think we ought to go back and get the rescue team? Surely they're there by now."

"I don't think so," responds Jon. "She's on a ledge no more than a foot wide. If she'd fallen asleep, she would have rolled off and I have no idea how much further down the bluff goes. For that matter, I have no idea how she stopped on that ledge."

George gets into the conversation. "How tall is the bluff? Have we got enough rope?"

"Bout 25 feet, best I can tell. No, we don't have enough rope. I figure we'll have to use the rope to fish her up the bluff, and it'll take almost all of it. But we also have to have help getting back up this last 35 feet. That plus 25 feet of bluff equals more than 50 feet of rope."

Charlie snaps her fingers. "I got it, guys! You've all got pocket knives, right?"

"Yeah," comes the chorus.

"Okay. Each of you find a small sapling, 10 – 12 feet of main trunk, and play beaver. Strip them except for the lowest good sized branch. Leave a "Y", 'bout a foot long on the short size. Got it?"

Mental light bulbs turn on and the men fumble around in the faint glow of their flashlights. Charlie stays on the edge of the slope and talks to Julie, telling her that they will be down to get her out, very soon.

Fifteen minutes later, the woodsmen re-appear with their trees. George winds up the rope and stuffs it into his pockets. "Charlie," he says, "Great idea. We make a temporary rail, huh?"

"Yeah, right on the ground so the saplings will be the strongest. Hook those Y's on the base of another tree, then we can use them to pull on, to get up. Tell you what, though. I'll feel a lot better with some kind of backup. Maybe use belts to lash the saplings. Yeah, that'll work."

Sam leads the downward expedition. He hooks his sapling onto a tree and lashes it tight. He works his way down the slope, using the sapling as a balance rail and it works well. He is followed by George, who hooks his sapling near the lowest point of Sam's. The two men move 10 feet farther down the slope. Jon and Charlie follow suit and join the first two, where Jon hooks his part of the "life rail" to a small tree. His estimate of 35 feet proves fairly accurate, as the last sapling–turned rail extends to the edge of the bluff where Jon's light shines bravely forth into the night.

"How are you doing, baby" asks Charlie.

"I'm doing okay, but I'm not a baby. I'm 10 years old."

"Sorry, I'll call you Julie. No, you're not a baby or you wouldn't have survived. Now guys, we're down here. What now?"

Jon shines his light down to illuminate Julie's perch. "There she is, guys. Not much room on that ledge. We could drop the rope down to pick her up, but I'm not comfortable with that. Nope, one of us has to go down to tie knots and help her. Plus to be there to catch her if something goes wrong. Pray that won't happen!"

Silence falls for a moment. Then, all four speak at once.

"I'll go down there."

"No, I will..."

"I'll do it..."

Then Charlie speaks. "No, guys. In spite of what Jon said a while ago, I'm the lightest. Even though I'm just a woman. It's not even close. I got you beat by 25 or 30 pounds. You three can lower me down. I'll secure Julie and you can pull her up. Then me. You did hear that–remember me! Okay?"

The three men can't argue with her logic, much as they want to. They fashion a loop to put under Charlie's arms and tie a smaller loop, higher up, for her to hold most of her own weight and keep the nylon rope from cutting into her. George gives her a kiss and the men prepare to lower her onto the ledge, 25 feet below. They tie the end of the rope to a tree as a last–gasp safety measure, but they pray it won't come to that.

Using two trees as pulleys, Charlie slips over the ledge. The men slowly, painfully, inch by inch, lower her into the dark abyss. Finally she yells, "Whoa, guys, I'm here. Let me get a real good grip, then give me some slack." She drops to her knees and stays there until the adrenaline flow stops. She looks up into the dirty, tear stained face of a frightened little girl.

Julie says, “You can call me baby if ya want to. I don’t mind.” She carefully reaches for Charlie and they share a heartfelt, if extremely careful, hug.

A shout comes from above, “Everything all right? She okay?”

“Yeah, just fine,” answers Charlie. Give me a minute and I’ll explain to Julie what we’re going to do. Julie, we’re going to get you up the same way the guys got me down here. I’ll stay down here until the guys get you up there, then they’ll pull me up. If that is all right with you. Are you still scared?”

“A little bit. But it’s better than being down here, in the dark, afraid I’ll fall off this ledge.

“Okay. Let’s put this loop under your arms. Like this. Is that comfortable?”

“It’s fine.”

“Can you reach the hand–holding loop I used? Let’s see, no, too far away. I’ll tie a new one, right about here,” and Charlie tugs on the new loop. “You ready, baby?”

“I guess so. I am scared, though.”

“I know, sweety. It’ll be over in just a couple of minutes. I’ll keep my light on you so you can see the bluff and not bump your knees, elbows or head. Be careful, okay?”

“Okay.”

“All right guys, bring her up!”

The rope slowly becomes taut and Julie starts up, trailed by a small shriek.

When Julie’s feet touch firm ground and the rope has been loosened, she begins to sob and laugh at the same time. The three men shed a tear or two of gratitude that the child is safe.

After comforting Julie and sitting her by a tree, where she can see what’s going on, they turn to the problem of extracting Charlie.

The retrieval of 60 pound Julie went without a hitch. The men had brought in the thin nylon rope hand over hand. Pulling up 120 pounds of Charlie proves more problematic. It takes a while to get the rope back down the ledge. Once Charlie puts the loop under her arms and grabs the upper loop with her hands, the men cannot get enough purchase on the thin rope to pull her up. They get her up two feet and she slips back one. Going down, gravity is their friend; going up, definitely an enemy. The men's hands become sore and rope–burned. They lower Charlie back to the ledge and she sits.

"Hey babe, we got to work out something better," says George. "Give us a minute."

"Don't have much choice, do I?" responds Charlie.

The three men talk over the problem. They shine their lights up the slope above them, then to the sides. It's fairly level to one side, along the bluff and they devise a plan. They cut a four–foot piece of tree limb, about three inches in diameter. Where the rope came over the edge of the bluff, they take it around a smooth–barked tree, to prevent abrasion, then tie it to the center of the four–foot limb. Jon and Sam arrange themselves on either side of the limb, a pair of mules, hooked to a singletree.

When all are ready, Jon and Sam start walking, the rope goes taut, and Charlie starts up. The rope hangs several times and they have to release the tension on the rope to allow Charlie to drop back a foot or two. Then they start back up. After 15 tension–filled minutes, George grabs his wife by the forearms and pulls her the last few feet. They collapse in a pile on the ground.

"Welcome, babe," George gasps out. "Glad you're back with us, in one piece."

"Me too, me too," she responds. "Those little hiccups in the upward process were a bit upsetting, to say the least."

Sam, Julie, and Jon join the party. Charlie reaches out and takes Jon's hand. The flashlights cast enough glow that she sees him wince in pain.

"What's wrong with your hand?" she asks.

"Nothing–it's okay."

"Let me see," and she spreads his fingers out to reveal deep, bloody grooves across the palm. "Damn," she says. "Let me see the other one." He holds it out and it's just as bad. She checks Sam's and George's hands and finds the same injuries. "Damn," she says again. "I'd better go on that diet, huh? We'd best get you guys to the first aid kit. I guess I'll be doing the hiking housework for a few days." She turns to the little girl. "Are you hurt, honey?"

Julie replies, "I'm all scratched up, and I'm hungry and cold and scared, but I'm okay."

"Here, Julie, put this on," says Jon, as he peels off his jacket. He zips it up and helps Julie to her feet. The jacket fits like a nightgown and reaches almost to the ground.

"Okay, gentlemen, now we have to find our way out of here. How are the flashlights holding out?" asks Charlie.

Jon's light is out–the others are dim but still okay. The group of five, with George carrying Julie, struggles through the brush and locate the trail. They cover the miles back to the ford much quicker than they came. The combination of trail, instead of brush, and light hearts, make walking a real pleasure.

They arrive at the search headquarters to find 15 or 20 people standing around a fire, in the light of the lanterns. Charlie yells out. "We've got her! She's okay!"

They get to the circle of campfire light as Julie's parents rush over, and the transfer of the child is made. Julie's parents hug the four hikers, and they tell the story of the rescue several times. One of the rescue team washes, dresses, and bandages the three men's hands.

The ranger and his rescue team lead the reunited family down the trail to civilization and Jon and friends wearily eat dinner and crawl into the tent and sleeping bags. Sleep descends for three of the hikers. Jon lies awake and stares, unseeing, at the roof of the tent. His mind drifts back to Russell Field and Gretel. Damn, he can't wait to talk to her. He slowly loses focus and drifts off to sleep.

In the morning, the hikers are enjoying the clear skies, coffee in hand. Jon says, "I don't know about you guys, but I feel good about last night. That delay didn't hurt anything. I sure wouldn't have wanted to spend the night out here all by myself, with no gear."

Charlie agrees, "Me either. That was a two-sided delay. Scared for the little girl on one side, happy on the other side at the result."

George says, "Jon, I haven't looked at the schedule for a day or so. How long is the hike today?"

Jon pulls out the guide. "Let's see, we're outta whack just a little bit. We're looking at about nine miles to Monson and re-supply. That is the last civilization we'll see for about 100 miles. We need to re-supply big time and make sure we get everything we might need. Nine whole miles. Not bad at all. We should be there soon after lunch. You got an itch for city life?"

George replies, "Yeah, that, plus we're fresh out of food after lunch today. Lucky, huh?"

"Lucky, hell," says Charlie. "It was absolutely perfect planning on my part, that's what."

"Yeah, yeah, yeah," says George. Let's motor out of here."

20

"SURPRISE! SURPRISE!"

Lunch is somewhat sparse, but the hikers barely notice. They're eager to get to town. To their surprise, a pickup truck is parked at the trailhead. The driver, sitting on the tailgate, waves his hand at them. "Howdy folks, need a ride into town?" he asks.

Jon mutters under this breath, "Damned entrepreneur. But I ain't fussin'. Let's take his offer–it's about three miles to town."

The driver turns out to be a real character and keeps the hikers laughing all the way to town. They've squeezed into the king cab at his insistence, even though they protested about their thru-hiker aroma. He said, "I ain't hearing of you folks sitting in the bed of my truck. Come on, get in. Where are you staying?"

"We made reservations at Shaw's Boarding House, but we're a day late. I hope they saved the reservation," says Jon.

"I 'spect they did. They're used to hikers' schedules. I know 'em pretty well. We won't have trouble getting you guys in there."

When the pickup pulls up in front of the Shaw's, another surprise. Keith and Pat Shaw are on the front porch waiting. They introduce themselves and welcome the hikers. Keith says, "I hope you guys plan to enjoy our all-you-can-eat dinner. It's special tonight."

Jon replies, "We've heard about your dinners and breakfasts from other thru-hikers we've talked with. You bet we'll be there. After showers, that is."

Pat says, "We've reserved spaces in the main bunkhouse for you folks. Follow me," and she leads them to the building.

It takes an hour for the hikers to scrub away the accumulated trail grime, and they dress in their last clean clothes. They bag their grimy hiking clothes, ready to find a Laundromat in the morning.

They leave the bunkhouse and head toward the dining room. On the way, Jon looks at the gravel-covered parking lot. "Damn, guys, look at all the local cars. The food here must be pretty good. The locals must all eat here. I'm starved!"

The hikers find the door to the dining room closed. They look at each other in surprise. "Damn, I hope they're still serving, and we haven't missed dinner. Let's see," and Sam opens the door.

They are greeted by a room full of people, who start cheering and applauding. A huge banner stretches across the room. It says, "**WELCOME!**" And, "**THANKS, THRU-HIKERS!**"

A small girl runs toward them and engulfs them with a hug. "Julie," exclaims Charlie. "You look a little more city-like than the last time we saw you. Hi, babe, good to see you."

A man dressed in a suit steps forth. "Folks, I'm the mayor of Monson. My name is Matthew. Welcome to our city. We arranged this little get-together to express our thanks for what you did yesterday. Joe and Dee Parsons, Julie's folks, want to say something. Come on up here to the front, folks."

Joe and Dee also come to the front, and more hugs are bestowed on the embarrassed hikers.

"Thanks, you guys, for finding Julie. The ranger told us later that the direction she was going was even worse than where she was. Bluffs, deep, fast creeks. She might have been badly hurt or killed. Oh God, thank you," and Dee covers her face to hide the tears of gratitude. "I've never been so scared in my life."

The mayor takes over, as mayors always seem to do. Particularly in places where there are a few voters gathered. "Folks, the Shaws here fixed a special feast today. Even better than usual, though that's hard to imagine. Step up–guests of honor first."

The feast is awesome and in many ways, gives Jon an eerie feeling. He says to Charlie, "Look at this spread. Unreal! But, I'm having a sensation of de'ja vu all over again. Where have I seen something like this before? Where?" He shakes his head. "Damn, I hate it when this happens. I'm too young to have galloping Alzheimer's. But I flat can't remember where it was."

He fills his plate to overflowing and is directed to the head table. He is joined by Sam, Charlie, and George. After a couple of bites, Jon slams his hand on the table. "I know where I saw this scene. Sam, do you remember that dream I told you about that night we shared a shelter with that crazy Beth and her friends. Remember? I was sitting in front of a table that looked just like this, only I was tied hand and foot? All I could reach was a bowl of macaroni and cheese?"

Sam laughs, "Yeah, I remember. Now shut up and let me eat. Do you want me to tie you up? Will you feel more at home?"

Jon busies himself with his fork and knife. "Nope, doing just fine like I am."

And the conversation wanes completely.

After dinner, there are more speeches and certificates given, which the mayor promises to mail home for them. The hikers return to their bunk area where they find that, in their absence, someone has done their laundry, and stacks of neatly folded clothes are on the table. A small card with the single word, "Thanks" is on top of one stack.

Jon says, "You guys reckon the hoopla is over? I'm tired of blushing."

The other three laugh, and Sam says, "It seems we're being lauded for blind, running luck. I've heard that it's as good to be lucky as it is to be good. I guess that's accurate." Conversations cease, exhaustion wins, and the heroes sleep.

The next day, they are still heroes around town, and they finally are forced to escape to the local theater, where they find and enjoy anonymity in the dark.

Over dinner, they discuss how they will handle the final leg of the journey–one hundred and six miles to the base of Katahdin. The schedule calls for 10 nights; eight in shelters, two in the tent.

Jon is looking closely at the *Trail Guide.* "Well, guys, Mother Nature and the absence of civilization have made our decision for us. There really aren't any resupply towns within easy reach of the trail. Let's supply for the whole 10 nights. Okay?"

The others agree, and they walk to the nearby grocery store. After their usual de-packaging procedures are followed, they hit the sack and enjoy what is to be their final night in civilization before the completion of the thru-hike for Jon and Sam, and the next-to-last leg for George and Charlie. Jon finds a phone and informs Andy of their planned arrival date at Katahdin.

Mixed emotions well up in them, once again. Happy, because of the near-success and accomplishment of their goal. Sad, because they will be going back to civilization and different paths in life. Sad, because they have heard from other thru-hikers that reunions are often planned, but seldom realized. Sleep that night is interrupted by dreams for all of them.

In the morning, after the Shaws' famous breakfast, the same man that brought them to town drives up. "Enough city life, guys?" he says. "Back to the boondocks, eh?"

"We'd appreciate it," says Jon. "Tell me something, though. Was your appearance out there two days ago fortuitous or planned? Are you a professional shuttler?"

The man laughs. "I guess I didn't introduce myself before. My name is Bill, and I'm the police chief of Monson. Nope, I was directed by our good mayor to sit my butt out there to make sure you folks wouldn't stay on the trail and slip by us, before we could express our thanks."

The hikers all laugh. "Tricked again," says Sam. "It was a nice trick though. Thanks."

"No problem," says Bill. "Now, let's move out." they did so and were ceremoniously deposited at the trail head. Big sighs all around, followed by big grins.

"Head 'em up, move 'em out" says Jon. "Rawhide, once again." Singing shatters the sanctity of the forest, as the friends start up the trail.

The final leg of the entire hike is called the 100-mile Wilderness. The first day of the Wilderness is a rough one. Fourteen miles seems forever after three days in the city. But the highs they are on after the fetes in town sustain them, and they arrive at Wilson Valley Lean-to at mid-afternoon.

They are joined in the shelter by other north-bound thru-hikers and camaraderie abounds. During philosophy hour, they discuss schedules. Some of the hikers plan to move faster than Jon and friends, some slower. They talk about meeting at Katahdin Stream Campground, the last night before the final 10.4-mile circle up and back down the mountain. Most of the faster hikers agree to wait two nights at the campground, but no more. If the slower folks aren't there by then, the rabbits will be gone. No more time to wait for the turtles.

The next two days' hikes are nine and 11 miles, and the seasoned hikers cover the ground with ease. Jon notices that he has become careful about placing his feet on the trail and in the streams. Falling and being injured now would be the same as a soldier being wounded the day before his evacuation home. That would be no fun, no fun at all.

They arrive at the Hermitage Shelter in mid-afternoon and join forces with some of the hikers they had met two nights before. Looking at the guide that night, Jon counts four mountains that they have to cross the next day. "Shucks," he mutters under his breath. "I guess I'd better warn Charlie, or she'll be on my back like a duck on a June Bug."

To his surprise, Charlie's response is simple. "Just four? So what?" she says. "Bring 'em on. Four mountains? No sweat." She goes back to her cup of tea, ignoring Jon. Jon, the unofficial tour guide, is surprised.

"That's it?" he says. "No bitching, moaning, complaining? I was beginning to look forward to your response to mountains. No fun! No fun, at all."

During the next three days, Logan Branch, Cooper Brook Falls, and Antlers Campsite are left behind, one by one. Adrenaline carries them on to Wadleigh Stream Lean-to. Now there are only three more nights to Katahdin Stream Campground. They are even more excited, because they had their first glimpse of Katahdin during the day. Singing, laughing and tall tales are the order of the evening, and all thoroughly enjoy themselves.

Even the turtles convert to rabbits over the next few days. Jon and friends find it difficult to be power hikers, because the area is so beautiful. The ponds, streams, and mountains are as pretty as anything they've seen to date. They are grateful that it isn't black fly time in northern Maine. Horror stories are told aplenty by south-bound hikers about the aggravating critters that will penetrate just about any screen you erect, just to get their drop of your blood.

The hikers move into Daicey Pond Campground. They register with the ranger and ask him about the availability of spaces at Katahdin Stream Campground, still 2.4 miles away. He punches numbers on a two-way radio and a squawk issues forth.

"Base camp, this is Daicey," says the ranger. "Got any tent space left up there in the jumping-off place?"

"Ten-four," says the radio. "They thru-hikers?"

"Sure are. Save 'em a place?"

"Ten-four. Name?"

"No Doubts Jon," announces Jon with a hint of pride in his voice. The ranger relays the new trail name to the campground.

"All set, folks. By the way, weather's been good up on Katahdin. Shouldn't have any problems. I hate it when I have to stop thru-hikers for days, or the rest of the season, because of weather conditions. So near, yet so far. That mountain can be a killer. Not now, though. The weather's magnificent. Enjoy your hike, and congratulations."

Jon and crew cover the two and a half miles as if on air. They set up their tent and discover that some of the rabbits have been there for a day and are getting real antsy to hike up the mountain. The faster hikers agree to wait one more day for the slower folks to arrive. Then, they would begin the last step of their journey. As a group. As a mob. Funny how the many-times welcome solitude of the AT goes away and is replaced with a desire for companionship at completion.

But, the next day, three of the faster hikers can stand it no longer and go ahead and make their final hike up and back down Katahdin. No apologies; they just couldn't help it. The desire to complete what they had begun months before has welled up in them, and they just have to hike. They have to finish. So, they go, asking those remaining to pass on their regrets to the slower hikers.

21

"FINI'"

The last straggling hikers arrive at the campsite, and the group decides to start early in the morning. The morning breaks clear and crisp, and after depositing their packs with the ranger, the final walk is begun. It is an interesting day. The hike up Katahdin is one of the tougher mountains they have ascended during the entire hike, but with the freedom that comes with no pack, all make it. The grade up the mountain is one of the steepest. The hikers scramble up 4000 feet during the five-mile hike, over and around huge rocks. They are grateful for the iron rebar that is driven in here and there for handholds at the toughest places. Conversation is minimal during the ascent of the mountain.

On the top, the view is spectacular. They stand in awe, as they turn in all directions to look at Maine, stretched out around them. Katahdin is the highest point for miles. Then, the celebration begins. Hugs, tears, yells. The hikers in the group from the northern U.S. quickly learn the fundamentals of the Rebel Yell, and the sounds reverberate from the peaks. Finally, the group starts back down the trail, feeling as if they are leaving a part of themselves on top.

The party continues, as the thru-hiker clan makes its way down the steep slopes of Katahdin. The cold air of the mountain has no dampening effect. Every half-mile, the men and women stop and exchange high-five's and hugs.

The camaraderie level is incredible, a level you would expect in a group of hostages successfully freed from a terrorist. In a sense, they have been held hostage by the Trail for five or six months and are now free. The ironic thing is, most don't really know whether or not they really want that freedom.

Jon turns to Sam. "Well, we made it. Tell me the truth. Six months ago, did you believe you'd be here? Did you have any idea at all that you would finish?"

Sam laughs, "No way! I was fat and out of shape, but I had to get away from that work stress. I thought when I started that David and Mike would kinda help carry me along, but when they ran off and left me, I had to do it on my own. That is, with your help! What about you, did you think you'd make it?"

Jon pauses for a minute to reflect on the back-at-you question. He scratches his beard and thinks. His response is slow and thoughtful. "No, not really. I mean, look at my track record. I'd never finished anything in my life. Who's to figure that a guy who couldn't even build a Cub Scout Pinewood Derby car could get his head together enough to hike 2000 dammit miles? Go figure! I can't."

George and Charlie are as happy as the others, but they can't forget that they have a couple of weeks left of hiking before they can call themselves true thru-hikers. They rejoice, anyway. They are close to success and they figure that they can make it, now, particularly with the main weather-dependent portion of the trip behind them.

Now it's Sam's turn for reflection. He stands by the trail for a moment, then says, "Jon, Charlie, and George, I'm still not real sure what I'm gonna do next. I mean, my boss says I can come back, but I'm not sure I want to. Trouble is, I'm fresh out of bucks. This cruise has cost me all of my pitiful savings. But, if I've learned nothing else this six months, it is that I can make my own decisions. I've been thinking for the last few days about an idea. I've got to go back to work to get some money. Maybe six months, that's all. Then I'm gonna go out on my own. Open a little architectural consulting business. I've got some good clients that'll probably go with me. I've got my own computer and architectural software, so I don't need much more. If stress tries to eat me up again, at least I'll be putting it on myself, and, if I make it, I make it for me."

As Sam finishes his soliloquy, he's got a huge grin plastered from ear to ear. Jon joins him in the grin fest. "Damn, bud, that's great! Sounds like you've made your call. If I need a house built in a few years, I know where to go for plans. Maybe something in an AT motif." He laughs as do Charlie, George, and Sam.

"Yeah," says Sam. "I can just see the central room in the house–lots of vegetation, sunlight, rock walls, maybe a huge walk-in rock fireplace, a few mice, skunks, moose, bear . . . "

"Enough, already! says Jon. "I'm not quite ready to start my house. You think you're low on bucks–I'm tapped out completely except for the last of the newspaper money which is going to George and Charlie. I guess it's back to Shorty's, for awhile anyway. Then I'm thinking about getting smarter. My B.A. in History's not worth a nickel as far as getting a job. I'm gonna go back to school next spring part time and get a Master's, maybe a teaching certificate. Then I can teach. That'll give me plenty of weekends and summer vacation, so I can keep on hiking. I'm thinking about the Pacific Crest Trail, and they've just opened up that new Ozark Trail in Missouri. You know, the one that Chattering Cricket was telling us about back down the trail. Anyway, that's what I'm thinking. After the last six months, I believe that if I want to go to the moon, by God, I can do it." Jon punctuates his declaration with a closed fist, pumping it in the air.

A series of high five's and "Yeah, man's" follow and Sam, Charlie, George, and Jon hug. The hug turns into a group hug as the two are joined by their eight companions who had ascended Katahdin with them and had returned. The eight haven't a clue as to what precipitated the hug, but they need no excuse to share the exhilaration they feel after completion of the trail. The stop-and-go trek down the mountain begins again, and the train of punch-drunk hikers continually bump into one another, as someone stops to say something to a buddy. Nobody objects.

The downhill hike ends at the ranger station parking lot at Katahdin Stream Campground, where they had left their packs early that morning, prior to the final leg of the hike. Yells ring out across the campground, as hikers spot family and friends who have driven north to collect their particular hiker. More hugs. Then, as they realize they are about to part company, there's another hiker group hug.

Jon steps back to catch his breath. He spots Andy's red pickup truck as it pulls into the parking lot.

"Hey, Jon, how the hell are you?" Andy yells out the window.

"Couldn't be better," is the response, and the two friends exchange a hug after Andy trots over to the circle of hikers.

Andy greets Sam and is introduced to George and Charlie. Jon stops and thinks and a look of sadness clouds his countenance. He says, "Well, one thing could have made it better. I'm mentally looking around for my hiking buddy, but I'll not see him again." A solitary tear trickles from his eye and tracks down his dusty face and disappears into his beard. "Nope, I'll not see him again."

"Well, wait a sec. I've got some news for you," says Andy.

"What the hell do you mean by news? Dead is dead is dead. Pookie's gone, and I'm used to the idea. I don't need any riddles. What news?" Jon's voice has gone up an octave and several decibels.

"Chill, man, I'll show you. Damn, the boy's not only gotten assertive, he's plumb aggressive." The last is said over Andy's shoulder as he trots over to his truck. He opens the driver's door, reaches inside, and picks something up off the seat. He covers it with a jacket and returns to stand in front of Jon.

"Okay, Andy, what in the hell are you doing? I said I didn't need riddles. Why did you have to bring up the subject of Pookie?"

"No riddles, it's simple. Here, I want to introduce you to someone. Meet Pookie-too." He ceremoniously removes the jacket to reveal a tiny ball of fur, completely black, except for two bright button eyes and a pink tongue. Andy dumps the puppy into Jon's arms, and Jon is immediately swarmed over by the squirming, licking, climbing critter. The puppy settles down and gives Jon the equivalent of a puppy hug, still furiously licking on Jon's neck.

"Where in the world did you get this little guy? And where did that name come from?"

"I told you it's simple. When the Pookster and Mollie were running and playing and chasing in Anita's back yard, apparently that sly guy caught up with Mollie at least once. This is Pookie's young-un, so I've been calling him Pookie-too. He loves to take walks, so there will be no rest for you once you get back to By-God Alabama. He's a smart puppy–I've already trained him to use the paper in the house. He may just be more house broken than you are."

Jon hugs the puppy until it yelps in protest. Pookie-Too has become even more special to him because of the connection to the Pookster. Flashbacks to Pookie as a puppy come over Jon in waves, and a couple of happy tears follow the tracks of the earlier sad one.

Jon walks over to the knot of hikers, who are still clustered, trying to avoid the inevitable separation. Pookie-too is passed from hand to hand. Each hiker receives a sloppy hello on ear, cheek, chin, or whatever part of a face the puppy can reach. Jon tells the story of Pookie-too's existence, and the hikers, all of

whom had heard of the sad demise of Pookie, rejoice once again. It still doesn't take much for a celebration to break out.

As Jon stands, grin plastered across his face, to watch the canine-human get-acquainted session, he is suddenly surrounded by a pair of warm arms in a tight hug. From the delicious aroma, he knows for a fact that the person was definitely female.

"Who, who . . . " stammers Jon as he tries in vain to turn around so he could see the person behind him.

"Who, who, who, hell, you sound like an owl. Your feet don't fit a limb. Who in the world did you think it was? Tarzan, I'm crushed. You have any more trail encounters? If I thought that you had, I just might get pissed," laughs Gretel, as she releases the wrestling hold. Jon spins around and envelops her in a bear hug.

"Damn, Gretel, I thought you were gone for good. I've thought about you a lot lately." He releases her, but holds tightly onto her shoulders at arm's length. He's afraid that if he turns loose completely, she'd disappear from his life once again. "But how did you know when I'd be here? How did . . . "

Andy, who had been watching the reunion in delight, laughs. "How did she know? Shit, man, at first she bugged me weekly, then daily about your schedule and when you'd be here. Plus, I've been sending her the articles from the newspaper."

Jon frowns at Andy and hits him on the arm. "You sumbitch! You never let me know she'd even called. I've been wondering if I'd ever see her again. I didn't know. You never told me . . . "

"Hell no, I didn't tell you. I'm not gonna say what she told me she'd do to me if I let you know she'd been in touch. Let's just say I would have had no kids or grandkids."

Jon laughs. "I understand. I do seem to remember that she's a bit on the pushy side."

Gretel hits Jon on the arm. "Pushy, I'll show you pushy. I really didn't decide to come up here until a couple of days ago. But, then I figured I had enough invested in you in time and in money from all those damned phone calls to

Andy, that I might as well be here for the finish. So, I took a couple days off from work and here I am."

"Well, you can't believe how glad I am to see you . . . "

"Hold on, Tarzan. Don't get carried away. I'm here, that's all. I'm still not ready for the 'me Tarzan, you Jane' bit. One step at a time, okay?"

"Okay, okay. Calm down. I'll settle for a step at a time."

Gretel softens the words, as she gives him another hug and a kiss. "Damn, Tarzan, that stroll up that little molehill made you a bit stinky. You ever hear of deo?"

Jon blushes. "I'm heading for the facilities. Since I can even smell myself, I think I'd better do something about that. See you guys in a minute," and he retreats to the bathroom after removing his toilet gear from his backpack.

Fifteen minutes later, he returns to the shrinking crowd. Most of the hikers depart reluctantly to pick up their changed lives. They're changed without a doubt. Now the challenge for them is to adjust and adapt to the outside world, which hasn't changed at all. George and Charlie share farewells and head for town and a bus south to Pennsylvania. They promise to let Jon and Sam know how things go with their last leg of hiking. They all exchange telephone numbers and addresses, as well as a few tears. They hope that their shouted "We'll get together" isn't just end-of-the-trail talk.

Jon turns to Gretel. "You think we can travel in convoy as far south as Boston? I've got a lot to tell you."

"Count on it, bud. You and Pookie-too plan on riding in my chariot."

"You got it," and Jon walks over to talk to Andy and Sam, currently deep in conversation.

"Andy," Jon begins, "Gretel wants me to ride with her as far as Boston, anyway."

"I know you hate the hell out of that. Sam and I were just trying to figure out how all of us were gonna fit in that baby pick-em-up truck. Since he's riding the big dog bus back to Memphis, I thought we'd save him some bucks and give him a lift at least as far as Knoxville. We head south there as he goes west."

"Damn, sounds good to me," exclaims Sam.

"Yeah, and I'll at least have some company on the drive to Boston, since my oldest and best friend is choosing the lure of a siren over me. Can't believe it." Then he looks at Gretel again. "Well, maybe I can believe it a little bit, anyway. Gretel, why in the world did you pick a dirty, bearded, stinky hiker like Jon, when you could have had a clean-living, good-looking city boy like me?"

Gretel laughs, "When I met this boy, I was in the same condition as he is now. Dirty, tired, and basically stinky. Besides, he was the only one there besides Pookie, so I didn't really have any options."

Jon blushes and Gretel, Andy, and Sam have a good laugh at his expense. He seems to have blushed quite a bit during the last hour.

"Hey, I didn't give her much choice either, after I body-slammed her to the turf of the AT," Jon unsuccessfully tries to cover his embarrassment.

"Enough, already. We've got muchos hours to Tuscaloosa. You say you're taking that mutt with you?" asks Andy.

"You betcha. That is, if Gretel'll have both of us."

Gretel laughs. "Still playing second fiddle to a Labrador Retriever. Some day I'll get my feelings hurt. Maybe."

After Jon and Sam sign their last trail ledger, the four humans and the small puppy head south. As they start on the trip, Gretel asks, "Jon, why don't you tell me about the trip?"

He starts his tale where he and Gretel had first parted company and ends at Katahdin. She is very interested and asks lots of questions as two hours pass. Up ahead, Andy's signal light indicates he wants to get off on the next exit, and Gretel follows. Andy pulls into a restaurant that proudly announces, "Buffet - all you can eat!"

They go in after parking Andy's truck and Gretel's car in the shade and they give the puppy water. As the temperature is getting chilly, they agree that he'll be okay.

Six plates of food later, Jon pushes back from the table and announces, "There, I guess that's all I can eat." Across the table, Sam is finishing his third dessert, and the two city folks are staring at the two thru-hikers in wonder and awe.

"Damn, son," says Andy, "I'm gonna have to up your share of the grocery bill 'fore you eat me out of house and home."

Jon says, "I'll slow up some once I get used to real food again."

Sam chimes in, "Yeah, and once we get the taste of macaroni and cheese and pasta and tuna fish out of our mouths and our memories."

After a discussion, the four decide to keep on driving and share the wheel so they can save money. The journey south continues and after talking non-stop for another hour, Jon leans his head back against the headrest in Gretel's car. Pookie-too is curled up in his lap, sound asleep. Jon closes his eyes. Flash-backs from the past six months run through his head, and he sleeps. The sleep of the self-confident.

BIBLIOGRAPHY
Books Quoted

Chazin, Daniel D., editor. *Appalachian Trail Data Book-1995.* Harpers Ferry, West Virginia: Appalachian Trail Conference, Inc., 1988.

Cook, Joe and Monica, editors. *Appalachian Trail Thru-Hikers' Companion.* Harpers Ferry, West Virginia The Appalachian Long Distance Hikers' Association, 1995.

Curran, Jan D. *The Appalachian Trail– A Journey Of Discovery.* Highland City, Florida: Rainbow Books, Inc., 1991.

Fletcher, Colin. *The Complete Walker III, 3rd Edition.* New York, New York: Alfred A. Knopf, 1993.

Irwin, Bill. *Blind Courage.* Waco, Texas: WRS Publishing, 1992.

Luxenberg, Larry. *Walking the Appalachian Trail.* Mechanicsburg, Pennsylvania: Stackpole Books, 1994.

Books Recommended for Further Reading

Antell, Steve. *The Appalachian Trail Conference Backpacker's Recipe Book.* Boulder, Colorado: Pruett Publishing Company, 1980.

Appalachian Trail Conference, Inc. *Comprehensive Plan for the Protection, Management, Development and Use of the Appalachian National Scenic Trail.* Harpers Ferry, West Virginia: Appalachian Trail Conference, Inc., 1988.

____________________. *The Appalachian Trail Conference Member Handbook.* Harpers Ferry, West Virginia: Appalachian Trail Conference, Inc., 1988.

Bates, David. *Breaking Trail in the Central Appalachians.* Washington, D. C.: Potomac Appalachian Trail Club, 1987.

Beeson, D.R. *In The Spirit Of Adventure.* Seymour, Tennessee: Panther Press, 1994.

Brill, David. *As Far As The Eye Can See.* Nashville, Tennessee: Rutledge Press, 1990.

Brooks, Maurice. *The Appalachians.* Boston, Massachusetts: Houghton Mifflin Co., 1965.

Bruce, Dan "Wingfoot". *The Thru-Hiker's Planning Guide.* Hot Springs, North Carolina: Center for Appalachian Studies, 1994.

____________________. *The Thru-Hiker's Handbook: #1 Guide for Long-Distance Hikes on the Appalachian Trail . . . with town maps and mileage data from Georgia to Maine.* Hot Springs, North Carolina: Center for Appalachian Studies, 1994.

Chase, Jim. *Backpacker Magazine's Guide to the Appalachian Trail.* Harrisburg, Pennsylvania: Stackpole Books, 1989.

Chew, V. Collins. A *Geologic Guide to the Appalachian Trail, 2nd Edition.* Harpers Ferry, West Virginia: Appalachian Trail Conference, 1988.

Cornelius, Madelaine. *Katahdin With Love: An Inspirational Journey.* 1990.

___________. *Appalachian Trail– How To Prepare For And Hike It.* Highland City, Florida: Rainbow Books, Inc., 1994.

Darvill, Fred T., M.D. *Mountaineering Medicine, A Wilderness Medical Guide.* Berkeley, California: Wilderness Press, 1992.

Douglas, William O. *My Wilderness: East to Katahdin.* San Francisco, California: Comstock Editions, 1989.

Fisher, Ronald M. *Appalachian Trail.* Washington, D. C.: National Geographic Society, 1972.

_____________. *Mountain Adventure, Exploring the Appalachian Trail.* Washington, D. C.: National Geographic Society, 1988.

Flack, James M. and Hertha E. Flack. *Ambling and Scrambling on the Appalachian Trail.* Harpers Ferry, West Virginia: Appalachian Trail Conference, 1981.

Foster, Charles H. W. *The Appalachian Scenic Trail, A Time To Be Bold.* 1987

Frome, Michael. *Strangers in High Places: The Story of the Great Smoky Mountains.* 2nd ed. Knoxville, Tennessee: University of Tennessee Press, 1980.

Garvey, Edward B. *Appalachian Hiker II.* Oakton, Virginia: Appalachian Books, 1978.

Hakola, John W. *Legacy of a Lifetime: The Story of Baxter State Park.* Woolrich, Maine: TBW Books, 1981.

Hare, James R., editor. *Hiking the Appalachian Trail.* Emmaus, Pennsylvania: Rodale Press, 1975.

Hemphill, Paul. *Me and the Boy.* New York, New York: MacMillan Publishing Company, 1986.

Hensley, Robie. *Appalachian Trail Journal.* Chucky, Tennessee: Robie Hensley, Publisher, 1992.

Hodgins, John. *An Appalachian Trail Sketchbook.* Batavia, New York: Hodgins Printing Co., 1984.

Houk, Rose. *Great Smoky Mountains National Park: A Natural History Guide.* Boston, Massachusetts, 1993.

Kephart, Horace. *Our Southern Highlanders.* Knoxville, Tennessee: The University of Tennessee Press, 1984.

Logue, Victoria and Frank. *The Best of the Appalachian Trail: Day Hikes.* Birmingham, Alabama: Menasha Ridge Press, 1989.

__________________. *The Appalachian Trail Backpacker's Planning Guide.* Birmingham, Alabama: Menasha Ridge Press, 1990.

__________________. *The Best of the Appalachian Trail: Overnight Hikes.* Birmingham, Alabama: Menasha Ridge Press, 1994.

MacKaye, Benton. *The New Exploration: A Philosophy of Regional Planning.* Urbana-Champaign, Illinois: University of Illinois Press, 1990.

Maret, Darrell. *The 1986 and 1987 Philosopher's Guides: Tips for AT Thru-Hikers.* Harpers Ferry, West Virginia: Appalachian Trail Conference, 1986-87.

Marshall, Ann. *Two on the Trail–Thousand Miles on the PCT.* Washington Trails Association, 1985.

Miller, Dorcas S. *The Healthy Trail Food Book.* The East Woods Press, 1976.

Muench, David. Uncommon *Places: A Celebration of Appalachian Trail Country.* Harpers Ferry, West Virginia: Appalachian Trail Conference, 1991.

Ogburn, Charlton. *The Southern Appalachians: A Wilderness Quest.* New York, New York: William Morrow & Company, 1975.

Peterson, Roger Tory. *A Field Guide to the Birds, East of the Rockies.* Boston, Massachusetts: Houghton Mifflin Company, 1980.

Prater, Yvonne and Ruth Dyar Mendenhall. *Gorp, Glop & Glue Stew Favorite Foods from 165 Outdoor Experts.* Seattle, Washington: The Mountaineers, 1981.

Ross, Cindy. *A Woman's Journey on the Appalachian Trail.* Charlotte, North Carolina: East Woods Press, 1982.

Sands, Mary. *Appalachian Trail in Bits and Pieces.* Pittsburgh, Pennsylvania: Dorrance Publishing Company, 1992.

Shaffer, Earl V. *Walking With Spring, The First Thru-Hike of the Appalachian Trail.* Harpers Ferry, West Virginia: Appalachian Trail Conference, 1983.

Thoreau, Henry David. *Walden or Life in the Woods and On the Duty of Civil Disobedience.* New American Library Signet Classic, 1960.

Warren, Michael and Sandra Kocher. *Appalachian Trail.* Portland, Oregon: Graphic Arts Center Publishing Company, 1979.

Watterman, Laura and Guy Waterman. *Forest and Crag.* Boston, Massachusetts: Appalachian Mountain Club, 1989.

Watts, May Theilgaard. *Master Tree Finder, A Manual for the Identification of Trees by Their Leaves.* Nature Study Guild, 1963.

Weidensaul, Scott. *Mountains of the Heart: A Natural History of the Appalachians.* Golden, Colorado: Fulcrum Publishing, 1994.

Whalen, Christopher. The *Appalachian Trail Workbook for Planning Thru-Hikes.* Harpers Ferry, West Virginia: Appalachian Trail Conference, 1992.

Wilshusen, J. Peter. *Geology of the Appalachian Trail in Pennsylvania.* Pennsylvania, 1983.

Author John M. Wilson is a Civil War historian, a geologist working in hazardous waste cleanup, and an active outsdoorsman. He has hiked many of the trails in the Great Smoky Mountains National Park, the Cherokee National Forest, the Appalachian Trail in Virginia, and the Ozark Trail in Missouri. He is also a Perpetual Deacon in the Episcopal Church. This is his fourth book, following a biography of William Porcher DuBose, soldier, theologian, and philosopher entitled *I Have Looked Death In The Face*, a collection of short stories about the Civil War and other subjects, *The Final Furlough*, and a novel about the Civil War, *Oh Yes, I Want To Go Home.*

John Wilson and Pookie Bear